Bathing & the single girl

BATHING AND THE SINGLE GIRL

Paperback ISBN: 978-0-9913046-5-3
E-Book ISBN: 978-0-9913046-4-6

Cover design by: JD&J

Bathing & the single girl

a novel

Christine Elise McCarthy

MULTUM IN PARVO
PUBLISHING

To my parents, Gail Rush and Alvan Long,
for a lifetime of support, creative
inspiration & ball-busting good humor.

To Miles Miller
for love, laughter & all-around badassitude.

And to Lauren Abramo
for her continued faith that there were people
out there who would enjoy reading this.

Contents

1: Funk soul brother	1
2: Hung	34
3: The albino	54
4: The valance	75
5: Booby nemesis	117
6: Devonevans	140
7: Irony & the yeti	198
8: Teen jesus	246
9: A girl named carlos	305

1 Funk soul brother

I WASN'T ALWAYS A MAN REPELLANT. I once had several successful relationships in a row. I use the term "successful" in the sense that these relationships were of the live-in variety and had lasted five or more years each. *Several.* If, you know, you allow that several can mean two. Each of the men in question was sent off into the world well trained in the arts of "why you call when you are running late" and "what happens in Vegas isn't going to happen in Vegas because you aren't going to that asshole's bachelor party" and other key tools required to maintain a happy pairing. Each of the men have subsequently met and married gorgeous and charming women (both European, by odd coincidence) who are ten or more years their junior. Each of the men has several children and even the late-blooming dreamer has a booming, prosperous business. In Paris. As a chef, no less. Where, though he is from Boston originally, his outrageously beautiful toddler speaks English as a second language and can order *moules frites* in French without feeling like a pretentious fraud.

Still, I don't know when exactly I became defined by the fact that I never have sex but it's safe to say that it happened. Okay, fine. Never might be an overstatement but when the periods of unwitting celibacy are measured in years and the periods of awkward, gratification-free sex are measured in weeks—I don't think a jury of my peers would convict me in the court of hyperbole.

Anyway, I look upon these men from my past and am genuinely happy that they are happy. I was invited to their weddings. I love their wives. I swear to God. But where the fuck is my sexy European guy who is ten years my junior and who is witty and quick and makes hand-cut pasta and loves dogs and seems to live only to help facilitate my dreams, both personal and professional? I'll tell you. Nowhere. European men are notorious cads who are raised in a culture that—while it teaches them to see beauty in women of all ages—teaches them to see beauty in women of all ages. That's a problem. Think about it. Do you really want the responsibility of keeping a hot French or Italian or Spanish guy so satisfied that he has no need to engage in the affairs his culture has taught him are his due? And with these guys, they might even cheat on you with a woman older than you are. Or a woman with hairy armpits. Or an older woman with hairy armpits. That is sure to devastate any self-esteem his initial interest in you cultivated. No. You can keep your Javier Bardem, Penelope. I don't need that shit.

I explain all this to illustrate—or maybe convince myself—that my celibacy is not the result of my having tastes too exotic or ambitious to be realized. Just gimme a dude close to my age, with a job, without a wife and hopefully carrying the same extra ten pounds that I am carrying and in the same denial I am in because, really, it is twenty pounds, who am I kidding? I have the great fortune of having always been drawn to guys my age and that has held true to this day. I see a paunch or a receding hairline or graying hair and I interpret that to mean he will not see my paunch, receding hairline and graying hairs. Spelled out like that, it is hard to miss the absurdity of such a leap of logic but fuck it. It doesn't matter because there is no such guy in my life to forgive or by whom to be forgiven. I am the girl who never has sex with anyone at all so I can participate in any kind of ridiculous fantasy of men my age and how they think, if I feel like it.

Recently, I made a grave mistake and Wikipedia'd "middle-aged." I'd looked the term up in an effort to comfort myself as I got ready for the birthday dinner my friends were forcing on me. I thought I'd see middle age defined as no younger than forty-five and go to—I don't know—retirement age. I thought I'd bask for a moment, pleasantly pondering the years I had before me that could still be defined simply as adulthood—years before menopause, Viagra, Depends and Denture Grip became the topics *du jour*. Years before Lifetime programmers were seeing me as their target audience. This is what I found:

"Middle Age is the period of age beyond young adulthood but before the onset of old age. Various attempts have been made to define this age, which is around the third quarter of the average lifespan of human beings.

"The US Census lists middle age as including both the age categories 35 to 44 and 45 to 50, while prominent social scientist, Erik Erikson, sees it ending a little later and defines middle adulthood as between 40 and 65.

"Prominent pundit Mit Xuamerf defines middle age as 'the period of 35 to 55.'"

What the fuck? Thirty-five? *You are already middle-aged*, screamed the voice in my head. That doesn't even seem fair. You turn thirty and then, just as you are waving good-bye to your youth behind you, you turn around and bam! Slam right into middle age? Why would forty even be an important milestone anymore? You're already middle-aged and slipping into the grave—so who cares? I wonder how old this Mit Xuamerf is. I imagine he is some snarky Asian-German (Mit Xuamerf?) Doogie Howser boy wonder type with a maturity beyond his years but without the life experience and resulting perspective of a freshman frat boy. How dare he even pretend to understand, let alone define, what middle age is? These are peoples' lives he is playing with by cavalierly tossing thirty-five out into the ether as the beginning of the end. The fucker. I'd like to kick his ass.

To compound my sense of lost youth, my theatrical manager of five years had texted me earlier that day, awkwardly—even for a text—dropping me as a client. Something about not being "able to do anything more" for me. He seemed to feel another manager might have more luck breaking down the increasing number of doors in Hollywood that had decided I no longer warranted access beyond the velvet rope. This is a depressing enough scenario when it is just a trendy nightclub deeming you unfit. When it is access to producers, directors, casting directors or, in short, work as an actress of any kind, then this rejection has a special and profound sting. It is a sting that strikes you right in the ego, certainly, but if your ego has taken the beating mine has in the last ten or fifteen years and is already punch drunk and on the ropes, it's the pain in the wallet that threatens to drop you to the canvas, and by "canvas," I mean "life under a bridge living out of a shopping cart."

So, here I found myself resentfully getting ready for a birthday dinner that had sounded like a Hellish idea even before I was aware that I had already squandered a measurable portion of my middle age. Now that I was so much closer to the grave than I had previously thought, I wanted to give up all pretenses of effort and just buy a pair of Pajama Jeans and a box of wine, curl up on the sofa and wait for my Social Security to kick in.

Stupid birthday dinner. I told my friend Eliza I was not interested in recognizing the passing of another year… another year without work, another year without a relationship and, scandalously, another year without even the most meaningless sex and now—another year down the dark side of the slope of middle age. Still, I had to make some gesture at giving a fuck so I tried on a few dresses. Horrified, I found that even my fat outfits were clinging to my mid-section like horny leg-humpers but without that exciting sexual element.

Just clinging in every ugly, desperate sense of the word. Was this the result of the sudden-onset middle age of which I now counted myself a bitter victim? More likely it was a result of the all-carbs-all-the-time diet I had been on for weeks. Extended unemployment and property taxes are a brutal combination.

Fortunately, I had become rather adept at a complicated financial shell game, shuffling short-term-interest-free credit card cash advances around between my other credit cards and my checking account. Sure, this was a slippery slope and my unsecured debt was mounting at a frightful pace but, so far, I had avoided paying the exorbitant interest rates that kick in if you aren't paying attention to dates. Still, despite my financial wizardry, I had literally found myself facing the choice between room (my mortgage) and board (fresh produce). So, I decided to embrace being part of the 99% and occupy my pantry. I was now several weeks into this self-imposed challenge to spend absolutely nothing more on groceries and, instead, eat all the food I already had taking up room in my cabinets and freezer. Initially, it was kind of an adventure in culinary imagination. Weeks into it, as my diet began to consist entirely of either brown rice or whole wheat pasta aglio olio (pasta, olive oil and garlic), my imagination was put to use imagining that I was eating something else. One might expect that I would delight in an excuse to get out, act like I was part of the 1% and add some roughage to the monotony of my diet… if only to stop my poop from looking the color of a hotdog bun. Sorry if that is TMI but an all beige diet has consequences and I don't see any reason I should shield you from that fact. Anyway, even the promise of multi-colored foods did not improve the appeal of this forcible birthday dinner.

Disgusted, I chose the least offensive dress I'd tried and added a forgiving, long sweater to mask my thickness. My tallest heels added enough length to my silhouette that I hoped the sweater lost its stink of "over thirty, camouflaging flaws" and achieved more of an air of "hot chicks get chilly, too." I was grasping. I knew it.

I decided I deserved a glass of wine while I prepped. It isn't called front-loading when it is your birthday. It is called celebrating. Wine was one thing I had decided did not fall into the category of groceries. That would be uncivilized. It would also be fiscally irresponsible because this was a Bevmo five cent sale week and it would be willful and silly not to stock up when I could get two-for-one bottles of Syrah. For my birthday, I had splurged and stepped it up a bit. I bought myself a two-for-one twenty dollar bottle rather than the dirty chard I am normally restricted to in the five dollar range. I gotta say, it still feels pretty ghetto unscrewing wine, even if you know it is a twenty dollar bottle. I comforted myself by pouring a glass far deeper than the polite five and a half ounces the airport bartenders and sushi bars cheap you out with. I could afford to, after all. I still had another unopened bottle winking at me from the counter.

I literally winked back because that is just exactly how much of a lonely loser I have become. I openly flirted with a bottle of red wine. At least I didn't talk to it. Talking is reserved for my three dogs: a French Bulldog, a pug and a Boston Terrier named, respectively: Crews, Fante and Ellroy.

"Who's the best mommy in the world?"

"You are, Mama! You're the best mommy!"

Yeah, that's me, too. Both voices. Out loud. The first line is spoken in my pet voice that I use not only with my own dogs but with any dogs to whom I speak in public. I am a bit of a breed snob so I don't just talk to any dog but if you have a pit-bull or a mastiff or any bully breed or a puppy—I use the international pet voice that dogs of all cultures recognize.

The second line is the answer to my question and uttered in a baby voice that I attribute indiscriminately to all my dogs. Don't worry. This voice is private. I won't walk up to you at the park and say, "Who's a good dog?" in the pet voice to your American Bulldog and then be presumptuous enough to put a voice—and words—into his mouth. And, frankly, I know the baby voice I use is kinda crazy. Come on. I do possess some degree of self-awareness.

Wine soothing my crankiness, I began to address my hair. Just because this is how my life works these days, when I plugged in the blow dryer, the socket spit sparks and smoke out at me and the bathroom went dark. *Jesus Christ*, I thought. I fumbled my way through the blackness to the circuit breakers and flipped my way back to illumination. Again in the bathroom, I tried the dryer once more. This time the outlet made no objection to penetration but the dryer was dead. I threw a dirty look at the heavens and cursed whatever God there might be for forsaking me yet again. *If this dryer still worked, I'd take a bath with it right now and end this bullshit nightmare of a life*, I thought. That might sound melodramatic but, over the last several months, some sort of slow-burn mutiny had been going on in my house. My last working television was a thirteen-inch, tubed number with a growing neon-green, blown-out area in the lower left corner. The DVD player hooked up to it had frozen a few days ago, jealously clutching the last disc of the last season of *The Wire*. Unable to coax the machine open, I'd had to tell Netflix I'd never received it. Last week my dishwasher hemorrhaged soapy, grey water onto my kitchen floor and shuddered its final cycle to an end, just as dinner guests knocked on my door. Yesterday, I'd accidentally hooked a toe in a small L-shaped tear in my duvet and tore the thinning, cotton fabric irreparably. My comforter now straddled my bed naked and ashamed, safety-pinned corner spitting down into the room every time I moved in the night. Today, the light in my refrigerator blew and I couldn't figure out how to replace the bulb. That was somewhat of a blessing, however, because at least it kept me from being able to see the growing, frosty ice patch on the back wall between the second and third shelves. Ice isn't supposed to formulate inside the non-freezer section of a Sub Zero. Its existence there is a dark promise that this item, too, is about to join the ranks of the stainless steel tombstones of functionless appliances in my kitchen. A month ago, the last time I'd had an audition, my printer decided to give up the ghost before I could print out the material I needed to take with me on the appointment. Among the other items in my house on strike or retired permanently are: my three-hole punch, my landline telephone, my Dualit toaster, the dishwasher, the knob on my underwear drawer (which is packed so tight with shit I'll never wear again, it is nearly impossible to pry open), my doorbell, the zippers on every pillow and dog bed on the premises (because one of my dogs has a powerful zipper-chewing fetish), my showerhead and the drain in my tub, one of the little legs on my wireless keyboard and the CD player in my truck. And now, my hair dryer. Just another "fuck you" from the universe at yet another unbelievably inconvenient moment. The hair dryer bummed me out particularly because it was a really expensive one that I had been given for free at a celebrity swag event, an event I'd been shameless enough to scam my way into. Sure, I'd had to explain to all the vendors who it was I used to be and that was humiliating, and then I had to pose for a photograph holding each of the free items I was given but I got to go home with a huge gym bag full of stuff I could no longer afford to buy for myself. Important things like an old-time popcorn popper, a hundred dollar aromatherapy candle, some hideous jewelry, a handmade, knobby scarf, a dog-friendly cap for water bottles, a pen that could translate whatever you wrote down and then say whatever you'd written out loud in one of five languages, sunglasses with a built-in Bluetooth device and a remote-operated, flying, Mylar fish. These things were the only barrier left in my life between me and an absolute crisis of self-worth. I'd gotten them for free, after all. Because somebody had been convinced, if even for just a few moments, that I was the kind of person you wanted your customers to see using your product. More likely, they had no idea who I was but were afraid of admitting that and of potentially offending an actual celebrity. I preferred to let these useless freebies serve as proof that I was still relevant, a style-maker and not just a hustler out there snagging items meant for the likes of the Kardashians and the casts of all forty *Law and Order* and *CSI* series.

I looked ruefully at the deceased appliance and then tossed it, with a little more anger than was warranted, into the trash can. I looked at my reflection in the mirror, sighed deeply, tied my wet hair back at the nape of my neck and donned a hat. What other choice did I have? Air-drying my shapeless cut into an uncontrolled fright wig? No. I then had a twenty-minute struggle to get my liner on straight using a mini-sized, free sample, designer eyeliner I'd gotten at the mall. I poured another glass of wine for myself. Sometime over the years, my eyelids decided they were afraid of heights or something and began creeping lower and lower until it was almost impossible to use wet liner and not have a matching line transfer appear where I used to have a crease. Gravity is a motherfucker, man, and that pinky-sized applicator wasn't helping the matter. Still, I insist on some standards and the hat and sweater were concessions enough to defeat so I applied and reapplied the liner until it was perfect.

Having come to half-hearted terms with my reflection, I said good-bye to my dogs (the kids) and got into the car to drive my fat ass to the damn birthday dinner. The restaurant they chose was a newish, hipster joint on Hollywood Boulevard. My friend Maxine had insisted that being seen in a local hotspot would be good for my career. As an actress, few things are more uncomfortable and demoralizing than well-wishing industry outsiders giving clueless advice.

"Do you have an agent?" asked in that mildly accusing tone that your dental hygienist uses when they ask if you have been flossing regularly and they are pretty sure you haven't been.

Um—yeah. I've been a professional actress for twenty years. You'd think they would know that, for sure, I'd already thought of getting an agent.

"You know what you should do? Write and produce a really cool indie movie and direct it and star in it and then do the festival circuit then parlay that into an edgy HBO series like that Lena Dunham did. Or into a show like *Friends*. I hear those guys got a million dollars an episode!"

You would be amazed at how often some version of that is run past me as a realistic resolution to my immediate financial concerns. Why didn't I think of being the highest paid actor on TV? It's such an obvious solution, now that you mention it! They make suggestions like that and then look at me waiting for some kind of V8 moment while I struggle not to respond with physical violence.

Maxine felt that "being seen" at Pho Bich Nga (spoken out loud at your own risk)—the new Soul Food-Pacific Rim fusion restaurant/night club rumored to be owned by, among others, Dennis Rodman, Sharon Osborne, Mickey Rourke, William Hung, Andy Dick and some Maxim cover girl—was going to restore me to my former glory, B-list though it might have been. I rejected this idea as completely as a hoarder fights minimalism. I argued that publicly celebrating my advancing putrescence in a room full of working, twenty-year-old actresses and moronic reality stars was not only going to do nothing to help my career but was also likely to render me suicidal. Worse yet, Maxine had informed me that our reservation choice was either 5:30 PM or 9:30 PM. Most of my friends have real jobs and real lives and would be unable to make the 5:30 PM reservation. I, on the other hand—having no real life—have usually had my first glass of wine at 5 PM, eaten by 6, am half in the bag by 7 and curled up in bed with a book or a movie by 8 PM. A 9:30 dinner for me feels like setting the alarm at 3 AM to get up for breakfast. Just craziness. I expressed this to Maxine who laughed it off like I must be

joking. This had the effect of making me feel even olde
I already did and that pissed me off.

"Fine, Maxine! This dinner sounds like grinding brok
glass into my eyeballs. But if making me feel really old and rubbing my face in my unemployment is your idea of a great way for us to spend my birthday, then fine!"

"Yay! I win!"

She actually said that. "Yay, I win!" So you can see what I was up against.

I pulled up to Pho Bich Nga and a valet waved me into the parking lot. Why do they have valets at restaurants with parking lots? I mean seriously. I have to spend ten dollars and tip a guy on top of that so he can move my car eight feet, change all the settings on my seat and steering wheel and steal my meter change? Fucking bullshit.

Another valet took a look at my seven-year-old Explorer and gestured that I should roll my window down, which I did. He was a giant Mexican badass, right off the set of *Oz*. He looked me in the eye for a count of several seconds, blinked a few times as if there was something I was supposed to say and then he asked me if I had a reservation. I assured him I did as I felt a flush of heat in my cheeks.

"A reservation at Pho Bich Nga?" he pressed, scrutinizing me like a poker competitor looking for tells.

Hearing "Pho Bich Nga" spoken out loud by a suspicious, fifty-year-old Mexican ex-con cheered me up. I laughed and said, "Yes. I know. I'm no happier about it than you are."

Resigned, he reached for my door without clearing his expression of evident distaste from my view. What? Like his bottom line is impacted by old ladies being allowed to mingle with the beautiful people? I chose to ignore his editorializing. Instead, I eyed my cup holder in the console brimming with quarters and realized there was nothing I could do about them out there in the open now—what with the border patrol breathing down my neck and looking for any excuse to turn me back. A man with this level of self-importance couldn't be a meter change thief and still feel superior, could he? Well, it was in Fate's hands now.

I grabbed my purse and threw my interrogator a smile intended to charm him into realizing we were pals. It was my best "Oh, you know you like me and even if you didn't know it before you know it now because I am irresistible" smile. He took it in and made me hold it until it twitched. Once he saw the crack in my veneer, he tipped his head and looked at me like I had just blamed a fart on the family dog.

"There goes your three dollar tip. Wanna keep going and whittle it down to one?"

I thought these things rather than uttering them aloud. I didn't know where this guy got his balls but, wherever it was, he'd gotten his money's worth. I felt like I owed him an apology or something but I was so baffled as to why, I couldn't begin to form a sentence. I muttered some guttural gibberish and added a short laugh like I'd imparted a witty riposte.

"That will be twenty dollars," Danny Trejo said, without even pretending to crack a polite smile.

"Twenty dollars?" I gasped before I could stop myself.

Danny Trejo didn't actually roll his eyes, but his face made some just-perceptible adjustments that implied he and I had had this exact conversation forty thousand times already and he was in no mood to have it again.

I was pretty sure I didn't have twenty dollars in cash.

"And I pay you now?"

"If you don't mind," he replied. He said it almost without inflection but it still sounded like a threat. Prison must be a terrifying place, I found myself reflecting.

I took out my wallet and found sixteen dollars there. Danny Trejo watched me count the money. He saw that I was short. Without looking up at him, I reached back into my meter change cup and counted out four dollars in quarters. Actually, it was three-seventy-five in quarters, two dimes and a nickel. I held my twenty dollars out, coins cradled in the bills, to the valet. The headlights of an incoming car swept over me and stopped like stage lights on my extended hands. I knew that my body language and cupped hands full of money made me look like I was in the act of begging from Danny Trejo. I thought for a moment about how much I hated Maxine for dragging me out here to this for what was sure to be only the first in a long night of similar humiliations.

Danny Trejo took my money and dropped it into a basket on his valet stand without bothering to count it. He ripped a parking stub and handed me my claim check. I stood staring up at him, waiting for some blessing, some absolution or something. I had to settle for what he gave me which was simply a quick jerk of his head, meant to flick me out of his eyesight.

Quickly, I clicked away in my trying-too-hard heels and as I recovered from a minor trip, I thought, *My dress is clinging to my back fat and I'm wearing a granny sweater, you fucker. Isn't there some part of you that could guess that Pho Bich Nga wasn't* my *first choice for me tonight, either?*

I'm gonna fucking kill Maxine when I see her, I festered. I turned from the parking lot to the sidewalk and headed toward the address I had written on a Post-it. The entire block from where I stood to Hollywood Boulevard was darkness. I walked to the corner, turned back around and stood there looking like a lost amnesia patient. Two giggling brunettes brushed past me headed in the direction of the parking lot from which I'd just come. *They are dressed like hookers*, I thought and then instantly reprimanded myself for being an old prude. But really. I swear I could see the tiniest hint of a hot-pink-clad pudendum occasionally peeking out from the impossibly short skirt of the girl on the left. I silently blamed the CW network and then looked back down on my Post-it for the address of Pho Bich Nga. When I looked back up, the girls had mysteriously disappeared. It was impossible that they could have reached the parking lot... but there wasn't any red velvet rope or signage of any kind between where I stood and the approximate point they'd vanished. I walked in their direction like a homeowner warily looking for a night-time intruder. Just as I reached the Bermuda Triangle into which the tramps had evaporated, a primer-black metal door which, until then, had been perfectly camouflaged within a primer-black unlit wall, smashed open before me, almost knocking me down. Two girls that looked just like the other two girls, if the other two girls had gotten expensive dye jobs and extensions, stumbled out and into me.

"Haha... oh, excuse me, ma'am," one said in a Southern accent without having taken more than a fleeting glance at me.

Feeling as conspicuous draped in my newfound middle age as I would standing there in a Bingo-themed Snuggie, I absorbed this new blow. I had just been dismissed as a "ma'am"—by this giggling twit who had probably just spent more money on two apple-tinis than I had on the eBay-acquired, "gently used" BCBG dress I was standing there straining. The most painful thing about it was how quickly I had been assessed. A split second on a dimly lit Hollywood side-street and I was a "ma'am." *I knew I shouldn't have worn this fucking long sweater*, I thought.

Oblivious to my shame, she and her friend headed toward Hollywood Boulevard and I looked up into the face of the bouncer. He was about to pull the door closed when we made eye contact.

"Oh. Do you have a reservation here?"

I looked back at him, grateful that I did not feel tears welling up in my eyes. That was one thing age was good for. Perspective. Or maybe I was just too dehydrated to cry. I pretty much live on coffee and wine and they are both diuretics. I can't even pretend to try to drink eight glasses of water a day anymore. It's...

"Ma'am?"

The bouncer brought me back to the moment at hand.

"Okay, what the fuck with this ma'am shit?" I demanded from the doorman as I tugged self-consciously at my ill-chosen

"You are not going to believe it."

I waited but she just stared back at me. Her expression was impossible to read. Was it terrible news? Something funny?

"What?!"

"Maxine can't make it. She doesn't feel safe driving here from Santa Monica in the weather."

"Weather? Weather? What weather? What? NIGHT?"

"It just started raining out as I pulled into the parking lot five minutes ago."

Now it was my turn to stare at Eliza with my mouth hanging open.

"You are fucking shitting me. She insists on dragging us to this fucking hipster anus of a restaurant and makes us take the nine-thirty reservation because she can't get here after work in time for the five-thirty and now she isn't even coming because she is afraid of the rain?"

She held her phone up so I could read the text from Maxine. It was true. She and her husband Nick were canceling because of the rain.

"She should have already been on the road before the rain started. Who leaves Santa Monica at nine-thirty for a nine-thirty reservation?"

"An asshole."

I ordered another glass of wine and thought guiltily about the stack of unpaid bills on my desk. I looked around the room and spotted an Asian man at the bar wearing a leisure suit peppered from head to toe in Louis Vuitton logos, like expensive little polka-dots. Why not just have a tailor sew dollar bills together and walk around wearing your money, literally? I stared at him with intense disgust, as if his ostentatious display of wealth was somehow connected to my inability to make ends meet.

"Want to order something to eat here at the bar?" Eliza asked, breaking me out of my irrational hate thoughts.

"Can we leave here and just go to McDonald's?" I asked, with complete sincerity.

"What? No way! We don't have to eat at the bar," she said, as if it was the bar specifically I objected to. "And you are not having a birthday dinner at McDonald's. Let's just get go to our table and order some internationally schizophrenic appetizers..."

Sebastian appeared as if he had read our minds.

"Would you ladies like to go to your table now?"

Eliza said we would and Sebastian led us around a corner into a room that looked like a House of Blues and a PF Chang's had parented an unfortunate love child. It was early New Orleans primitive country folk Tiki Chinese. Not a single patron was in there. We walked past empty booth after empty booth until we had walked across the entire room. Sebastian led us up a flight of stairs and indicated a big table with ten places set upon it standing by itself in a dark room. It was about fifteen degrees colder up there than it had been in the bar.

"Sebastian, do you think we could maybe just have one of the booths downstairs?" I asked. "A table maybe somewhere south of the North Pole?"

"I'm afraid we don't have a booth large enough to accommodate your whole party."

"My whole party has been reduced to a party of two. Half the table got spooked by the rain."

Sebastian shifted just perceptibly and cleared his throat.

"Yeah, unfortunately, we are all booked up tonight. All the booths are reserved. It *is* Tuesday night," he said as if that explained everything. "I suppose I could see if we have had any last minute cancellations due to the severe weather."

He stood looking at me and I got the distinct impression that he was waiting for me to say, "No, don't bother. This dark table up in the Arctic is already more than we deserve." I didn't. He managed to contain his sigh of annoyance and went back downstairs. When he was out of earshot I turned to Eliza.

"Good thing we took Maxine's advice. A couple of hours at this table and I'll be hosting next year's Oscars."

"Well, who knows? I heard your boyfriend Justin Timberlake is one of the investors here. Maybe he will show up tonight," she offered, as if Justin Timberlake simply showing up was going, at once, to make every dirty dream I'd ever had about him come true. If only.

"Fuck Justin Timberlake."

"You love Justin Timberlake."

"Until I found out his mother is—like—my age. It's one level of wrong to have a crush on a teenager with a Jew fro but it is whole new level of yuck when he could be your son. I don't need Chris Hanson showing up with Perverted Justice while I'm trying to seduce Justin with chocolate chip cookies and sweet tea."

"His mother is your age? That isn't even possible. I mean, how old are you?"

I shrugged noncommittally. My age was my business and I was irritated that she was cramping my drama with her fact finding.

"Well, practically my age…"

"Okay, lady. You need to stop pretending you are ancient and decide to have a good time. We're here. We might as well have some fun."

Sebastian returned and informed us that our "VIP" table was as good as it was going to get for us at Pho Bich Nga.

"Thank God I brought this sweater," I grumbled, but I waited until Sebastian left before I put it back on. I was tying it around my waist to mask its length when, out of nowhere, a busboy appeared and began clearing all but two place settings. He did this with an energy that made his movements feel like an assault. I was afraid to look at him in case he mistook eye contact for an invitation to fight. I did a double take on a piece of framed art over my right shoulder. It was a wildly over-the-top caricature of an Asian man wearing Lennon glasses and a bellhop hat, huge buck teeth about to chomp into a slice of watermelon. It confused me.

Sebastian had dropped two menus onto the table before he bounced down the stairs. I downed my wine and picked a menu up. Eliza didn't seem to have even tasted her wine. She could nurse a single glass for hours. It was infuriating.

I opened the menu. It was written in like a 10 pt. Asian-themed font on top of a very busy Mammy and Rastus background. I needed my reading glasses, my iPhone flash-light app and a sociologist to begin to decipher the contents. I caught the prices and the CitiMortgage logo lit up like neon in my mind. I chose to ignore the intensifying guilt I felt sitting there waiting to order overpriced food when I knew I really should have been in the kitchen downstairs talking to the manager about applying for a minimum-wage job.

"This is incredible. Sixteen kinds of meat-based Pho and soul food. Even the veggies have pork in them. It's like a culinary orgy of fat and cholesterol in here. The only thing on this menu I can eat is a side of red beans and rice or the thirty-two dollar mac and cheese appetizer."

"Wow. Teriyaki bacon-wrapped sweet potato donuts?" Eliza read, looking at me with an expression of horror before continuing to flip through the menu.

"I've been living on grains and pasta for over a month now. I'm shitting rice cakes," I added. "And what could possibly make a mac and cheese appetizer worth thirty-two dollars? Where's Sebastian? I need another glass of wine."

"He's probably running a credit check on us to see if we can afford the entrees here."

"Did you see the 'Porterhouse in a bone marrow and butter bath' for the low, low price of seventy-eight dollars?"

"I did. And did you notice? For that price you also buy the right to pay twelve dollars each for any pork-fried veggie side dish you might fancy."

We sat there sipping wine and mocking the menu contents until we had exhausted all potential for humor there. After fifteen minutes and still no sign of Sebastian, we decided to break out of the second level exile to which we had been shunned and confront the beautiful people with our existence. We walked back through the main dining room. Two booths had people seated at them. The bar, on the other hand, was quite crowded. There were two vacant seats at the bar but there was a guy sitting in between them. Determined to milk something acceptable from a disastrous evening, even if that ambition was as low rent as simply wanting to sit at the bar next to my only birthday dinner co-celebrant, I approached the guy and tapped him on the shoulder.

"I'm sorry, but is anyone sitting in the seats on either side of you?"

He turned and looked at me with huge blue eyes which were set off by an amazing quiff of nearly white hair. I'm not one that typically goes for towheads but something about his face made my heart pitter pat. He appeared to be in his early thirties. He looked at the seats beside him and turned to me and shook his head.

"Well, would you mind terribly moving over one so that my friend and I can sit here?"

"Fo shizzle," he replied and scooted over a seat. Eliza and I bellied up to the bar.

"This your first time here?" he inquired.

"What? We look like we don't belong here?" I snapped back defensively and reflexively removed my granny sweater.

"Whoa, Cuz. I was just making small talk."

"I'm sorry," I said as I tucked my sweater beneath me and wondered if I'd really just been addressed as "Cuz." "It is my birthday and it hasn't been a very good night so far."

"Happy birthday! Let me buy you guys a round, Big Willie style." He smiled a shy smile that was in contrast to his urban verbiage and he touched my shoulder. He called the bartender by his first name (Thaddeus) and I ordered a glass of champagne. Eliza was still pawing her first glass of wine.

"Thanks. That is very sweet of you. So, you must come here a lot, huh? You know the bartender by name and all."

He nodded as he sipped what looked like a gin and tonic but more likely involved exotic tinctures and artisanal liqueur and probably set him back thirty bucks. I eyed the candied lime astride the rim and wondered if it was made of fruit or Chuckles. You could never tell with hipsters these days, what with their irony and irreverence. Thaddeus placed a glass of champagne before both me and Eliza, made some hat-doffing, semi-bow gesture and moved away.

"Ya dig, my Thaddeotis. Celeb mixologist. I'm all about livin' nappy, yo. Know what I'm saying?"

I did not. Undeterred, I forged ahead.

"Can I ask why you come here? This place sucks."

"Co-owner Mos is my OG homie skittle, son," he explained and touched my cheek.

I tried to put an expression on my face that 1) suggested I understood what he had just said and 2) looked noncommittal enough to suggest that I agreed with him—whether what he'd said had been good or bad and 3) hid the fact that I was secretly swooning every time he touched me. Eliza kicked me under the bar. I grabbed my champagne and took a long swallow, trying to distract my platinum wigga from seeing in my eyes that I had no idea what the fuck he was talking about.

"My name is Ruby. This is my friend Eliza."

"Word. I'm Bunker." He smiled again and pierced me with those baby blues. He reached out and removed an invisible bit of lint from my dress. It was all I could do not to press my heaving bosom into his retreating palm.

"Bunker? Really? Bunker? Eliza, did you hear that? Isn't that unbelievable?"

"Yes. I have been listening and yes, it is unbelievable."

Her sarcasm was lost on me.

"My dog! I had a dog named Bunker. He just died last month. His name was Edward Bunker."

I said that to Eliza, as if she didn't already know.

"Facheezie on the reezie! That is some crazy shiznit, Holmes. My middle name is Edward," interjected Bunker, and then he touched my champagne glass. I took it to mean I should finish the glass. I drained it and, as I chewed the green-tea infused lychee that had been at the bottom of the flute, I gestured to the bartender that I was ready for another. I was very excited about this Bunker business.

"This is amazing! Are you a fan of Edward Bunker?" I asked him and, without even waiting for his response, I turned back to Eliza. "Can you believe this, Eliza? Isn't this crazy?"

"Craaazy shiznit, fo sho," Eliza quipped. I heard her mocking tone that time. I mean—she never said shiznit at home. I threw her a little warning stink-eye. A fresh glass of champagne was before me. Bunker touched it twice and then touched my cheek again. He looked directly into my eyes when he touched me. I blushed and grabbed my drink. My head was swimming with wine and champagne and the crazy odds that I would meet a cute guy that shared a name with my recently deceased dog. And on my birthday. It had to be sign. I looked at Eliza and I could tell she saw the hearts bursting above my head. I fixed her with the "Wow, can you believe my luck?" look.

"I'm gonna go to the ladies' room. Ruby, will you come with me?"

"Go ahead, Shorty. I'll watch your drinks." He touched my shoulder again.

I giggled a thank you, took a huge slug of champagne. Standing up, I suddenly felt the impact of the five plus drinks I had had in probably just over an hour. Hoping Bunker was watching us, I tried very deliberately to suck in my gut and be sure I did not stumble in my heels. I could hardly wait to get into the privacy of the bathroom and discuss these exciting new developments.

"Oh my God! I LOVE him! And his name is Bunker! How perfect is that? Isn't this crazy?"

"Word, Dawg," she said and flashed me a gang sign.

"I know, but, I don't know. Maybe he is trying to talk black to... compensate for... being practically an *albino*..." I said, stumbling into an end to a sentence I had begun with no formed conclusion. "Andheissocuteandhekeepstouchingme-andhisnameisBunker!" I thrilled.

"I don't know who is more retarded, you right now or Yo MTV Raps out there." Eliza was laughing.

"You don't think he is cute?"

"I guess he's okay. You know who he is, right?"

"No. Who is he?"

"He is an actor. He was in that movie about the kangaroo that became President."

"THAT'S Jerry O'Connell?"

"No, the other kangaroo movie. The impossibly dumber one..."

"Dumber than? ...oooh..." I exhaled my realization, deflated by this new information. "But still. Tonight sucks. My life sucks. My career is on life support, I'm hopelessly broke and I haven't kissed a boy in five years." I let that soak in for both of us before I continued. "Fuck it, Eliza. He is very cute and every time he touches me I think I am going to faint."

"I saw him on Oprah a long time ago. He has Tourette's syndrome," she said gingerly, as if it had great meaning. I stared blankly back at her. I was pretty buzzed. Then it dawned on me.

"Oh! You think that's why he hangs out here?"

"What?"

"You know. Shouting out 'FUCK' and fucking... blurting out racial slurs... might not seem so offensive in a restaurant with 'Nga' in the name and bizarre, culturally insensitive art on the walls... right? I don't know if you've noticed, but it's like a racist free for all in here."

of Kraft at home? It is enough to fill a mattress and it was practically free."

"I'm buying, but I get it. Are you okay? Or is this just standard 'birthdays suck' malaise?"

I knew that, ultimately, it had very little to do with my birthday. Birthdays don't suck if the rest of one's life is humming along at a satisfying pace but playing the birthday card was my easiest way out of a conversation I didn't want to have.

"Yeah. I'm okay. Some birthdays just seem to hit you harder than others, no? I guess this is one of the bad ones."

"I totally get it," Eliza sympathized. "Twenty-six threw me for a loop, too." She smiled, trying to lighten the mood.

"Yeah. Twenty-six. Several of my twenty-sixth birthdays bummed me out, too," I quipped and laughed weakly.

As I considered the absurdity of actually being twenty-six, I looked around the bar again, trying to decide if anyone in the room had even reached that age yet. I felt like Carol Channing chaperoning a prom.

"Let's just pay the bill and mercy kill this night. Do you mind?"

"Of course not. But don't you dare even make a move for the check. This one is on me. It's your birthday."

Fifteen minutes later and an eighty dollar bar tab for four drinks and we were out in the rain, squeezed together under the teeny umbrella at the valet podium. Eliza's car came right away. I thanked her and made her leave. I felt myself weaving a bit as I stood shivering in my granny sweater, which I now let hang to full length trying to maximize its warming qualities. I counted and realized I'd had something like seven drinks in about ninety minutes and no food. The term "alcorexic" came to mind. I admired -rexics of many varieties. I take my hat off to anyone that can not eat all day, and skip dinner, saving calories just for drinking at night, as I had inadvertently managed this evening. I have a lifelong admiration for anorexics, too. Not eating at all is an incredible feat. Bulimia just doesn't compare. Bulimia is like getting a little lady bug tattoo on your bikini line where anorexia is a full back piece. Or a face tattoo. You gotta respect that kind of commitment.

Danny Trejo pulled up in my car. I moved quickly, trying to time it so I could get into the car as soon as the he vacated the door. I miscalculated and smashed right into him. I surprised myself as much as I did him and stumbled backwards. Tipsy and on six-inch heels, it took me a baby step or two too many to steady myself. I tried to cover by fumbling in my purse for a tip.

"Are you sure you are okay to drive, ma'am?"

I was instantly incensed.

"Again with the ma'am? Are you kidding me?"

I felt rain pouring down my face, compromising any chance of my being taken seriously. He looked at me and kept the keys in his hand as his arm dropped to his side.

"What? First you didn't want to let me in and now you don't want to let me leave? *Senor*."

I spat the "senor" at him as if it were a scathing retort to his use of "ma'am." He was not scathed. He continued to stare at me. I literally sputtered the heavy rain that was threatening to waterboard me.

"I'm sorry. I'm fine. I live really close. Just up on that hill," I pleaded, pointing in the general direction of my house which was, actually, not that far away. *Too far to walk in these shoes*, I thought. Too far to walk in the rain.

"It's my birthday," I said, breaking under what felt like his relentless grilling but was, in reality, probably three seconds of silence. He shook his head, handed me the keys and walked away.

"Wait. Your tip..."

He dismissed me with a wave without even turning to look at me. He was right. I did suck. And we both knew I had no money in my wallet for a tip.

I got in the car and drove past the valet stand playing with my stereo so as to avoid any accidental eye contact with the most disdainful valet in Los Angeles history. Because the CD player was, of course, broken—I punched at the presets a few times. Eventually, I happened upon an ad for a new miracle pill, the Well Tab. Well Tab. A benign name full of impossible to fulfill promises. Obviously, a non-prescription drug with a name like Well Tab was just a scam preying on all the aging, malcontent, unemployed, underappreciated, disaffected and disenfranchised people all over America desperate, as I was, for some quick fix. For an escape. But while I knew Well Tab couldn't provide the feelings of relaxation, positivity and strength that it promised, the ad did make me nostalgic for the good old days when a self-respecting woman trapped in a dead-end life could at least indulge in a secret Valium addiction, away from the judgmental eyes of valets that belonged to Neighborhood Watch and MADD. *I seriously need to investigate the viability of restoring prescription drug abuse to respectability. Even to fashionability. Now that would return a purpose to my days and might even provide a solution to my money woes,* I thought. Then I pulled out into traffic and carefully navigated "the drunk way" home.

2 Hung

ONCE SAFELY IN MY HOUSE, my spirits were lifted tremendously by the tail wagging and stinky fish kisses of my kids. I completely forgot about my plan to become the Tony Montana of an emerging Hollywood Valium scene, collapsed onto the floor and let the dogs have their way with my eyeliner. I tried not to think about the broader disappointments of my life and chose, instead, to focus on the smaller humiliations of that single evening. That fucking albino. Why had I let myself get so excited? That wasn't really a question that I didn't know the answer to. I needed distraction. I needed something, anything, else to think about besides money, bills, my career. I needed someplace to focus my attention that did not create anxiety so intense that it felt like I was in the early stages of a stroke. And in fairness to myself, an accidental, five-year dry spell can really cloud one's judgment. The tiniest spark has the potential to flare up into a bonfire. Tonight, the spark produced nothing more than one of those little fires Benihana chefs wow tourists with four hundred times a night.

I thought about my unused sexual apparatus. I wish I could have known twelve years ago that I was going to break world records and set new standards, redefining the term "single girl." If I had been able to see the future, I would have hired a documentary crew to immortalize the details. Twelve years ago, my last relationship ended. It ended abruptly and painfully and I needed a year of wound-licking to recover. I then had a brief dalliance with a guy who turned out to be a junkie and, well, what does the "and" part even matter? Junkie is enough, no? By brief I mean less than a month. By dalliance I mean constant fighting and some awkward sex. For the record, junkies are not super satisfying rebound material. Even before you find out that they are still married and the wife doesn't know they are broken up. So, I took the next two years off. Don't get me wrong. I like sex as much as the next guy, assuming the next guy isn't Michael Douglas or David Duchovny. But, I need some pretense of a relationship—even if it is just an agreement to be monogamous—for the sex to be any fun because—really—sex is the cherry on the banana split relationship. Without the bananas, ice cream, chocolate and whipped cream—all you have left is the cherry and a big, commercial jar of maraschino cherries sounds really gross to me. In the two years after the junkie, I didn't meet any ice cream desserts that seemed worth the calories they represented. Still, two years in, even freezer burned pudding pops start looking appealing—so I broke down and gorged a bit. Classic dieting blunder. And when you are in gorging mode you seldom make the healthiest choices.

So, a few days after my third anniversary of being single, and at the risk of spreading this food metaphor out too thin, I grabbed exactly the kind of junk food one does when they have skipped too many meals. Convenient, fast, readily available and the sort you regret immediately afterward as you sit, nauseated, swearing "never again."

This regret was so deep that, once I'd cut bait, I lost any remaining interest in the kind of boys that I had selected almost exactly because, while they each had their merits, they were as easy to cut out of my life as they had been easy to invite in. Four more years passed before I began to feel restless again. They should have support groups for these sorts of issues. Again, I chose poorly and had achieved a new low. The experience illustrates perfectly why I have never understood one-night stands. This guy was not a one-night stand, but bear with me while I explain. I had been seeing him several weeks before inevitability made me inquire about a certain mysterious tattoo he had on his arm. It took a bit to wrangle the answer from him… red flag, I know. He finally confessed it was a band logo of some kind. Music, people's taste in music, is important to me, so I pressed for an explanation. He swore up and down that the tattoo was a youthful indiscretion and that he had completely rejected that band and that part of himself that allowed him to be a tattooed fan. I was worried but I knew he had a short shelf life anyway and his expiration date was rapidly approaching so I decided not to dwell on it. Later, as he forced me to watch the same Jerry Garcia YouTube footage for the umpteenth time, trying to convince me that I had wrongly written Jerry off as a result of my lack of exposure to his band rather than because they sucked really, really hard, I realized that I was, in fact, fucking a fucking Dead Head. That was a Grateful Dead tattoo on his arm. And then I saw his new canary-yellow Mustang. Inexcusable. Two huge strikes. I couldn't wait for a third. I had to wash my hands of him immediately. So, my point is, just imagine the sorts one might wake up next to if they allowed themselves to make completely uninformed, knee-jerk choices, hammered, in a dark bar and with no reconnaissance whatsoever. No. Mr. Deadhead was horrifying enough and he launched me into the longest stretch of celibacy so far, the five year stint I was cresting now.

As I reflected upon my ignominious romantic resume, I'd polished off the twenty-dollar bottle of red I had opened earlier. I looked at the remaining unopened bottle of twenty-dollar red and told myself I had already consumed plenty for one night. I told myself it was time for bed.

I woke up in the morning feeling like my tongue was coated in fur. Because it was. I had fallen asleep on the dog bed in my office and my pug Fante's tail was buried in my mouth. I sat up sputtering and gagging on dog hair. Nausea rolled up my throat and I just made it to the bathroom as a torrent of hot red wine filled the toilet basin. The only thing worse than puking red wine is trying to puke doughy things that ball up in your stomach, like peanut butter sandwiches or pizza. More accurately, I guess, those things are harder to puke—when you have eaten them to the point of bursting and then you want to purge. They come up, if they come up, pummeling your throat like little fists of rebuke for having eaten them to begin with. Yeah, I dabbled in the art of purging but it doesn't define me so let it go.

Wine and bile erupted from my mouth and nose. My brain tested my skull's commitment to physically contain it. More red wine and bile splashed the bowl and then there was some dry heaving before I collapsed back onto the cool of the bathroom tile. I focused on breathing through the pain of my burning sinus and throbbing head. I tried to remember how I ended up on the dog bed but thinking caused more pain. Two of my dogs gathered around me looking very concerned while the third lapped up splashed wine puke from the floor. There was an empty bottle of red on the counter by the tub and a fingerprint-smudged glass beside it. Seems I'd decided a bath was in order last night. Hot bubble baths are an excellent component to a night of excessive drinking—assuming you desire the added dehydration they cause to maximize your suffering the next day. I tried to remember if that was the same bottle I had opened before I went out to dinner or if, God forbid, it was the damning evidence of having consumed the second bottle. Based on the puking, which I seldom do, it was the second bottle. Today was going to be a very bad day.

I crawled back to my office and curled fetal on the dog bed. I gazed up at my computer in a futile effort to determine the time. Oh, fuck. My computer. What had I done? Who had I Facebooked? I had been trying to break myself completely of the habit of drunken social networking but the problem was—I was always drunk when it came time to enforce the policy. On good nights, I indulged my fetish for white-wine-fueled domain name acquisitions but on bad nights, like last night no doubt had been, I stalked people on Facebook and Twitter. I took the opportunity to tell them exactly what I had thought of them in seventh grade or relentlessly clicked their "like" buttons and chimed in on thread after thread or jumped in on trending topics, often with people I did not know at all, an act that can haunt you for weeks.

Terror provided me with the required motivation to get up and assess exactly how much damage I had done. I looked on AOL and determined that I hadn't emailed anyone from that account. AOL was pretty much useless now that I am the only person in America that still uses it and since they discontinued the "from AOL to AOL" email UNSEND feature. Unsend had been a Godsend in the past when I had woken up to see I had been over-served the night before and had chosen to settle several scores, real and imagined, via email. I will forever mourn unsend.

Next stop—Twitter. They should offer breathalyzer apps for these social networking sites. Blow a certain number, and the site will just archive your posts until you are sober again and can review if you really do want to tell your old boss that he can suck your ass for supporting John Boehner's policies. Maybe, sober, you won't find it so unbearably offensive that a total stranger is a huge fan of Victoria Jackson. Maybe, in the sober light of day, you won't need to threaten that person with actual physical violence involving both her hair and her taint. I'm just saying.

So, heart racing, I scanned my tweets. Apparently, the character limit on Twitter worked to successfully curtail any real damage I might have done. I found one Tweet only, with a hundred and forty nearly space-free characters strung together from which nothing intelligible could be gleaned beyond the hashtag *#birthdaysuck*.

The Facebook icon leered malevolently at me from my Google homepage. I'm sort of a begrudging Facebook member, learned about me, the more upbeat he seemed to sound. Maybe I did love Hunter.

"Okay," Hunter continued. "All I need now is the number on line seven of your tax return from last year and we can wrap this refi up."

I couldn't believe how easy this was going. Maybe my luck was turning, after all? I dug through my files and retrieved the form requested. Line seven—wages, salaries, tips etc. I read Hunter the number there: $11,203.

"Okay," Hunter chirped in response. "And what other income do you have? Income properties, dividends, alimonies, that sort of thing?"

I explained that eleven thousand was it. My total income. Most of which had come in the form of tiny residual checks of under forty dollars, before taxes, from television shows I had done over a decade ago. Hunter was certain I did not understand the question.

"Okay, well, tell me the number you see in the line showing your adjusted gross income. Line thirty-seven."

"Line thirty-seven? It says negative seventy-five thousand, eight hundred and four dollars."

"Negative? As in minus?"

"Yes. Last year was worse. It's been really hard. Thank God for unemployment insurance. And refis," I said and allowed myself a small, optimistic but self-deprecating giggle.

"You have no other income you can claim?"

"No. I wish."

"Well, I am afraid I cannot proceed with this refi based on that income."

"But, I'm confused. I am refinancing it to get a lower payment."

"Yeah. I'm sorry. There's nothing I can do based on that income."

"What if I do not take out any cash or consolidate the credit card debt? What if we just do a straight refi for a new thirty-year fixed at the way lower rate?"

"Yeah, I'm sorry. You do not qualify for that."

"I don't qualify to make a lower payment? What sense does that make? It is a lower payment."

"You need to show more income."

"But Citibank FedExed me an invitation to refi. Based on my long credit history with them. With you."

Crickets from Hunter.

"This doesn't make any sense. Citi already owns my loan. We are already in a relationship. Citi has already taken the risk on me and I have already proven myself worthy of that risk. Not one late payment in my entire life."

"I understand that, but we need to see a stable income so we can be assured that you are good for the loan."

"But you are already on the hook for the loan. If I default on the current loan or on the loan I am applying for now, either way, it is Citi that will be eating the loss."

"I understand that."

"So, if it is default Citi fears, wouldn't lowering my payment decrease the possibility of that happening?"

"Your income and assets do not qualify you for this loan."

"Does it sound logical to you that a person isn't qualified to make a lower payment? The same bank. A lower payment. How can anyone not be qualified to pay less?"

"I'm sorry."

"What the fuck?"

"I'm sorry. If you remember some additional income you may have, feel free to call us back."

"Remember? Suddenly remember what? That I have a six-figure income I forgot about?"

"I understand you are disappointed. We will keep this application open. If your financial situation changes, call us back. Now, you have a great day, okay?"

I decided to punish Hunter by hanging up on him. It wasn't very satisfying but it was all the rebellion I had in my power.

Immediately after I hung up, the phone rang. It was my mother.

"Hi," I answered, in my most dejected tone.

"Hey! How was your birthday dinner? Did you look fabulous?"

My mother has always been my greatest supporter. She thinks everything I do is amazing and is genuinely baffled that the rest of the world doesn't think I am more talented than Kate Blanchett and more beautiful than Naomi Campbell. While this might sound sweet and endearing, and, of course, it is on many levels, there is a strong element of delusion in her confidence that my rise to fame and fortune and worldwide adoration is still inevitable. She doesn't seem to realize that her absolute conviction that I will still achieve stratospheric success does not magically create opportunity for me, nor does it satisfy bill collectors.

"Hello? Collection agency? Yes, this is Ruby Fitzgerald. I just wanted to let you know that my mother is really sure that this is going to be my year. She told me it is all going to turn around very soon so—no need to keep calling to remind me of my overdue debts. They will all be repaid, with interest, as soon as the rest of the world finally realizes what they have been missing out on by ignoring me completely. It's just a matter of time. My mom just said so. Okay?"

"No, Ma. I looked old and fat and it was all I could do to get the valet to allow me into the parking lot."

She laughed this off.

"I'm sure you are exaggerating. I'll bet you looked gorgeous. Did you meet anyone famous? You never know who might have seen you! This could be the jump start you need to get your career back in gear."

Part of me was grateful that her confidence in me was so unshakable. The rest of me was furious that she refused to read the writing on the wall. That latter part of me was desperate for someone to acknowledge that I was in a really dangerous place. That part of me wanted a realistic game plan from someone about how I could ever again support myself as an actress or, and this is something I hadn't fully admitted even to myself, give me an idea of what else I could possibly do for a living.

"My career? I haven't worked in—like—six years."

"That's not true. You did that movie last year."

"Yeah, right. It was a couple of days' work for a hundred dollars a day. It hardly counts."

"It counts and this is all gonna change soon. Your career is going to be bigger than ever."

"My career consists of four auditions a year to day-play women who are always described as, 'Once pretty—but now beaten down by life,'" I said, truthfully. "And I can't even get those jobs. Why do you think that is? Huh? It is because I actually am getting beaten down by life! And people can smell it on me. Nobody wants to be around that," I said and couldn't help but laugh at my sudden realization of how awful and how true it was. My only other option was to cry.

My mother laughed with me, as if my rant had been a melodrama played for comedy.

"It sounds like I'm being funny but I'm not kidding. It's just, I think I might be done. Honestly. Think about it. There isn't a TV show on my résumé that is still on the air. I'm one of those black-and-white headshots you see hanging up at the dry cleaners amongst dozens of other dust-covered headshots. I'm one of those has-been, anonymous actors from the seventies."

"No. You weren't even acting in the seventies," she said, refusing to see any significance in what I was saying.

"I don't mean literally. Come on, Ma. The fact of the matter is, I haven't earned enough money to put me over the poverty line in nearly a decade. Thank God for home equity loans or I would have had to give up on this a long time ago. But my loan is maxed out and I have zero liquid assets. And there is no reason to think my career will ever revive, even marginally. There is far less reason to expect it to recover to the point that I can reliably support myself through it. But what else can I do? If you think my acting résumé looks dated and unimpressive, you should see my regular résumé. Retail cashier? Twenty years ago? At a store that has long since literally been torn down. I don't think I can get a real job. I have no skills, no references, no experience."

"You have waitress experience."

"What?"

"Yes. You were a waitress for a while."

"No. No, Ma, I wasn't. I was never a waitress."

"Yes, you were. At that fancy place. Remember?"

"Oh my God!" I yelled, finally figuring out what she was talking about. "No. I wasn't a waitress, Ma. I played a waitress. On TV!"

"Oh. Right," she said, realizing her mistake, and she laughed. "I don't know why they canceled that show. I thought it was really cute..." she said and drifted off into memoryland.

"What am I going to do?" I asked, continuing my rant. "I don't have any more wiggle room. I'm completely broke. I have a mid-five-figure credit card debt. I already live on little more than bulk-rate carbohydrates and I drink wine that tastes like salad dressing. I haven't purchased a non-essential item that costs over twenty dollars in years."

"You just need to stay positive," my mother insisted. "It has to turn around."

"That's just it. It doesn't have to turn around. And I have been positive. I have been wearing the blinders of positivity and absolute certainty and trudging forward for, some would say, too long now, only to get myself deeper and deeper into debt waiting for the dream to kick back in. And it hasn't."

"It will. I can't understand why it hasn't already."

"Exactly. You have been giving me this pep talk for more years now than my original career lasted. And you don't need to understand why my career is dying to acknowledge that it is."

"I don't know... maybe..." she said, unsure how to finish her sentence, and I could feel through the phone how badly she wanted to be able to fix my life.

"I qualify for Welfare, mom. And I have for ten years now."

That sobered her up. It even sobered me up. There are few things more depressing than having to convince someone else how fucked you are. In the end, they never truly understand it and can, at the very least, dismiss whatever discomfort your reality brings them and escape into the myriad but lesser discomforts of their own lives. You, however, have just effectively given a D and C to whatever corner of your soul harbored the last vestiges of your self-preservational denial.

We both held the line in silence for a few moments and absorbed the total hopelessness that was my future as an actress.

"Ugh," I said, finally. "I'm sorry. I don't mean to be a huge bummer and I know you are trying to help, but I really do need to accept reality here and figure out some way to pay for the rest of my life."

"I'm sorry. I wish there was something I could do."

Her tacit admission that my life really had hit a wall suddenly made it ten times more real for me. Sympathy can be devastating. I started to cry. I didn't want her to know it.

"I know. I know. Thanks," I said in a choppy staccato. "I gotta go. I'll talk to you later. Okay?"

"All right. You hang in there. It's gonna be okay."

"I know," I replied, lying. "Thanks."

I hung up the phone and cried myself into a near-migraine. Finally spent, I willed my thoughts away from bankruptcy, foreclosure, exile. Away from thoughts of grinding, minimum-wage jobs with ball-busting teenage bosses. The first pleasant thing my thoughts fell upon was a cold beer. I looked at the clock on my computer. It sneered a too-early-to-start-drinking 11:11 AM at me. I decided that 11:11 seemed meaningful, like a sign. I also decided that I didn't care what my computer thought of me. I went to the kitchen and opened a Corona Light. Halfway through the second beer, I began to regain some of my critical ability to live in denial. I could, I observed, begin to face my life again with a posture that didn't insist on being described as "slumped."

Later, at my desk, as I nursed my hangover with another beer and began the process of stacking the bills in order of their priority, I got a new friend request on Facebook. My heart picked up its pace when I saw the name. It was from The Albino! I sat for a few moments, basking in the glow of the as-yet-unaccepted friend request, before clicking the link. Almost immediately, I got a message from him.

"Thanks for friending me, Shorty. I just wanted to apologize for leaving suddenly last night but my cellie started blowing up and I had to go help a brother out. Can I make it up to you tomorrow night? At Pho Bich Nga…?"

The next night was Valentine's Day. The idea of running the PBN gauntlet again and sitting in a room full of romantic douche-bag couples was not my idea of a fun way to spend the evening. At least, that's what I told myself. I wrote him back pointing out that the next night was Valentine's Day and asked if he was sure he wanted to hang out that night. He said he knew and that it didn't bother him if it didn't bother me. Or at least, that's what I think he said in his HipHop-ese. With a flood of imprudent enthusiasm, I wrote him back.

"Why don't you just come over my house? I don't live far from the restaurant and I can cook us some dinner here!"

He immediately agreed, I gave him directions and the plan was set.

As soon as I hit send on the confirmation of details, I regretted agreeing to see him again at all. What was I thinking? Fear began to set in. I hadn't been on a date in years. What if I'd forgotten how to do it? What was The Albino going to expect of me? Did I need to shave my legs? Should I shave other things? I didn't even know this guy and now he was coming to my house. What had I done?

I decided to make a trip to McDonald's to take the edge off my panic and maybe finally end my waning hangover. There is nothing like McD's. It is the only fast food chain I patronize. I've been a fish-eating vegetarian for over twenty years but McDonald's remains my own personal crack. I have to pretend I do not know that there is beef tallow in the French fries and block out the fact that McD's are a great supporter of the factory farming that spurred my vegetarianism to begin with, but when I am hung over, McDonald's is my best friend.

I ordered a #1 Big Mac value meal with fries, a diet Coke (gotta save calories somewhere) and a Filet-O-Fish. Once out of the drive thru, I pulled over on a side street like a drug addict jonesing for a fix. I took several big gulps of the best fucking diet Coke I had ever tasted while throwing furtive glances around to make sure I was not being watched. I opened the fish sandwich and scooped all that tartar sauce up on the top bun. This would serve as a bowl and dip for the fries. I grabbed the golden goodness of the square fish stick looking back at me and threw the bottom bun of the fish sandwich in the bag. I took the top off of the Big Mac and threw it in the bag. I removed the burgers and put them aside for my dogs. I placed the fish patty on the middle bun piece and flipped it over onto the bottom bun and its remaining ingredients.

Special sauce, lettuce, cheese, pickles, onions and a filet of fish on what was once a sesame seed bun. I rammed it into my mouth and nearly fainted with pleasure. Every cell in my body reacted negatively to the toxicity and I felt zits popping out on my face as I chewed. I didn't give a fuck. I dipped a handful of fries in the fatty tartar sauce and forced them into my mouth before I swallowed my first bite of sandwich. I was disgusting. I felt the shame of a tweeker turning her first trick for drugs. My eyes flashed a scan of the horizon searching for the PETA police. My pants felt a size tighter. I finished that food in less than two minutes, literally drinking the last bit of fries from the cardboard container. It was glorious.

Slouched in the car, high from whatever it is in McDonald's food that made Morgan Spurlock's liver begin to shut down in Supersize Me, the plan to dine with The Albino seemed like it might actually be a fun adventure.

I decided to go immediately to the supermarket and shop for groceries. I wanted to devise a menu to impress but that I could also claim had been casually thrown together. Walking around Gelson's killed my trans-fat buzz. How can a jar of mustard possibly cost twelve dollars? Pasta sauce in a jar for fourteen dollars? I wanted to make the meal seem lavish while not leaving me short on my now-even-larger mortgage payment but the prices on the shelves, even the red-tagged sale items, left me with sticker shock. I priced fresh seafood and discovered that wild caught salmon for two was going to cost $50. It was cheaper to eat it in a friggin' restaurant. Why hadn't I agreed to meet him out for dinner? He probably would have paid. I'm just such a retarded control freak. I can't let people take care of me and I am so weirded out by the idea of a date at all that making it happen under my roof feels like the only safe way to do it. I'm not sure if it was the "Karma Chameleon" soundtrack being piped into the store or my hangover that was thwarting my efforts to concentrate and come up with a meal plan but thirty minutes of aimless wandering and discouraging prices later, I noticed all I'd put into my cart were several different sugary beverages and a mixed case of electrolyte waters. Shopping full but dehydrated will do that to one's selections so maybe I should lay the blame there. I decided at last to make hand-cut pasta because flour was cheap. I thought a pink sauce with some shrimp would be a mainstream choice and feel mildly decadent. I bought arugula and a nice shaved parmesan, a gorgeous hunk of brie and crusty bread. I still had red wine at home from my Bevmo sale purchases, at least one of which I was pretty sure was palatable. It was a simple meal but the pasta and sauce would both be made from scratch. I would even pink the sauce with a fancy, homemade ricotta rather than simply using heavy cream. I would make up with caring and attention to detail that which was missing in imagination. I spent over $120 and walked out with two small grocery bags. How is that possible? I pushed the hot wave of guilt and adrenalin down into a nice, tight ball in the pit of my stomach and walked across the lot to my car.

I went home, cleaned up the bathroom, fed the dogs, got into bed while it was still only late afternoon and watched *Bridget Jones*. Yeah, rough life having fucking Hugh Grant and Colin Firth fight over you despite the fact that you are—gasp!—thirty pounds overweight. I've always felt that romantic comedies are substantially damaging to the collective female psyche. For women, they are emotional pornography. They are a total mind fuck and I recommend they be viewed with caution. They teach women to need, want and expect men to swoop in to rescue us, but only once our spirits have been appropriately broken by the various slings and arrows of life and by our own feminine caprice and incompetence. They present this very sexist attitude toward women and wrap it in a fucking Matthew McConaughey or Ryan Reynolds bow and we eat it up and then expect real life to live up to the bullshit fantasy. Don't let them fool you into believing that your suffering and loneliness will be alleviated by a guy, if only you suffer long enough and, more importantly, suffer bravely enough. If you think about it, it was probably a guy that made you suffer and feel lonely to begin with. Why look to another problem to fix what the first problem caused?

I went to sleep at 8 PM, uncommonly sober, praying I would lose ten pounds in my sleep, praying that I had made the most impressive menu choices for the next night and praying that The Albino and I would have a fantasy evening and, despite myself, praying that he would be the beginning of the end of all my suffering and loneliness. Fucking Bridget Jones.

3 The albino

I HADN'T WANTED TO LET The Albino know that I usually eat dinner at five o'clock so I suggested he come over at 6:30 PM for cocktails, but I didn't see any reason I shouldn't still keep my regular five o'clock date with my first glass of wine. I considered putting a 2 Live Crew CD in the player for Bunker and then realized that, of course, I'd never owned one. I settled for an R.L. Burnside record, instead. Parched, I poured my third glass of wine as The Albino arrived, promptly at the designated time.

As I attempted to open the door, the knob came off in my hand. After what felt like an hour of fumbling, I was able to screw it back on and get the door open. Flustered and more than a little embarrassed, I greeted my guest. I was relieved to find that his platinum hair and blue-eyed combo was exactly as striking as I had remembered it. That is not always a given when you have a pattern of forming physical assessments of people and rating their attractiveness while you are half crocked.

Immediately upon entering my house, he was enthusiastically greeted by my kids. His reaction couldn't have been more dramatic if he'd been made of straw and my dogs were balls of fire. I hadn't noticed how tall The Albino was the other night because I had never seen him standing, but watching him jump and flail like The Scarecrow from the *Wizard of Oz*, I put his height to be at least six two. I noticed he was one of those guys that carried a ridiculous amount of stuff in his pants' front pockets. It gave his upper thighs rather disturbing chipmunk cheeks.

"I'm allergic to dogs! I'm extremely allergic to most breeds of dogs!" he screamed, suddenly whiter than the Jonas brothers.

I apologized as I scrambled to collect my kids and lock them upstairs. Once they were safely away, I rejoined my agitated guest. He was engaged in the futile effort of removing the airborne dog hairs that mercilessly attach themselves to everyone who enters my house as if we were all human intake ducts. I wasn't sure if I was supposed to hug him, kiss him on the cheek or fist bump him so I pretended we had already done that bit. I breezed by him, beckoning him to follow me to the kitchen—which he did.

"Hollah! If I was hip you had dogs, girl, I would–a brought my Bennydrill, yo!" I think he said. I wasn't really listening because he was behind me and I was trying to concentrate on making my ass look good.

We turned the corner and entered my kitchen. Cooking for people is my favorite thing to do. Despite my many mutinying appliances, I am very proud of my kitchen. I designed it myself, complete with a Viking range that is nearly as big as my bed and used to entertain guests far more often. My own lovingly made hand-cut pasta was beautifully displayed as it sat drying on my granite countertop.

"Help yourself to a glass of wine," I suggested as I took a warmed baguette from the oven. I attempted to pose seductively as I began cutting the bread to pair it with the brie which was room temperature and just begging to be one with the parts of my thighs that I nightly pinched with such disgust. I turned to get my wine and be sure he was settling in and saw him standing there staring at the wine and cheese. I placed some steaming bread by the brie, picked up my glass and looked at his cutie face. I thought I saw the beginning of a hive on his cheek but it was more than I could deal with so I ignored it.

"Help yourself. There is a glass right there."

"Sorry, brah. I can't, um..."

"What's wrong?" I asked, picking up the gorgeous bottle of red and holding it poised over his empty glass.

"I'm allergic to red wine."

Oh, God.

"No problem. Do you want something else to drink?"

I tried to look calm as I did a panicked mental inventory of any other alcohol I might have had in the house to serve him. I knew I had a gallon jug of Southern Comfort, though nobody I knew would ever accept responsibility for bringing it into my house, let alone agree to drink any. I'd had it for a decade now. I had coconut rum left over from my father's last visit, but I was pretty sure I had only canned, diet tonic to use as a mixer. How could I provide him with the craft cocktails to which he was accustomed?

"I don't want to be a bother."

A bother? Having to get through this night with a completely sober date would be the greatest bother of all. What are you? New? *It is a good thing he is cute and that I am beaten down by life,* I thought, inwardly mocking myself. Outwardly, I chose different words entirely.

"Stop. It's no bother at all," I soothed as I dug through my liquor cabinet. "I think I have some Malibu and... hmm... let's see," I stalled as I blocked his view with my body and pushed the Southern Comfort out of his sight. I didn't want him to think I was trashy. "I have a nip of Sapphire here, mudslide mix, Vermouth, a bottle of Absinthe..." I said, with extra enthusiasm on the word "Absinthe." Hipsters drank Absinthe, right? "And... um..." I trailed off as I dug deeper and tried to imagine what kind of degenerate would have nips of gin and mudslide mix in their cabinets.

"Do you have any Pinot Grigio?"

"I do not," I answered without adding that I thought Pinot Grigio tasted like vented spleen and, because I was raised right, I didn't ask him why he hadn't brought a bottle of wine with him to begin with, as civilized dinner guests do. I chose the high road instead.

"Damn. I am fresh out of Pinot Grigio but I think I know where we can get some!"

Ten minutes later we were at my favorite neighborhood wine store. Rite-Aid is your best bet to get a decent price on what I call table wine. It would appear that ten bucks is special-occasion-only stuff for the average person doing their grocery shopping at a drugstore. Forget about buying a bottle under five dollars, those shelves are always completely sold out. But, because people that drink $20-$25 dollar bottles of wine don't go shopping for it at the local pharmacy, I've seen delightful chardonnays there marked down to half what Costco charges for the same bottle and, hence, almost within my price range and a good option when one feels the urge to splurge.

So, while my hustler frugality wasn't on the top of my list of things to reveal to The Albino right out of the gate of romance, shit happens. Who was he to judge, anyway? He hardly had any fucking pigment. Furthermore, he let me pay for the two bottles of the Santa Margherita Pinot Grigio he had pointed out as his favorite. I let him slide because he had sprung for those rounds at Pho Bich Nga and they probably cost him his rent money but I made a mental note all the same.

Back in my kitchen, I poured us both a very deep glass of vino and encouraged him to try the brie.

"The bread is not warm anymore but the brie looks ridiculous," I said and dug into the brie in an effort to lead by example. Plus I was really nervous and eating helps that. I shoved a day's worth of carbs/fat in my mouth at one go.

"I'm allergic to dairy," he said.

Grateful he was making a joke about the situation so far, I laughed and then tried to speak through the orgasm in my mouth.

"Seriously, have some brie and I will get the salad together," I mumbled and turned toward the opposite counter to do just that.

"Honestly, I am allergic to dairy, Pood."

My back was to him so I allowed my face to drop for a beat. I guzzled some wine, swallowed the brie, adjusted my expression and turned around. I couldn't think of anything to say except, "What the fuck, dude?" but that didn't feel like an appropriate thing to say to a guest I hardly knew so I simply stared at him like he was an alien.

He looked genuinely apologetic and was tapping the wine glass and the brie plate rhythmically. I thought I saw his head twitch. Ugh, right. Tourette's. My heart again went pitter pat and my next instinct was to comfort him.

"No! That's okay. Really."

He took a deep, deep drink of white wine. It made me proud. He put the glass down, touched the rim, touched the brie plate and I saw an undeniable head twitch.

"Really? Allergic to dogs, red wine and dairy. Wow. Are you allergic to pasta, too?" I giggled, trying to lighten the mood.

"No," he said with a weak laugh and looked down sheepishly and touched his glass. He seemed so vulnerable, despite a vocabulary from a Compton episode of *Cribs*. Fucking ticky heartbreaker. How could I resist?

"Well, is there anything else you are allergic to that I should know about?"

"Well, uh... seafood?"

I decided that being super good-natured about this was the wisest course of action because I had a growing suspicion I was being Punk'd. I glanced around the kitchen looking for some evidence of hidden cameras.

"Okay! So let's see. My plan was to serve you red wine and cheese—not gonna work. Then I had an arugula salad with shaved parmesan—cheese—not gonna work. Then I had a ricotta-pinked red sauce with shrimp and home-made pasta for you—not gonna work. Do you realize that if you eliminated dogs, red wine, cheese and seafood from who I am—I would cease to exist?"

No response beyond a twitch-o-the-shoulder.

"Pardon me for asking, but what *do* you eat?"

"I eat a lot of salad and chicken and, you know, In-N-Out. Regular stuff."

"Wellll... I don't eat meat. So, what the Hell am I going to feed you tonight?" I asked in my best "I'm just bustin' yer balls and this is all really okay with me" tone. I looked to the door for Ashton but, so far, he was a no show.

After we determined where the foods we both ate intersected and compared that (limited) list to what I had in the house, we eventually sat down to a meal of pasta with arugula, garlic and olive oil and garlic bread. He made impressively short work of the Pinot Grigio while I tried to pace myself a tad, having already consumed half a bottle of red before he'd arrived.

I am not sure if I was just getting used to it or if he actually tapered off the wigga-speak but it seemed to stop, mostly. The dinner conversation was largely about where he was from (all over, army brat), how he had gotten into acting and our experiences as actors. He touched things randomly all through the meal (literally touched them), and even though I knew he was not touching me out of any affection, inexplicably, affection was what I took from it every time he did it. As soon as dinner was over, he asked if there was somewhere outside that we could sit and talk because the dog hair was killing him. I noticed that he did, in fact, have a few hives and I happened to have a nice patio so we adjourned.

As I turned around to close the French doors behind him, he grabbed me and planted a solid, twitch-free tongue sandwich right on me. I hadn't kissed a guy in five years and the impact this physical contact had on me cannot be overstated. My pants about fell off. If he hadn't had such a tight grip on me, I might have collapsed. The kiss lasted a hundred years and that was a hundred years too short. When the kiss finally broke, The Albino loosened his grip on me and looked at me just the way you want a guy to look at you in that moment. He touched my cheek and I decided to believe it was a caress and not an uncontrollable OCD impulse. He touched his own brow and touched my cheek again. His cell phone rang from within his overstuffed front pockets. He stepped back away from me, dug his phone out and flipped it open.

"What up, G?"

While he mumbled rap lyrics into the phone I took a moment to wonder what the Hell I was doing. While not literally being an albino, he looked to be a lot younger than I was and he talked like a suburban mall kid. He was allergic to my dogs and, therefore, my house. He was allergic to dairy, red wine and seafood. That is tantamount to being allergic to my mouth. How could this possibly work out even in the shortest term?

I heard him end his call with a very street, "*I'll hit ya on the hip, blood.*" He then grabbed me around the waist and asked, "Where were we?"

Boom. Another killer kiss and my doubts were drowned out by the sound of crashing surf in my ears. When the kiss finally ended, I was suddenly shy. He looked me in the eyes and I blushed deeply. I looked at the ground and literally kicked at invisible dirt. It had been so long since I had kissed someone, these two moments with The Albino really opened the emotional floodgates. "I love this guy!" echoed out from some neglected corner of my brain. "I love this guy so much! And he has the same name as my dead dog! He is perfect for me! How could anything possibly go wrong, especially in the short term?"

Squirming under his scrutiny, I moved in to kiss him. Just as our lips met, his cell phone rang again. Again, he answered it.

I took the opportunity to go inside and get us each a full glass of wine. My mind was swimming with incomplete thoughts and concerns about the rest of the night. How far does a girl go on a first date these days? I walked back out to the patio promising myself I would not let The Albino get past second base no matter how badly I might want to. I was giddy as a schoolgirl.

"Here you go. I got you another glass of wine."

He put his phone in his pocket and took the glass of white.

"Sorry, gotta jump, babe. That was my bro…"

He was explaining but I wasn't listening. I felt myself nodding understandingly.

"No, yeah. Of course. That's totally cool…" I heard myself saying and before I knew what had happened, The Albino was gone.

I woke up the next day to an email from The Albino. It was a flowery thank you for the previous evening and a perfunctory explanation involving his homie and blah blah blah. It didn't matter. The new email took all of the sting out of what had felt like a rejection the night before. I invited him over that night and he accepted.

I went to Rite-Aid and stocked up on more Santa Margherita that I could not afford. I bought stuff for a Caesar salad and a simple pasta alla checca and made homemade garlic bread. I again allowed myself to be very excited.

He showed up at about 5 PM and I immediately plied him with the Pinot Grigio. The fur in the house, in the carpets and in the furniture made him break out in hives very quickly so we again went out to the patio. We made out for what seemed like the best week of my life but it was probably closer to an hour. My face was getting raw from the scruff of his beard so I thought it might be a good time to take a break and eat dinner.

"Whoo! Well! Whattaya say we go into the kitchen and have something to eat?" I suggested.

He pulled out his phone and, as if on cue, it rang. He, of course, answered it. I went to the kitchen to give him some privacy. A few minutes later, he came into the kitchen.

"I gotta take off… blah… blah… blah…"

More urban youth speak meaning he had to go, more veiled disappointment on my end, another effusive email in the morning and another date to get together. This pattern repeated for a week or so; The Albino came over, we drank wine, we made out mercilessly, he answered a lot of calls and texts and inevitably left far earlier than I'd hoped and never once did we progress beyond first base. This was the sort of affair typically reserved for seventh graders in finished basements.

Once, we were going at it seated in my bathroom. I don't know why we were in the bathroom, maybe to avoid furry things, I don't know, but we were. Sitting, straddling his lap, I felt his cell phone vibrate from within his pants front pocket before I heard it. He froze and I opened my eyes to see him staring right back at me, lips still pressed to mine in the aborted kiss. As we stared at each other, I slowly realized, I was supposed to get up so he could answer his phone, which, like a douche, I politely did.

"Sup, homie-cide?"

I looked in the mirror as he took the call. Horrified, I beheld my face, cheeks and chin just this side of actually bleeding and I promised myself I was going to take this shit to the next level if it killed me. I am no sexual predator, not with five years of celibacy under my belt, but I was poised to add another five years if something didn't change and change soon. When he ended his called and patted his lap for my return, I got into his lap and put my arms around his neck. I looked deep into his eyes and said, "I have an idea."

He waited for the idea while alternately tapping his own brow and my cheek. I put on my most seductive temptress voice and indicated my bathtub built for two that was right next to us.

"Let's take a bubble bath..."

"A bubble bath, huh?"

"Yeah! I'll draw a nice deep bath, we can get some more wine and we can, you know, get in the tub."

"Word! Sounds sweet, babe," he said while tapping something in Morse code on his brow and my cheek.

Wow. That was easy.

"Okay, well, why don't you go down and pour us some more wine and I'll hook us up here."

He left the room, I turned the taps on and dumped a huge quantity of shampoo into the stream of water. As I watched the suds build up, I felt my insecurities swell in direct proportion. What had I gotten myself into here? I hadn't planned this new development nor, more mysteriously, had I prepped for it. I tried to remember the last time I had trimmed the snatch patch. Was I sporting a forty pound, winter bush? How would I look naked? Naked from behind? Did the back of my thighs look like powder-pink ballet tights filled to capacity with lumpy oatmeal? Did this development mean I was going to have to have sex with him tonight? I remembered an old *Cosmo* article about how to look ten pounds thinner instantly and, since it was too late to "buy a bigger bed" in which I would look smaller (actual advice), I quickly lit candles and turned off the lights. I didn't feel any thinner but it was definitely darker. I was somewhat calmed.

The Albino returned and handed me my wine.

"Oooh, chillin' in the candle light, eh, shorty?"

"Yeah. Where's your wine?"

"Babe, bad news. I gotta jump. My cellie's blowin' up, yo."

More of the same crap—his *bro*, the *hizzie*. I couldn't understand the actual sentences but I recognized his familiar inner city youth code and knew that it meant, again, that he was leaving. I adopted my standard, casual attitude toward his sudden departure.

I walked him to the door and we said our goodbyes. I fetched the bottle of red from my kitchen and polished it off alone, in my bathtub built for two.

In the interest of economy and to preserve some shred of my own dignity, I will not detail each of the subsequent "dates" with The Albino beyond sharing that I suggested that damned bathtub so often it became almost confrontational. My friends began calling me "Bubbles" and I grew steely in my resolve. I bought every bottle of pinot Grigio on the Rite-Aid shelves in an effort to weaken his will but The Albino proved to be a better man than I was. Eventually, he broke me and I stopped responding to his affectionate morning emails with increasingly combative and, ultimately, futile invitations to bathe.

"Why do you think he wouldn't get in the fucking tub?" I asked my girlfriend, Mack. Now, Mack is a gal that can get the job done. She never seems to wear a bra and I'm not sure if that is the magic of her method but her success rate made her a natural source from which to seek romantic advice.

"Does he have a tiny penis?"

"I have no idea. Things never got that far."

"But you sat in his lap and made out and stuff, right? Couldn't you feel anything?"

"Honestly, no."

Her expression said, "Well, there you go."

"That doesn't mean as much as you might think. He packs so much crap into his front pockets, the bulges on his thighs act as bumper guards for his package."

"Maybe he is gay."

"Then why would he come over and make out with me?"

"I don't want to hurt your feelings but maybe he's just not that into you."

"I know, but then why come over every day for weeks?

She thought about that a bit and then shrugged. It made no sense.

"Maybe he has a vagina!" I blurted.

"I think you'd know if he was a girl, Ruby."

"Nuh-uh! Have you ever seen Buck Angel? Buck Angel looks like a super butch Danny Masterson but he has a full-on God-given vagina."

Since there is no way to convince anyone about the magical, awesome human that is Buck Angel without photos, I found his website and showed Mack the evidence.

"Oh my God! Buck Angel is a totally hot guy... with a totally shaved beaver! Maybe Bunker *is* a woman!"

"I don't know if that answers more questions than it raises."

"Okay, whatever. So, what are you going to do now?"

"I don't know. This is ridiculous. I've gone five years without finding one guy worth kissing, I spend three weeks ramming my tongue down the throat of a person with indeterminate genitalia and ablutophobia and now I am..."

"Wait," Mack cut me off. "Ablutophobia?"

"Fear of bathing. I looked it up."

"Five years is insane. You need to get dicked down, sister."

"That's a charming expression."

"True, though."

"Yeah. I know," I conceded "But how am I supposed to meet anyone? I never work anymore and I'm too old and too broke to hang around in bars. What else is there?"

"eHarmony?"

"I tried that two years ago when you kept insisting, remember? They rejected me."

"I don't remember that! They rejected you? Why?"

"I don't know. I got some letter saying that I was not reliably predictable or something and that they didn't feel they could match me with anyone. [*The actual letter: 'Our matching model could not accurately predict with whom you would be best matched. This occurs for about 20% of potential users, so one in five people simply will not benefit from our service.'*] While I kinda found that flattering, another part of me was freaked out that a service that makes its money by agreeing to enter your information into a computer lottery with a bunch of losers was afraid to throw me in the mix. They think I am so awful that they need to protect their subscribers from wasting precious seconds looking at my profile. What is that about?"

Mack was laughing. I couldn't help but notice her breasts seemed to laugh along with her, unrestrained as they were in her loose-fitting T-shirt.

"And then I submitted an application to that reality TV show that fixes people up," I said, tearing my eyes from her chest and looking pointedly into her eyes. "And they rejected me. Then I applied to a group dating thing where they send like twenty people out to a wine tasting or a pottery class and they all mingle…"

"That actually sounds pretty cool."

"Yeah. Rejected. Then this high-end 'attractive people' New York dating service got my info somehow and emailed me an invitation to apply to their newly opened Los Angeles chapter. This one costs a lot, like two grand a year for membership plus the cost of the group events it plans. They have a whole submission process that involves a written form and then an interview and then who knows what—some gauntlet. Very exclusive. I didn't even make the first cut for the one-on-one interview with their staff."

"That's crazy."

"No shit. What am I? The Elephant Man? Fucking Sarah Jessica Parker is a beauty product spokesperson and fashion icon and I am not allowed to 'break the ice' on an internet dating site with a fat, bald, divorced middle manager from the inland empire? What the fuck?"

"I don't know. How's work? Any auditions?"

"And that's the other thing. No auditions. None. Or, so few and for such insignificant stuff that it is tantamount to none. I mean, six auditions a year is not the kind of schedule that leads to meaningful employment. I used to have six auditions a week. It's a numbers game. You need to go on fifty auditions to book one job. At the rate I'm going, I will book a guest star spot in seven or eight years. Do you realize that, even with the occasional residual check I get, I have only earned more than ten grand in a year a few times in the last decade—often less than that?"

"Wow. How have you been living? Are your parents sending you money?"

"My parents don't have anything. They don't even have a savings account. I was living on a home equity loan for most of the last several years and, lately, on credit cards and cash advances."

"That's no good."

"I know. I don't know what else to do. Acting has been my only source of income for my entire adult life. I don't have a back-up plan. And the hardest part is that I live a really inexpensive life. My mortgage is cheaper than any decent apartment I could get that would work for me and three dogs. Am I really supposed to sell my house to move into a studio apartment that costs more than my current mortgage?"

"You're right. That isn't fair."

We sipped our coffee and reflected on that for a moment. I marveled at how long I had been surviving and remaining hopeful about my future with only my belief in some sort of ultimate, cosmic fairness as support. I tried to look into my future and see it without the whimsical concept of fairness coloring the imagery. A flip book of never previously considered outcomes flashed before my eyes. If life is just a lottery of things, some good but some almost unimaginably horrible, just a totally random distribution of blessings and curses that can happen to you at any time and for no reason, how do any of us ever walk outside our doors without expecting an anvil to fall on our heads? How do any of us ever have the gall to observe people dealing with an easily identifiable challenge, blindness, for example, or some other physical handicap, and not be moved to tears that we were lucky enough, so far anyway, to have not been dealt that hand? Is it fair that anyone should be blind? Where did I get off thinking it might not happen to me, maybe even today? I suddenly felt so arrogant for taking anything for granted and I realized that my believing in fairness was like anyone believing in God: it can often be comforting but there is no evidence in the world that either exists. In fact, there is overwhelming evidence that neither exists, but sitting there really absorbing that reality filled me with such horror, I literally shook my head to change my focus. Mercifully, Mack broke the silence.

"In other news, are you going to the St. Patrick's day party at Mike's next week?" she asked.

"Yeah. Free food and free booze. Count me in. Maybe in a room full of shit-faced strangers I will be able to find a guy without a vagina who will take the baton from The Albino and be willing to maybe touch my boobs."

"Be careful not to set your expectations too high there."

"You think you're kidding," I said and indulged in a deep sigh.

She nodded knowingly but her breasts were motionless, somber in the face of my predicaments.

I USED NOT TO BE a huge fan of St. Patrick's Day. As a native Bostonian, March 17 meant a parade I avoided, drunken Southie guys starting fights, people puking green beer in gutters and a lot of "Kiss me I'm Irish" buttons. However, having been away from Boston for more than half my life, the holiday took on different significance. In Boston, there were seventeen pages of Fitzgeralds in the phone book. In Los Angeles, people asked me how to spell my last name. St. Patty's had become a sentimental connection to my roots. And, I'd discovered, it is a lot more fun when you are one of the ones puking green and not the sober person trying to avoid stepping in it.

Mike Moran's Limerick Social Club tattoo parlor was ground zero this Paddy's day. Mike is the perfect mix of Tom Waits cool and long-lashed, Bambi sweetness. He is spun sugar in a heroin wrapper. He personifies timeless style. It was not unreasonable to think Mike might have a handsome, tattooed pal that I could sink my teeth into so I decided to go to the party with an open mind.

By the time Eliza, Mack and my married-since-high-school friends Wayne and Kate arrived, the joint was hopping. Mack was wearing an "ERIN GO BRALESS" T-shirt and a nametag sticker that read "Hi! I'm Erin." And yes. She was braless. We were able to twist our way to the bar and then retreated to a corner to drink our beers and criticize the crowd. Mike found us and treated us to a warm greeting. I swear I could feel the air stir every time he blinked his giant cow lashes over his enormous blue eyes. He was impossibly debonair. He spoke very slowly and with a musical cadence. The last word of each sentence was elongated and allowed to fade away at its own pace, like a train whistle in the distance. Even the simplest sentences sounded like Bukowski or Burroughs and Beat poetry when delivered from his lips.

"Hey, Ruby, babyyy... How you doinnng? Happy St. Patrick's daaay...."

"Happy St. Paddy's to you, sir," I said, beaming big hearts of love at him.

Mike greeted the rest of the gang, made some small talk with us and then turned his attention to me again.

"So, Ruby, a friend of mine over there thinks you are the bee's kneeees... He wants to meet yooou..."

"Uh-oh. Who? Which guy?"

He pointed to a guy across the room with a boyish face that didn't look a day older than sixteen except for the fact that nearly every bit of exposed skin, his hands and neck and even his cheekbone, was tattooed.

"The illustrated man over there? In the plaid shirt?" I asked and looked at Mike with concern.

"Nooo, not Orange County body suit over theeere..."

"Orange County body suit?"

"That means the only parts of his body that are tattooed are the parts that show when he is dressed," Wayne explained as he slipped his arm around Kate's waist, pulled her in tight to his side and cupped his hand over her ass. Despite having been married for a hundred years already, these two still behaved like horny teenagers in the throes of newfound passion. They were not above the occasional swingers' party or old-fashioned wife-swap, either. I wrote it off as their manner of rebelling against their traditional careers as real estate agent (Kate) and attorney (Wayne). I didn't need to manufacture such excitement in my life, I told myself, because my career provided plenty of that. Even though it didn't. Maybe I was just a prude.

"The rest of his trust fund body is pristine. He is faux gangsta," Wayne continued.

"Not him, Rubyyy," Mike said, nodding agreement with Wayne. "The tall drink of water behiiind hiiimmm..."

He indicated an exceedingly thin guy who was leaning casually up against the wall. My heart skipped a beat as I drank him up with my eyes. He was a dead ringer for my most recent object of lustful obsession, Tennessee-born musician Justin Townes Earle. I was relieved to see the guy wasn't looking at us so I took the opportunity to give him the once over twice. He was well over six feet tall, maybe 6' 5" or so, and wearing heavy glasses, deeply cuffed Levis, wingtips, a white shirt with the sleeves rolled, revealing heavily tattooed arms, a bandana at his throat and a brimmed hat with the brim flipped up. He was a vision in Billy Reid. He was perfection.

"What is his name?"

"His name is Niiick. He is one of the carpenters helping me design the new shop, honeeey. I think you'll really like hiiimmm."

I looked back over to Nick and saw that he was approaching us. My heart started to race.

"Hey, Mike! Aren't you going to introduce me to your friends?" he asked and he smiled at me. He was adorable and his confidence was disarming. Introductions were made. He was immediately very likeable. I nervously guzzled my beer.

"Hey, shorty. You need another beer. Let me get you one."

Oh God. Another with the "shorty" shit? He reached out and put his arm around me and I surprised myself by letting him lead me away from my friends and toward the bar.

Two hours passed in a minute. He was charming and smart and funny. He was a gentleman that kept getting me beer and little plates of green appetizers. He was delightful, almost exactly my age and never used The Albino's phrases like "that is so fly" or "chill-axing" throughout our entire conversation. I decided the "shorty" thing was a fluke and that I really liked him. We were deep in conversation when my crew told me they were leaving. They were my ride so I had to leave, too. They stood around with me and Nick for another hour forming their own opinions and then we prepared to leave for real. I gave Nick my card, melted into his very strong goodbye hug, thanked Mike for the party and went home on cloud nine.

Nick and I talked on the phone a lot over the next several days. He was on a big construction job out in Malibu and we couldn't find a chance to get together as soon as I would have liked. I tend to have a salty sense of humor and can generally hold my own with the guys. I have always had a lot of male friends and I am not sure if it was my comfort level that made Nick be so open with me or if things like Howard Stern's show have just changed our culture dramatically but Nick told me stuff you might not expect a man in the earliest stages of courtship to share. Among other things, I was told of multiple experiences with prostitutes and that he preferred oral to traditional sex. I was grilled pretty mercilessly about my own sexual preferences with particular attention given to my feelings about anal sex.

Over cocktails in my kitchen, I confided in Kate.

"He has a tiny dick, Kate. I know it."

She howled with laughter. Kate, despite having been married for more than twenty years, still had sex with her husband at least once a day. While that sounds like a lot of responsibility to me, I bristled as she laughed at my plight.

"You already saw his penis?!" she asked, exploding again into her trademark laughter. Usually, Kate was a gratifying person to say funny things to because she laughed easily and with abandon. I didn't find this situation to be particularly humorous.

"No. I haven't even seen him since the party but I am just getting a way strong vibe that this man is going to be a record breaker. How fucked up would that be? I don't have sex for five years and then I finally meet a guy I like and he's swinging a…"

I paused to think of small things that swing. I couldn't think of anything fast enough.

"What if he is swinging something that doesn't swing at all—but—like—just pokes its little turtle head out?"

More laughter from Kate. Maybe throwing her head back with her mouth open like that all the time kept her in the prime of mouth-dookie fitness. While I considered that possibility, she composed herself and continued the interview.

"Why do you think he has a small dick? Did he tell you that?"

"No. I hardly think he'd volunteer that info in casual conversation. But he seems to have spent a lot of money in his life on hookers. He also prefers oral sex to regular and he is obsessed with fifth base."

"And that means?"

"Fifth base is anal…"

"I know what fifth base is," she said, cutting me off. "What do you think these confessions reveal?"

"I bet he likes oral and anal because his dick isn't big enough to generate friction anywhere else. And I can't stop thinking about Dutch's saying…"

I made a gun with my index finger and my thumb pointing up.

"Short guy and…"

I flipped the gun so that it looked like the letter L.

"…tall guy."

I repeated the gestures until she got it.

"Oh! Dutch thinks short guys have big dicks and tall guys have small dicks?"

"Exactly. And Nick is very tall."

"Dutch is your director friend, right?"

"Yeah…"

"And Dutch is short. He is sort of invested in his own theory, no?"

She made a good point.

"I loved him," Kate continued. "And so did Wayne. Eliza liked him. Mike vouches for him. And you like him. Right?"

"Ah, fuck it. I really do like him. I haven't liked someone this much in forever. He is age appropriate, he has a job, looks delicious and I never have sex ever ever ever anyway so maybe I can live without it forever."

"I don't know how you do it. I don't think I've gone a week without…"

"A-a-ah!" I cut her off. "I know! I know."

"I think you should just embrace the back door action and let Nick throw butt darts at your balloon knot."

Kate buckled over laughing at her own joke. I suddenly felt decidedly queasy.

• • •

THAT NIGHT I TOSSED and turned in my bed, obsessing over my financial situation. The problem seemed huge, overwhelming. My one manner of decent income, working regularly as an actress, might actually be forever outside of my reach. And as I had lived out my denial of that fact, I had let my debt mount to a point that no minimum-wage job that I might actually get would begin to cover even my minimum payments. My heart sped up its pace in objection to these thoughts, these scenarios without apparent solution. Nausea swelled and I wondered if I was having a panic attack. Forcibly, I redirected my thoughts. I thought about Nick. Tangentially, I remembered how I'd once seen Shaquille O'Neal's sneaker on display in a sports medicine office. It was six inches longer than the full length from my elbow to my fingertips. All I could think about when I saw that shoe was that if he was remotely proportionate, he must have a penis like a butternut squash. I thought about the next night, my first live date with Nick, and I prayed, literally prayed, that he would have at least a "nothing to write home about" penis, one you might find on any average guy. I didn't need it to be proportionate to his height. I didn't need a Tommy Lee but I sure as shit was hoping I wasn't going to be dealt a micropenis. (Google it. Yikes.) You might argue that God has bigger concerns in the world than my rancid little sex life but, I say, even if there is no God, it doesn't hurt to ask.

4 The valance

UNWILLING TO MAKE THE SAME MISTAKE I had made with The Albino, I quizzed Nick at length about what foods he ate and any items that could potentially throw him into anaphylactic shock. Good news! He wasn't allergic to dogs. He wasn't allergic to red wine or dairy or seafood but he was a recovering sufferer of type 2 diabetes. Apparently, he had once weighed a great deal more than his current one-sixty and needed a strict diet to keep his weight down and the diabetes at bay. He could not eat white foods including: breads, pastas, potatoes and rice. That eliminated seventy-five percent of foods I ate on my Depression-era budget. He couldn't—or wouldn't—eat a lot of different fruits and vegetables. His idea of a gourmet meal was Boston Market. But—he was a Southern Comfort drinker. Score.

After two weeks of chatting on the phone like high school girls, we finally set a night to get together in person, at my house. Dinner for our first date was a series of culinary compromises on my part that matched the ones from my first dinner with The Albino. The only lettuce Nick would eat was iceberg. I tried to class it up by preparing a wedge salad with vegetarian bacon bits. The only seafood he would eat was clams and he could not have a white chowder so I made, to my own horror, a Manhattan clam chowder. I cheered myself a bit by splurging on fresh, in-the-shell Cherrystones. The only vegetable he liked that felt remotely special was steamed artichokes so I made homemade garlic mayonnaise for dipping. I dusted off the jug of Southern Comfort and even decanted a small portion. To further my Justin Townes Earle fantasy and to set the mood, I put William Elliott Whitmore and Jason Isbell CDs in the player and pressed shuffle. If you are wondering why I didn't put one of Justin Townes Earle's records in the mix, let me explain. If you have an Elvis Costello doppelganger headed over for dinner, you don't put *This Year's Model*, *Spike* and *Painted from Memory* in the changer. You want to maintain some subtlety.

So, dressed in my most flattering retro fifties frock, Bettie Page bangs freshly trimmed to meticulous perfection, I hit the play button and waited for the first song to start. Nothing. I looked at the panel on my nineteen-eighties-era component CD player and saw the shuffle display spinning wildly. I pressed stop. Nothing. I pressed eject. Nothing. Fuck! Another mutineer. I pressed the power button and shut off the receiver. I wanted to pick up each of the four components before me, raise them each over my head and smash them into a thousand pieces on the floor but, instead, I stood there and tried to breathe deep, calming breaths as I counted to ten. Somewhat appeased, I realized I could plug my iPhone into a pair of old computer speakers and get a little musical atmosphere that way. Jason Isbell was crooning "Songs That She Sang in the Shower" and I was putting the final touches on the table settings when I heard the knock on the door.

He came in with such a confident energy, I was put immediately at ease. He was dressed in a cream suit, a button-down shirt with a neatly knotted bow tie, white buck shoes and tortoise shell glasses, his hair greased back in a style that would have made Elvis proud. It was like I'd custom ordered him off the Internet. *This is already going so much better than it did with The Albino*, I swooned.

I led him to the kitchen as he admired my home and art and all the little details about. The dogs danced around and under his feet and he seemed charmed by it. I offered him the Southern Comfort. He asked what other things I had and proceeded to help himself to my liquor cabinet. He inventoried the contents and asked if I had any vodka. All he needed was Absolut vodka for Absolut Confusion, he told me.

I watched him open my freezer and look for vodka as I tried to decide if I was impressed by his ease or offended by his presumptuousness.

"Bingo! Vodka."

He proceeded to make an icky cocktail from what seemed like the remnants of several other icky cocktails. He mixed Absolut Vodka, Green Apple Pucker, Malibu Rum and Southern Comfort. I was amazed that I happened to have those ingredients at all and that, when he'd seen them, he was inspired to construct something made from them. He put ice and the abominable mixture into a pint glass, leaned against the counter with his drink and smiled a huge smile at me. He had his Absolut Confusion. Now it was my turn as I watched him sip it.

"So, what's cooking, good looking?" he said so nonchalantly I was discomfited.

I poured myself a glass of wine. He watched me do it and then picked up the bottle to read the label.

"You are a wino, eh?"

"Yes. I am afraid I am. Do you not drink wine?"

"No. Never got into it."

"Okay, well, help yourself to another of those things if you want it. Don't wait for me to offer it, okay? Sit down. I'll serve the salad."

Salad went over well. Conversation was easy and fun. I served the chowder and the artichokes together. I placed a steaming bowl of soup before Nick.

"Oh, what's this?"

"Clam chowder."

He pointed at the bowl and looked up at me like a five year old.

"But what's..."

"It's Manhattan chowder. I would have made New England but you said your diet forbids white foods"

"No, I like Manhattan clam chowder better. But why are there conch shells in it? I think I can hear the ocean."

"Um... those are clams. It is clam chowder."

He looked at the chowder as if it was his last meal and it had been vandalized.

"Look, I can take those fresh clams out of there. There is canned clam meat in there, too."

Without saying anything, he pushed his bowl closer to mine. I sat down, retrieved all the fresh clams from his bowl, put them in my bowl and I pushed his chowder back to him. He tore off an artichoke leaf and dipped it into my homemade aioli. His reaction upon tasting it was dramatic.

"Whoa! Wow! What is that?"

"Aioli."

Blank stare from Nick.

"Garlic mayonnaise," I explained. "I made it from scratch today."

He got up and got a big glass of water and downed it. He refilled the glass.

"You don't like it?"

"It's not that, chitlin. It is just really garlicky, don't you think?"

He didn't like it. But I liked being called "chitlin." A lot. I'm such a retard.

"Well, what do you usually dip your artichoke in?"

"The usual. Butter. Mayo. Ranch dressing. Blue cheese dressing."

By chance, I had the first three and I had blue cheese dressing left over from the wedge salad. I arranged a little dipping bowl of each in front of him. He seemed happy. I poured another glass of wine. Nick attentively watched me do it.

The evening progressed very pleasantly from there. My batting average feeding these guys wasn't very good but I tried not to dwell on it. I finished a bottle of wine and made Nick a third cocktail. He was very gracious about the meal, thanked me for it profusely and sipped his Confusion. He thanked me so much, in fact, that what had started out like another disaster began to feel like a success.

As it got late, he helped me clean the kitchen. He opened another bottle of wine and poured me a big glass. We chatted some more about forgettable but pleasant stuff. I was liking him more and more and just when I started to think he did not like me back, he swooped me up and kissed me. Without breaking the kiss, he lifted me up and set me on top of the countertop. More kissing. Very nice. Then I remembered my suspicions. I have never been a girl so bold as to go there without a great deal more build up than had occurred so far, but I thought I might have a situation on my hands and I wanted to know if I did, sooner than later. Seated as I was on the counter and with him pressed against the cabinets beneath me, there was not going to be any sort of reconnaissance opportunities—except for the most aggressive gal—so I just enjoyed the kissing some more. Finally, he stepped back an inch or two.

"So listen, shorty. I've had a lot to drink tonight and I live way out by the airport. If I promise to behave, do you think it would be okay if I stayed here tonight? I can sleep on the couch or on the floor with the dogs or whatever. I just can't afford to get a DUI and Johnny Law is out there in full effect these days."

"Okay, first of all, there are a few conditions. One—you cannot call me 'shorty,' anymore. Okay?"

"Okay," he said, confused but agreeable.

"Secondly, my kids don't sleep on the floor. They sleep in the bed with me."

He nodded, listening for the rest.

"That's it. You can stay on the couch."

"Thank you!" he said and gave me another long kiss. There was something about him that made me feel safe. It was a nice feeling.

After several minutes, I broke the kiss and said, "Okay, sailor! It is getting late. Let's get the couch made up for you." As I said it, I put my hands on his belly to push him back from the counter. It felt like I was pushing a Shar Pei—hands full of loose skin yielded before my light pressure. I froze the expression on my face, hoping it still looked romantic and playful. I resisted the overwhelming desire to pull my hands back and recoil in horror. Nick was talking but all I heard was the voice in my head saying "keep your expression upbeat" and another voice counting and wondering how many seconds I would need to leave my hands there so it would seem like I had experienced nothing unusual. After what felt like an eternity, I braced myself and pushed Nick back more firmly. It felt as if I'd pushed two inches into gathered fabric before he felt me pushing and stepped back. Quicksand. His entire midsection was quicksand. Then I remembered he told me he had lost a lot of weight in the past. Micropenis and a fleshy valance framing it. Yum…

"…where do you keep your sheets or blankets or whatever." Nick was still talking. He hadn't noticed my freak out. I am a professional actress, after all.

"Yes, of course," I recovered and we went off to make up the couch.

I kissed him goodnight at the sofa, keeping it quick under the pretense of not wanting to "get in trouble" with him there in the living room. He was an absolute gentleman and agreed that we should call it a night. The delightful vision of him sitting on the couch in his pants, his shirt and tie loosened to reveal a wife-beater and Sailor Jerry tattoos running across his chest, fucked with what I felt about what I'd discovered about his midriff. I just could not catch a break.

I went to bed with my kids curled up beside me and I vacillated between self-pity and self-loathing. Why did this elegant specimen with impeccable fashion sense have to be increasingly and outrageously unappealing physically? And why was I such a judgmental cooze? Two dueling realities twisted my brain in knots: 1) he was a great guy that really knew how to mix and match his separates and 2) I was pretty sure I never wanted to see him separated from them.

Then another thought came to mind. Maybe I had too highfalutin an idea of myself, my own appeal and exactly what kind of a guy I could reasonably expect to land. The fact that my last real boyfriend had been prettier than I was and under thirty when we broke up might have been skewing my expectations to an unhealthy degree. Twelve years had passed in the interim. Maybe my taste in men wasn't keeping pace with my own reality, my own advancing decrepitude. Maybe I thought I was an eight but, in reality, was only a five? Maybe my tastes in men ran along lines that were now forever out of my reach? Compared to a man realistically in my league, a man in the throes of his own balding, spreading middle age—maybe a cute, hip Justin Townes Earle lookalike with a skin valance and a cornichon penis was trading up?

I had twisted dreams that night, though all I could remember specifically when I woke up in the morning were intermingled images of slapping sails on a ship and okra.

I WENT DOWN AND WOKE NICK WITH A KISS. He pulled me on top of him and I sat on him, straddling his hips. I tried desperately to avoid placing my hands anywhere near his midsection. That left his groin and his shoulders and I wasn't ready for more bad news, so I placed my hands nearer the latter and we made out for a bit.

"Uh-oh. Now look at what you've done to me," Nick teased and looked toward his nether region. My eyes followed his and I wish I could say I was surprised to find something immediately visible to which he might be referring. He was pointing out his undetectable morning wood and I found myself mourning wood.

My mind went to a day in the seventies when I, as a thirteen-year-old romantic, asked a free-loving hippie friend of my mom's what she would do if she found she had married a man with a one-inch penis. She said that would never happen. I insisted she had to go with the hypothetical and answer the question.

"I would divorce him immediately," she finally said.

I judged her harshly then as a heartless whore, and I could not help but think now that she would enjoy my current dilemma very much. Touché, hippie lady. Touché.

"Uh-oh, indeed!" I blurted.

I jumped up off of Nick pretending that I was not ready to finish what I'd started, which was the truth really, but for different reasons than he likely guessed. Men are amazing creatures. If someone, one person, somewhere, sometime ever told them they were the most handsome or the best lay or had the biggest dick or—whatever—then that praise, even if it flies in the face of the obvious, becomes for them forever empirical fact. Women are the opposite. Thousands can tell them they are gorgeous or smart or talented or that they do not have a fat ass but if one person says the opposite, it is the negative opinion only that they will forever hold as truth. Someone, sometime, somewhere must have said something nice about Nick's body and he believed it. God bless his heart.

The remaining details of the morning are unimportant except that Nick continued to be so affectionate and lovely, I was racked with guilt and began to second guess myself again. His greased hair was sexy and sort of disheveled from sleep. His dress shirt was casually untucked and unbuttoned at the neck and kinda wrinkly. Suspenders hung limply from his waistband. Goddamn, he looked good. Maybe I was being an ass. Maybe I ought to practice a little gratitude? Maybe I hadn't had sex more than a handful of times in twelve years precisely to prepare me to be thankful for any penis at all? As they say, beggars can't be choosers. The universe can be a blunt teacher.

Nick had a job to bid that day and I had an increasingly rare voiceover audition, so I walked him out to his car. Standing outside kissing me goodbye, he looked so cute climbing into his primer black, 1960s Chevy pick-up that I forgot about his saltwater taffy midriff and heard myself inviting him back over that night. I heard him accept the invitation and he drove away blowing me a kiss.

All that day, I thought about how nice he was and how much I liked him. I tried to let myself feel all the excitement about it that I would under normal circumstances but, every time I began feeling butterflies of excitement, I remembered the valance and the absence of anything evident on the stage beneath the curtain. I told myself that I was likely acting out of fear and that I had not yet absolutely confirmed the extent of his shortcomings. Maybe the valance had somehow obscured my view of his acceptably average manhood. Maybe he "dressed down"—like Buffalo Bill in *Silence of the Lambs*—maybe that was why Nick's "uh-oh" moment this morning had a completely different meaning for each of us. Maybe his junk was tucked? I wondered how many other women ever hoped that a guy they liked intentionally sported a man-gina as I left for my audition.

Let me take a moment here to talk about auditions. I used to have them a lot. I used to work a lot. Now I seldom get audition opportunities and the bulk of the auditions I do get are either for commercials or voiceover jobs, two fields in which

I have never had any real interest, but money is money and money is something I need very badly. So, I drive two hours in rush hour to Santa Monica to wait two more hours at a cattle call to, finally, be allowed to show some client or other that I can chew cereal realistically or say motherly things to other people's kids believably or project intestinal discomfort convincingly. The jury is in and it has determined that I cannot. Apparently, I cannot do these things or dozens of other everyday things with the authenticity required, nor can I utter everyday sentences like "Wipe your feet, Jimmy!" and exude the proper degree of warmth, chagrin or bemusement. I have never, ever booked a voiceover or commercial job in my life and I am now convinced I never will. Still, dutifully, I jump through the hoops put before me without even a wisp of a sense that I might get one of these gigs. I just do it so I can keep calling myself an actress because, at this point, it is the only proof I have. That, and the overdue notices I keep getting for my unpaid union dues.

After my exercise in futility, I stopped by a book store to peruse a few diabetic cookbooks and maybe steal a recipe or two for that night's menu. As I considered some, I felt someone staring at me. I turned to see an enormously fat, older woman beside me, gazing into my face with her mouth hanging open. There were several thick hairs sprouting from her chin. They stretched out nearly an inch in my general direction like the tendrils of a climbing vine. I feared I was in imminent threat of being body-snatched. I moved back a few steps and the rest of her came into view. She was morbidly obese with unbound pendulums hanging to her waist with the words "I Wish These Were Brains" emblazoned on her shirt at about fourteen inches above where her flapjacks were currently residing.

"You know that show—*Cooterville, PTA?*" she sputtered at me from a mouth that seemed void of teeth.

I did know it. I had done several episodes of the show. It was the most high-profile job of my career and, though it happened almost twenty years ago, it was a role I was still often recognized for. It seemed I would never live down the character of Pinky Browntown. I obviously had a fan on my hands.

"Yes, of course. I know the show," I said, only a tiny bit patronizingly.

"Well, I hope this doesn't offend you but you look just like that girl that played Pinky 'Downtown' Browntown."

"Ya think?"

"Yeah. A way older version—but you look a *lot* like her. I hope that doesn't hurt your feelings."

"No. Why would that hurt my feelings?" I asked as I absently pulled several cookbooks off the shelves and clutched them to my chest, subconsciously creating a shield.

"I don't know. Because nobody likes her, I guess. I always did but everyone I know hated her but I related to her a lot maybe because I always thought we looked alike..."

"Yeah, I can see that. It's uncanny," I deadpanned. I don't know why encounters like this, interactions with clueless or rude fans, bum me out so much, but they do. This one was mild, compared to some I'd fielded in the past, but I was instantly reduced to a shy middle-schooler unable to hold her own against the school bully. "Okay, gotta go. Gotta make dinner," I said, showing her the cookbooks I held to prove it and I hurried away from her as fast as I could.

Home again, I made my daily trip to the mailbox, or what I call "The Evil Box of Financial Ruin." Reaching into that thing and looking at its contents every day felt like a dare right out of *Fear Factor*. In fact, the idea of eating giant hissing cockroaches or sheep balls left me less nauseated than the dread of opening unexpected but official-looking missives. Predictably, there were several bills mixed in with the supermarket mailers and political campaign letters and more than one of the envelopes had declarations on the front announcing to the world that these were bills that were way overdue. One was from CitiMortgage and I knew it contained the statement for my newly reset payment. My stomach twisted and my heart began to race. I had no money to pay the mortgage with this month. I'd used the last of my home equity line to pay it last month. I was living a hundred percent off unemployment and credit cards now. I put the envelopes, unopened, on top of the growing stack on my desk and distracted myself by preparing dinner for my date with Nick.

For this meal, I decided to be frugal and safe, if not imaginative. I prepared the same meal as the night before but with all the nice touches eliminated, as Nick's kindergarten palate required and my wallet appreciated. I wore an old vintage dress and retro platforms that I hoped would prove our fashion compatibility. Nick showed up early, three hours early, and I was surprised again at how much I enjoyed him. Again, he was dressed impeccably and he was more complimentary about dinner than he had been the first time. It was so enjoyable, I completely forgot about all the bad news piling up on my desk. He paced up his "making himself at home" behavior, which I was also surprised to note didn't offend me at all. He put his feet on the table and I even let him have the remote control. We were like an old married couple—but one that still liked each other.

This story played itself out very similarly for almost every day over the next week or so with Nick staying on the couch each night. Nick was nicer and more charming each day than the last. I kept the physical part of our relationship very light because I really liked him and new relationships are fragile. I kept his hands above my waist and my own hands nowhere near his. Maybe I am alone in this but if something goes wrong in the early "getting to know you" stages, it can just slam the door to a potential relationship shut forever. It can be anything, really; an offensive joke, bad breath, unfortunate shoes. Whatever. But when it happens, it can be as final as death. I call men that fall victim to this circumstance "in the Howard Dean zone." The valance was challenging enough and I was afraid that if my fears about Nick were confirmed before that trial period had expired, he would be forever relegated to the Howard Dean zone. I wanted to give Nick the best possible shot. I wanted to give myself the best possible shot. He was a nice guy and I was in no position to fritter away a keeper. I had gone five years without sex. How difficult could it be to wait a few more weeks?

Finally, one night after a particularly romantic dinner, I was perched atop the counter and we were making out. I decided I liked him enough to risk stepping it up. I broke the kiss for a moment and asked, "Wanna take a bubble bath?"

"What?" Nick asked. "You wanna take a bubble bath?"

Shit. It was out there now. I had to sell it. I didn't want another Albino debacle.

"Yes! A bubble bath! It'll be fun!"

"I don't know..."

Caught up in the moment, drunk and desperate not to strike out on the damn bathtub thing again, I grabbed Stretch Armstrong by his deflated middle and tried to shake some enthusiasm into him. I could have taken that extra skin, wrapped it around his back and terrorist fist-bumped myself behind him. There was so much give, I nearly lost my balance on the counter. I immediately loosened my grip and, in an effort to mask why, began clapping with delight about my idea to bathe. Flapping like a mental patient had the added benefit of keeping Nick from reading any of the revulsion that must have flashed across my face.

"Come on! It'll be fun! Make yourself a glass of Confusion, I'll get some wine and we can take a *bath* together!" I clapped several claps longer than was already awkward. There followed a very uncomfortable silence.

Nick looked back at me solemnly. Fuck. He'd seen it. I had hurt his feelings. He was such a nice guy and I'd just embarrassed him. Humiliated him. I had no idea what to say to fix it. What could I say? "Oh, don't worry, Rubber Bandman. I think those African elephant ears you call love handles are super hot!" Without any more sophisticated plan, I winged it. I ignored his mood change.

"C'mon. Grab your drink. Let's go! I am not taking no for an answer!" I said as I hopped off the counter and bounced toward the bathroom.

As I bounded up the stairs, it dawned on me that the bubble bath would be the perfect way to prove I was not completely grossed out by him. This bath would prove I was cool with the valance. I owed him this bath. The bath would be our salvation! And who knew? With a few more drinks in me, maybe I could motorboat the valance. Crazier shit has happened. Like my five years of celibacy.

I ran the bath and dumped half a bottle of one of the many unused foaming bath salts I'd purchased during my Albino period. I programmed my iPod to play an old Anita O'Day record in a loop. I lit candles. I sipped my wine. I realized I needed this bath to happen as much to prove to myself that I was not grossed out by Nick as anything else. The tub was nearly full before I noticed Nick had not followed me upstairs.

"Nick!" I screamed like a harpy. "Nick! Come on up here!"

"You have your bath, babe! I wanna watch the game."

The game? The fucking game? What the fuck? On what planet does a guy turn down an opportunity for mutual nudity with a girl?

"Nick! What? Do you have the gay?"

No response.

"Nick! Get up here and get your clothes off and get in this goddamn bubble bath with me. RIGHT FUCKING NOW!"

That might sound harsh but I was getting a complex.

The tub was full and the bubbles were a foot deep. I have a great tub. I turned the water off and realized I could hear the game still coming from the TV in the kitchen. All this delay was letting my revulsion set in a way that might not be reversible. I tried to drive it out of my mind by chugging the balance of my drink.

"Nick, come ooon! And bring the wiiine," I whined.

The TV went silent. I heard him push his chair back and the fact that I was going to get naked with this guy slapped me back to reality. Nobody had seen me naked in over five years. I had only been hanging out with this guy a few days, really. How had I gone from born-again virgin to rabid bath slut so quickly?

I heard him start up the stairs and suddenly remembered the flaws of my own midsection. In a frenzy, I ripped my clothes off and jumped into the tub without first testing the water. The water was hot, very hot indeed, but I had no time to acclimate my lady parts—Nick was in the room.

"Here's your wine, bossy," Nick said and topped my glass off as I suppressed the urge to spring back out of the tub and dance the heat of the water from my blanched flesh.

"Nude up, bitch. Get in," I challenged in what I hoped sounded like a playful tone and then audibly breathed in my pain.

"No. But I can hang out in here with you."

"What? Do I disgust you? Do I have a bat in the cave or something?" I asked and covered my nose.

"No!" he laughed. "Look at you in there. You are beautiful."

I had no time to absorb this. I was on a mission from Hell to get some fucker in that Goddamn bathtub if was the last thing I did. I was already naked, for Chrissake. Don't invitations from naked women usually go better than this?

"Then come on in here with me. The water is perfect," I lied. I couldn't feel my body from the waist down.

"I don't like to take my shirt off," he winced.

Ah! So he knew he had more in common with Dali's watches than was ideal. I was overcome with drunken sympathy.

"I did. I took my shirt off. I'm nekkid in here. Tooootally nekkid. There are bubbles aplenty... if you are shy."

"I never take my shirt off."

"Not even when you shower?"

"You know what I mean."

I had to make this happen or, I swore, I was going back to being (read: remain) a sexless troglodyte. What was with these guys I was attracting? They just made this being trampy thing way too difficult. I blamed free internet porn... and *There's Something About Mary* for teaching guys everywhere how to rub out the easy one before they went on dates, rendering them immune to desperate women trying to rid themselves of the stink of unfuckability. I made a mental note to flame the Farrelly brothers on their IMDB page. The twats.

"Okay. Keep your shirt on, then," I suggested. "But get in here."

A no, yes, no back-and-forth ensued. In desperation, I got on my knees in the tub under the pretense of reaching out to pull him to the tub but it was, in actuality, a deliberate, if momentary, reveal of some boobage. I could work it—in a pinch. Don't underestimate me.

The peek worked.

"Okay. I'll get in but I am keeping the shirt on."

"Whatever makes you happy," I said encouragingly, pretty sure I didn't want to see what was under there anyway. I watched him take off his shoes and socks and drop trou. After carefully folding and placing his clothes on the leopard ottoman, he pulled down his boxer shorts which, I noticed, appeared to be Ralph Lauren. I was trying to decide if he bought everything he owned from the Double RL line when I realized Nick was standing in front of me wearing nothing but his wife-beater. Kneeling as I was in the tub, my eyes were exactly at crotch level and I found myself staring straight down the barrel of what I can only compare to a flesh colored C battery nestled securely in an aggressively manscaped flesh mound. In all the drama about the valance and the bath and the T-shirt and my own insecurity about being seen naked, I had completely forgotten my worst fears and my prayers and, it seemed, so had God. I was eye-to-eye with the smallest penis I had ever seen on an adult in my life and it was perky and winking its existence at me from the center of a meat pillow in the shadow of a Hitler mustache. I was cockeyed in more ways than one. The valance became a sentimental memory.

He dipped his toes in the water.

"Ouch! Fuck! This water is hot!"

No chance he can blame that spark plug on the water temperature, I thought. I busied myself sipping wine and playing with bubbles until his junk was out of sight. I was afraid if I made eye contact with it again, I might get locked in a staring contest, a deer caught in headlights.

The bath was a blur of him talking and me pretending to listen while I tried to come to terms with the new information I had. When the water lost its heat, I reached out to add more hot water but, as I twisted, the tap came off in my hand. I looked at the piece of chromed metal and then up at Nick with an expression that must have suggested I did not recognize the object on my palm.

"Don't sweat it, Mama. I can fix that for you," he said, smiling at me over a mountain of bubbles. "Why don't you pop out and give me five minutes alone in here."

Ah. He didn't want to get out of the tub in front of me. I jumped out and quickly left the room to give him his privacy. He asked to borrow a dry T-shirt and he opened the door a tiny crack so I could pass it to him. While I put on a pair of boxer briefs and a T-shirt, I pouted about the unfairness of this situation. My professional predicament was bad enough and now, it seemed, I couldn't catch a break in the romance department to save my life. *At least I'm not blind*, I thought and then threw a nervous look at the heavens, almost expecting twin lightning bolts to come down and punish me for my entitlement and ingratitude. Then I began to think about Nick. He was such a nice guy and he was a real guy, complete with real man-skills. He was going to fix my faucet for me, for Chrissake. Maybe he could fix some of the *everything else* in my house that was breaking all around me on a daily basis here in Grey Gardens. I think that kind of thing is super sexy. But he had been dealt a pretty bad hand in the physicality department. Even that old trick of cutting the pubic hair short hadn't worked to create an illusion of size or, God forbid, it had. Maybe he's a grower, not a shower, I considered. Maybe he was the victim of my rush to judgment. He didn't seem embarrassed by the size of it. Maybe he knew something I did not. Or maybe I should express my appreciation for my, perhaps temporary, ability to see by being generous with Nick and his little pee-pee. I had a knee-jerk thought that if I were kind to Nick maybe I'd earn back the right to regular work as an actress. The concept of "what goes around comes around" was proving to be a very difficult one for me to let go of. I forced myself to answer the question, "Would you be so charitable to Nick if you knew there would be no ultimate reward beyond the act itself?" By doing so, I effectively guilted myself into proving to myself that I wasn't just a total douche. Unable to control the reflex, I thought, *because douche-bag actors don't get to have regular work*. Then I remembered Tom Cruise and had to put another mental check in the "proof that there is no God or universal fairness" column.

Nick came out of the bathroom just as my need to prove I didn't suck peaked. He announced that my fixture crisis had been successfully resolved. Awash with disproportionate gratitude, I led him to my bedroom where we started fooling around. It was like navigating a field of land mines. Foreplay is brutal when you are afraid to put your hands anywhere on the other person's front. At a loss for other options, I slipped my hands under his boxers and grabbed two robust hands full of his ass. Curtains in the front, curtains in the back. The man was a walking window dressing department. I wondered if the fat version of him could possibly have been worse.

Nick reached for my hand and brought it around to the front and placed my hand directly upon on his package.

"I'm sorry, baby…"

Oh God, I thought as I curled my fingers around his mini gherkin. I felt like a pedophile. I tried to think of something, anything, to say in response to this apology. Then I realized he had something else to say.

"You probably already noticed, but…"

A suicide pact seemed like the only way out of what was going to be the most uncomfortable situation of our lives.

"Anyway, I'm sorry. But I have really small balls."

I actually did a slow-mo head turn and "Can you believe this shit?" look over my shoulder to a non-existent witness.

"I'm sorry, baby. You probably noticed that I have really small *balls*," he says? Guess what? No! No, I didn't. As a matter of fact, I didn't notice your balls at all. I mean, even if you do have really small balls, that would matter because? Because chicks are totally into nut sacks? Really? When was the last time you saw a scrotum aisle at the sex toy store? There are no "Celebrities with big gonads" websites. Is there anything less pleasant that accidentally catching an eye full of some guy hanging brain at the beach or while spotting you bench pressing? I think not. Don't believe what you see in porn, guys. Girls don't really want your balls in their mouths. The only people on Earth that give a fuck about your balls, gentlemen, are you.

"No! No, you don't," I finally said, hoping I sounded turned on and then started kissing him so as not to blurt out, "It's not your balls. It's your wiener, dude! You are packing a fucking party frank!" And he really was. Hard, it was the size of a super-plus tampon, and those things are made so chicks can't feel them when they are inserted. Extrapolate from there.

I never thought I'd be so grateful for the threat of STDs but, after a brief make-out period, I managed to avoid the situation escalating further by pointing out his history with hookers and our lack of a condom. He was as gentlemanly as ever and I got no argument from him. As a consolation prize and because I was too lazy to make up the sofa again, I let him sleep beside me and the kids. I even let him have my side of the bed. Looking back, I believe this was the moment Nick thought he had me hooked.

In the morning, Nick kissed me awake and said, "We gotta do something about how bright it is in this room. I could get a sunburn on my ass while I sleep."

The mention of his drapey ass resulted in a reflexive sour expression on my face. And I like a bright bedroom. I am a morning person. I live in a little tree house and one of my favorite things about it is that, due to its perch on the hilltop, none of the windows need privacy barriers.

"I don't like window treatments. I don't have curtain rods. I like the room sunny."

"I have some black construction tarp. I will bring it over later today and staple it up."

"Construction tarp? That will look like shit and you are not stapling into the plaster."

"Well, we gotta figure something out."

He could have tacked his lower abdomen over the windows and still have had enough freedom to climb back into bed and under the covers with me. Black tarp, my ass.

I got up and went to brush my teeth. He came into the bathroom behind me with a toothbrush, mouthwash, deodorant and a towel that did not belong to me.

"Where'd you get all that stuff?"

"Brought it in my overnight bag," he said and held up a gorgeous, brown leather duffel bag with a prominent Ralph Lauren logo tooled into the side. "I'm particular about my towels. You got an extra drawer somewhere I can put this stuff when I'm done?"

Stunned by these new developments, I went in the other room and cleaned out a drawer, then went downstairs to make a pot of coffee. Demanding and superior, who was this new Nick?

"We gotta make some other arrangement with the dogs. That bed ain't big enough for the five of us," Nick said, entering the kitchen.

"There is plenty of room in the bed. I love sleeping with my dogs," I bristled. "Want some coffee?"

"No. Blech. Got any Red Bull?"

"No."

"We should probably get some. What are you up to today?"

"Not much. I was going to take the dogs for a hike maybe."

"Can I ask you a big favor? I need to get some stuff out of my old place and bring it to my new place. It would be great to use your truck."

Caught off guard again, I agreed.

Two hours later we were packing up what felt like an infinite number of milk crates filled with forty tons of vinyl records, several garbage bags full of his dandy duds and what seemed like fifty hatboxes from a rented room in El Segundo and dropping it off at a crash pad a few miles away.

Until that day, I had heard the term "crash pad" but I had no real concept of what it meant. A crash pad is an apartment near the airport with *way* too many twin beds crammed into it for airline personnel to crash on when they are in town for one night. This particular crash pad had a *Hollywood Squares*-style honeycomb against one living room wall. The honeycomb was made up of sixteen or twenty plastic storage bins, each neatly labeled with the name of the person that owned its contents. There was a complicated graph on the wall representing each bed in the apartment and names and dates representing reservations for them. There were four bedrooms, three of which had three beds in them and one with two. They were tiny beds, beds that looked half the size of a twin, glorified cots, really. We were moving stuff into the room with two beds.

"So, you are going to live here?"

"Yeah, it's great. Really cheap."

"Um..." I said and wondered if I could live in a place like this. I wondered if I might actually have to someday. My heart fluttered and picked up its pace. *Is this what a panic attack feels like*? I wondered to myself. I don't know what the expression on my face looked like but Nick saw it and got defensive.

"What? There is a recession, you know. Times are tough all over."

"Except wherever it is you buy your Grand Ole Opry clothes. You must be keeping several stores afloat single-handedly," I snapped back and tried to remember the last time I'd bought a new piece of clothing.

"Moving here is my way of cutting back. And don't you like how I dress?"

Fuck. I had to admit, I did. And it was his money. His life. If a crash pad worked for him, who was I to judge? I was a has-been actress dressed in years-old, eBay-acquired "hand-me-downs," playing Three-card Monte with credit card debt and about to default on my mortgage. The day might come where I wished I could afford a bed in a depressing apartment for disparate transients.

"Okay. But how are you going to get all those records in here? With those stacked in here, you won't be able to walk into the room," I said, adjusting to a friendlier tone.

"I was hoping I could put some stuff in your garage, just temporarily." Nick, too, sounded friendlier, now. "That's cool, right, biscuit?"

"Are you fucking high?" was what I was thinking but I heard myself say, "Okay, I guess so. Temporarily..."

He'd called me "biscuit," after all. Damned folksy endearments. They were like crack.

We dropped off the garbage bags of clothes and the hatboxes at the crash pad and headed back to my place with the records in the back of my truck.

"Oh, damn! We should stop and buy some wine flavored condoms, too!"

I need a bigger glass of wine than you're serving, I thought and said, "Great idea!" and then changed the subject.

"Why are you renting a bed in a crash pad? Don't you have a successful contracting business?" I began to worry that his ample free time might be the result of something other than being able to make his own hours.

"I told you. The economy..."

"Yeah, but still. A crash pad? It's worse than a youth hostel," I said, risking offending him again. But seriously, those living arrangements were not okay.

"Well, like I told you, I used to be into hookers and... you know..." he said and trailed off as if he had explained everything. He hadn't.

"How many hookers have you been with?"

"Well, it wasn't just hookers. It was hookers and I had a small issue with gambling and the IRS is on my back."

Great.

"Wassup with the hooker thing? What's the appeal there?" I asked, trying to narrow my focus.

"They are all access. All access on the first date."

"All access?"

"Three holes, no waiting."

Wow.

"That's romantic."

"Hey, what do you want? Me to lie?" he laughed and patted my knee. "Don't be threatened. I can be *patient*, too," he said and looked me in the eye, meaningfully.

"You already put enough junk in my trunk for one day, champ. Let's not get overconfident."

"You know what else is really hot?"

I was certain I did not want to know.

"One time, this chick was going down on me and then she just suddenly pushed my legs up and went to town on my ass."

My throat began to close up in revulsion.

"I never thought I'd be into that but it was smoking. You should try it..." he said, and looked at me, nodding encouragingly as if he'd just asked, "Who's up for frozen yogurt?" All I could think was that finding his anus in the folds of his ass valance would be like digging—with my tongue—for the center of an especially dense and, likely, humid meat rose.

In a cruel twist of coincidence, he bought me a rose from a street vendor at a freeway ramp with my meter change. I couldn't bring myself to look directly at it. Back at the house, I helped him load the milk crates into my garage. It was difficult to mask my growing resentment.

We went inside and I poured myself a glass of wine.

"Kinda early to start on the sauce, no?"

I chose to ignore that remark and changed the subject.

"Hey, let's look at those diabetic cookbooks I bought for you last week. You never even looked at them. Maybe you could go through them and highlight the recipes that sound good to you. That way, you know? I can cook for you and not include ingredients you don't like and not include things you shouldn't eat."

"Yeah, about those cookbooks..."

"What?"

"I don't know. Just seems a little... bit... much."

Confused look from me.

"I just think a lotta guys would run in this situation."

"In what situation?"

"Buying cookbooks for me. It is kinda stalkery and suffocating. Most guys my age would call that a serious red flag. I don't think a lot of guys would stick around."

"A lot of guys would be flattered that someone gave a fuck," I said aloud but silently added some really hurtful name-calling.

"Okay, if you say so. It explains some stuff, that's for sure."

"What the fuck?"

"I'm just saying—it might explain why you are single."

"What? Being nice to you? Wanting to cook for you? Wanting to help you out with the diabetic thing? That's bad?"

"I'm just saying."

I glared at him. C battery fucker.

"Okay. Okay. I'm sorry. You're right. Let's go through these books and make a plan for dinner."

"I actually cannot tonight. I am meeting the girls for happy hour at... our... regular place."

This was not true but I needed to get away from him for a while and clear my head. Where was sweet Nick? Who was this asshole? Justin Townes Earle would never act like this.

"Okay, cool. I gotta go to my new place and get unpacked, anyway. Maybe after you see your friends you can come by and we can chill at my pad tonight."

Yeah, cuz that's gonna happen. I am going to sleep on a cot in an apartment in El Segundo with six stewardesses on a layover from Milwaukee. Jesus.

LATER, ONCE NICK HAD TAKEN OFF, I called Mack to bring her up to speed on my romantic misadventures. Maybe she would have some advice.

"You are exaggerating!" she exclaimed once I'd filled her in.

"Nope. Not even a little bit."

"Have you had sex with Nick yet?"

"No. I can't have unprotected sex."

"Buy some condoms, silly."

"I can't. I'm afraid to."

"Nobody at the drug store is going to care."

"No, not that. I am afraid that a regular condom will fall right off. Honestly. It would be like putting a forty-gallon garbage bag on a fire plug. And I am afraid to buy extra-small condoms because it might hurt his feelings."

"Oh… my…" she trailed off and laughed.

"I'm pretty sure I cannot go through with this one."

"Fine by me, but if you really like this guy, my advice is, don't write him off too quickly. Maybe he is acting like an asshole as a defense mechanism. Maybe he is afraid that you will dump him now that you know about his chilito. You know, a little 'you can't fire me because I quit' kinda thing."

That was definitely a possibility and it softened my feelings toward Nick again. An image of him dandied up in his county-fair best flitted across my mind's eye. He sure looked good—dressed.

"And… if his dick is as small as you say, he might have developed other skills to compensate," Mack continued, bringing me back to the conversation. "Perhaps he is a cunning linguist."

I hadn't thought of that. It was somewhat comforting to consider. I decided to suppress my doubts, try to be more understanding of Nick's potential insecurities and potential yet-to-be-revealed talents and forge ahead. I could be selfless if there was something in it for me.

NICK CAME OVER THE NEXT NIGHT and we made dinner. Over our short time together, Nick had become increasingly critical of my drinking. His latest trick was to drink only water or diet Coke and to count the glasses of wine I had. Out loud. I'd responded playfully at first, but it quickly turned into a real issue. I became a player on the stage of "wine theater." Wine theater entailed masking how much I was drinking by having several bottles of wine open simultaneously, preferably with at least one "hidden" on the counter amidst the olive oils and balsamic vinegars. With multiple bottles from which to pour, it was almost impossible for Nick to track my consumption. It also involved filling the wine glass to the brim because Nick perceived that as one drink whereas he perceived several smaller, civilized pours as many drinks, even when they added up to less than one full glass. The fact that I was forced to do this and in my own home had the effect of making me feel like I had a drinking problem.

"Have you ever considered that you might have a drinking problem?" he asked, as if he could read my mind.

"Yes, and I am not an alcoholic," I said and poured myself a full-to-the-rim glass from the bottle he was monitoring. The phrase "surface tension" was appropriate at that moment on every level.

"You should watch that show *Intervention*. You might learn a few things about yourself."

"I love that show and the thing I learn from it over and over is that I do not have a problem. Those people are out-of-control degenerates, oblivious to their own excesses," I said and then, oblivious to the irony, sipped the wine from my glass as it sat on the counter because it was too full to lift without spilling.

Nick sipped his ice water and looked at me over the rim the way a shrink does when they want you to realize you have just answered your own question. All the sympathy for Nick that Mack had revived in me immediately evaporated. Even his *To Kill a Mockingbird* wardrobe couldn't save him now.

"Whattaya say we do dinner out by the beach tomorrow and then sleep at my place for a change? We always sleep here at your house."

"Why would I want to leave my dogs alone all night and sleep on a cot in a tiny apartment with paper-thin walls and nine roomies when we have a whole house right here and complete privacy?"

"So, what are you saying? You never want to just come spend some time on my turf? My placed isn't good enough for you? Got a problem hanging out with some folks that actually work for a living?"

I stared back at him, speechless. I couldn't tell if he was calling me a snob or if he was mocking my unemployment—or both.

"It's not *all* about you *all* the time, you know," Nick said with supreme self-righteousness, and he cupped and shifted his junk as if either one of us believed there was anything there.

I knew then that I wanted out of this deal with Nick worse than I wanted him to actually be Justin Townes Earle. Or Justin Long. Or Shelley Long. Or Shelley Winters. Or Jonathan Winters. You get my point. Christ.

Later, as he tried to initiate romance in the sack, all I could think about was that obnoxious hand gesture politicians use. They make a fist and use their thumb for emphasis because some poll somewhere must have said that viewers find this more polite than old fashioned pointing. As he dry-humped my thigh, it felt like a midget public speaker was repeatedly trying to make a really important point to my hip. It wasn't especially seductive. Neither was watching him rub one out.

Men are shameless.

THE NEXT MORNING I pretended to get a call from my agent. I pretended it was amazing news. I pretended I had been offered a job on a miniseries that would take me out of town for months. I pretended there was a possibility this miniseries would become a TV series. I pretended that I thought it was unfair to ask him to wait for me and our break-up was inevitable so we might as well accept it immediately. I pretended this upset me greatly. I pretended to cry. He bought it completely.

Just because I haven't worked in a long time doesn't mean I can't act.

A FEW DAYS LATER, with no men or auditions or social obligations providing distraction, I decided finally to face my biggest fear and deal with the financial realities of my life. I got a glass of wine and sat at my desk and opened every last bill in the stack there. I scanned each credit card bill for charges that could be eliminated from my future. The only monthly charge I had left in my life that was billed to a credit card was my one-DVD-at-a-time Netflix subscription. I went online and canceled it. I called the phone company and scaled my cell plan back to the least expensive they offered, scaled cable down to the cheapest basic package and canceled my landline. When I hung up, I thought about that cable bill and the fact that cable is, no matter how we have become accustomed to feel, in fact, a luxury, not a necessity, so I called back and canceled that, too. It was actually kind of liberating. *I'll read more*, I thought. Reading is free. I felt empowered.

There is no getting around driving in Los Angeles, hence, no avoiding car insurance, so I went online and paid the six-month policy on a credit card. Same thing with my gas bill—on the credit card. *Nobody could chide me for wanting to drive legally and for wanting warm water,* I thought, defending myself to nonexistent critics. I had just enough money in my checking account from my paltry unemployment insurance to pay the minimums due on each of a half dozen credit cards with a collectively staggering balance. This wasn't nearly as bad as I'd feared. I was awash in a sense of accomplishment. I even allowed myself to feel hopeful about my ability to micromanage my spending into some miraculously affordable zone and, therefore, avoid a future competing with illegals selling serapes and Chiclets at the end of freeway ramps.

I stared at my mortgage statement. Alone, it was more than all the other bills I'd just paid combined. I opened my desk drawer and dug out a recently secreted-away letter from one of my credit card companies inviting me to another interest-free cash advance. "Consolidate bills! Pay off your higher rate credit cards! Or just access some extra cash!" the letter suggested to me from the heading. *Okay*, I thought, *I will.* I went online, signed in and clicked on the "transfer balances" button. A new screen popped up reading, "Unable to Complete Your Request. Balance transfers aren't available for your account at this time. If you have any questions, please call us 7 days a week using the toll-free phone number on the back of your card."

My heart began its now-familiar flutter up to a high gear and revved there in my chest for a minute while I stared at the words which were screaming at me on the screen in a bold red font. Not available? I looked at the date on the letter inviting me to this temporarily interest-free money-party. It was three weeks old. I felt like I was having a heart attack. In an effort to calm myself, I told myself this must be a mistake. What could have happened in three weeks to clue them in to the fact that I was a credit risk? I'd been a credit risk for years at this point and that never seemed to bother any credit card company on Earth. Why would they cut me off now?

I called the bank in question and after I typed in my credit card number and password and the last four of my social, I navigated my way by pushing ones and fives and, finally, a zero, where I finally reached a person who promptly asked me for my credit card number, password and the last four of my social. My heart increased its pace and my stomach kicked into gear to join it. My organs conducted a drag race on the anxiety track to Strokesville while I tried to speak in a civilized tone to the agent on the line. I willed myself into dropping the fight I wanted to have about the whole "typing in all your personal information so they can serve you better" crap only to have me repeat to a real person every single bit of info I had spent five minutes sharing with their computer. Instead, I addressed the far more pressing matter of the credit cut-off.

"Your account is not eligible for balance transfers, Miss Fitzgerald."

"But I have a three-week-old letter here inviting me to a balance transfer."

"Oh, yeah, well, our computers spit those things out often as far as ninety days in advance of the date you receive it."

"And?"

"And in the interim, our account managers must have reviewed your account and decided you were no longer eligible."

"But why? I have never made a late payment."

"I am not in that department, Miss Fitzgerald, and so I am unable to share with you the potential factors that brought our team to their decision."

"I am confused as to why I am being punished when I have never made a late payment and this credit card has a zero balance."

"Their assessment was not necessarily negative. You are not being punished."

"So, are you suggesting that they reviewed my account and, as a result of my stellar record with your company, chose to reward me by cutting off my credit line?"

"Your credit line is open. You are free to use your card anytime."

"But I cannot make a balance transfer with an interest-free grace period?"

"No."

"Can I apply or request or whatever to have my account assessed again with the balance transfer option in mind?"

"No. These are done randomly, not by request."

"So what you are saying is, I am free to use the card at my current, like, twenty-percent interest rate but..."

"Twenty-nine percent on this card," the agent corrected.

"Twenty-nine percent interest? So I can use it if I want to pay twenty-nine percent interest on what I spend?"

"If you pay your balance off every month, there are no interest fees."

"I know that," I said and sat there boiling over with righteous indignation. After a moment of the resulting silence, the agent spoke again.

"Do you have any other questions I can help you with?"

"No," I spat, bitterly.

"Okay. Have I provided you with excellent service today?"

I gave an irritated and dramatic exhale of disgust and then a completely insincere "Yeah."

"Wonderful! Would you be interested in filling out a short satisfaction survey..."

I hung up the phone before the agent could finish. I then went online and paid my mortgage with money borrowed at usury rates from a loan shark named J.P. Morgan Chase.

THE FOLLOWING WEEKEND, Eliza and I attended a friend's wedding. More accurately, we were at the wedding of a woman with whom Eliza used to work and whom I hardly knew. If I'd been asked to give a speech about the bride, all I could have said with confidence was that her name was Suzy, that she used to work with Eliza and that she always dressed in things that brought the greatest possible attention to the worst flaws of her anatomy. And, to be completely accurate, we were not at the wedding but at the reception.

"How is it that we got invited to the reception, but not the ceremony?" Eliza complained.

"I don't know why I got invited at all. I don't even know Suzy's last name."

"But seriously. What are we? Red-headed stepchildren? What is that about?"

"I don't know. But I do know that, while there is rarely an open bar at the ceremony, there is often a long-winded religious figure with an open mic. I think we dodged a bullet."

"True dat," Eliza conceded, somewhat begrudgingly. "Do we still have to give her a gift?"

I nodded that I thought we did and sipped my Negroni.

"So, I still can't believe Nick turned out to be an asshole. I'm sorry."

"Eh, you know, it's for the better. I swear to God, Eliza. He is a swell dresser and all but I've come across bigger penises changing diapers. Call me superficial, but I don't think I could have signed up for that for the long haul. It was shocking."

"But he is so tall..."

"I'm not exaggerating. It was smaller than my thumb."

"Hard?"

"Yes! Hard," I said and halted further questions with a wave of my hand and a defeated shake of my head. Then I remembered something. "Hey! Didn't you have a date this week?"

Eliza's demeanor changed instantly and she looked at me with great seriousness.

"What? You had that date? Right? With that advertising guy?"

Eliza bit her lower lip and nodded her head slowly.

"What?!"

Eliza continued her nodding. The nodding took on an ominous meaning.

"What?! You are killing me. What the fuck?" I asked and laughed nervously. Eliza wasn't typically the great mistress of mystery.

"Something happened."

Now it was my turn to get serious.

"What? What happened? Something bad?"

"Something huge."

"Something huge? And you haven't seen fit to bring it the fuck up until I asked?"

"I'm sorry, but I have been ruminating on it all week. I wasn't sure what to make of it at first."

"Oh my God! What happened? Huge is intriguing as fuck!"

"Okay. I had that date on Wednesday night. Right?"

I nodded, rapt.

"So, we went to dinner and it was okay. He was really nice and he was easy to talk to and it was fun."

"Are you going to tell me you broke your dry spell? How long has it been? Did you have sex? Hasn't it been years at this point? Oh my God! Was it good? Was he the huge part?"

I shot questions at her like an automatic weapon.

"Just listen, will you? So, we end up back at my place and we are on the couch having a drink and one thing leads to another and we started fooling around."

I literally let out a squeal of impatience.

"And the next thing I know, he is going down on me."

I clapped my hand over my mouth.

"And you know, he does that for a while, until—you know—until I was done..."

"Aaahahaha!" I laughed, throwing my head back in delight and slapping both my thighs. "This is the best story ever! So then what? Did you blow him? Did you have sex?"

"This is the weird part. After he did what he did, he got up, thanked me for a great night and left."

I sat there staring back at her with a blank expression.

"What do you think of that?" Eliza asked.

"He left? He blew you and left? What the…? What? Is he a hooker?"

I asked these questions as much to the universe as to Eliza, my brow knitted and palms upward in supplication.

"Yes," Eliza responded, deadly sober.

"Yes, he was a hooker? You paid him?!"

"No! He is not a male prostitute and no, I didn't pay him. Are you nuts?"

"So, wait. He went down on you, you came and he left?"

"Yes."

We both just sat there a moment as Eliza let the full impact of this information sink in.

"Have you seen him again since?" I asked, finally.

"No. He won't return my texts or emails."

I started to say something and then realized I had no idea what to say, so I shut my mouth again.

"But here's the weird part."

"There is something weirder in this story?"

"Ruby, I think I am a lesbian."

I indulged in a cartoonish Scooby-Doo shake of my head in response to this spectacular bomb drop. I let out an abrupt guffaw and then resumed my confused expression.

"A lesbian?!"

"Shh! Keep it down. But yes. I think I'm gay."

"Why? What the… oh no. Wait. Is that a thing, again?"

"A thing?"

"You know… a fad. Is it trendy again?"

"No. It is not a thing. But it's pretty fantastic, Ruby, to just have someone go down on you. No penis issues. No balls. No hairy backs. No awful condoms. No… bleachy… ejaculate."

"Ejaculate?!"

"You seriously need to keep it down, Ruby," Eliza said, scanning the room for eavesdroppers. Satisfied that nobody had heard me, she continued. "Anyway, I have been thinking about it all week. I've never had a long-term relationship with a guy. Don't you think that is pretty significant?"

"You have never had any kind of relationship at all with a woman. Don't you think that is pretty significant?"

"Significant, perhaps, but for the reasons you are suggesting? Or because we are cultured to grow up assuming we are straight?"

Eliza paused after her last question and nodded at me slowly, eyebrows raised in that expression that says, "You can't deny the logic in that now, can you?"

"Are you attracted to women?"

"I think baby dykes are super hot."

"Okay. I think you have lost your fucking mind. Babies? And how can you even tell if a baby…"

"Not babies. Baby dykes."

"Um, what the fuck is a baby dyke and how the fuck do you know the answer?"

"I was on the internet all week. And according to Nappy-Dugout.com…"

"Nappy dugout? Wait. Nappy fucking dugout? Okay, that is so frigging awesome, I can't stand it!" I squealed in delight. "Nappy-Dugout.com? Do they sell T-shirts? If so, I have to have one!"

"According to the website," Eliza pressed on, ignoring my outburst, "a baby dyke is like—a young, tomboyish lesbian. They are toughs. Tattoos, low-riding pants. I think…"

"Like Pink?"

"Pink is gay?"

"I don't think so, but do you mean girls that look like that?"

"Okay, yeah. Younger, though, and really masculine."

"If you like them masculine, why not just, I don't know, date a guy?"

"Ruby, I need you to take this seriously. I am a lesbian now."

I blinked back at her for several moments.

"Eliza, I'm not sure you have thought this thing through properly. You do realize, right? That as a lesbian, you don't just walk around having Samantha Ronson lookalikes munch your box. I'm guessing that, at some point, some chick with pubic sideburns is going to expect a reach-around. And by reach-around I mean they are going to expect you to go ears-deep in their ham wallet. Are you ready for that?"

"Think maybe you are being unnecessarily boorish here?"

"Seriously. Chewing your way through some dank, ruby fruit jungle sounds good to you?"

"It does," she insisted, defiant.

I reacted maturely to this declaration by indulging in a grimace of disgust. Then I remembered something.

"You don't even like seafood!"

"That's nice. Thanks for being so supportive," Eliza pouted and sipped her cabernet.

"I'm sorry. I don't know why I said that. I guess I am just still in shock. I mean, you just told me you discovered you were gay by researching on the Internet. On a site called Nappy Dugout, no less."

"That is not what I said. I said…"

"Hi, girls! Are we having fun?"

It was the bride, Suzy, coming over to pay her respects. Suzy wasn't a fat woman but she wasn't thin, either. She had a swimmer's broad back and shoulders and had chosen a dress with breathtakingly unflattering, capped sleeves that maximized the girth of her arms. The scooped neckline made her upper body appear as brutish as a linebacker's and the empire waist hung limply from her ample bosom adding the illusion of advanced pregnancy. As my eyes wandered south, I noted that she had very muscular legs and had, as was her wont, chosen a dress that ended at the widest spread of her calves. The tiny ballet flats she had selected only exacerbated the thickening effect. The phrase "ham hocks" came to mind as I eyed her. I had a sudden impulse to blurt the words out. I thought of The Albino and his Tourette's. I grabbed my wine and gulped some down. It was then that I noticed a man beside her that I assumed was her new husband.

"Congratulations, you two!" I chirped, once I was sure my ham hocks impulse had passed.

Eliza's head whipped around and she looked at me like I was crazy.

"Oh, silly! This isn't my husband. This is my cousin, Bobby. Bobby Nemunaitis. Bobby is a police officer in Salt Lake City. Bobby, this is Eliza and Ruby. You know, Ruby is the movie star I told you about."

Ah! That explained my invitation to this shindig. I was a movie star.

"No, Suzy! Stop it! I am absolutely not a movie star," I chided Suzy and then turned to Bobby. "Nice to meet you, Bobby."

"Ruby was the star of *Cooterville, PTA*. You know? Remember that show?"

Bobby beamed star-fucking admiration at me, then sheepishly shook his head no. What is with these people that are impressed by just being told that someone is famous, even if they have no idea who the person is themselves?

"I'm sorry. I don't watch a lot of television," Bobby apologized.

"That's okay. Neither do I. I don't even have cable anymore," I added bitterly. "But Suzy! Look how beautiful you are!" I gushed, changing the subject. "That dress is... unbelievable," I added, truthfully.

"Really? Thank you! I designed it myself. Stuff right off the racks never fits me properly, you know? It is always so unflattering."

"You designed it yourself?" Eliza said, in evident wonder. "It's really some dress!"

You had to listen very carefully to hear the snarkery in Eliza's voice. Neither Suzy nor Bobby suspected a thing. They both just stood there, grinning like village idiots.

"Sit down. Join us," I said, gesturing to the vacant chairs at our table.

"Oh, I'd love to but I have to greet all the other guests. You know? No rest for the wicked."

"Especially on your honeymoon," I said, attempting something at humor, but once the words were out there, I realized I had no idea what the fuck I was talking about. I cleared my throat.

"Actually, that is why I brought Bobby over here. We leave for Jamaica tonight and Bobby is here for two more days. I was hoping you could show him around a little. You know? Show him where the stars hang out."

"Ah, yes. The stars," I said. You didn't have to be listening carefully to hear the snarkery in my voice. Suzy and Bobby grinned back at me, oblivious.

"Yeah, Ruby. Why don't you take Bobby out to the star hangouts?" Eliza mocked.

"Yeah, Eliza! You should come, too. You might get lucky and run into Ellen. Or Martina Navratilova."

"I love Ellen!" Bobby said. "I love how she dances at the start of every show. She is really fun, you know, for a lesbian!"

"I know," Eliza agreed. "Most lesbians are such downers," she added, her sarcasm ratcheted up significantly. I looked at Suzy and Bobby for a reaction. They were still all smiles and nodding agreement. Suzy and Bobby couldn't scrounge up fifty IQ points between them.

"So, it's settled! Okay, I'm going to go work the room, as they say. You know? Have fun!"

Suzy moved away with all the grace of a stockyard mammal, leaving Bobby still grinning and hovering over us.

I wanted Bobby to go away so I could grill Eliza on her newfound lesbianism and her thoughts on whether baby dykes got into Vajazzling but Bobby didn't appear to have any immediate, pressing engagements. Resentfully, I repeated the invitation that he join us and, finally, he did. A waiter came by and refreshed our drinks. Bobby was drinking water.

"So, ladies. Are either of you married?"

When we both said we were not, Bobby made that face you make when you wish you could take your foot out of your mouth. I was instantly and deeply offended.

"What?" I demanded.

"Nothing. It is just that single women tend to take it hard when their friends get married."

"Really, officer?" I asked. "Is that true of all the ladies out there in Salt Lake City?"

"Hey, don't shoot the messenger. And it is true everywhere."

"Are you married?"

"Yes."

"To how many women?"

"Ruby..." Eliza warned.

"No, Eliza. Bobby here seems to know a lot about women and weddings. And he lives in Utah. My question is fair."

"Just one. But I am Mormon, if that is your next question. Are you guys divorced or never married?"

"I don't know why this is any of your business, but I have never been married."

"Me, either," Eliza added.

"Can I ask why not?"

"I'm a lesbian," Eliza blurted.

"That's right! She's gay! And this country, Utah in particular, discriminates against same-sex marriages," I added defiantly. "Eliza here is not free to marry the... you know... vagina-packing tomboy of her dreams. I suppose you think that is okay."

"Vagina-packing?" Eliza asked, looking at me again as if I'd come unhinged.

"That explains why Eliza isn't married. I'm guessing your high-strung, movie-star personality might have something to do with why you have never married. Or maybe your friend's wedding is simply taking its toll on you."

"For your information, being married hasn't ever been a goal of mine."

"You prefer just shacking up with guys?"

"Shacking up? Where'd you come from? 1968?"

"She's not married because she hasn't yet met the man she wants to marry."

"Ah," Bobby said and nodded, patronizingly.

"It's true," I spat at him.

"Isn't that clock ticking kinda loud and fast these days, though?"

"Again, I don't know why this is any of your business, but I don't have a clock. I don't want kids so I can wait as long as it takes to find the right guy."

"Oh. So you are one of those women that thinks no guy is good enough for you," he said and he winked at Eliza.

"No. That is not what I said. But I don't feel like I need a man to complete me," I explained and scanned Eliza for signs that she was on Bobby's side in this. "I am waiting for a guy I cannot talk myself out of, not one I can talk myself into."

"That sounds like therapy-speak."

"Fuck you."

"Calm down, movie star," Bobby laughed. "I'm just yanking your chain. Right, Eliza?"

Bobby reached into the breast pocket of his coat, produced a card and handed it to me.

"Here's my card. Give me a call tomorrow and tell me where we are going to meet up. I'm really looking forward to meeting the stars with a star on my arm," he said as he stood up. "Now, if you ladies will excuse me, I am going to do some time with my grandparents. And maybe I'll see you out on the dance floor later, Eliza."

He winked at me and was off.

5 Booby nemesis

"HIS NAME IS BOOBY NEMUNAITIS," I texted Kate the next day.

Kate: Sounds like another name for breast cancer.

Me: Typo. Bobby. Not Booby. I keep wanting to say his last name as Nemesis.

Kate: Booby Nemesis is good. I'm keeping that.

Me: Eliza and I are meeting him out at the Frolic Room tonight. Please come. I am inviting Mack, too. I don't want to do this alone. This guy really is my nemesis. Everything he says pisses me off.

Kate: Oh? So, you aren't going to invite him to your house and make him a dinner he won't eat, invite him to bathe and then not fuck him? LOL

Me: It's not a date and shut up.

Kate: Okay. I love the Frolic Room. But I cannot come out. Wayne just added a porn channel to our cable service. I think he has a big night planned.

Me: Gross. I don't know how you do it. He needs sex more than every other guy on Earth combined. You are a saint.

Kate: Oh, I make it worth my while, horny.

Me: I'm sorry. Did you just address me as *horny*?

Kate: LOL! No. I meant *honey*. Hahahaha. Anyway, as I was saying, horny, if I'm going to be servicing him night and day, I might as well enjoy it, too. You know what I mean?

Me: Okay. Ew. Thanks for that visual. I can skip lunch now. So, are you are sure you can't come out?

Kate: Yeah. I need to go buy batteries for my pocket rocket.

Me: Are you doing this to me on purpose?

Kate: Hahaha!

LATER THAT DAY, Eliza and Mack and I were nursing drinks at the Frolic Room. Eliza was dressed in a black men's suit and a black, ruffled tuxedo shirt unbuttoned just to the point where you got an occasional glimpse of the top of her bra.

"So what's new and exciting?" Mack asked.

"Didn't K. D. Lang here tell you?"

Mack looked at Eliza and Eliza responded by rolling her eyes.

"Tell me what?" Mack asked me.

"Eliza decided she has the gay."

"Really?" Mack said with unmasked delight. "Cool!"

"Actually, the term we prefer is *queer*."

"We? The royal we?"

"Have you taken a lover?" Mack asked, eyes popping out of her head.

"*Taken a lover*? Who are you people?" I asked and looked scornfully at them both from as far up my nose as I could angle.

Before Eliza responded with more than a shake of her head, Booby walked through the door, joined us and promptly ordered a Bud and a shot of Goldschläger.

"So you are a cop in Salt Lake City, huh?" Mack asked when introduced. This was a tame opener for Mack. She sometimes opened with "Do you think my left implant feels too hard?"

He confirmed that he was a police officer and ordered another shot. I tried very hard to think of a few non-controversial topics we could all politely discuss, topics other than why I wasn't married. Mack brought up her boobs twice and, for the first time, I wished she'd do it more. It kept Booby's attention very successfully and my spinsterhood seemed unlikely to come up.

It wasn't long before Booby was lapping us big time. He'd had four shots of Goldschläger and three beers before I finished my second drink. After I ordered my third drink and Booby did his fifth shot, I decided to go next door, grab some tacos and bring them back to the bar. Booby was half in the bag and getting loud and I thought some food might help. Eliza and Mack shared a look with each other as Booby followed me out of the bar. As we were walking out, I heard Eliza ask Mack, "Have you ever heard the term *baby dyke*?"

Booby took one look at the taco shop and stopped me from entering with his hand to my chest.

"This is where you wanna get food?"

"Yeah. They make *the best* tacos. They are famous."

Booby peeked in the window at the cook and the sole customer on one of the four stools at the counter.

"Looks awful perpy in there."

"Perpy?"

"Perpy. As in perps. And they are probably illegal, too."

"Oh, for Chrissake. They're fine. We come here all the time."

I pushed past Booby and entered the shop. Booby followed and looked at the two guys in there as if they fit the description of his mother's rapists. I ordered eight tacos of mixed variety. Booby turned his attention to the grill.

"Is that cat?"

"It's *carne asada*."

"Is that Mexican for 'cat'?"

He put air quotes on cat. I tried to imagine what the fuck he thought he meant with those quotes.

"Why don't you go back to the bar and relax? I'll handle this here," I eventually said.

"You sure you are gonna be okay in here alone?" he asked and threw a dirty look toward the guy at the counter who was busy eating and ignoring us.

"A hundred percent sure. Go." I physically shoved him out the door.

Five minutes later, I was back in the bar with a bag full of tacos. I handed Booby one and passed the bag to the girls. He unwrapped the taco and made a sound of disgust.

"This isn't a taco! I'm not eating this."

"What are you talking about? These are the best tacos in L.A."

"This is not a taco. I eat tacos all the time back home. Where is the shell? What is that mystery meat? Cat?"

"Yeah, that cat joke never gets old. These are authentic tacos. Real tacos don't have a hard, molded shell like a Pringle and ground beef in them, you know?"

"This is not a taco."

You try to convince a guy from Utah that the Mexican guy running his own taco stand knows more about tacos than Old El Paso does. I couldn't be bothered. I was busy hatin'.

"Ugh, and they stink," he said, wrapping the taco up again and throwing it across me and into the bag Eliza was now holding.

What was wrong with me? How had I become a magnet for assholes? Or maybe I turned men into assholes. Maybe five years of celibacy was an underrated achievement. Five years of dodged bullets.

Booby pounded several more shots and two more beers while the rest of us ate the tacos. By the time we were making excuses and getting ready to bail on him, he was legless.

"Okay, Bobby, we're going to get outta here. School night and all for the ladies and I have an early audition," I added, lying. My heart objected to the mention of my obsolescent career by fluttering briefly and skipping a beat or two before settling back into a steady and ignorable rhythm. Increasingly, any mention of money or work or auditions or bills or my future resulted in palpitations or nausea or both. It was enough to drive one to drink. I thought about another drink but quickly dismissed the idea as it just meant more time with Booby.

"Wha? Wait! Whereseverybodygoin'? Let's go hang out someplace where the stars are at," he slurred. "I'm buying!"

"That's very generous but, really, we can't," I said, Eliza and Mack immediately backing me up.

"You're the boss, Pinky. I guess if we are making like an abortion and heading out early, I'm going to go drain the main vein."

He stumbled back to the restrooms. We watched him use the bar stools as walking sticks and slam into the ladies' room. We paid our tab and went outside to wait for him.

"Jesus, where do you find these guys?" Mack asked. "He was totally staring at my boobs all night."

"Make like an abortion? Who says shit like that?" I asked in disbelief.

"That business with the food was the final straw. He really sucks," Eliza chimed in. "And I thought Mormons didn't dri..."

A petite woman who looked more like a fourteen-year-old boy brushed past us. Eliza stopped talking mid-sentence and ogled the woman openly until the girl disappeared into a restaurant two doors down. Eliza caught me watching her stare.

"What?" Eliza asked defensively.

"He's a Mormon?" Mack asked and looked to me for an explanation. Mack hadn't caught the exchange between me and Eliza.

"Yeah. But tonight he is like some out-of-control frat jock. Anyway, I'm sorry. I only did this as a favor to Suzy… who I don't even really know… so… I mean, I don't even know how these things keep happening to me. This is why I never go out. Because…"

I stopped talking as Booby stumbled out the door of the Frolic Room talking on his cell phone. He crashed into a crowd of *Wicked* fans leaving the Pantages Theater next door. This spun him into an older couple and Booby grabbed the woman for balance. The man shoved Booby off of his wife and Booby twisted his ankle on the curb and fell to his knees, half on the sidewalk, half in the street. His cell phone skittered into the gutter and down into the sewer. The three of us watched this unfold with our mouths literally agape. Theater patrons threw him dirty looks and stepped over and around him.

"Are you okay?" I finally managed to ask as I went over to help him up. He was gazing mournfully down the hole into which his cell has disappeared.

"My phone…" he said, pointing.

I followed his gaze but I could not make anything out in the darkness.

"Gimme your number," I said to Booby. "I'll call you and we can see where your phone is."

Booby stood up and recited his number. I dialed and, in a few seconds, we heard Billy Squier's "Stroke Me" chiming from beneath the street. All four of us peered into the drain and watched the phone light up with each ring and vibrate its way into the mud. The ringing stopped at about the same moment the phone finally sank out of view. Nobody moved for about five seconds and then, as if on cue, Eliza and Mack and I burst into laughter.

"Nice ring tone, dude."

"Somebody did that to my phone as a prank yesterday and I don't know how to fix it," Booby slurred.

"Well, I guess you can consider that problem solved," I quipped and we gals laughed some more at Booby's expense.

"What am I gonna do now?" Booby moaned.

"Was it insured?"

"No, I mean, I am supposed to stay at a friend's house in Santa Monica tonight. He was gonna drive me to the airport in the morning."

We all stared at him, uncomprehendingly.

"He texted me his, um, address. I'm supposed to take a taxi back..."

It was beginning to become clear.

"I don't know his number or his address. They were... you know..." he tapered off. He pointed into the sewer and looked to the three of us for answers.

"Oh, shit! What are you going to do?"

His expression could not have been more blank. Then he threw up in his mouth, leaned toward the sewer and blew the puke into the gutter at about the same location his phone was last seen.

After a difficult conversation with Drunky McDrunkerson, we concluded that he would come back to my place for the night and that I would drive him to the airport in the morning. I was none too pleased about this scenario but he certainly was not the responsibility of Eliza or Mack, and the newlyweds were off honeymooning in Jamaica. We had no other people in common. So—this plan was the only reasonable one we girls could come up with after we decided that, for sure, just making a run for it and leaving him there would be kinda bad form. Instead, Mack agreed to follow me to my place and help me get Booby settled in. Eliza waved goodbye to us and headed toward her car mumbling something I didn't catch about Beaver-Book.com.

While Mack and I had discussed her staying over at my place for the night as a safety measure, it turned out that was unnecessary. Once Mack and I navigated Booby from my car to my house, he indicated a need for a bathroom. I pointed him to it and seconds later our ears were assailed by the sounds of violent puking. I say assailed because he screamed like an angry lion as he emptied the contents of his stomach. He came out of the bathroom and joined us on the balcony.

"I feel much better..." he said and then bent at the waist over the railing and roared some more vomit into my yard. These were waking-the-neighbors, call-the-police level sound effects.

What an amateur, I thought.

"What a cunt," Mack whispered and then added the non sequitur, "Hey, do you think I look fat in these jeggings?"

I pretended not to hear her use a word as offensive as jeggings.

"Dude, is it important to alert everyone from here to Utah that you can't handle your liquor?" I scolded.

Booby's response was to treat my garden to another ten decibel Goldschläger shower and stumble back from the rail. He fell onto his ass, legs spread as if to begin a stretching warm-up and looked up at us smiling. He then curled up in the fetal position and went to sleep. I stepped over him, closed the doors to the balcony and locked him outside. The lion safely in a cage, Mack decided to sleep in her own bed that night. She went home and I crawled into bed with my kids.

I was awakened at dawn by the sound of knocking from my balcony. My dogs went shithouse and were throwing themselves at the French doors. It took me a few seconds to remember the night before and realize what all the commotion was about. Booby was up.

I went to the balcony and let him in.

"Good morning." he said.

"Morning."

"I am so embarrassed. Did I do anything last night that I need to apologize for?"

"No, no. Don't sweat it. How are you feeling today?"

"Not bad, considering. Better than I have a right to."

"Yeah, well, my lawn probably has the hangover you earned."

"Ah. So it was like that?"

I nodded, noting that I had a bit of a hangover myself.

"Well, come on in. What time is your flight today?"

"It is at nine AM."

"Nine? What time is it now?"

"I have no idea. I can't find my cell phone."

I filled him in on the whereabouts of his cell phone and checked the time on my own. It was almost 7 AM. We had to hustle.

"Can I get a handful of Advil or something from you? My head is killing me."

"Good idea. I am right there with you."

I led him to the linen closet that also served as my medicine cabinet. I only had two Advil left and insisted Booby take them.

"No, I feel terrible! I cannot take your last Advil. You must have something else in there. Please look."

I dug around in the semi-darkness, found an old bottle of generic liquigels in the back of the closet and swallowed three horse pills with a handful of water.

"Satisfied?"

Booby was appeased and downed his Advil.

"Okay. We'd better roll if you wanna make your flight."

As I put on my socks and shoes, I was overcome by a tsunami of otherworldly nausea. Seconds later, I was kneeling in front of the toilet, dry heaving. A full minute of retching and a teaspoon of expelled bile later, I emerged from the bathroom sweating heavily.

"Are you okay?"

I told him I had no idea what was going on. I had gone from a mild, tolerable hangover to praying for death in just minutes. I spent four of the next five minutes bent over the toilet. My body was reacting violently to something and whatever it was that my body wanted to purge was refusing to be displaced. I looked at the bottle the liquigels had come from and discovered that they were women's multivitamins and not pain relievers. Anyone who knows anything knows vitamins on an empty stomach are bad news.

Concerned that Booby would miss his flight, I forced myself behind the wheel of my truck and we headed toward the airport. We stopped at my local donut shop so I could pick up a bagel and try to quell the nausea with a bit of food. Booby got a coffee.

I nibbled the bagel as we headed south on the 101. The smell of Booby's coffee was more than I could bear. I rolled down my window to circulate the air which, as it happened, was a stroke of luck. As soon as the window was down, bagel-puke flew out of my mouth and down the outside of my car. I tossed the remaining bagel into the back seat.

"Are you sure you are okay?" Booby asked, looking very worried.

"I don't know. This is crazy," I said lamely, wiping thick sweat from my forehead. Secretly certain that I was dying, I was bitterly humiliated that a guy I considered to be an insufferable tool was going to be the last person I saw in this lifetime.

At some point on the 110 South, things went from bad to worse. I had to pull over into a breakdown lane that was only as wide as my truck. I leaned out the window and green bile erupted, Linda Blair-style, out of my open mouth. Sitting as close to rushing traffic as we were, my puke was caught in the draught and whipped across my right cheek and out after the passing cars.

"Ugh, it smells like vitamins!" Booby complained.

I dropped, panting, back into the driver's seat. I swiped my forearm across my cheek. My abdomen began cramping.

"You need to drive. I can't. I can't. You need to drive."

"But I don't know the way."

"YOU NEED TO DRIVE!" I screamed in his face, perfecting the image of a person in need of an exorcism. I turned away again and promptly puked a new horizontal stream out the driver's window.

That scared the shit out of Booby and he opened the passenger door the few inches that were possible before hitting the sound barrier wall. He squeezed out and around the car like a human squeegee as I crawled over the console to the passenger side. My stomach was audibly percolating. Booby was behind the wheel and looking at me with justifiable shock and horror.

"I feel awful. I made you take those pills. Oh my God. Do you need to go to the hospital?"

"Just drive!! Take this to the 105 West. Then you can follow the signs to the airport."

My body was shutting down. I could barely keep my eyes open. I opened the passenger window but was relieved to note that the urge to vomit was gone. It was then that I knew that the demon inside me had selected a new action end. I put my feet onto the dashboard in a desperate effort to push the brewing trouble up.

What seemed like sixteen hours later, we pulled to the curb outside Booby's airline terminal. He got out of the car and ran around to open my door for me. My stomach felt as though all my internal organs were in the process of rupturing.

"Come inside the terminal. Maybe you can rest in there or find a doctor."

As soon as I stood up outside the car, I realized I'd made a terrible mistake. I slammed the door shut and then bent at the waist in a ninety degree angle. I had to do something to rekink the hose that had been unkinked by my standing, or risk a torrent of exploded organ-matter running down my thighs.

"Just go. I'm fine. Really. You'll miss your flight."

"I can't just leave you here. I feel responsible. Come inside..."

I cut him off, "RUN, Booby, RUN! *Save yourself*!"

If I had been the second coming of Jesus Christ standing before him then, his expression could not possibly have registered more confusion or awe. He didn't even try to argue anymore. He just turned on his heels and speed-walked his way inside the terminal. He never dared look back.

I walked as quickly as I could to the driver's side and clambered in. I put the car into drive and sped back toward the freeway. Before I was even off airport property, my bowels commenced a hateful release. When I remember it today, it is accompanied by the same sound Booby had made the night before as he yakked into my yard but, realistically, that is unlikely. A quiet rumble and then a muffled but explosive "rooomaboombamooovvv!" Immediately, my pain decreased by half and I was two inches taller in the seat. The car filled with a noxious poopy-vitamin vapor. *Fuck it*, I thought, *there's no going back from here*. I released the hounds. Another sloppy "vroomaboomammmvvrooombbbppp...ppllppp" made itself heard. When it was over, and it was over mercifully quickly, I was so much taller on my perch that I had to actually reach down and lower the seat setting. I felt hot sloppy-Joe oozing its way up the back of my pants from the pressure of my sitting upon it. My crack was a vile conduit to my waistline. I didn't care. I didn't need to puke anymore and I was no longer in any pain. All I felt was total relief and complete exhaustion.

At home, I undressed in the garage and threw everything I was wearing away. I considered keeping the shirt and bra because they were undefiled but finally decided against it. I wanted no witnesses to this event. None. So, nude but still sporting the evidence of the shit taco I had become, I used the shirt to wipe my car seat with Armorall, tossed it with the other soiled items, buried it all under a torn-open trash bag and walked like a bow-legged cowboy inside to shower.

After ten minutes of scrubbing like a rape victim, I stepped out of the shower, lobster-red from the heat of the water. The bottle of vitamins was still sitting on the sink. I picked it up and read the label. They were expired. Really expired. Seven years expired. I made a mental note to respect labeling more in the future and crawled into bed. While I waited for sleep to overtake me, I thought that even in drastic situations like today, one could find a silver lining if one were inclined. I fell asleep congratulating myself that, at least, I'd probably lost a few pounds that day.

SOMEHOW, A MONTH WENT BY and a renewed stack of unpaid bills had accumulated on my desk. Again, I poured a glass of wine and began the heart-stopping process of opening each and absorbing the bad news. Utility and telephone bills, homeowner's insurance, union dues, seven or eight maxed-out credit cards with deviously low minimum payments. I looked at the little chart on each outlining how long it would take to pay them off with just minimum payments and the real cost of doing that and felt a crushing weight on my chest. Worse yet, there wasn't room on any card, or among the cards collectively, to pay my mortgage this month. My heart lurched painfully into overdrive and my breathing became quick and shallow. Certain I was having a heart attack, I did what anyone in panic mode and afraid for their life would do. I called my mother.

"Hi!" she answered cheerfully.

"Hi," I answered and burst into tears.

"Hey! What is it? Is everything okay?"

"No. I'm done. I'm completely done. I can't pay my mortgage. I'm going to lose my house!" I wailed.

"What happened? Why?"

"Because I'm broke, that's why."

"But you said your mortgage adjustment wasn't bad."

"It isn't bad, if I had any income at all."

"Well, aren't you still getting unemployment?"

"Yeah..."

"How much is it?"

I told her and I told her what my mortgage was.

"Okay, well, let me see. That's, um..."

"Not enough! Not enough is the number you are looking for. It isn't enough to cover my mortgage, let alone my second, my utilities and phone and minimum credit card payments and car, house and health insurance or property taxes and gas for the car. And dog food. And anything else that always seems to come up month after month. Every month some new, unexpected expense. A broken crown, shots for the dogs, new brakes on the car. Shit like that. Every friggin' month. And I have to eat, too."

"How have you been doing it until now?"

"I had a home equity line of credit and then, when that was maxed out, cash advances on credit cards. My cards are all maxed out, or very close to it now, too."

"Living on credit cards is bad."

"I know! But what other choice did I have? Who could have guessed ten years ago that ten years would go by in which I barely earned ten grand? I kept thinking things had to turn around, you know? It isn't like I don't have a SAG card. It isn't like I didn't have a long and pretty lucrative career. My belief that I can work as an actress isn't some totally baseless, fantasy pipedream. And it isn't like I'm the fucking Elephant Man here. How can it be that in ten years there hasn't been a single role that I am right for?"

"What does your agent say?"

"She says that she calls and tries to get me in and everyone says, 'I know her. I love her. She's not right.' If they loved me, I'd have been in their office in the last ten years. Now, you know, they haven't seen me in so long that the person they are remembering probably isn't right for the role. The person I am now is, but they have no idea who I am and… ugh. Whatever. What am I going to do?" I demanded and launched into tears again.

"Do you need me to lend you some money?"

"Unless you have fifty grand you can let go of for a few years, no."

"Well, I don't have anything like that but I could maybe send you a thousand. Would that help?"

"It would help but so temporarily it wouldn't make any real difference and you'd be out of what must be your entire safety net. Then, two weeks later, I'd be right back here again and you'd be broke right along with me."

"Have you tried pulling more money out of the house? Don't you still have a lot of equity there? Maybe you could refi and lower the payments?"

"Those would be great ideas but I already tried and the bank said I don't qualify."

"You don't qualify for a lower payment?"

"No."

"What sense does that make?"

"Don't get me started. I'm beginning to think it is a big bank conspiracy to kick people out of the few remaining homes in America that are not under water so the banks can sell those homes at a huge profit. The trick is not to get foreclosed upon. The trick is, sell before the bank smells blood."

"Are you going to sell the house?"

"I don't want to! I bought it so long ago and when I was working all the time. I could never afford this house now or ever again, in all likelihood. I don't want to sell this just to end up renting a studio apartment that costs more than what I pay to own this. It seems so incredibly unfair that the bank gets to punish me in reaction to the crisis that they caused. I didn't buy more house than I could afford. And now it is probably worth two or three times what I paid and I have probably thirty or forty percent equity. Conservatively. The equity alone should qualify me for a refi. I don't want that equity in a bank account collecting .00002% interest while I rent some fucking Melrose Place apartment in a hideous, 1980s pool building with paper-thin walls. I don't want to live next door to Jack Wagner! I want to live here. If I pulled fifty grand out, refied the loan to a new thirty-year fixed at some rate in the high threes instead of this ass-raping 6.5% I am paying now, the cash, lower payment and unemployment could keep me afloat another year or two and maybe my career would finally miraculously revive. Or worst case scenario, I use that fifty K to bring the house back up and running and suitable for buying eyes and sell it for the price it deserves. But as it is... ugh. How did this happen? How did I become a complete and total loser?"

"You're not a loser."

"But I am. I am a fucking has-been loser. I have been for years. I've just been in denial. Every year that passes, the chance that acting will ever again be my sole and adequate source of income grows smaller and smaller in the rearview mirror. Do you realize there isn't a single show on my résumé that is still on the air?"

"Yeah. You told me that before."

"See? Now I am a boring, repetitive has-been loser."

"You are not a loser! Stop saying that. I think repeating that to yourself is more damaging than you know."

I didn't respond. I sat there silently pondering the corner I'd painted myself into. The corners of my mouth were pulled down as if by anchors into a frozen caricature of a drama mask and tears flooded past them onto my desk.

"I'm gonna have to sell the house," I finally said, devoid of emotion, and wiped at my tears. "I'm gonna have to sell the house and move into a meth community, start hoarding cats and work at the ninety-nine cent store ringing up purchases of novelty ice-cube trays and generic brand Doritos called 'Daritas' or something to grey-looking women shuffling around in filthy slippers and ill-fitting wigs."

"Stop it. That's not going to happen. And there is nothing wrong with novelty ice-cube trays. I have a flamingo one that makes the cutest, retro-looking ice if you use pink lemonade."

"Are you really talking to me about pink flamingo ice cubes?" I asked in disbelief but, secretly, I couldn't help but imagine how cute they must look, bobbing around a tall glass of regular lemonade. "I'm having a life crisis here. I won't have anywhere to chill ice, anyway, from my new digs under the freeway overpass."

"Are you really considering selling the house?"

"No. I don't know. I don't know what else I can do. I tried the refi thing and was completely stiff-armed. So, this month, for the first time in my life, I won't be able to pay the mortgage. I am going to default. This month."

"What happened to your photography business?"

"I think 'business' is an overstatement, Ma."

The fact is, I had dabbled a bit in real estate photography, shooting high-end houses for websites and those glossy fliers real estate agents use at open houses, etc. It was a nice little supplement to my income but never an income in and of itself. But the advent of digital had turned everyone into a photographer, it seemed, and now those agents that used to hire me either did it themselves, or got that service free as part of those crazy three-hundred-sixty degree moving camera shots of rooms they provide now on websites. I had attempted to break into headshot photography, too, but the competition there was worse than it was actually being an actor. Without several iconic people well-presented on your website, it was hard to get someone to choose you over some guy that shot the likes of Jennifer Lawrence and Robert Pattinson. So my headshot business was at a bit of a dead end, too.

"And at this point," I continued, "I'd need to upgrade my camera and invest in some lights, et cetera, neither of which I can afford. And photography isn't going to provide the big infusion of cash I need to save me now, anyway. Right now, I need a miracle."

"You know, doesn't your union have some kind of emergency relief for actors who are in trouble? Didn't you tell me that a friend of yours appealed to the union and they paid his rent for a while?"

She was right. Such a thing did used to exist and a friend of mine had been helped by it. He lost his apartment in the end but the union aid postponed it for a few months, until he could figure out other arrangements.

"Yeah, you're right! I wonder if they still have anything like that. I'm going to look into that right now. Thank you!"

"Okay. Good luck. And I love you. It's all gonna be okay. All right?"

"I hope so. I love you, too," I said, hung up and immediately began Googling actor aid.

Three hours later, I had found and applied for three different actor relief programs through the various union funding sources. The people I spoke to were all incredibly kind and understanding. No attitude. No judgment. No sneering quips about the legitimacy of still referring to myself as an actor after a decade of near-total unemployment. Instead, they all expressed how impressed they were that I had kept my house of cards intact this long with only the scarcest income, income they could each confirm directly from the SAG database. They made applying for charity an ego-boosting experience. Better yet, two weeks later, between them, they paid my mortgage for a month, my huge water and power bill, the second six-month installment of my car insurance and my property taxes for the second half of the year. It was a miracle but a miracle that only postponed the inevitable by a few months, if not weeks. But for the first time in a long time, I could think about my bills and not have an anxiety attack, so, it seemed, they had also postponed my impending death by stroke.

• • •

A WEEK LATER, still drunk on the success of my applications for charity, I was again trying to get drunk the old-fashioned way. I was awaiting delivery of my fourth drink at the opening night party of the Hollywood Completion Fund Film Festival in beautiful beachfront Santa Monica and trying to figure out if Eliza's new haircut reminded me more of a guy from Kings of Leon or Adam Lambert. She was wearing a Western-themed outfit that looked like she'd nabbed it at a *Brokeback Mountain* trunk sale. She sat back, slumped in her seat with her legs spread wide in what, I imagine, was her fledgling attempt at adopting a more male physicality. It seemed unnecessarily gauche to me. Or maybe some part of me was just jealous that she was able to embrace such a huge shift in how she defined herself. I eyed her casually and considered for the first time that maybe she was brave, and I was the crazy one, miserable and white-knuckling my grip on my definition as "actress" right into the poorhouse. Maybe I needed to loosen up a bit, let go of this idea of who I was and see what the world might have to offer in other fields. A new feeling came into me then but was gone again before I could figure out what it was. Was it relief? Or was it something people feel when their dreams are finally beaten completely out of them? I couldn't be certain. A waiter caught my eye and I thought, *Maybe I should become a waiter.* I waited to see if that fleeting feeling returned as I considered a life in the service industry but that feeling proved to more elusive than I'd hoped. I looked again at the waiter and tried to guess what he earned.

"So, yesterday," Eliza said, interrupting my thoughts and stirring the ice in an empty highball glass with her index finger, "I read on Clamsnackers that GayJayDate is one of the best online dating sites and..."

"I'm sorry. I need to back you up here. *Clamsnackers?*"

"Clamsnackers," she repeated matter-of-factly, and sucked the moisture off her stirring finger. "It is a lesbian blogging site. And they said that queer Jews have a great success rate on GayJayDate."

"Eliza! You are killing me. You are a holiday Jew that has never kissed a girl. You can't even say the word 'pussy.' How are you going to wrap your mouth all up on one? Have you thought about that? You realize that joining Team Lickalotapus means more than a fashion makeover, right? Now, you are taking advice from a site called *Clamsnackers* to help you find a baby dyke with payos and tzitzit? Honey, I think you might need an intervention."

Before Eliza could find the words to express her disappointment in me, Mack staggered over with an unfamiliar guy helping her carry our cocktails.

"Hey, ladies! I want you to meet Devon Evans," she said, handing Eliza a drink. "He is a famous surfer from Hawaii! Devon, that Last Word you have is for her," Mack added, pointing to me. Devon handed me my drink.

Devon Evans. While his face was unfamiliar to me, I certainly knew his name. All of my guy friends in Boston used to worship him in the early eighties. He was a surfing icon in the seventies and even starred in a few big budget, beachsploitation films in his prime. Seems he was quite a fetching young man in the day but years of meth addiction and an apparent fetish for homemade tattooing had taken their toll. Standing before me now was a man that looked more like he belonged in an episode of *Lock-Up* than on the cover of *Teen Beat*.

"I know who you are!" I blurted out enthusiastically. "My guy friends love you!"

Devon Evans's smile said he had come to take that reaction to his name for granted. His smile also revealed that Devon and his dentist had long been estranged.

"Devon Evans, madam," he said to both me and Eliza, taking each of our hands in turn and kissing them. "And you are?"

"I am Ruby and this is Eliza. Eliza is going through her lesbian phase," I volunteered, for no explicable reason. "How do you know Mack?" I asked as I eyed the tattoos he had on his skull on either side of his Mohawk. Mack was a rich girl from Marin who was far more familiar with tennis than with seventies beach culture and her taste in men was more *The Bachelor* than *America's Most Wanted*.

"He was behind me in line at the bar and we started talking," Mack replied and I caught her quickly look down at her tits, making sure, maybe, that they were still there.

"Sit down. Join us!" I said, probably more exuberantly than was required.

I am seldom star-struck and I am not sure that is the right term for what I was feeling this evening but I was uncommonly excited to be at a table with this guy. I couldn't wait to tell my guy friends that I had met the legendary Devon Evans. Over the course of the night, I must have taken thirty photos of myself with him to support my story. Pushing fifty, he was delighted by the attention he was getting from a table of enthusiastic gals and the photos show all of us getting more drunk and stupid with each successive shot. Eliza even paused her efforts at establishing her new persona and embraced the shenanigans that were Devon Evans, among them a penchant for sticking his tongue out ala Gene Simmons and posing making devil-horn hand gestures. He was pure class.

When it was time to leave, Devon slipped each of us his card. He had clearly mistaken our attentiveness for physical attraction. None of us were so broken down that we wanted to go there, but I got it in my head that shooting his portrait for my photography website would be an enormous coup. Maybe this was just the sort of iconic presence I needed to launch a full-blown headshot or portrait business. Maybe Devon Evans was my savior. Maybe I could become the next Annie Leibovitz. Overnight.

With no time to waste, the next day I called the number on the card Devon had given me. It was the number for his surfboard shop—Devon Evans Pipeline Surf—in a town somewhere in California that I had never heard of. Nervous, I recited my prepared speech silently as the phone rang.

"Pipeline," a guy answered sounding very bored.

"Hello, is Devon Evans in?" I ask, heart in my throat.

"Nah, brah. He ain't here right now."

"Do you know when Devon Evans will be around?"

I heard myself say "Devon Evans" the second time as if his name was "Devonevans." It was like saying, "Is John F. Kennedy available? No? Well, do you know when John-FKennedy might be around because I really need to talk to JohnFKennedy."

"No, dude."

"Um, can I leave my name and number? I would like to speak to Devonevans about an art project."

He took my name and number and I hung up, feeling like a ginormous dork. An hour later, my phone rang. It was an unknown number with the same area code as Pipeline's.

"Hello?"

"Hey, babe!"

It was Devonevans. I reminded him who I was, specifically which of last night's three women I was, and explained that I wanted to shoot his portrait for my site. He was into the idea immediately but made a passing reference to his lawyer while saying "yes, yes, yes" the entire time. It worried me that he thought there might be contracts or money or anything legal passing between us. I shoot portraits alone and in my house with natural light with a ten-year-old digital camera. This was no *Teen Vogue* Top Model photo shoot he was agreeing to. I decided to ignore it and press on.

"So what do you wanna do?" he asked.

"Well, I just need to know when you are free and when you can come to my house for a few hours."

"I'm still in L.A. now and could hook up tonight."

I had a birthday party that night for one of my guy friends and it struck me that half the guys I had wanted to brag to about Devonevans were likely to be in attendance. What if I just showed up with Devonevans as my guest? People would shit!

"I actually have a birthday thing tonight but it is at the bar at the W. Do you want to stop by there? I'll be there at seven. We can talk about the portrait then."

"Sweet," he said and we hung up.

6 Devonevans

ELIZA AND MACK were at the W Hotel bar when I arrived. Mack's breasts told the room that maybe it could be a little warmer in there, while Eliza's outfit said "I own the entire *The L Word* box set." I filled them in on the recent Devonevans developments, including my "Devonevans" faux pas on the call early that day. From that moment on, they would only refer to Devon Evans with the one-word version of his name. My guy friends, Dutch, Jim and Gene, joined us seconds before Devonevans arrived.

"Devon, you remember Eliza and Mack. These are my old friends Jim and Gene and Dutch." I turned to my friends. "This is Devonevans."

Dutch had no idea who it was he was meeting but Jim and Gene looked like Rolling Stones fans being ambushed by Mick Jagger. Their faces began a synchronized evolution involving a slowly slackened jaw and an accompanying widening of the eyes. You could almost smell smoke as their brains overheated trying to figure out how I was the one making such an unexpected introduction.

Devonevans moved to greet the gals and planted a wet one right on my mouth. I am not a lip kisser on my own but I will usually go along with whatever the other person instigates. I regretted it this time immediately. Not only were his lips literally wet but he had breath that would gag a maggot. In self-preservation mode, my entire body involuntarily recoiled back the foot or so that remained between me and the bar. I took a deep breath of fresh air, a safe distance from Devonevans, and looked down at my shoes, pretending to look for the nonexistent thing that had made me lose my balance. While I did this, Devonevans clouded up and rained down upon my female companions. When he stepped back, I saw that Eliza's and Mack's faces looked much as Jim's and Gene's had only seconds before but for a completely different reason. It was then that I saw Devonevans reach out to me as if to take me under his wing. To protect myself, I turned my back to him under the pretense of ordering him a drink.

"What are you drinking, Devon?" I asked over my shoulder.

"Platinum Patron rocks. Double."

I was grateful to hear this. Tequila would improve and maybe disinfect his stink hole. I ordered his drink and a house red for myself and talked awkwardly over my shoulder, refusing to turn and face him until I had the eighty proof mouthwash with which to fend him off.

While I waited for the drinks, I watched the bartender going through her motions. I wondered what bartenders earned. Making drinks all night couldn't be that hard and at these prices, the money had to be fairly decent. I projected an image of myself in her place, mixing drinks, flirting with customers for better tips. I was surprised to note that the vision didn't totally depress me. Then I looked at her outfit, the same one the other female bartender was wearing: the lowest of low-rider, skintight black jeans and a cropped black vest. Six inches of taught tummy complete with elaborate tattoo work were exposed, more when she reached up for something, and not the teensiest belly roll, not even when she bent over. I was assaulted by the vision of my own abdomen exposed in that manner; just a big, fleshy fanny pack in the front, obscuring the top button of my skinny jeans and four inches of plumber crack in the back. That would be sure to hurt tips, assuming it didn't serve as a barrier to my being hired at all. Man, it was hard out here for a pimp.

Dutch leaned in and interrupted my contemplation. He whispered, barely audibly, in my ear, "Please tell me you are not fucking this gator," meaning Devonevans, I intuited, and not the hot bartender girl. I shook my head in an emphatic no. Dutch relaxed and stood back with the other guys. Dutch had a tendency to be very protective of me. It was sweet.

At last, the drinks arrived and I turned to hand Devonevans his while easing myself to a safe spot between Eliza and Mack. Soon the boys were deep in conversation so we girls took the opportunity to excuse ourselves and head off to the ladies' room.

"Holy fuck! I actually gagged!" Mack said, once we were out of earshot.

"Who has mouthwash or toothpaste? Teeth whitener? Lysol? Anything. I… I… I.." I panicked. "I need something to decontaminate my face!"

"He is like a walking Western Exterminator fogger. I might hire him to treat my house for termites," Eliza commiserated.

"It was so wet! It was like getting slapped in the mouth with a decomposing chicken liver!" I said. "I don't remember him being like that last night? Do you?"

Nobody did. Nobody had an explanation. We all splashed water on our faces and scraped our lips raw with the brown paper towels that were dispensed from the wall.

"Eliza, you might want to think about that Devonevans kiss and the reality of tonguing taint. I think they just might be in the same league."

"You are such an asshole," Eliza said, but I saw the tiniest hint of worry in her eyes.

"Okay. Let's circle the wagons when we go back out there. Nobody stray from the herd. He might pounce if he senses weakness," I strategized and, wise and wary, we returned to the group.

We successfully avoided any more contact with the portal to Hell that was Devonevans's mouth, and Devonevans had several more double Patrons. That might have had a part in dispersing the funk but, either way, we spent the balance of the evening without any further life-threatening events. Devonevans proved to be very entertaining, from a safe distance.

When it was time to leave I asked for my tab.

"I'm going to go to the head while you take care of that," Devonevans said and walked away.

I couldn't believe I hadn't anticipated getting stuck with this outrageously excessive bar tab but I justified paying it as part of the cost of doing business in the portrait world. *You gotta spend money to make money*, I thought, consoling myself.

Outside the W, I waited with the others for the valet to deliver their cars. I had parked on a side street in order to save the ten dollar cost. Before he left, Dutch made me promise I would not hook up with Devonevans. I assured him, his fears were unfounded. It wasn't long before it was just me and Devonevans standing there on the sidewalk.

"Okay, Devon. Thanks for coming out tonight."

"Where's your car?"

"Oh, I parked around the corner. Your car will be here any second. I'll call you tomorrow about the pictures. Okay?" I said and leaned in, cheek first, to press the side of my face to his as a means to say goodbye.

"I'm around the corner, too. I'll walk you."

Oh, man. When we got to my car, I made some fuss about being cold and jumped inside as fast as was humanly possible. I closed the door and rolled the window halfway down.

"So, I'll just follow you, all right?" Devonevans said.

Follow me? Had the others made some additional plan for the evening that I had missed? Was I more drunk that I thought and blacking out a plan I had made myself? Did he think we were going to shoot portraits right then? I looked at him and asked, as innocently as Cindy Lou Who, "Follow me where?"

Devonevans looked back at me and said nothing. We blinked at each other for several seconds when it suddenly dawned on me.

"Follow me to my *house*?" I said, too stunned to mask my horror.

"Yeah. It is a long drive to Carpinteria."

Unable to recover in the least, I stammered and shook my head repeatedly, "No, no, no… I… no."

I stared at him feeling like a thirteen-year-old girl in way over her head out on a date with a forty-year-old guy. I didn't care. I couldn't budge. He was not following me home. It crossed my mind that this could get ugly.

"Okay. Gimme a call tomorrow and we will talk about the pictures."

He leaned in to kiss me through the partially open window. So relieved that this had concluded on a friendly level, I met his mouth with my lips. His expensive tequila was worth every cent. He lips were still disturbing, but his breath now just smelled like my spent money.

A woman of my word, I called Devonevans the next day. We chatted a bit and tried to figure out our calendars and how to get this portrait done. I noticed that the coming weekend was Memorial Day. I was hosting a big supper. Maybe I could get him over before dinner, shoot him and let him stay for the meal. This seemed a brilliant tactic to avoid alone time with the surf legend and also achieve my end.

"What are you doing Sunday? If you are free, maybe you want to come over. We could shoot the pictures and you could stay for dinner. I am having a lot of people over. It will be fun."

"I'd love to grind some munch with you and your peeps. Thanks!"

"GRIND SOME MUNCH? Hahaha," Eliza laughed when I recounted the conversation to her later via text.

Eliza: *Grind some munch* is going right to the top of the list of my favorite new expressions. Devonevans rules!

Me: He is much nicer than he looks.

Eliza: Nicer than he smells, too. LOL

Me: I need to be sure I have some tequila around for him. He'll wilt lilies with that stank of his.

Eliza: I can't believe you invited Devonevans to Memorial Day! This is going to be the best Memorial Day of our lives! You are going to marry Devonevans.

Me: Don't get carried away. I just need to get the frigging portrait taken as soon as possible. I don't want him to think we are dating or that I want him to grind *my* munch, if you know what I… ugh. It's just too gross to even think about.

Eliza: Hahaha.

MEMORIAL DAY ARRIVED AND I TRIED to find something to wear that looked dressy but that Devonevans would not mistake as an outfit intended to impress him. I settled on cuffed jeans rolled high, platforms and a T-shirt through which one could just make out the faintest hint of my leopard bra. Between cooking and cleaning and trying to be ready for Devonevans's early arrival time, I had no time to properly do my hair and make-up. I resorted, as I often do, to a hat and mascara and then tried to calm my nerves. Devonevans was due an hour before anyone else and my plan was to take him to a spot on my patio that works great for portraits, shoot a roll of b&w and a roll of color, maybe a roll of 120 and then get the party started. I was being forced to shoot him with film, the far more expensive option, because a recent inspection revealed that my digital camera did little more now than flash an unknown error code whenever I touched the shutter. I couldn't catch a break to save my life. At least I had film cameras as back-up and some outrageously expired film from the vegetable bin in my refrigerator. Devonevans was due at 1 PM.

At 2 PM, Eliza walked in. She was dressed in a royal blue, velvet zoot suit and had a blue-and-gold ascot tucked neatly into a brocade vest. Her hair curled on the sides into little ladylike sideburns, and I wasn't sure, but I thought I saw the faintest hint of a mustache on her upper lip. She caught me staring and, anticipating my question, said mysteriously but definitively, "Mojo Juju," then handed me the knob from the front door. I could tell from her tone that I was supposed to let that cryptic answer go unchallenged. I did. I had other worries.

"Ugh, thanks. This fucking house is falling apart all around me and I am too broke to do anything about it. I don't know how I will ever be able to sell it in this condition," I said and set to putting the knob back on.

"You are selling your house?" Eliza responded in shock. "Why? What?"

I realized that I hadn't ever confessed the extent of my financial troubles and the solutions I was considering to anyone but my mother. I also realized then that I didn't want to. It was humiliating and my plans were still so unformed that the last thing I wanted to do was get into some information tennis match, with Eliza suggesting every simplistic solution that I had obviously already considered and deemed impossible or ineffective, and then my shooting down every bit of her well-intended advice with my brutal realities until I'd convinced both of us that suicide was my only feasible way out. That's not fun. Especially at a Memorial Day party.

"No. I'm not selling the house. I just meant that I couldn't even if I wanted to. It is falling apart all around me."

"Okay. Good. You scared me. So?" she asked, changing the subject. "How did the photo session go?" Eliza pressed, pretending she wasn't looking deeper into the house for some sign of Devonevans.

"Relax. He hasn't shown up yet," I told her, fumbling with the door. "Maybe he is blowing me off."

"I hope not! I have been looking forward to a Very Devonevans Memorial Day all week!"

By 3 PM, the knob was back in place and all my other guests had arrived, but Devonevans was still a no-show. The house was filled with the music of Howlin' Wolf and Son House and abuzz with the Devonevans news. I was surprised how many people, male and female, were excited to meet him. People were eager to marry me off to him.

"You haven't even met him yet," I pointed out, "and I have no intention of anything going on with this guy."

"I had his poster on my wall in seventh grade," a female guest gushed. "I thought he was dreamy. I can't believe he is actually going to be here, at your house, for Memorial Day! This is the best Memorial Day ever!"

"That's what I said," Eliza agreed and adjusted her package.

"You did not just do that," I said in horror.

She ignored me and man-walked her way over to the bar.

Wayne and Kate arrived with their three sons, the eldest of whom was actually carrying a Devonevans surfboard.

"Max wants Devon Evans to autograph his board," Wayne explained. "Is he here yet?"

"You know he did jail time in the nineties, right?" Kate added as if a prison sentence and a mid-sixties orgy with The Stones were on par.

I had not known about the Big House but I had no time to get to the bottom of it because Devonevans had entered my home. He stood just inside the front door looking around, taking in his environs. He was silhouetted by sunlight from behind and I couldn't help but notice that his silhouette was empty-handed. Who raises these guys? As he stepped deeper into the room, I got an opportunity to take in the vision that was Memorial Day Devonevans. He was wearing a pair of navy Dickies cut off at mid-calf and some Jackson-Pollack-looking fucking Crocs. He was also wearing a red-and-white satin jacket that looked like stolen wardrobe from a roller derby movie and no shirt of any kind. His hairy nipples caught me staring.

"Devonevans! You made it! Come on in," I said.

He came in and planted a wet one on my mouth. I cannot report what it smelled like because I was holding my breath from the moment I saw it coming until he withdrew to a safe distance. I heard the fidgety excitement of my guests behind us in the dining room and I actually heard someone stage whisper, *"Devonevans is here!"*

"What happened? I thought you were going to be here at one for the photos."

"Sorry. I was up in the canyon scouting a cool location for the shoot. I found a great spot up by the Hollywood sign. It's kind of a hike but it will be worth it."

I had no idea what the fuck he thought this portrait was going to be and I had nothing to say in response except, "Cool. Come on in. Let me get you a drink."

We entered the dining room and it felt like we were interrupting a game of statues already in play. Everyone was frozen in their version of casual disinterest.

"Hey everyone, this is Devonevans. Devon, this is everyone," I said by way of introduction. "What are you drinking?"

"Got any tequila?"

"As a matter of fact..."

I went off to fetch his drink. When I returned, he was happily holding court in a circle with five of my friends. When I handed him the tequila, I heard him saying, "I like the way this satin feels, you know, directly on my skin." I noted the

"Devon Evans" logo in swirly seventies font, faded on the back of the jacket.

"Thanks," he said, taking the tequila. "Do you mind if I use your john?"

I led him to the stairs and pointed him up.

"Top of the stairs, straight ahead."

As he walked up the stairs he looked back down at me and, without breaking his stride, said just as casual as you please, "By the way, I have a huge cock and I am going to tear your shit up." With that, he walked out of my view.

Shell-shocked, I returned to my guests. I told Eliza and Mack what Devonevans had just said.

"BEST. MEMORIAL DAY. EVER." Eliza chanted.

"Stopsayingthat! I am not going to fuck Devonevans."

"Come on! Do it! You can make him pop a few breath mints first. How long has it been since you've had sex?" Mack asked.

"Five years."

"And who was that?"

"Harry."

"Right. And did you actually have sex? Wasn't he the 'get in, get out' guy that stuck it in for a second before you changed your mind?" Eliza asked.

"Yes."

"And how long was it before that?"

"Stop! I am not sleeping with..." I drifted off as Devonevans approached us.

The huge cock quote made the rounds at the party very quickly. I was under a lot of pressure to get confirmation. I've found that people are pretty open-minded about who is a suitable person to have sex with when it is somebody else's vagina on the table. It is like the definition of "tasteful nudity." People have a very broad definition of that term until they are the ones that have to get naked. In the case of nudity, "tasteful" simply means "not me doing it." It seemed a similar rule was being applied to my chocha.

This Memorial Day was different than other, mellower ones I had hosted because everyone got all caught up in the Devonevans rock-n-roll holiday vibe. People who hardly ever drank were smashed. Kids were posing for photos with their tongues out and flipping the bird in group shots. Everybody was louder than usual and laughing more often. Dinner was at 4 PM and people were still lingering around until after 11. At midnight, I began shooing them out of the house. Devonevans was walking people to the door and thanking them for a great day as if he'd been my co-host. It was then that I realized I was likely in trouble but was just drunk enough not to be too concerned about it.

Inevitably, the decision was made that Devonevans was going to spend the night. I made it clear that there would be no funny business, but try getting a boozed-up "rock star" to buy that you mean that. Even I wasn't sure I meant it, but I wasn't ready to admit that to myself. Yet.

Once we were in bed, inevitably we began fooling around. I was relieved to note that his breath was no worse than my own must have been after a twelve-hour shift of red wine consumption. I was thinking about this when I realized Devonevans had my hand and was guiding it inside his shorts. I cannot say for sure if it was my experiences with The Albino or the C battery or the wine or pressure from my friends or Devonevans's own bragging, or a combination of them all, but something weakened my will to resist. I found myself allowing my hand to be led to his groin. What I discovered there was shocking.

Guys, my best advice to you is to set low expectations in women. If you really have a huge cock, we'll figure it out. Saying "See this? This is *big*" is unnecessary if it really is big, and you're not gonna convince us if it's not. Bottom line, if you say you have a huge cock, you had better deliver. Why not say you've got an average one and then let us be pleasantly surprised?

In the case of Devonevans, there was an unusual twist. While his penis itself might well have warranted the adjective huge—it was dwarfed by his balls which undeniably demanded it. They were like two pliable coconuts stored in a moist, hairy bag. Tangelos at the very least. It reminded me of Tom Arnold's response to Roseanne's accusations that he had a tiny penis.

"Even the Goodyear blimp looks small in the Grand Canyon," he'd said.

It's all relative, is my point. Devonevans would have needed a penis like an oversized daikon to gets those balls to proportion. So, Devonevans, if you are reading this, I am not complaining about the size of your dick but it is your balls you really need to prep people for.

Reconnaissance accomplished, I withdrew my hand and, after a good deal of playful argument from Devonevans, I finally had to say, "Seriously. No."

"You know what they say, though?" Devonevans asked, cheekily. "No means yes and yes means anal." Then he winked.

I was properly scandalized.

"What? What the fuck?"

"Settle down, baby. Don't get your panties in a bunch. I'm just joshing you. Goodnight!"

And with that, he gave me a peck on the lips, rolled over, let out a short, high-pitched fart and fell immediately to snoring.

Really?

I looked at my ceiling, through it really, to whatever divinity might have been up there laughing at my expense and thought, *What did I ever do to you?*

• • •

In the morning, Devonevans suggested we get coffee at what was, unbeknownst to him, my favorite coffee joint. I liked that he was aware of a neighborhood "secret" despite the fact that he lived an hour away. At the Tropical, we each ordered a café con leche. The cashier rang it up and we owed $3.75. Devonevans pulled a wad of cash and some coins from his pocket and counted out $1.75. He slid the change toward me saying, "You got a large. They cost two dollars. I only got a medium."

Does everyone think an actress can live forever on money they made on a TV show twenty years ago? Nobody anywhere has ever retired after shooting ten episodes of anything. Do they all think the meals I provide cost me nothing? Why were these men I was seeing such unrelenting freeloaders?

I paid my $2 and we walked out to our cars. He promised to call me later and we went our separate ways.

Over the course of the next week, Devonevans must have called a dozen times. We had a few conversations and I was still trying to pin him down for the damned portrait session. If I didn't pick up when he called, he'd leave long messages about the minutia of his day. It was oddly intimate, despite the fact that we hardly knew each other. It made him seem vulnerable and redeemed his cheapness a great deal in my eyes.

The following weekend, I was at my book club with a gang of women who were adamant that I break my celibacy streak with bocce balls. They demanded to hear some of the messages he'd left the previous week and they swooned and reacted like they were watching cute YouTube puppy videos. While we were listening, Devonevans called. I let it go to voicemail. Once I was notified that he'd left a message, I played it back for us all to hear together.

"Hey, honey. It's me. I am down in L.A. and I was hoping you were home. I wanna come by and see you tonight. I haven't seen you since Monday. So call me back if you are around. It'd be fun to hang out. Okay. Well... I miss you and stuff..." and he closed with a kiss. I ended the call.

"I miss you and stuff!" they all mimicked as one.

"OMG, you so totally gotta let him grind your munch. Call him back and tell him to come over. Right now!" Eliza insisted from beneath her backwards baseball cap. The matching track suit she wore had already gotten a less than gentle ribbing from me.

The whole room supported Eliza's position on Devonevans and ganged up on me, demanding that I leave immediately and get my groove back.

"He hearts you, Ruby! You have to call him back now."

Is there anything ickier than saying "heart" in that manner? I didn't have time to make that point before somebody grabbed my phone and pressed the call back button and handed me the phone. I was going to end the call again but I heard Devonevans answer.

"Hey! I'm glad you called me back. Are you around? Can I come by?"

I looked around the room at the faces peering back at me and heard myself saying, "I'm not home right now but I can be in twenty minutes." The room erupted silently like a rejoicing football crowd on a muted TV.

As I collected my purse and said goodbye to my friends, Eliza pressed something into my hand. I looked down and found a box of Trojans looking back up at me.

"I told you guys! I am not going to fuck Devonevans!"

"Yeah, yeah..." they pooh-poohed and shoved me out the door.

Devonevans was already outside my gates when I pulled up. Once inside, I got us a both a drink. Before I could even finish my first glass of wine, he took me by the hand and started to lead me up the stairs. Things were moving far too quickly for me. I needed to slow the pace of this evening at any cost. I resorted to my old standby.

"Hey, wanna take a bath? A candlelit bubble bath?"

I was relieved to find he was into that idea. No argument at all. I started the water and added bubbles and excused myself to fetch the tequila and a bottle of wine. After putting on a little Lightnin' Hopkins, lighting candles and refilling our glasses, I couldn't think of anything else to do to stall so I just went for it. I got my clothes off in record time and submerged to my neck in the bath. Devonevans undressed more slowly, not feeling the same apprehension about nudity that I did. People who were sexually active in the seventies seem to have an entirely different attitude toward their own bodies than we later bloomers, a more nonchalant attitude. I wasn't convinced their positive opinions of themselves were entirely realistic. Anyway, I took the opportunity to reexamine his downtown, hoping that perhaps I'd imagined his testicular elephantiasis the week before. He stood before me, arms akimbo, and I was afforded an opportunity to take it all in. The best I can do is downgrade the comparison from coconuts to tennis balls. *He needs to call Guinness*, I thought. *Or a doctor.*

We stayed in the bath for at least an hour while I pounded wine and tried to psyche myself up for my first sexual encounter in over five years. What was I waiting for? Actual middle age? My fifties? Who'd want me then—with grey pubic hair and a menopausal gunt? Then I thought about Maury Povich and his paternity show guests. I remembered one slattern in particular, wheelchair-bound due to her immense size. Her chair was virtually engulfed by polyester-encased meat. It almost appeared as if she was rolled out on stage on her own—a seven-hundred-pound Hoppity Horse on an invisible conveyor belt. She was having a fifth potential baby daddy DNA tested. Apparently, four other guys had slept with this woman who was too fat to stand unassisted—and in a short enough period of time that they could all have been the father of her child. None of these men denied having had sex with her and she seemed to feel no shame admitting the assembly line fuckfest she had conducted. So—guy number five was getting tested and—as I sat stupefied—he, too, was absolved of responsibility, which meant no less than six guys had found this enormous woman irresistible. Six guys had given it to her old-school in a period of a few weeks at most—days, in reality, if paternity were really a possibility. And aren't any of these people familiar with the phrase "safe sex?" You might want to break out a condom when the third guy in a single afternoon is WD-40ing you out of that chair with a copy of the *Kama Sutra* in his other hand, lady.

The idea that Hoppity Horse was unashamed of her body and had, some might say, an overactive sex life while I was a romantic ascetic suddenly bothered me. It crossed my mind that I was pitying the wrong person and I considered that the longer I let this go on the harder it would be to ever break out of it. I decided to take the presence of both a willing man, albeit with a pair of candlepin balls, and a box of unexpired condoms under my roof at the same time to be a sign.

With a good wine buzz and new determination, I entered the bedroom with Devonevans excited about what I was about to do. *Why shouldn't I be?* I thought.

A few minutes of fumbling around on the bed and it, apparently, was game time.

"You got any condoms?" he asked.

I jumped up, crab-walked my way out of the room to avoid giving him the full view of my naked rump, and fetched the condoms Eliza had given me. Back in the bedroom, I handed him the box as I scuttled under the sheet. Before I had finished arranging myself to my best aesthetic and alluring advantage, he was on top of me. It actually caught me off guard. He positioned my legs abruptly and I heard my gynecologist's voice, "This might be a little uncomfortable," in my head. I was jolted back to reality by unceremonious penetration and then the full weight of Devonevans upon me.

"I'm gonna hurt your insides," he growled.

Ew.

He buried his face in the pillow by my left ear. I tried to maybe kiss him or something—after all, *inter*course is an *interaction*, no? I did not feel like a participant. I was getting the breath pounded out of me by a hundred and eighty pounds of dead weight pumping like an industrial generator. If only the pillow could have completely muffled his grunting sounds of effort that filled the room. The word "rutting" looped, alone, on the chyron of my mind. I focused on that as I tried to tune out the slapping sound of his giant balls against my ass. After about a minute of this bliss, the pace of the grunting slowly increased until it stopped. Devonevans rolled off of me and flopped onto the bed with a final guttural umph.

I resisted the urge to say, "Yes, sir! You sure 'nuff tore my shit up!" I was too stunned to crack wise. I was bummed that this guy was now forever on my résumé and that this rather underwhelming encounter was how I broke a five year celibacy streak.

"Uh-oh," Devonevans said.

I looked at him and saw that he was holding up the condom. Why are used condoms so unbelievably gross? Under typical conditions, everything that a condom has touched or contains has probably been in your mouth at some point. Isn't having "the kids" contained—like heroin in a balloon—the easier way out? I don't have an answer. I just know used condoms are very high on the disgusting scale, way higher than a garden variety blowjob, which I wouldn't necessarily call disgusting at all. I'm just saying.

Devonevans seemed to want me to take the condom from him.

"Dude, what? I don't want it!" I said.

"I'm not giving it to you. I am showing it to you."

"Okay. I see it. Nice work!" I offered, confused as to what he wanted me to say.

"It's broken," he said and he dangled it closer to me for inspection.

"*Broken*? Why is it broken? What did you do?" I asked, squirming in an effort to avoid anything dripping on me.

"I told you I have a huge cock. You shoulda bought Magnums," he said and then mercifully removed the condom from my view and dropped it on my nightstand.

That's gonna leave a ring, I thought as I jumped out of bed and began jumping up and down frantically.

"Are you doing calisthenics or something? Because... you aren't that fat."

"I'm trying to get the friggin' jizz out," I explained, trying to ignore the insult ringing in my ears. Then I thought about what I was doing. I didn't want my contents pouring out onto my bedroom floor. It is lovely hardwood and deserves more respect than a secondhand money shot.

I hurried to the bathroom and was relieved to see we had neglected to drain the tub. I plunged back into the water and did everything I could think of to flush myself out. Devonevans came in to see what I was doing.

"Go get that condom off the table, would you? Wrap it up in toilet paper and flush it. I don't want my dogs digging it out of the trash. And wipe off the table, too. Okay?"

He dutifully obeyed my command and then disappeared into the bedroom. I waited for him until the water was tepid and then got out, dried off and went into the bedroom myself. Devonevans was sound asleep, intertwined with all three of my dogs and snoring loudly.

Fucking mouth-breather, I thought, but the vision of him with my dogs made me like him again, so I got into bed with them and fell asleep.

In the morning, we repeated our trip to the Tropical. When it was time to pay, I wanted to see if he would stop me. He did not. This parsimonious a-hole couldn't spring for a four-dollar breakfast after I had let him mate with me? I could have been pregnant already with a little Devonevans and he couldn't pay for a cup of coffee?

* * *

"The condom broke and he still didn't buy your coffee?" Eliza marveled that night at the Frolic Room. This evening, Eliza's outfit seemed to channel Melissa Etheridge: a denim shirt, tight Wrangler corduroys and Western boots.

"Where did you buy those condoms, anyway, Tex? The fucking ninety-nine cent store?" I asked, nursing my second drink.

"I got them at the gas station near my house. The expensive gas station by the freeway. I bet they have a pretty good turnover there. And I checked the date on the box, too!"

"What if you have a baby with skull tattoos?" Mack asked.

With Mack, you could never know for sure if a question like that was sincere or a joke.

"Oh! Would you actually have the baby? If you were pregnant?" Mack asked before I could address her first question.

"I'm not pregnant. And I don't think even an evil, vengeful God would pull a stunt like knocking me up with Devonevans's kid the first time I have had sex in five years."

"Did you teabag him?" Mack asked, cracking herself up.

"I don't think I could do that even if I had the ability to unhinge my jaw."

"So, what was it like? Aside from the condom thing," Eliza asked.

"It was like a grudge fuck."

"What do you mean?" Eliza asked, wincing, growing certain that she didn't want the answer.

"It's better if I show you."

I got off my stool and walked over to Eliza. I pressed my body flat against her, pinning her against the wall. I put my mouth close to her ear and grunted like a pig while I bumped her with my hips. She pushed me off, laughing. Mack was laughing, too.

"That is awful! Really?"

"It was a good ole-fashioned, Jackson County yard fucking," I said resignedly.

"Maybe you should consider sleeping with women," Eliza suggested, with a purse of her lips and a sassy, Jackée neck sway.

"Maybe you should actually sleep with one before giving that advice to the rest of us."

"For your information, I have been instant messaging several women on GrrlonGrrl.com."

"Yeah. Because that's the same as going shrimping south of Dixie," I said, in maybe somewhat of a nastier tone than was required. It wasn't her fault that my life was unmanageable and that I had worse luck with men than Liza Minnelli.

"Shrimping south of Dixie?" Eliza challenged, evidently more offended by my vulgarity than my churlishness.

Out of curiosity, I had secretly gone to Clamsnackers.com and had been rewarded with an arsenal of muff-diving euphemisms. I had no intention of admitting that to Eliza, though.

"Yeah. Figure it out."

"Did I ever tell you I gave a guy a forty-five minute blowjob?" Mack blurted.

"Why? What the fuck?"

"He just wouldn't cum."

"Was he high on coke?"

"Or Viagra?"

"I don't think so because he couldn't get hard for the first twenty minutes or so. I was using every trick in my book and forty-five minutes later, when I couldn't feel my face, I got pissed off and quit."

"What an asshole!" I said.

"You think I should have kept going? I was counting the songs that played while I was doing it and promised myself that if he didn't cum by the end of the tenth song I was just gonna stop."

"No, he is the asshole. After five or ten minutes, he should have given you the tap."

"Really?"

"Definitely," Eliza agreed.

I loved that nobody stopped me to ask what "the tap" was.

"He is a fucking asshole to make you work all that time. He must have known it wasn't going to happen pretty early on."

"I give a great blowjob, too," Mack pouted.

"I'm sure you do, girlfriend. I am not blaming you. Promise me you will never do that again. Cut'm off after no more than ten minutes."

"Okay. Good to know. Can I ask you guys something?"

Eliza and I looked back at her, waiting.

"If a guy is going down on you, how long do you guys take to cum?"

"Are you asking if the ten-minute rule applies when the situation is reversed? Because..."

"...it doesn't!" Eliza and I said in stereo. We laughed and revealed our ages by high-fiving each other. I immediately regretted what we'd done and scanned the bar for witnesses. Nobody was watching. It was early evening and the only other person in the dark room was a day drinker wrapping up a ten-hour shift of nursing High Lifes.

"Okay, but, how long?"

Suddenly shy, I deferred to Eliza.

"Um, I don't know. I guess it depends."

"On what?" Mack pressed.

This time Eliza looked to me.

"Um... things like how into it I am, how good at it he is, whether the dogs are in the bed or the phone rings... if I am too full or if I feel fat..." I said, and Eliza was nodding agreement.

"Or if he is one of those people that sticks their tongue inside you over and over like a rattlesnake..." Eliza added.

"Oh! I hate that! They try to fuck you with their tongue or something?" Mack asked and stuck her tongue in and out, mimicking the snake tongue action. It was more upsetting to see than it was to experience.

"Yes! What is that about?" I said. "And don't stick your tongue in my ass, either. It is very distracting. At best."

"So, how long, if none of those things happen?"

"I don't know but I'm going to say more than ten minutes," I offered.

Eliza shrugged. I took that as agreement.

"If Eliza ever pulls the trigger with one of these chicks from Lezilicious.com, maybe she can do some research and get back to us," I said, ever the ballbuster.

"Okay. Please do," Mack said to Eliza with complete sincerity.

Why was I the only one that found Eliza's new sexual identity and wardrobe tour de force suspect? And hilarious? And a personal challenge?

"Because Brian tells me I take too long," Mack continued.

"Is this forty-five minute blowjob guy?" Eliza asked.

"No, that was years ago. Brian is the guy I'm seeing right now. You met him."

"No, I know who Brian is. I just wanted to be sure he wasn't Mr. Forty-Five. Go on."

"I hate this story already, Mack. What is Brian's problem?"

"He says I take too long so, the other day, I counted songs and I was able to cum during the third song."

"Okay. First of all: three songs is probably under ten minutes, so good for you. And B: I can't believe you were able to cum at all with a stopwatch running and counting songs!"

"Really? That seems fast enough?"

"Yes," Eliza assured her. "Plenty fast. Why are all the guys you date such assholes?"

"At least he buys me coffee," she quipped.

"Hey! Why are you picking on me? Eliza said it! And Devonevans..." I trailed off at a loss as to how to defend him and unsure I wanted to.

"...has a huge cock and is going to tear your shit up!" Eliza and Mack mocked in unison.

My cell phone rang.

"Speak of the devil," I said when I saw who it was. When the message came through we all listened to it on speaker.

"Hey, baby! Just calling to say hi! I had fun and stuff last night. I hope you bought some bigger condoms! I told you I would bust it out. Anyway, I stayed in Hollywood today doing business and I was hoping you were around. Gimme a jangle when you get this. Smooches!"

"Call him! Tell him to come here! Call him back!" Mack and Eliza chanted. "We want to see him! We want to see Devonevans! We miss him and stuff!"

I eventually gave in and called him back. He said he would be there within a half hour.

Immediately regretful, I complained, "What did I just do? I don't want another donkey fuckin' from Skinflint."

"He doesn't have to come back to your house. We can hang out here and then all leave and go home alone."

"Easier said than done. Thunderballs won't try to follow you."

Forty-five minutes and three drinks later, Devonevans still had not shown up. I was feeling pretty tipsy when Eliza said she had to go. I made her wait another fifteen minutes. As we sat there, the day drinker stumbled by us on his way out. He stopped behind Mack and stood there swaying and staring. When it became impossible to pretend we were unaware of him, we turned around to face him.

"You are tight," he said to Mack.

Pot. Kettle.

"Your ass looks tight as fish pussy and that shit is watertight," he continued.

Mack looked back at him, nonplussed. "Thank you?"

"Don't thank me," he said and turned around and left.

Devonevans was pushing in the door as Fishpussy staggered out.

"Ladies! Wassup?"

Devonevans greeted the girls and then took a stool next to me. He ordered his Platinum Patron and the girls doted on him for a bit. He held court like King Jinglefarts. When Eliza finished her wine, she begged off, citing work the next day, and left. Mack lingered for another drink and then began getting ready to go, too.

"Okay, guys. It's getting late. Let's get outta here."

"You're right. We should probably call it a night," I said and stood up.

"What? I just got here. Let's get another round."

Mack insisted she could not. I had already had plenty to drink and knew I would regret another but Devonevans indicated to the bartender that we wanted another drink. Mack went and paid her tab, mouthed "I'm sorry" to me behind Devonevans's back and left.

Devonevans and I slid over a few seats the two stools closest to the wall. Our drinks arrived.

"So, did you go buy the bigger condoms today?" he asked, sipping his tequila.

I told him I had not.

"Well, I did! Who's your daddy?"

Oh God! I knew it. I was pretty drunk but no amount of alcohol was going to make another barnyard rape sound appealing. I could've killed those girls for making me invite him out with us and then bailing on me.

Devonevans ordered another tequila and smiled at me.

"Looking forward to later?" he said in what I can only guess was his best attempt at sounding seductive.

"Yeah, wicked," I said, hoping I sounded enthusiastic.

He pulled me stool closer to his and leaned in to kiss me. I went along with it briefly and then pretended I was shy about the public display.

"Okay. Okay, I get it. Let's get outta here then and head back to your place," he said.

I needed time to think of an excuse, some way out of another sleepover. I wasn't sure I wanted to be done with Devonevans completely but I was completely sure I wanted to go home alone that night.

"No. Let's get another drink and um… um… I'm going to go to the ladies' room. Order me a drink," I said and stumbled my way through the dark bar to the bathroom.

In the bright light of the restroom, I realized I was way more drunk than I had thought. I definitely did not want the drink I had just ordered but I needed a stalling device and a drink was the simplest solution. Looking in the mirror, I decided I would tell him I was house-sitting for a friend and not going back to my own home. Satisfied with my plan, I returned to my seat.

Devonevans was grinning widely when I returned. He patted my stool, indicating I should sit down by him, which I did.

"I'm gonna get all German porno on you tonight!" he grinned. "Ever heard of a blumpkin?"

I wasn't exactly sure what a blumpkin was but the only time I'd ever seen German porn it was a tenth-generation VHS tape of leather guys squeezing "fresh-from-the-oven" human fecal matter between their teeth like little kids do with Jell-O. It was enough to put hair on your chest.

"Oh! Dang! I forgot to tell you! I am house-sitting and I am not going home tonight."

"So I'll come with you," he said, matter-of-factly, and sipped his drink.

Drunken pandemonium in my head. How was I going to get out of this? He wanted to follow me to my fictional house-sitting place and do a blumpkin—whatever the fuck that was. I looked at him while I tried to silence the "blumpkinblumpkinblumpkinblumpkin" in my head. I would have joined the circus and hit the road right then if it would have gotten me out of that situation.

"See what I have for you," he said and pulled my hand under the bar toward his lap. I expected to get a handful of Magnum condoms and suppressed a roll of my eyes. I was unable to suppress my shock when, instead of a handful of condoms, I got a handful of Devonevans. Big, giant glass cutter, loosed from the confines of fabric and decency, pressed into my unsuspecting palm. He moved my hand up and down on it and I knew then how to get out of bringing him back to my house.

"YOU GAVE DEVONEVANS a pity handy under the bar? Here? In the Frolic Room?" Kate howled with delight.

"Yup. And I am not proud."

"I am! Last night?"

"No, last week. Remember the night I invited you to join Eliza and Mack and me here? That night."

Kate was crying, she was laughing so hard.

"Do you know what a blumpkin is?" she asked, wiping her tears away.

I confessed I did not.

"It is when you blow a guy while he is taking a shit," she managed to blurt before bursting into peals of laughter.

"Oh my God! Is this what I am reduced to?" I wondered in horror. "Please tell me you don't give those to Wayne!"

Composing herself, Kate assured me she did not.

"So, a public pity handy? I'm proud of you! How did that even happen? Was it crowded in here? Did people see?"

"Kate, it is the single grossest thing I have ever done but I didn't know what else to do! The thought of having his mango balls slapping my taint for a romance-filled ninety seconds and him grunting like a truffle pig—I just couldn't do it."

"Did anyone see you?"

"It was a weeknight and we were the only people in here. The bartender was busy on the other end of the room stocking the bar and we were over there," I said, indicating the end of the bar by the wall, "so I think we actually pulled it off."

"I'll say you pulled it off! Mama's little girl is all growed up!"

"Ha, ha," I responded, humorlessly. "Anyway, I don't know what I was thinking except that anything was better than bringing him home again. He had his big wang out and put my hand on it and the next thing I knew, I was just yanking it like I was plunging a toilet."

"Wooo hoo hoo!" Peals of laughter from Kate. "How long did it take?" she asked, nose pinched and shoulders up at her ears.

"Not long. Thank God."

More laughter from Kate.

"What about... I mean... where did he... the...?" she asked.

"I think he had a napkin and I guess he caught it or something. I don't know. All I know is I will never look at my hand the same way again. A hand job, Kate? You know how I feel about those."

"I know. You think, why try something on a guy he can do so much better himself. But I don't agree. Sometimes, a hand job becomes a very viable option. Sometimes you just don't have time to get undressed again and, you know, your jaw's still sore from the morning session or you haven't showered since the last round and..."

"Okay, Kate," I interjected. "Please stop. I get the picture. But wait. This story gets even better. After that sordid pity handy business was completed, it was definitely time to go. I asked the bartender to close the tab and bring us a check, at which point Devonevans said, 'I'm going to go wash my hands while you take care of that,' and he got up and left."

"He left?"

"He went to the men's room and left me to pay the bill!"

"You gave the man a hand job under the bar in public and he didn't even spring for the drinks?"

"Ain't that some shit?"

"What did you do?"

"I waited until he came back. He came back and asked if we were good to go and I said he owed forty-five dollars for his tequila shots. He stood looking confused for a minute and when I didn't budge, he pulled out his wallet and put forty dollars on the bar. 'That's all the cash I have,' he said. I paid the balance of the check and we left."

"Did he come home with you?"

"No way! I told him I was house-sitting and not allowed to have guests so he went home. On the drive back to my house I got so mad, I called him and read him the riot act on his voice mail. I busted him for not being willing to even buy me a coffee and I told him I wasn't into hanging out anymore and to have a nice life."

"Did he call you back?"

"Two days later he called to say he missed me and stuff and asked why I was 'getting all menstrual' on him and asked why I left such a bitchy message. I ignored the call. I'm done."

"Can't say I blame you there."

"What the fuck, Kate?! Who are these guys? Is that all there is out there for me? These guys are intolerable. Five years of celibacy and I get prison fucked and then give a public hand job? Is this really what I am reduced to?"

"You know what you should do? Come to this swingers' party with me and Wayne next weekend!"

"Are you kidding me?"

"No! It is supposed to be really classy and the other couples, I heard, are hot."

"While I can think of many responses to your invitation, the simplest and most immediate thing I feel I need to point out is that I am not part of a couple. And I'm not hot."

"You are a babe. Any guy would be lucky to fuck you."

"Yeah, thanks, Kate, but, you know, for once, I'd like to be the lucky one in the scenario. Not the charitable one. And anyway, I repeat, I am not part of a couple."

"Single women are allowed to attend. No single men, though."

"Then who would I be swinging with?"

"Other couples, of course!"

"Oh, of course. Well, whatever. I have no interest in swinging, single or coupled or tripled or otherwise."

"Suit yourself. So... maybe you should try Match.com or something. This girl I work with just married a guy she met on there."

"Oh my God with the fucking internet dating! What is with everyone? I think I'd rather take my chances in a threesome."

Kate smiled and nodded her encouragement that I, in fact, should try a threesome. I ignored her and continued.

"Where do people meet people—you know—people our age?" Kate asked. Fair question. She'd been off the market for eons.

"I think a lot of people either meet people at work or through friends. I haven't worked a job for more than a few days in years and I have known my friends for so long now, I already know everyone they know. Not for nothing, but it gets old living alone, eating alone, eating alone *all the time*, drinking alone and doing one hundred percent of everything that ever gets done in the house alone. Lonely, Kate. It can get fucking lonely. And, in all honesty, I'd like to have a guy around to take the fucking trash out once in a while or pick up something for me that I forgot to get at the grocery store. Someone to zip up my dress. Someone to unzip my dress. Someone to have sex with regularly. Not as regularly as you and Wayne, mind you, but with some reasonable frequency. Someone to resent for always hogging the remote. Someone to hug when they are sad. Warm skin. A familiar form to spoon."

"You have the dogs."

"Yeah, but they can't do any of those things, Kate. Call me crazy, but I want more from life than total self-reliance, isolation and internet porn."

"I bet that Devonevans blumpkin sounds pretty good right now, eh?"

"Not even with your dirty mouth," I said. "And I never even got to take his stupid portrait. Ah, whatever. One portrait of a grungy, old, seventies poster boy probably wasn't going to launch me into the ranks of the Mario Testinos of the world, anyway."

"No. Probably not," Kate agreed and, suddenly somber, added, "Ruby, are you okay?"

I couldn't even look at her. I could feel twenty years of friendship and compassion radiating out of her. I knew if I looked at her, I'd cry. I didn't want to cry, especially at the Frolic Room. That seemed too pathetic and sordid, even for the woman who had given a public pity handy there the week before. So, instead, I meditated on the beer in front of me, playing with the bar napkin and making designs in the condensation on the glass and I confessed.

"No. I'm so unbelievably not okay. I'm completely broke. I'm seconds from defaulting on my mortgage and I'm in five-figure credit card debt."

She put her hand on my back. Her sympathy burned a hole through my shirt.

"Don't. Don't or I will lose it."

She removed her hand.

"I'm sorry. I... just... don't know what I am going to do. I am just flailing around wildly. These guys? What the fuck? A photography career? Why not become a sculptor or an author or some other impossible-to-make-a-living-at artistic endeavor? Why not play the lottery as an attempt to subsidize my income? The odds of succeeding are probably better."

"Nothing in the pipeline work-wise, huh?"

"No. And no reason to ever think there will be again. And you know what? The only part of me that cares is the part that wants the mortgage paid."

"That seems like it must be a pretty big part, though."

"Yeah, but what I mean is, when I became an actor, I had big goals. I wanted to be in great films, work with people I respected and earn their respect back. I wanted to amass a body of work, you know? Something to be proud of. But I think, at this point, that ship has sailed. Now, all I can hope for is grinding out a living and even that is becoming more and more of an apparition on the horizon. And I don't know what I can do to fix it or help myself or change the course of my life. And I'm really scared. That is the word that defines my life these days. Scared. I'm going to lose everything and I'm going to do it alone. That is the scariest part. Succeeding alone might be unsatisfying on some level because of the whole 'no one to share it with' thing but, let me tell you, Kate—failing alone is fucking terrifying. I don't want to be homeless alone."

"You are not alone. And you are not going to be homeless. You will always have your family and you have me and Wayne. You are always welcome in our home. You know that, right?"

"I know. Thanks."

"No. Really. We have an extra room. If you need to sell your house, I will handle it for you, for free. And if you need somewhere to land until you figure out your next move, you come stay with us. The dogs, too, of course. I'm serious."

"I know you are," I said, knowing she was absolutely sincere. "Thank you."

We both sat quietly with our drinks and I thought about her offer. Maybe she was, too. It sorta sounded like an extended pajama party. I envisioned cooking for them every night and sitting around a table over dinner with them, sharing a bottle of wine with them, being a family with them. And while I knew I would never take her up on it, because I could never really quit acting, I could never really accept the idea of selling my house—because these two things defined me—and I could never really accept being a charity case—still, the idea of an option—any option—took the edge off my terror and I felt the pain in my chest, pain that had become a full-time affair, lessen just a bit. Just enough. And I felt just a little bit braver and I felt incredible gratitude that Kate was my friend.

SO, ONE MORNING LATER in the month, I was again facing the relentless onslaught of overdue bills. And once again, I faced an unpayable mortgage. I managed to stretch a few paltry residuals and my unemployment benefits to cover my cell bill, utilities and the minimum payments on my credit card balances. It struck me that "balance" was an interesting word to call mounting debt. What would they call it once I could no longer balance it and it came tumbling down all around me? Bankruptcy, I guessed. Foreclosure was another guess. My chest began its now-too-familiar objection to thoughts of financial matters and squeezed in on itself while my heart sped to a pace that seemed dangerous. I tried to do some breathing exercises to prevent the stroke I was certain was coming, but I couldn't even get air to fill my lungs, let alone the deep stomach breath I'd been taught in yoga classes. I was becoming light-headed when the phone rang. It was my agent, Kim.

"Hi, Ruby! Good news! I have an audition for you."

"Really? Great! What is it for?"

"It is a new show called, I don't know, um… *Cops with ESP Vs. Vampire Teens*, or something."

"Okay, that is hilarious," I said, laughing. "That's like *Teenage Mutant Ninja Turtles*."

I could hear her typing furiously.

"Okay, here it is," she said when the typing had stopped. "It is actually called *Sexy Dicks with ESP Vs. Gangster Vampire Teens*."

"You have to be kidding me."

"What? It's supposed to be like a *The Mentalist/Sopranos/Twilight* hybrid. It's getting amazing buzz. You are lucky I was able to get you in."

I was in no position to pass on any opportunity but the title of the show alone made me ask myself, for the first time seriously, if this was really the way I wanted to spend the rest of my life. Did I want to continually live on the razor's edge of financial ruin, doing breathing exercises to put off an inevitable stroke, praying for an audition for a job I only wanted because the check would clear? Wouldn't working at Costco be easier, and more lucrative? At this point in my career, a guest-star spot on a show called *Sexy Dicks with ESP Vs. Gangster Vampire Teens* would not advance me one inch toward my original career goal of amassing a "body of work." But it might pay my mortgage for a month or two, so I kept my existential angst to myself.

"Thank you," I said, rather than, *I can't believe what a total failure my life is*. "What is the part?"

"Marge, fifty-two. Once a handsome woman, Marge's face and posture show the effects of a life lived hard. Dowdy and in need of a root touch-up, Marge is an unexpected woman to be in charge of a sexy escort service. Having a regular client who also happens to be a powerful politician, Marge has been kidnapped by the head of the teen vampire crime syndicate, Demone Malvagio. During a long torture session at the hands of the teen vampires, Marge finally gives them the information they require. Actress must be comfortable with tasteful nudity and simulated sex. One thousand dollar, one-day guest star. All actors must agree to these terms before reading."

I wanted to cry.

"Sounds like a great role, right?" Kim chirped.

"Um, Kim, I'm nowhere near fifty-two."

"Don't be thrown by that. They are probably going to go younger. How old are you these days, anyway?"

"Too old to suddenly start doing nudity and simulating sex. For a thousand dollars."

"It says tasteful. Tasteful nudity. This is a great show!" Kim said brightly, to encourage my enthusiasm. "And you could really use some new tape for your reel," she added darkly, to discourage any objections.

I couldn't imagine putting a nude scene, tasteful or otherwise, on my reel to be published on my website. I couldn't imagine doing a nude scene at all. I'd gotten this far in my career with only a handful of bathing suit scenes and counted myself lucky. Ten-plus years and twenty-plus pounds later was not the time to start nuding up for posterity.

"Kim, I don't know. I need money desperately and I really would like to book a job, but oh my God. This is just brutal."

"Why don't I email you the material? You look it over, go in, knock it out of the park and then, once they offer you the job, you can be better informed to make the decision. This casting office hasn't seen you in a while. You want to go in there and remind them of how great you are. Right?"

"Who's casting?"

She told me and my records indicated it had been nine years since they had seen me for anything. They were a huge office and cast a dozen shows a year. Not going in could be a big mistake.

"Okay, fine. Send me the material. When is the appointment?"

"Today at four."

I looked at the clock. It was 11 AM.

"Today? Can't we push this until tomorrow or something?"

"Today is the last day they are seeing people for this role."

This was likely untrue but it was every agent's rote response to the request I'd just made. I don't know why I ever bothered to ask anymore.

"Where is the appointment?"

"Santa Monica."

Again, I don't know why I ask anymore. If the appointment is anywhere near rush hour, it is in Santa Monica. This meant I needed to allow a good ninety minutes to get there. That left me three and a half hours to shower, dry my hair, put on make-up and learn the material before I had to leave. Nothing like being in a hurry to amplify what is already a stressful situation.

"Why don't you text me when you are done and meet me for a drink afterwards? I haven't seen you in a while. I want to see how you are holding up."

I agreed to this plan even though I knew she just wanted to see if I had gotten fat, which I had. But what are you going to do? A minute later I had hung up with Kim and printed out the sides she had emailed me. There is no better way to illustrate the horror of what I had before me than just to show you the scene itself.

FADE IN:

Int. Gangster Vampire Lair—Night

Moonlight from a tiny window slices through the dark lair, illuminating DEMONE MALVAGIO, 19, snarling malevolently in the terrified MARGE'S, 52, bloodied face. Marge looks scared but strangely defiant.

DEMONE MALVAGIO

Tell me where you keep your little black book, bitch, or I will let Luna finish you off.

LUNA INSANGUINARE, 16, looms in a dark corner giggling wickedly. Her shirt is soaked in blood. Is it Marge's? We can see Luna's erect nipples straining the wet fabric, announcing her arousal and her bloodlust.

Marge, tied to a chair and unable to move, takes her eyes from the sneering Demone to get a look at Luna. Luna smiles in response to Marge's evident terror and her fangs drop down like a two-pronged dental erection. Marge looks back, in supplication, to Demone—her eyes begging him for mercy. Demone presses Marge's face to the right with his spookily long and pale fingers and reveals two purple holes in Marge's throat. Marge whimpers. Demone looks at her with what seems to be deep sympathy. Is he about to cry? He then uses a jagged, razor-sharp nail to slice Marge's shirt and bra open right down the center. Marge lets another moan escape but, this time, we are unsure if it is the sound of fear or pleasure. Her milky-white breasts, completely exposed, heave in the pale moonlight.

DEMONE MALVAGIO

Ambrosio Pellegrino was a MADE vampire! Your corrupt politician clients will have to pay for what they did to him!

Marge responds by spitting in Demone's face. Demone just laughs and licks the spit from his own face with a bizarrely long tongue. Smiling, Demone parts his cape and begins to unzip his trousers.

DEMONE MALVAGIO

And *you* will have to pay for *that*.

Demone straddles the seated Marge and from a three-quarter angle, we can tell, if not see, that he is forcing Marge to fellate him.

DEMONE MALVAGIO

Give me the information I desire! Or else you will join the ranks of the damned!

Marge tries to speak but her mouth is full. All we hear are grunts and gurgles.

DEMONE MALVAGIO

What? What are you saying, Margie

darling? Are you trying to tell me something?

Luna giggles in the corner, nibbling her thumb talon. Demone thrusts into Marge's mouth several times as she continues to make sounds of protest. Or is she protesting? Demone finally pulls out of Marge's mouth and violently pulls her head back by her hair.

DEMONE MALVAGIO

Didn't anyone ever tell you it is rude to speak with your mouth full? Now, what is that you are trying to tell me?

A gasping Marge looks, wild-eyed, up into the grinning Demone's face. Luna approaches and leans in to Marge's stricken face for a closer inspection. Luna is loving this show. Marge opens her mouth to let out a primordial scream and…

MARGE

(exploding into hysterical tears)

Take me! Take me now! Make me one of you! I want to live forever! I want to be beautiful again! I want to be a vampire! Take me! Please!

Off the shocked expressions of Luna and Demone, we fade to black.

Seriously. That was the scene. The other scene required that I, as Marge, pretend to wake up from unconsciousness and find myself still bound to the chair. This time, however, I am gagged. I begin to try to struggle to free myself. After a few moments, I notice several teen vampires peering at me through the darkness, at which point, I burst into maniacal sobs. My crying triggers their attack and they swoop in on me to finally drain me of my last drop of blood. The last shot is of my lifeless body, slumped in the chair.

Two scenes. Eight lines. Eight lines if you allow that one or two words can be defined as a line. Primarily, the audition involved: pretending to be bound and/or gagged, pretending to spit in a vampire's face, pretending to blow a vampire while also trying to speak, moaning and whimpering in a way that sounds both turned-on and petrified, pretending to die, oh, and of course, bursting into hysterical sobs. Twice. The only thing better than the audition was the fact that, if I were to be hired, I'd get to do all that again, but with my shirt off, cameras on and seventy-five crew members watching.

Chest pressure and the accelerated heartbeat returned as I considered what this audition could possibly do for me. The thousand dollars wasn't even a Band-Aid on my financial wound and it would only be nine-hundred after I paid Kim her ten percent. So, the money was no real impetus. The role itself was degrading even without the milky-white, heaving bosom reveal. The only reason to go in was to get myself in front of those casting people again, for the first time in nine years, so they could see what I looked like now and that I don't play fifty-two. But I'd have to do that while sitting in a chair, unbound, pretending to be bound and straining, ungagged but pretending to either be gagged by a hanky or by a vampire penis, pretend to spit in a face that is not in front of me, burst into sobs on two different occasions and then slump over and play dead like a well-trained terrier. Just try the pretend-bound-and-gagged-and-struggling part where you are right now, in whatever chair you might be seated.

Feel like a retard? Wanna do that, and more, seated in a room with fluorescent lighting, five impatient producers, an HD camera recording and a casting director reading the vampire dialogue, deadpan, from ten feet away and never once looking up at you?

Me, neither.

I called my mother in a panic.

"I'm done," I cried. "I am so done. I can't do this actor thing anymore."

"Why? What's happened? What's going on?"

I told her.

"It doesn't sound that bad. You've done stuff like that before."

"No! I haven't! I have never had to blow a vampire while bound to a chair with my tits out in front of God and everyone for nine hundred dollars!"

My mother laughed. The absurdity of the situation even made me laugh.

"I can't go in there. All I will succeed in doing is embarrassing myself. And that is the best case scenario. The worst case scenario is that I get the job. Then what? Do the job? Topless for the first time in my career now? While playing a haggard fifty-two year old?"

"Fifty-two? You can't play fifty-two. You can't play forty-two."

"At this point, I can probably play forty-two. Stress is killing me. But that isn't the point. So, I either go in, make a fool of myself and that casting office waits eighteen years this time before ever bringing me back in, or I do a good job, whatever the fuck that is, and I get the job and have that shit on my résumé and floating around on the internet and on MrSkin.com ad infinitum, or I get the job and turn it down, thereby pissing the casting director off and having that same eighteen-year moratorium on auditions for her that I already mentioned. So, I either go in and never see her again for eighteen years or I take the job and become granny porn forever. I can't go in. I have to pass."

"Are you sure?"

"No, I'm not sure. I need the work. I need the money. But everything in me is screaming no-fucking-way to this. That's why I'm sitting here having a heart attack."

"Then don't go."

We both sat in silence for a few moments.

"It's just not fair," I said, defeated, and started to cry.

"No, baby, it's not," my mother consoled me. "You are really talented. I don't know why nobody out there seems to see that. Yet," she quickly corrected.

"I feel like I am having a heart attack. I swear to God."

"That's not healthy. This strain you are under is going to start taking a real toll on you."

"I know, but what am I supposed to do?"

"I don't know. Have you ever seriously thought about giving up acting?"

I had—but only hypothetically. I threatened it all the time but I never meant it. Not in any real way. In the beginning, there was no reason to question it because I was doing very well. Then as my employment slowed, I'd watch other actors I knew quit, and I watched them with genuinely confused, almost pitying eyes. As my employment slowed further, I watched people throw in the towel and I envied them for having whatever gene made quitting possible, but I still never really considered quitting myself. Lately, as I looked at other people doing jobs—waitresses, the mailman, cashiers, radio talk show hosts, manicurists, dog walkers, Pilates instructors, flyer distributors, whatever—I always tried to imagine myself doing those things to subsidize acting. I never looked at other jobs as something to take the place of acting, not really.

"I defaulted on my mortgage this month," I said flatly, composing myself. I knew she knew this already but I needed to get used to saying it out loud.

"You didn't answer my question."

I hadn't, deliberately, but I let her push me into a conversation I didn't want to have.

"Kinda. Not because I don't want to do it anymore but because it doesn't want to do me anymore. Half a dozen auditions a year? For a day or an episode of a show here and there? Even if I booked every job I read for, which has never happened to any actor ever, I wouldn't break twenty-thousand a year. That isn't enough. But I can't think of any other job I could realistically get that would cover my bills, even as cut back as they are now."

"Have you ever thought about moving home?"

At first, her question didn't register. The word "home" had meant where I was currently sitting, Los Angeles, for so long, it took me a minute to realize she meant Boston.

"No! No, I have not. I can't move back to Boston!" I shot back, deeply offended.

"Why not? We have room here. You could sell your house there, move home with a nice little nest egg and then take your time finding something else to do that will make you happy, with no financial pressure."

The idea seemed absolutely preposterous to me. Move home? Live with my parents? I hadn't lived at home since I was eighteen. Only losers move home after they have lived on their own. I thought I was a loser but I wasn't that big of a loser.

"I can't move home, Ma," I said, my tone clearly calling her insane.

"Why not? Do you realize eighty-five percent of college graduates move home to their parents? Eighty-five percent. And some of these are Ivy League kids. There is no shame in it."

"Ma, I am old enough to be the parent these kids move home to."

"No, you're not."

"Yeah. I am. Do the math."

She did.

"Okay, so you are not a recent college grad. I just think you might need to start broadening the scope of things you will consider as a solution to your situation. The stress you are under is really unhealthy."

I had no comeback for that. Several times a day, I had anxiety attacks that I actually feared might escalate to a stroke. I was living in near-constant physical pain caused entirely by the emotion attached to trying to maintain both my career and my house. Was anything worth that? Did I love acting so much I was willing to die for it? But who was I if I wasn't Ruby, working actress and proud owner of a modest home? I didn't want to be Ruby, McDonald's minimum-wage employee and proud resident of a crash pad.

"Yeah, well, I don't know. I can't talk about this now. I need to get ready."

"So you are gonna go to the audition?"

"No. But I am going to meet my agent later, as was planned. I need to figure something out."

"Okay. Go meet her looking amazing."

"Okay. I will."

"What are you going to wear?"

I think these conversations about how I looked and what I wore, et cetera, were a way for her to feel supportive and involved but they always felt like a test to me.

"I'm going to wear that pink dress with the black shrug," I might say.

"I think that blue dress you have hits your leg in more flattering spot," she'd counter. "You want to show people what great legs you have. And that dress shows your boobs off, too."

I didn't have the emotional resilience right then to field this version of my mother's support. To her detectable disappointment, I told her I would figure it out and said goodbye. I dug through my medicine cabinet for a two-year-old prescription I had for Xanax. The prescription was for twenty pills, prescribed for pain and sleeplessness. There were twenty left. I took one and felt certain I was one step closer to making my debut on a "Faces of Meth" website.

A FEW HOURS LATER, I stood inside the door of a dark bar and grill and waited for my eyes to adjust to the light. I assessed the impact the Xanax was having. I was disappointed to note that I didn't feel any different but also relieved that I didn't have the sudden urge to turn five-dollar tricks in alleyways or rob a pharmacy. Then I realized that the weight on my chest had lifted and I could actually get a deep breath of air into my lungs. *Hmmm,* I thought. Maybe my fear of immediate drug dependency and subsequent prison time for forging benzodiazepine prescriptions was premature—melodramatic, even.

"Ruby!" Kim called, interrupting my thoughts, but the room was still too dark for me to make anything out clearly.

"Over here at the bar," I heard her say, so I headed toward the backlit wall of alcohol. By the time I got there, I could clearly see Kim at the other end and an oversized martini glass in front of her. I walked over and sat next to her.

"So? How was the audition? Did you nail it?"

"Did you read the material?"

"No. But this series is very hot and getting a lot of buzz. They are going for an edgy, HBO, boutique-y, *True Blood* meets an updated *Police Woman* but with a sixth sense set in a post-apocalyptic *Jersey Shore* kind of thing. They are shooting it in L.A. but it takes place in Detroit. They really want to push the boundaries. Don't tell anyone I told you, but I heard they are in negotiations to get Sean Young and Gary Busy to do a three webisode arc," she said and sipped her drink as though she hadn't said a single, unbelievably insane thing. "So," she repeated, setting her drink down, "how did it go?"

"Pushing boundaries just means more nudity. And, again, you didn't actually read the material, did you?"

A bartender came over and I ordered an eight-ounce glass of wine, the largest of the three options available. When did restaurants start selling wine by the ounce and who the Hell gets a three-ounce glass? The world was going to Hell in a hand basket.

"Kim, there is no way you read the material you sent me."

"No. I didn't. Why?"

"The audition involved pantomiming being bound and gagged, spitting in someone's face, sucking off a vampire, crying hysterically and dying. Oh, and I think there were about ten words to say, or grunt—and grunt ambiguously, mind you. A horny-but-afraid-for-my-life kinda grunt. You know the kind," I said with heavy sarcasm.

I then put my hands behind my back as if bound, opened my mouth as if gagged and thrashed around looking wild-eyed, pretending to spit intermittently and pretending to gag on an invisible cock, and then struggled some more as if trying to free myself. Finally, after some faux crying, I slumped over dead. I looked like a porn star being executed in the electric chair.

Kim laughed uproariously.

"And they say you're not funny!" she said and laughed some more.

"Who says I'm not funny? Where the fuck did that come from?"

Kim ignored my questions.

"So? How did it go? Did they love you?

"I didn't go, Kim!"

"What?! Why not? It was a great part!"

"It was not a great part. It was simulated sex with my tits out, no dialogue, lots of crying and nine-hundred dollars. And it is for a *webisode*! I'd hoped never to say the word 'webisode,' let alone show up on one, middle-aged and topless, blowing a teen vamp named Demone Malvagio."

Kim, to her credit, laughed at this, too, rather than castigate me for being self-sabotaging. After all, what did it mean to her? Ten percent was one hundred dollars and even she had to know, somewhere deep in her shallow soul, that it wasn't a good part and that nobody wanted to see me naked.

"Okay, so I'll call casting tomorrow and make up some excuse for your no-show. Tell me, what else is new and exciting in your life?"

"Nothing. Tough times at the Fitzgerald house. Going on three years without a job here, you know?"

"I know. It is so slow all over town. Nothing going on."

That is what all agents say any time it is slow for *you*. It has no basis in truth. I forgave her lie in return for her not throwing the blown-off audition in my face as evidence of a pattern that had caused my financial crisis.

"And," she continued, "everything is young. If you were in your twenties it would be different."

Also bullshit. When I was playing twenties, I was told that everything was high school or that if I were old enough to play the parent of a high schooler then there would be tons of opportunity.

"Wait. You did that indie movie, *High School* something or other, just last year."

"*Getting High School*. Yeah, last year and it paid a hundred bucks a day. And I worked like five days. Believe it or not, I've already gone through that money."

"You are funny!" Kim said and laughed lightly, as if I'd made a droll joke.

"Stand up and turn around," she said, sounding really friendly. "Let's get a look at you!"

She had me stand, take my coat off and turn for her. This was a common device of hers used to stoke my insecurities about my weight, hair, skin—anything to turn the tables on me so I'd stop questioning her about her ability to get me meaningful work.

"You look great," she said finally. "You can totally still play mid-thirties."

This was also a subtle jab, a reminder that I was getting old disguised as a compliment. While she seemed willing to forgive our differing opinions on the value to my career of engaging in simulated sex in webisodes, she wasn't above putting me in my place in other ways.

"How old are you now?"

"Thirty-five," I deadpanned.

"Thirty-five? Didn't I come to like—your thirty-seventh birthday last year?"

"No."

"Yes. Remember? You had that cocktail affair thingy at that cute bar in Union Station. I could have sworn you were thirty-seven. Or was it thirty-nine?"

What happened to thirty-eight?

Kim knitted her brow, appearing to consult the crystal ball of her mind and, through it, ascertain my real age.

"I thought you were older than I am," she said, still seeming to be looking inward. "What year were you born?" she asked suddenly, and turned her full focus back to me. I felt naked and squirmed in my seat.

"What year?" she repeated and, assuming an innocent pose, sipped her martini and peered over the rim of the glass at me.

"What's up with the gotcha journalism, Katie Couric?" I asked, sounding more defensive than I'd hoped.

"Okay, well, whatever. Have it your way. If you won't do *nudity*..." she said and paused. The word "nudity" had been pronounced with special emphasis meant to indicate that I was being a huge baby. She let the incomplete sentence hang there a bit so I would have time to absorb a nice portion of the responsibility for my never working again because I am too much of a prude to do nudity. "You know?" she finally continued. "Just wait a few years. Pretty soon you will start getting into the mom roles and things will pick up."

"I can play a mom now, no? When my mother was my age, I was in junior high."

"No, you look too young to play moms yet."

Again, bullshit. Everything an agent tells you is calculated to lower your expectations for yourself and intended to break your spirit and your every moral boundary—all while sounding flattering and supportive. I didn't bother arguing. I ordered another eight-ouncer.

"Sooo... how's your love life?" she asked, changing the subject. "Anything going on there? Got a guy?"

"No. But I did go out with a couple of different guys recently. Which is sort of a change of pace for me."

"That's nice!"

"Sure. Really nice. If by 'nice' you mean unbelievably hideous."

Kim laughed and ordered another double martini. She looked at me mischievously over the giant olive she was gnawing.

"What?"

"I have a guy for you!"

"No, no. Honestly, I'd really rather get my career on track, you know? I am broke and stressed and I am not going to be good for anyone right now. No guys. I just need to work."

"Blah blah blah! This guy is great!"

I decided to ignore the fact that my agent, my only access to future employment as an actress, had just pooh-poohed my desire to procure said employment.

"He saw your headshot on my desk and thought you were hot. He asked me for your number. Can I give it to him?"

"No. Who is this guy? Not an actor?"

"No. His name is Eddie. He used to be an actor but he directs sitcoms now."

"Eddie who?"

"Eddie Flagon."

"Eddie Flagon!? No way!" I said in horror before remembering that Eddie Flagon was her client and maybe a good friend. "No, I'm just not… dating. Anyone."

"You just said you were dating around."

"I never said I was dating around. That sounds like a euphemism for prostitution. I said I had gone out with a few guys."

"So? Go out with this one! Eddie is great!" she repeated.

Eddie Flagon was a comedian from the eighties famous for his achy-breaky mullet and unpredictable behavior. He had all the physical appeal of Gallagher and the likeability factor several rungs on the ladder below Gilbert Gottfried. He had been the star of an enormously successful movie franchise similar to *Porky's*. Thirty years ago, it seemed people with crimped hair and huge shoulder pads could not get enough of him. Mercifully, Eddie Flagon went out of style right about the same time as *Miami Vice*.

"Look, just let me give him your number."

"Wait, isn't he the guy that jerked off Jim Hanna's exotic goat on *The Johnny Carson Show*?"

"It was a koala and he only diddled him a little. That was just schtick, anyway. He is really sweet in real life."

"No. I'm sorry. Anyway, I need some time off from guys."

"Didn't you tell me last time we were together that you hadn't had sex in over four years?"

"Five. Yes. But I broke that streak," I said, again just a smidge on the wrong side of defensive. How did she keep managing to do this to me?

"Oh! So you got back in the saddle?"

"Um… yeah. Once," I said with a heavy sigh, as if I were finally confessing my involvement in a heinous crime.

"Was it *amazing*? I bet sex after that long was amazing. Tell me it was amazing!"

"It was amazing, all right," I said, devoid of enthusiasm, and sipped my wine.

"No good?" she asked, and when I shook my head emphatically no she added, "Girl, you need to get The Rabbit!"

Bear with me if you already know about The Rabbit. The Rabbit is a vibrator that has several bands of rotating pearls at the base, a Playboy-bunny-head-shaped clitoral stimulator, a bent tip meant to stimulate the G-spot that rotates in the opposite direction from the pearls and all of these features have variable vibrating and speed settings. I think they give courses at the city college for women to get a license to own one of these things. If they don't, they should, because they seem more complicated to drive than a fork lift and seem to have more in common with heavy machinery than a human penis. They should create a division of the Teamsters for people that own these.

"No. I am not a toy girl. And someone who has sex as seldom as I do runs a serious risk of becoming addicted to a toy like that. I like sex. I like men. I like sex with men. I don't want to go five years celibate and then finally find a great guy and be disappointed that his dick isn't bent like a toilet bowl brush and that he can't vary the speed and intensity level of the different parts of his johnson."

"You are insane. The Rabbit is the greatest thing ever. You know what I do sometimes? I spin it backwards and use that clit thing on my ass."

I got a fleeting mental image of one of those battery-operated personal fans spinning against an anus. I didn't hang out with Kim enough to know if these were her double martinis talking or if she was always so free with such intimate details, and you might be surprised that anything shocks me, but this information, and from my agent, handily met my definition of TMI.

"Well, that sounds... dangerous, mostly." Those bunny ears look like clippers poised for a clitorectomy.

"So what do you do to get off?"

I wasn't comfortable giving my agent the skinny on my masturbation habits so I tried to say something that sounded like an answer without revealing anything specific.

"Have you ever Googled 'free porn'?" I improvised. "It is amazing what is on there. I don't know how parents sleep at night. A friend of mine has a nine year old that was doing a report for school on camels and she was scarred by what came up when she Googled '*camel toes*.'"

Not one to be thrown off the scent, Kim ignored my camel toe diversion.

"So you like porn? I like it, too. I like to watch gay guy porn. Have you ever seen it? Hawt!"

I actually had seen gay guy porn. I sought it out specifically when a genuinely lesbian friend informed me that she and her friends were all about the guy-on-guy. This perplexed me. In the name of research, I found some random movie online and I have to admit, it is appealing. The guys are all fit and it is penis city. If you like to look at penises without distracting labial roast beef sandwiches always mucking up the view, gay guy porn is for you.

"Yes, I agree. I like interracial porn, too," I heard myself volunteer. Or was this the Xanax/wine combo talking now?

"Like black guys?"

"Yes. Black guys."

"And white chicks?"

My glass was empty. I definitely needed another drink. I ordered one and pressed on. I'd already come this far, what the Hell?

"Yeah, sure. Why not? If they are white, I can pretend they are me," I said, adlibbing. I didn't really have any preference but I wanted to throw her some red meat.

"You are into the chocolate, huh?" she said, making it sound as kinky as her rabbit-bunny-ear-ass maneuver.

"Yeah, well, actually... I mean, I like black guys but it isn't a fetish or something. I like white guys, too. Any kinda guy. Just not in porn."

"Black guys are huge, right?"

"Most guys in porn are pretty big. It isn't that."

"Spit it out, girl! What is it that you like about black guys in porn?"

"I don't want to say. It will just sound racist."

"Come on. What?" she leaned in conspiratorially.

"I like black guy porn because I assume... oh my God this is so racist!"

"What?"

"It is gonna sound way racist."

"*What?*"

"I like it because I assume..."

I couldn't believe I was about to say these words out loud. This could not come to any good.

"I like it because I can assume... that the black guys are all Democrats."

Crickets.

"You know? The white guys are always so pink and jocky and their hair looks conservative and all I can think is, *that guy voted for McCain or Romney*. It is a huge turn-off."

Kim erupted into laughter.

"Okay, why aren't you on a sitcom?" Kim asked.

"I'm not on a sitcom, my agent, my darling, because nobody thinks I'm funny and I can't get an audition to save my life. Remember?"

"Oh. Right," she said and continued laughing. "Wait, what about Ron Christie?" she asked, suddenly serious.

"What about Ron Christie?"

"Ron Christie is a black guy and he is a Republican."

Involuntarily, I imagined a naked and coy Ron Christie inexplicably tweaking his own nipples.

"Great. Thanks. Now all I have left is gay guy porn. Like my sexual world wasn't claustrophobic and dysfunctional enough."

"Okay. You are definitely going to meet Eddie Flagon. My house. Tomorrow night. I am having a little cocktail party and I want you to come. Eddie will be there. No pressure. You can meet him and decide for yourself."

"Thanks, but I can't," I said, unable to think of a decent excuse to offer.

"I will not take no for an answer. We have a new agent at the office and you need to meet him, too. He'll be there. Tomorrow night at my house. Seven o'clock."

I tried to think of some believable commitment I might have that would get me out of this but my mind was a blank. A Xanax-and-wine-addled blank.

"And hey, you owe me. For not going to that audition today."

Ugh. She went there.

"Okay. Fine."

"Great! And wear a dress that shows your tits off and makes your waist look a little smaller, okay? There will be people there that can give you a job."

I took down her address and promised myself I would not eat anything until the party.

* * *

The following evening, weak from hunger but no thinner, I began the torturous process of selecting an outfit. I finally decided upon a dress that basically served as a shelf for my boobs. I crossed my fingers and hoped that my well-presented rack would draw interested eyes north and away from the thickness that was my waist. I put on an agonizing pair of strappy shoes that I reserved for evenings I intended to end early. I stopped at the store and spent a week's grocery money on a lesser champagne, took a Xanax and headed to the party.

I am often the first guest to arrive at soirees but I was relived to find that night was an exception. Things seemed well under way when I walked in the door. I handed Kim the bottle of bubbly and poured myself a glass of red from an open bottle I recognized as a ten-dollar Trader Joes staple. Kim hurried off to welcome another guest so I made my way to the hors d'oeuvres. As I was shoving a third huge slab of baked brie into my face, someone tapped me on the shoulder. I turned to face an avuncular gentleman who looked to be about sixty. He was a bowling ball of a man; about five foot nine, very heavy by anyone's standards, and balding. The hair he did have had been bleached white with the faintest traces of marshmallow-peep yellow streaked through it. His eyebrows had thinned to the point one might say he had none at all. He was wearing a faux-Shepard Fairey Joe the Plumber T-shirt—I could only assume, ironically.

"I'm sorry. Do you want some brie?" I asked while also trying to chew and swallow.

"No. I just wanted to introduce myself."

Embarrassed to be caught eating and then talking with my mouth full, I made it worse by wiping my hand on my hip and reached out to shake his hand.

"Hello. I'm Ruby."

"How's that brie?" he asked, smiling shyly.

"Too good. I wish you'd have some so I don't eat it all myself. I'm already big as a house," I said and then heard myself.

"Who you telling?" he said and made a "look at *me*" gesture. Not sure what to say to that, I let out a too loud but noncommittal, all-service "Ha!"

He let me off the hook by laughing, looked at my nearly empty glass and asked if he could refill my drink. Not wanting to be seen refilling it myself so soon, I accepted. When he stepped away, I piled appetizers on a tiny plate and promised myself not to make any more fat references. I found a seat on a small sofa, sat down and continued eating.

"Here you are, darlin'," he said and handed me a deep glass of wine.

"Thank you, sir," I said and reached for the glass. From my position beneath him, I could see up his sleeve to his ample bingo wing and coy back boob peeking out from beyond it. Distracted by this visual, I knocked my empty glass over as I took the fresh one he was offering me. Both hands occupied, I watched helplessly as the empty glass rolled off the coffee table. Instinctively, I kicked my foot out in a Xanax-guided effort to catch the glass with my toes. I failed. The glass shattered on my foot and broken glass fell all over the rug.

"Oh my God! Now look what I did!" I said and put both my plate and glass of wine down. I knelt on the floor and began picking shards of glass from the carpet.

"Be careful," he warned. "Let me do it."

I refused to let him take over and we were both still on our knees when Kim approached.

"What happened?"

"Kim, I'm so sorry," I apologized.

"It was me," he interrupted. "I was distracted by the lady's charm and clumsily knocked an empty glass off the table. I'm so sorry! Do you have a vacuum?"

"Don't be ridiculous. I'll have the caterer clean it up. Do either of you need another drink?"

We told her we did not. The caterer appeared before we could call him and cleaned the broken glass with a handheld vacuum. We stood aside so he could do his job.

"You didn't have to take the blame but thank you."

"Nonsense. I was the one that broke the glass," he said and winked in a way that suggested we were a team. I liked this guy. Then I noticed he kept sneaking looks at my feet. I seldom wear strappy shoes because I have fat feet that tend to swell. An hour or two on my feet or in the heat and my insteps look like raw bread dough with abundant active yeast. Challah-like mounds of flesh strain the straps and my circulation becomes dangerously impaired. Feeling self-conscious, I shifted my weight.

"I think you cut your foot," he finally said.

I looked down and saw why he had been staring. Blood was pooling in the nail bed of my big toe. It wasn't immediately obvious because my toenails were painted red.

"Oh, shit! I guess I did!"

"Come on, follow me."

He led me to the bathroom where he proceeded to clean and bandage my toe. For the next hour or two, he led me around, introduced me to people and made sure my glass was always full. Everyone in the room seemed to know and like him a lot. I felt like a college girl being shown off at a party by her proud Daddy, albeit a proud Daddy who was trying to get his precious baby drunk.

Eventually, my Easy Bake feet did begin to rebel against the restraints that were my shoes. Already uncomfortable because of the cut on my toe, I decided to take this as a sign that I should say my goodbyes.

"Did you have a good time?" Kim asked as she walked me out the front door.

"I actually did. Your friends are lovely. Thank you for inviting me."

"Isn't Eddie great? Didn't I tell you? I knew you guys would hit it off."

"Eddie is in there? Which one was he?"

"The one you spent the whole evening with!"

"That old guy? That is Eddie Flagon?" I asked, incredulous. Eddie Flagon couldn't have been that much older than me but he looked old enough to be my father.

"Yes! Who did you think he was?"

"I didn't know. I didn't hear his name at first and then he was so nice to me, by the time I realized I wanted to know his name it seemed insulting to admit I didn't already know it."

"Well, that was Eddie. He's a Democrat. Volunteered for the Obama campaign. And he wants your number."

Eddie really had gone above and beyond and took very good care of me that night but I couldn't imagine dating him.

"Kim, no. He is very nice but…"

"Come on. He just coming out of a painful break-up and you are the first person he has expressed any interest in."

"Great. So, what? I get to be rebound girl for Granddad?" I regretted saying that as soon as it was out of my mouth. Eddie had been nothing but generous to me and I was being a douche.

"I'm sorry, I might be pushing forty but I'm not ready to start dating a guy who looks sixty."

"I thought you were thirty-five."

"No. I'm twenty-six."

"Whatever. Look. He is all grown up. Let me give him your number. You tell him you have a boyfriend or whatever you want. But for me to tell him you won't even let him have your number is really insulting."

I am one of those girls with enough dysfunction in my self-esteem to think that I am flattering myself to think a guy wants to hang out with me so just so he can fuck me. Now, intellectually, I understand that I am flattering myself to think guys want to hang out just to be pals, but somehow that information seldom seems to inform my decisions.

"You are right. And maybe he just wants to hang out, you know? Who knows?"

Kim knew but she also knew to stop talking once she'd gotten what she wanted. Did you forget she is an agent?

"Great! Okay, drive safe!"

Drive safely, I thought to myself. "Thanks again," I said out loud.

I looked at my novelty breathalyzer on the console in my car and decided it didn't have anything to tell me that I wanted to hear. I put it in the glove compartment and carefully drove myself home.

7 Irony & the yeti

Early the next day I got a call from an unknown number. When I checked the voicemail, it proved to be a call from Eddie Flagon. He left a very sweet message about how nice it was to meet me and he wondered if I would let him take me to dinner. He went on to explain that he was flying out of town later that day to spend the weekend doing a few Monster Truck Comedy dates. He told me that if he didn't pick up between 5 and 6 PM it was because he was on a plane.

I waited until I knew he was on the plane to call him back. I thanked him for taking care of me the night before but deliberately avoided referencing the dinner invitation. I was such a pussy. I knew I didn't want to go out with this guy. There was exactly zero physical attraction. When he called me at seven, I again avoided his call. His message said that he would be working from nine to ten or so but that he was looking forward to talking with me.

I called him back at nine-thirty. This went on for three days. I deliberately called when he said he would be busy, or I texted him excuses for being unable to pick up. I used explanations like being at the movies or at a dinner party. I even pretended I had to go to church. No excuse was too outlandish but the reality was I was home alone the entire weekend.

As the days wore on, I ignored the growing realization that I was dragging this out way too long. I had made this guy jump through every hoop of communication and persistence I could think of and he complied every time. By Monday, I knew I had to actually answer the phone.

When the call came Monday morning, I picked up.

"Wow! You are a hard person to get hold of!"

"Haha, sorry. Crazy weekend."

"No problem. I'm just glad to finally hear your voice."

I asked him how the weekend had gone for him and we made other small talk and then he popped the question again. I felt so guilty about avoiding him all weekend that I decided I owed him a damned dinner.

"Great!" he said. "When are you free?"

"Any time, really..."

"How about tonight?"

No time like the present, I thought. I wanted to get it over with as quickly as possible, anyway, so I agreed to dinner that evening.

I deliberately dressed down, jeans and a sweater, in an effort to appear casual. As I approached the restaurant, I saw Eddie Flagon walking toward me. As he got closer, I saw he was wearing a beret and sucking on a soggy Cuban.

"Hello," I said.

He bent down and gently extinguished the cigar before greeting me with a double cheek kiss as he exhaled a cloud of sickening smoke.

He looked shorter and older than I remembered and he looked nauseated to the brink of puking.

"Are you okay?"

"Yes, of course," he said but his voice cracked. I realized he was terrified. I saw his hand tremble as he slipped the cigar in the breast pocket of his jacket. It made my heart hurt and my vagina recoil. My heart began to race and I cursed myself for not bringing my new best friend, Xanax, along on this date.

We went inside and were quickly seated. I ordered a glass of wine and Eddie ordered coffee and a diet Coke. I knew what this meant and I couldn't believe I hadn't noticed at the party that Eddie was sober. Eddie was so bizarrely awkward it made me nervous. He sat there wincing and left me to take the reins, so I regaled him with question after question about his past, his career, and I laughed too long at his jokes. He quickly got around to his last break-up. He told me they had been together for ten years. She was much younger than him and wanted children. He told me he loved her so much, he would have done anything to make her happy so he bought her a four-karat ring and proposed. She told him she needed space to think and moved out of their home that night. She never came back, not even for her stuff, and that was eleven months ago.

"Wow. Did she ever explain why she left?"

"No. She packed a bag and left. She hasn't returned a call in all this time. I am dealing with her business manager now to arrange the sale of our house."

"That is some fucked up shit."

"What size shoe do you wear?"

"Nine. Why?" I asked, lost as to how this could be relevant.

"She has more shoes than Imelda Marcos. I thought, if you wore the same size, you could come over and go shoe shopping. She doesn't seem to want any of her stuff… but she wears a six and a half."

"Thanks. But, um…"

"That would be too weird, right? I know. I am sorry."

"Nooo! That's okay," I reassured him and sipped my wine. "She sounds like a sociopath. Better to find out before the wedding, right? And I think you are doing great. It took me forever to recover from my last real break-up. Look at you—out with a chick already. Bravo."

"She's a good girl. I just have to force myself to move on. I wish one could actually die of a broken heart."

Wow. Fun date. Still, the more he whined, the more he reeled me in. I'm a sucker for someone that needs rescuing, maybe because I was in need of more than a little rescuing myself.

"I try to remember the bad times like—when she wouldn't allow me to accompany her on vacations or to her movie premieres or to visit on the set."

"Oh… she's an actress?" I asked, tenderly, in my best "Oprah's here, baby. Let it all out" tone.

He told me who she was but I had never heard of her. I nodded, though, like her name meant something to me. I'll call her Emily.

"My therapist told me to go out on a bunch of dates, no matter how painful it is, until I work Em out of my system. You are the first woman I have asked," he said, dolefully.

I was so caught up in his drama that I was flattered by this revelation. I didn't feel, as I should have, that he'd just told me I was a social Dulcolax, helping him soften and pass the stool that was "Em."

By the time dinner was over, I had consumed a full Big Gulp of his Kool Aid. He loomed in my wine-soaked mind as this tragic, romantic figure—an abused dog who approached strangers with a submissive dribble of pee but also a hopeful wag of his tail.

Eddie paid the bill, which was refreshing and a huge relief, and insisted on walking me to my car. Once there, he produced a CD from his jacket pocket. He asked if I wanted to hear some of his stand-up. I said, "Sure," and the next thing I knew, he was in the passenger seat of my truck, sliding the disc into the player. I'd forgotten that it was broken until I saw the player spit it back out at him. Eddie accepted this rejection with defeated resignation, as if it had been inevitable. I couldn't help but notice his hand shaking as he reached to retrieve the CD. He made no move to get out of the car. I tried very hard to keep conversation flowing and upbeat. I assured him that the stereo was a broken piece of shit but he remained silent and inconsolable. In the constricted environment of my car, his palpable nervousness began to fill me with panic.

"Okay, well, thanks again for dinner. It was lovely," I said, hoping my tone both gave him the will to live and the urge to get out of my car.

No movement from Eddie, just insecurity radiating out of him and bouncing off the window.

"Um, so, I have to be up early and..." I drifted, awkwardly.

He looked at me with the most pathetic expression I have ever seen on an adult and I heard him say softly, out loud but to himself, "Oh God..." and then he leaned in to kiss me.

That quiet "Oh God" he had uttered utterly robbed me of any option other than to allow the kiss. I had to take this bullet for humanity. To save Eddie's life, I had to let the kiss happen.

And happen it did. That kiss happened *to* me. The only part of Eddie's body that wasn't trembling with fear was the cigar-and-coffee-flavored Swedish Fish of a tongue he flopped into my mouth. He was one of those guys that thinks a French Kiss is the act of sticking your tongue as deeply into the other person's mouth as is physically possible and holding it there, motionless. I felt like a kidnap victim with a dirty gag rag filling my mouth to muffle my screams.

Eventually the assault ended and he leaned back to assess my response. I feigned shyness and looked into my lap. My vagina took this opportunity to remind me that she had known he was a bad choice from the moment she had seen his trembling hands at the top of the date.

"Um... so... I had a really good time, tonight," he said.

"Me, too. Thank you."

"Maybe we can do it again? Soon?"

My cooch did not like the direction this was going but I couldn't think of a way to respond and get out of ever doing anything remotely like it again. I was too consumed with the effort not to wipe my tongue with my sleeve. It was disorienting that the evening had taken this completely unexpected course. I'd come to dinner to give him a polite brush off, not to escalate things to the physical level. How had this happened? How had I gotten in over my head so quickly? Again. It just confirmed what I had always known—that I am not cut out for this traditional dating bullshit. I was proving, as I instinctively knew I would, to be a complete failure at policing my own boundaries if I perceived that someone else's feelings might be hurt by it. This was not a healthy dynamic. Or maybe I was underestimating the toll my general stress level was taking. Either way, I just seemed to be making bad decision after bad decision when it came to men.

"Okay," I said to break the weeks-long uncomfortable silence and instantly berated myself for being such a coward.

"Tomorrow, maybe?"

"Maybe, yeah."

My vagina threw her hands in the air in disgust.

Eddie leaned in again but, merciful God, he just planted a peck on my cheek and, finally, bid me goodnight.

The next day, I spent hours Googling Eddie and watching YouTube clips of his comedy and career since the eighties. I was desperate to find something, anything, that would justify my giving this guy a chance, even though it was a chance I felt manipulated into giving him. It seemed easier to find something worthy in him than to navel gaze and determine the source of my own inability to put my own feelings ahead of his. So I was pleasantly surprised to find that his comedy was smart, edgy and really funny. Funny goes a long way. Guys like Lewis Black and Zach Galifianakis, while not movie-star handsome, are totally bone-able because they are hysterically funny. Who wouldn't want to manhandle the guy from *Between Two Ferns*? So, seeing Eddie on stage, confident and riffing about politics, was just the thing I needed. By the time I left to meet him, I had talked myself into a budding crush on Eddie Flagon.

Dinner that evening went much as the first, but Eddie was visibly more at ease, if no more upbeat. While he droned on and on about how good he had been to Emily, I sipped my wine and noticed his man boobs draping his abdomen like mammoth jowls. They made even his chest look depressed—like that old Droopy Dog cartoon. A thick shock of salt-and-pepper hair curled out from the neck of his shirt. My fragile crush was no match for these obstacles. Was this really all I could expect from the dating pool at my age? With his Mona Lisa eyebrows and deeply lined smoker's face, Eddie suddenly looked to me like a fat version of Robert Blake in *Lost Highway*. While he looked to be in his sixties, in reality, he had to be only somewhere in his early fifties. Still, where had the men in their thirties and forties gone? How had I missed twenty years' worth of guys? Was I supposed to accept jumping from my twenty-eight-year-old ex to this Botero Baretta here without a fight?

Adding insult to injury, I'd seen a good friend's husband in a commercial for an erectile dysfunction drug earlier that day. I'd always considered Viagra to be something old people used, not my peers. This new information freaked me out. *Is it true*? I asked myself. *Is it even possible that if I ever have regular sex again it will be with a medically induced faux boner?* And I winced as I wondered if the reason those people were always in two separate bathtubs in the ads was because everyone's junk was sore from trying to tame one of those famous four-hour erections. And what was with those other ads, where a woman is painting a foyer or some shit and her husband walks in with, I am just guessing here, an ill-timed hard-on? The moment is unexpectedly "romantic," so what happens? The walls of the house fall away and they walk hand-in-hand out to the woods and sit on a rock by a creek. Erections and hiking, the ads seem to say, are inevitably linked. Did this mean that if Eddie popped a blue pill, I could expect him to want to go wait out the erection in the forest, communing with nature? Is the outdoorsy thing supposed to be some metaphor I am just not getting? Or do old people need the threat of getting caught to make sex interesting? I was lost.

When dinner was over, I heard myself agree to do it again the next night. He celebrated by ramming his tongue into my mouth and leaving it there to rest for a few minutes. It had gotten quite a workout sniveling about Emily all night so I tried to be understanding and leave it undisturbed. When the power nap concluded, Eddie withdrew his tongue like a sword from its sheath. This pattern was repeated every night for a week.

Then the inevitable occurred. Eddie adopted that pained expression of his and asked, "Do you think it would be okay if I had sex with you?"

Listen, Low T. I'm all for gentlemanly behavior but asking "Would you mind awfully if I put my penis in you later?" is tough to respond to. A girl wants to be swept off her feet, caught up in the moment. It's fine and dandy to be polite when you are asking for a ride to the airport, say, or for another packet of Splenda, but when you are asking to have sex for the first time a little more passion might be in order.

"Um… don't mind if you do."

I said that. I actually said, "Don't mind if you do."

His agonized expression did not alter to reflect the fact that I had just courteously accepted his offer of a sexual encounter. If anything, he looked even sicker. Without saying another word to me, he gestured to the waiter that we wanted the check. We were at my house ten minutes later.

This was his first time inside my house. Unsure of how to proceed, I got a glass of wine for myself and gave him a tour. He seemed genuinely impressed with my taste in décor.

"How is your house decorated?" I inquired, sipping wine.

"Well, Em decorated it so it is entirely in her taste. She wouldn't allow me to put anything of my own out. It is all in storage."

"Em sounds like a lotta fun. No wonder you wanted to marry her."

"Where's your bedroom?" he asked, instantly filling me with butterflies. I guzzled the rest of my wine and poured another.

"This way..." I said and led him upstairs wondering, yet again, how I'd found my way to a second sexual encounter that, yet again, I wasn't remotely sold on and was quite certain I would regret. *Yes, regret. Maybe not today, maybe not tomorrow. But soon and for the rest of my life*, I thought.

We entered my room and he sat on the edge of my bed. He looked around at the art on the walls. At a loss for anything better to do, I sat beside him. I looked around the room, too, and remembered that I was on the brink of losing it all. This small niche I'd carved out for myself, my sole source of reliable comfort, might soon go away. Eddie rubbed my back and I let myself pretend it was because he knew what I was thinking and that he was comforting me and not just readying me for a mounting. He took the wine glass from my hand and put it on the nightstand. He stood up, took some impressive initiative and dimmed the lights, sat back on the bed, pushed me down and proceeded to impale my face with his tongue while grinding his pelvis into my thigh. So much for sympathy. As soon as I could do so without rousing suspicion, I disengaged myself from the ashtray and filled some time by sucking in great mounds of neck meat, moving on his throat like one of those pet sucker fish that clean the insides of tropical tanks. He undid the top of his pants and slid my hand inside. What I discovered there warrants no particular description and, at this point on this evening and in my romantic career in general, I was relieved.

I slid my hands up the back of his shirt. A wave of revulsion washed over me. The man had more back hair than Bigfoot. Why are men allowed to have an acre of dense forest growth anywhere on their persons but God forbid a girl has a visible pubic hair or a little leg stubble? My hands ventured further northward to his DD back boobs. Not sure what else to do, I gingerly cupped them. "More than a handful's a waste," some say, and now I knew what they meant. I tested their heft a few times and was less disturbed by the sensation that I was having my first lesbian experience before Eliza had had hers than I was by all that back hair threatening to get entangled in my jewelry. I casually slid my hands back in the southerly direction.

Eddie suddenly made a sound like a Chewbaca mating call and pulled his hips from my thigh.

Eddie, it would appear, had blown his load in his pants.

"I'm sorry. That's so embarrassing," Eddie pouted. "First time with my new girlfriend and I jizz in my pants."

I assured him that it was fine and, frankly, it was. I didn't need things to progress any further for one night. Or ever. It was the sudden introduction of the word "girlfriend" that really spooked me.

A few days after the premature ejaculation episode, Eddie invited me over to see his house. It had sold and he wanted to show me the Em museum before he began packing it up for her. I found the house on the west side, a little rose-covered cottage with arbors and trelliswork everywhere. It looked like a house Snow White might live in. There were a few half-packed boxes on the stairs. Eddie was standing at the door when I walked up the path. He had a cigar in his mouth so I was able to avoid a kiss.

Inside, it seemed impossible this could be a museum of his ex, unless his ex was a well-heeled tween. Everything inside was white, including the pickled pine floors. The only hints of color were provided by hundreds of Hello Kitty collectibles: Hello Kitty pillows on the white Shabby Chic sofa,

Hello Kitty quilts framed on the wall and a Hello Kitty coffee table book on the white lacquer coffee table.

"I know you said your ex was a lot younger than you but... exactly... how young *is* she?"

"Oh, you mean the Hello Kitty stuff?"

"Uh, yeah..."

"I know. It is a bit over the top but she was really into it. A lot of this stuff is more valuable than you might think."

"Don't you feel like a character lost in a world of anime?" I asked, wandering deeper into the house, looking around in wonder.

He didn't respond so I turned to face him. He was looking at a picture of himself and a young girl. They were smiling at the camera from over a cake that read, "Happy Sweet Sixteen Emily!"

"Is that your Emily?"

"Yeah. That's her. There was more to her than Hello Kitty, you know," he said suddenly and bizarrely defiant.

"How long ago was that picture taken?" I asked in as neutral a tone as I could muster.

"Twelve years ago," he said, then placed the picture face down, indicating the talk about Emily was over.

I did the math in my head as he led me upstairs. Twelve years? That would mean she was seventeen when he started going out with her. And twelve years ago, he had to have been somewhere near forty. Yuck.

We entered the master bedroom dominated by a massive canopy bed draped entirely in white with an assortment of stuffed Hello Kitties on the comforter. The walls were a mosaic of framed portraits of Emily. Emily in a bikini. Emily with George Clooney. Emily with Barack Obama. Emily with Katy Perry. Emily on various red carpets. I noticed there were no pictures of Emily with Eddie.

Eddie showed me her master closet. It housed an elaborate shoe display system, complete with sliding panels and white velvet rests for her shoes to relax upon. It was a pretty impressive shoe collection. I was glad we did not wear the same size because I definitely would have broken down and taken a few pairs. I imagined myself out at a premiere, prancing in a pair of her stolen stilettos and then running into her on the red carpet.

"Ruby, this is my ex… blah blah blah…" Eddie would be saying while Em stared daggers at my feet.

"Are those *my Jimmy Choos*?" she would demand from me and, without waiting for an explanation, grab a fistful of my extensions and drag me to the ground. The paparazzi would have a field day.

Yeah, it was probably for the best that she had delicate fairy tale feet and I had evil stepsister flippers.

Tour complete, Eddie walked me back to the door.

"Don't you want some help packing boxes and stuff?" I asked, surprised at being pushed out the door so soon after my arrival.

"No. Thanks. This is a very emotional time for me and I just need a little space," he said, voice trembling, then he took a big draw off his cigar.

I was over all this Em and the break-up shit. There is grieving and then there is wallowing.

"Sierra is coming over in a few minutes to help me, too. She's not really comfortable with you so…"

Sierra was his personal assistant whom I had never met. It wasn't news to me that she existed but the fact that she had issues with me was news.

"She… what? What's her problem with me?"

"She was very close to Emily. Sierra is still hoping we get back together," he said and then scanned the street for approaching cars.

"We? You and Emily or you and Sierra? Did you have a thing with Sierra?" I asked.

"Not really."

"Not really? That is like not really being pregnant. You either did or did not."

"See? This is exactly what I was trying to avoid. You have nothing to worry about with Sierra. I don't like fat chicks. I just wish you could move past this. It would make this whole situation so much less complicated. You shouldn't feel so threatened."

"I don't feel threatened by Sierra. I don't even know Sierra. I couldn't pick her out in a line-up of two people… unless one of the people was male or thin."

"That's mean."

"What?"

"She is very sensitive about her weight."

"You were the one that just called her fat. Anyway, I don't have any issue with her."

"Okay, okay. Settle down. I just thought it was pretty passive aggressive of you to not include her more," he chided.

"I don't *know* her."

"Well, it would be nice if we could all hang out together for once—like adults. Maybe this week at your house? Maybe you could make us dinner."

"This is nuts. I don't know Sierra and you already told me she hates me so why would I invite her?"

"Hate is a strong word. Don't be so dramatic."

"I'm going to stop talking now because I don't know what the fuck is going on."

"You are right. It is best that you go," he said, and I saw his chin quiver.

I snuck a last look at the house as I drove away and saw Eddie with his face buried in a huge Hello Kitty pillow, shoulders racked with sobs. It was then that I saw Eddie's sell-by date stamped on the top of his balding head.

Almost as if he could sense my energy shift, Eddie showed up at my door that night to explain and apologize for being a dick earlier.

An hour later we were fumbling around in my bed together, engaged in our version of foreplay, which really amounted to little more than him trying to stick me with that tent spike of a tongue and me trying to avoid the pinning. Eventually, he wiggled out of his pants to reveal what appeared to be a teeny, tiny pair of faded denim Daisy Dukes beneath. I reached out to touch them in wonderment and realized that what looked like skintight blue jean nut-huggers was actually a pair of cotton boxer briefs made to look like cut-off shorts. Even knowing this, it was an intensely disturbing visual. They seemed better suited to a man that pursed his lips and regularly used the adjective "fierce" and not on a rotund, fifty-something comedian from the Monster Truck Comedy tour. *Sometimes people take this "ironic attire" thing too far*, I thought. I was still in my dress when he pulled me up on top of him. I knew Eddie was a big guy, as wide as he was tall, but trying to straddle him really drove that fact home. Sitting on him at his hip level, my knees did not touch the mattress beneath us. I lost my balance and put my hands on his belly for balance. His middle moved beneath me like soft dough in whichever direction I tipped. Just when I thought I'd regained my balance, a tiny shift in weight from either of us sent me kneading all over his torso. Eventually, I found that by grinding my pelvis into his as an anchor and using the tops of my feet against the mattress, creating a tripod, I could stabilize myself. He must have mistaken my crotch grinding as an indication that I was aroused or something because he was tugging away at my dress, trying to get it up over my head. Frustrated by the belt around my waist, he gave up and turned his attention to his own shirt. With what seemed like an incredible amount of exertion, he tugged it over his head and flopped back onto the mattress gasping for air. I looked at the furry beast beneath me. His body hair was dense and almost entirely white. I was about to have sex with Bumble, the Abominable Snowman from *Rudolph the Red-Nosed*

Reindeer. I removed my rings as a safety precaution lest they become hopelessly entangled in the Yeti's coat.

He lost his shorts, pulled me back on top of him, pulled my panties aside and shoved himself inside me with all the romance of corking an overturned flask. Wham! Eddie's hand firmly gripped my hips and pushed them down hard to meet his thrusting pelvis. He pumped away in short, hard thrusts. He was a championship paddle-baller slapping his way to victory. Eddie did not utter a sound. His eyes were squeezed shut; his upper and lower lips had disappeared inside his clenched teeth. He looked like he was trying desperately to push out a shy turd. When I couldn't look at his grimace any longer, I leaned forward, lost my balance on his mohair mush-mound and face-planted into a pillow. The fall was perfectly timed because, judging by his trademark Chewbaca gurgle, I had narrowly avoided getting a front row view of his orgasm face. Grateful to have dodged that bullet, I counted to five so my revulsion wouldn't be apparent, rolled off of him and adjusted my underwear. With the exception of my shoes, I was still fully clothed.

"So," he finally said, catching his breath. "Did you cum?"

"Um… no… but… it was really nice…"

"Nice? Ouch."

"I'm sorry," I said, apologizing, I guess, for my lack of responsiveness. "It'll take me a while to be relaxed and really get into it."

He seemed satisfied with that answer.

We hung out a lot over the next few days and settled into a routine. Eddie bought a lot of meals and I got a bunch of nuance-free rammings, each followed by an increasingly accusatory "So, did you cum?" satisfaction survey.

"Have you *ever* had an orgasm?" Eddie finally demanded acerbically, disappointed by my most recent response to his sexual stylings.

"Yes."

"With someone else in the room?"

"Yes."

"Well, I'm not sure what else I can do here," he said, throwing his hands in the air.

I've seen dogs fuck with more imagination, I thought, but it seemed counter-productive to say that to his face. Instead, I said, "Yeah. I know. You are doing everything so right."

Perhaps he'd picked up on my sarcasm because the next time we had sex he shocked me by changing it up. He made the bold move of getting on top. Unexpectedly, I found myself on my back, his massive, white-haired man boobs swinging over my face like low-hanging, repellant fruit. I was examining my nails behind his back boobs and thinking about Koko the gorilla and her incredible sign language vocabulary when I felt the palm of his hand brush across my cheek.

That could not possibly have been what I think it was, I thought. *There is no way he just hit me... is there?* Eddie was pounding away in silence as if nothing unusual had happened. Just when I was convinced I'd imagined the slap, swack! This time there was no mistaking it. I had just been hit, hard, in the face by an open hand.

"NO!" I said emphatically. I could not think of any other words to say out loud. This fucker had just hit me. Intentionally. In the face. He did not acknowledge that I had spoken and continued pressing his squeezy-faced, mechanical lust upon my person. It wasn't long before he went rigid, purred like Chewie and rolled off me gasping. My thoughts were frenzied and my face and neck flushed crimson with rage. Then, from somewhere, someplace very far away I heard, "So," and some heavy breathing. "Did you cum?"

"I CAN'T BELIEVE HE HIT YOU! You are not having any luck with this dating thing, are you?" Eliza commiserated over cocktails, as she played with her wallet chain. Today's outfit consisted of low-slung chinos, a wife-beater, an oversized Pendleton and a pair of Timberlands. The T-shirt read "LESBIAN IN TRAINING" in army drab *M*A*S*H* font.

"No. So far I've had a gender-unspecific Albino, The Valance with a crudités phallus. You know, even the word 'phallus' is too generous for that thing. His penis isn't even as long as the word. Then I get medicine balls and an aging Bigfoot who's into S&M. What the fuck?"

"I'm telling you—you ought to try J Date," Eliza said and swirled her wine in the glass.

"I think J Date—and GayJayDate—are racist or bigoted or something."

"What? How?"

"They are dating sites for people that prefer to date—and will only marry—Jewish people. It offends me."

"Why?"

"It seems the same as saying you would be okay dating a black guy but you would never marry one. How about White-Date.com? Doesn't that sound racist to you?"

"It actually does when you put it that way, but it is a religious thing. That is different. Religion is important to some people."

"Well, that is just another reason I should not go on J Date. Not only am I not Jewish, I am not religious. I don't want to go out with some guy who would, categorically, reject me as a serious romantic interest simply because of my position on popular mythology."

After pointing out that my categorical write-off of religious folk made me guilty of the same sort of thing, Eliza finally let it go and pretended to agree that my assessment was fair.

"Even for you, Eliza. Even if you really were a lesberado…"

"Ruby, I told you…"

"I know. You are a lesbian. Who never has sex with women."

"I wasn't having a whole lotta sex with men, either, and nobody challenged my heterosexuality. Why is straight the default presumption?"

She had me there.

"Well played," I conceded. "So, anyway, doesn't GayJay-Date just narrow the field exponentially? You see the shit I am dealing with and this is with my choices unfettered by self-imposed filters like what religion they are. Why make it that much more difficult to find the right person? Aren't the odds stacked against us drastically enough already? What are the odds that any of us will meet someone single, someone we also find to be reasonably attractive, and that this someone is likeable enough that love is even a potential possibility? And then what are the odds that that person, if we ever find them, doesn't then have some genital deformity or the need to slap a bitch?"

"I still can't believe he hit you," Eliza said.

"He did me a favor, actually. I was like Patty Hearst with Stockholm Syndrome. The slap brought me back to reality. I should have cut bait after the first time he garaged that Fiat of a tongue in my mouth but I was powerless, Eliza. *Powerless*!" I insisted dramatically.

"Well, try a nondenominational dating service."

"I have! Remember? eHarmony. They rejected me. And I only even tried because you guys insisted. I think the whole process is pathetic and doomed."

"Oh, right. I still don't understand why they rejected you. Hey, I have an idea. Why don't I give you my eHarmony account? I'm not using it anymore. Just change the settings and add your own photograph and then see who they match you up with. What can that hurt?"

"Haven't we been over this already? I just don't believe in matchmaking. The fact is, even when it comes to movie stars, we don't all agree which ones are appealing so why would it be any different with hedge fund managers or unemployed baristas? And I never let friends set me up because

I am always end up deeply offended by their idea of who is right for me and then I have to explain that I think their favorite cousin smells like pennies or feta cheese, or something. I swear to God, it's like people think the only thing I need to have in common with the guy they are suggesting is that we are both single. It's bullshit. Life is lonely enough without constant reminders that even your best friends have no idea who you are."

"Just do it for fun then. You never know."

Fun. Right. I did know but I pretended to agree to do it just to shut her up.

"What about you, homie? How's life as a pillow queen?"

"What's a pillow queen?"

"A woman who lets women go down on her but won't return the favor."

"Really? Um, fuck you, and how do you know that term?"

"I'm very cosmopolitan, sister. Very LGBT friendly. I'm nearly fluent in Gaybonics."

"Good to know. Well, since you asked, I signed up last week for an account on TheLicker-Cabinet.com and…"

"The Licker Cabinet? With a CK?"

Eliza let out a sigh of impatience.

"Oh. My. God. I have to have a T-shirt that says that, too!"

"I'll be sure to get right on that for you."

"Said the nun to the priest. Or to the nun, in your case."

Not amused, Eliza just stared at me. In fairness, it was a pretty lame joke.

"Why am I friends with you?" she finally asked, deadpan.

"I'm sorry. So, Licker Cabinet. You signed up. And? Any hawt baby dykes there filling up your inbox? If you know what I mean?"

I laughed like a jackass at my second terrible joke. Maybe there was a little something inside me that secretly wanted to punish her for again suggesting I online date. Maybe I was being kind of a dick on purpose. It happens.

"You don't even know how almost fired you are."

"I'm sorry. I'll be serious," I apologized and donned my most sincere expression.

"Anyway, yes. There are a bunch of women on there that seem amazing."

"Have you met any of them?"

"Not yet. It's kind of intimidating."

"I bet. At the risk of sounding insensitive, are you really sure about this?"

"About what?"

"I don't know... uh... giving someone's panty hamster a tongue bath?"

"Why would you think that might sound insensitive?"

"I'm sorry. I'm not trying to be an asshole..."

"Really? Because you're succeeding. Wildly."

"I'm sorry."

"You've said that four times in almost as many sentences. Maybe you should just stop talking. In fact, you know, I'm gonna go."

"No! Eliza, wait."

"I gotta work early tomorrow, anyway."

"No! I wanna hear about The Licker Cabinet."

Eliza put a twenty on the bar.

"I'm not mad, okay. You don't understand and I'm just not in the mood."

"I'm sorry, Eliza. I really am. I'm just in Hell and taking it out on you."

"Eddie sucked," Eliza said, softening. "You know you can do so much better than that."

"No, I know. It's not him. I don't want to get into it but I'm in deep shit financially and it is stressing me out beyond belief and, as a result, I'm this completely miserable bitch just walking around being a douche to everyone."

"You are not a miserable douche. And I know how you feel. I took a ten percent pay cut last month."

"I know. And that sucks. But this is worse than that. I have no income at all. Unemployment is not even covering my minimum expenses and I am behind on my mortgage payments and, just, ugh. It's too much. Believe it or not, I even had fantasies of moving in with Eddie and living happily ever after."

"You liked him that much? I had no idea."

"No. I didn't. That's my point. I never thought Eddie was remotely a viable keeper. It's just, I'm afraid I'm going to lose my house. My career is gasping for breath. I'm facing a future that just looks like shades of darkness. No idea where I will live. No idea how I can pay for it. And I have decades of life left to pay for and I'm suddenly caught in the throes of middle age facing a ground up reconstruction of every element of my life. I could throw up just saying those words out loud. And then I look at you and I see you reinventing yourself and with such panache. I might make fun of you a lot but, I think, maybe I'm just jealous. So, bravo to you, Eliza. And I apologize for seeming so unsupportive. Sincerely. I'm sorry. And I support any version of you that makes you happy."

"Thank you. That means a lot. And if there is anything I can do to help you, even if it is just to be a sounding board, I'm here."

She offered help sincerely but in such an offhand manner, I knew instinctively that she had not really heard or believed the gravity of my situation. If she'd really heard me, she'd understand that there was nothing anybody could do. This was all on me. My choice, then, was to either relentlessly hammer into her how grave it actually was until I'd impressed upon her that she couldn't possibly save me—even if she wanted to—or just suck it up and move the fuck on. While the latter option left me feeling helpless, alienated and hopelessly disconnected from one of my closest friends, the former option would have left us both feeling that way. I decided to let Eliza off the hook. She hadn't caused my problems. It wasn't her job to even fully comprehend them, let alone fix them.

"Okay. Thanks," I said. "And I really do want a Licker-Cabinet T-shirt. You think you can make that happen?"

"Fuck you."

"Okay. Never hurts to ask."

THE FOLLOWING WEEKEND, Mack asked me to be her wingman at a shindig in Beverly Hills. The party was being hosted by a mutual actress friend, Kelly, and Kelly's agent was going to be in attendance. Mack wanted to meet this agent in a casual atmosphere and attempt to charm him into representing her. Free food and booze in Beverly Hills sounded good to me and I desperately needed distraction, so I agreed.

We arrived early and made a beeline for the bar. An hour later, we were feeling no pain and the house had filled up with guests. The crowd was made up mostly of people in their sixties and seventies, which was odd because Kelly was our age, but that did not stop either me or Mack from feeling altogether too comfortable. It was a nice change of pace to be the kids in the room and kinda fun to get so much appreciative attention from a crowd full of wealthy old men. Mack and I were good together at these sort of events because we were both able to survive alone in the room for stints and then reconvene to exchange notes without either of us ever feeling abandoned or responsible for the other one having a good time.

Three hours into the evening, I was hammered and hunkered down in a kitchen banquette with three older ladies who apparently all shared the same plastic surgeon. Their faces reminded me of the costumes once worn by acts like the Andrews Sisters: three ever so slightly altered versions of the same pattern. Tight, swollen and shiny was the theme here. We were discussing the differences between men and women.

"The defining difference," I proposed, "is that women would not be able to have an orgasm while raping a bleeding victim who was crying and begging them to stop."

The three women nodded and made "I never thought of it that way" sounds.

Encouraged, I continued.

"You know? I mean, what is that about? A vicious gang rape and all the guys have orgasms? I can't have an orgasm if the phone rings in the middle of… you know… whatever I'm doing."

"Don't you hate that?" Betty agreed enthusiastically. "But Chad always has to have that damned smart phone on the nightstand."

"You are awful!" Suzanne gasped and looked over her shoulder to see if anyone had heard Betty.

"What?" I asked, confused as to what Betty had said that had been controversial.

"Betty's husband's name isn't Chad. It's Herb," Dottie explained.

"God, I hate Herb," Betty said.

"Everybody hates Herb," Suzanne said.

Betty didn't argue, wrapped her store-bought Angelina Jolie lips around an electric cigarette and took a long drag. I waited for the faux cinder tip to go dark and for Betty to exhale the aerosol mist before I snatched it from her like we were sisters and took a hit myself. Exhaling, I handed it back to her while directing my attention to the other ladies. We were thick as thieves.

"You know what else gets me?" I said, leaning forward. "Funky ball musk."

"Oh! Don't get me started!" Dottie agreed and refilled Suzanne's glass from an open bottle of White Zinfandel on the table.

"What is funky ball musk?" Suzanne asked, eyes widening the minute amount that her infinity of Botox allowed.

"That is exactly my point!" I said and looked to Betty and Dottie for support. All three women were looking at me like I was preaching the Gospel.

Dottie downed her cognac like a shot and, without breaking eye contact with me across the table, held the empty glass up in the air as if there was a wait staff there to notice and refill her drink. Impatient for my answer, Suzanne got up and grabbed a bottle of Jack Daniels from a nearby counter and slammed it on the table in front of Dottie. Dottie poured herself a full snifter.

"What is funky ball musk?" Suzanne repeated, sotto voce.

"The fact that you do not know makes my point perfectly," I said, very self-satisfied. This was a fantastic party. "Funky ball musk is…"

I stopped talking as a terrifically handsome, if very conservative-looking, young man entered the room. He went to the fridge and got two beers.

"Go on…" Suzanne prodded.

Betty noticed me looking at the man who was now standing by the table.

"Oh, hi, Daniel. Daniel, you know Suzanne and Dottie. This is Ruby. Ruby, this is my grandson, Daniel."

"Hello, ladies. Looking lovelier than ever, I see! Nice to meet you, Ruby," he said and reached out to shake my hand. He pierced me with ice blue eyes and I actually blushed as I took his hand. There was something superior about the way he looked at me but not superior in a way that I found insulting. It was superior in a way that made me want to dirty him down to my level—old school in the sack.

"Daniel, now that you've met, get out of here. We are talking girl talk."

"I can see that. You all look very conspiratorial over here. Like a coven."

"Oh! Let's get a picture!" Suzanne blurted, fumbling through her purse. When she couldn't find her camera, Daniel pulled out his phone and took a shot of the four of us. There followed a drunken debate about how to distribute the photo amongst us all. Ultimately, Daniel texted it to me and I promised to email it to our hostess who would handle the rest of the distribution.

"Very nice to meet you, Ruby. And don't let these ladies get you into trouble," Daniel said, and I blushed again.

"Daniel! Get lost!" Betty shouted. Daniel winked at me and crossed paths with an approaching Mack as he rejoined the party in the rooms beyond.

"There you are! What are you guys talking about?" Mack asked, squeezing into the booth with us.

"Funky ball musk. Get us some more wine, will you? I'm parched," I said, finishing what had to have been my seventh glass of red.

Mack found a bottle of merlot on the counter and refilled our glasses. I took a healthy swig and continued.

"As I was saying, funky ball musk is that cellar smell of a guy's balls. All guys have it, some worse than others, unless they are freshly showered or doused in cologne," I added, thinking I sounded rather professorial.

"How do you know what their balls smell like?" Suzanne asked.

I blinked back at her uncomprehendingly.

"You smell it when you go down on them. You can smell it on your hands after a blowjob, too, especially if he is one of those guys that likes a lot of ball action," Mack explained.

"Does Herb like a lot of ball action, Betty?" Dottie asked and then guffawed loudly. Suzanne looked like she'd seen a ghost and sipped her wine.

"I'll have to ask his secretary," Betty replied.

Suzanne suppressed a spit-take with her hand and pink wine shot out her rhinoplastied nose. Once we got Suzanne cleaned up, I continued.

"The point is, all guys have funky ball musk but women, in aggregate, *do not talk about it.* Women are mature about such things," I added, willfully unaware of my own hypocrisy. "Men? No so much. If a guy makes a tuna joke, everyone in the world knows he is referencing stinky pussy. Our whole culture accepts this ridiculous, chick-hating myth that women's twats smell like fish. Douches? *Strawberry* douches? Really? And those vaginal deodorant sprays with ads like, 'I found out the hard way that not all feminine sprays are the same.' The hard way? How? By walking into a crowded room and having it part like the Red Sea because of her banky hanky stanky panky? I've never heard someone say, *Hey! Who's dirty vaj is ruining my bridal shower*?"

Nobody had anything to say to that so we all sat and sipped our drinks.

"So, wait. Do you guys all give blowjobs?" Suzanne asked the table in disbelief.

"Not to Herb," Betty replied and put her palm out to Dottie who promptly gave her some skin.

"Blowjobs come standard," Mack added.

"She once gave a forty-five minute blowjob to a limp dick," I told the table.

"Forty-five minutes? Why didn't he give you the tap?" Dottie asked, disgusted.

Mack shook her head and shrugged.

I turned to Suzanne. "You don't give blowjobs?"

"Not after marriage. That is just something you do to get them to buy you a ring," she said matter-of-factly.

Mack and I cracked up but stopped when we realized nobody else was laughing. Then, in unison, Dottie and Betty pointed to their crotches and said, "You can put it here," then they pointed to their asses and said, "You can put it here," then they pointed to their ears enthusiastically and added in sing-song, "You can put it heeere, but you can't put it *here*," and they pointed inside their mouths, shaking their heads no. This was obviously a regular joke between them.

"Shut up!" Suzanne insisted and finished her wine.

"Suzanne! You take it in the butt but you won't suck a dick?" Mack asked, stunned.

Suzanne's throat turned red but the skin on her face must have been pulled too tight for the blood flow to reach there. Her face remained a taut, white mask.

"That's crazy!" Mack squealed, delighted.

"Don't knock it if you ain't tried it," Suzanne said peevishly.

"Ooo! You got some sass, girl!" I said, impressed, and refilled Suzanne's wine.

"All I'm saying is, I am not the prude everyone thinks I am, just because I don't want hot mucous squirting into my mouth and pubes in my teeth."

That was a sobering thought and it silenced the table. I elbowed Betty and she reflexively handed me her electric cigarette. I took a drag and looked around at everyone as they reflected upon Suzanne's words. Their expressions suggested they had just discovered fresh road kill on the table between us.

"That was really gross, Suzanne," Betty finally said.

"Have you ever noticed that scrotum skin can move all by itself" Mack inquired.

"What do you mean?" Dottie asked.

"If you stay really still and just stare at a guy's balls, you will see the skin creeping all around and getting smooth or all pachydermy and his nuts move, too. Like a fleshy lava lamp."

"Chad is uncircumcised!" Betty blurted out as if she was sharing the exciting news that she'd just gotten engaged.

"That is disgusting," Dottie said.

"I don't mind it. I think it makes him seem exotic."

"He is exotic, Betty. He is from fucking Malaysia," Dottie scoffed.

"Minnesota, Dottie. And I don't believe in unnecessary surgery. It isn't natural."

"Right, Joan Rivers," Dottie said with heavy sarcasm and drained her Jack Daniels.

As the ladies bickered, Mack and I excused ourselves, pretending to need the restroom.

"Whattaya say? Should we get out of here? I'm pretty drunk," I stated and took a giant swig of wine.

"I'm ready, too. And I gotta drive. Let's find Kelly and say thank you."

We walked around the house looking for Kelly, refilled our glasses at the bar and said flamboyant goodbyes to everyone we passed. Unable to find Kelly, we stood at the door and Mack called out, "Kelly! Wherever you are, thanks for a great party and bye-bye!"

We stumbled down the hill to Mack's car, got in and headed home.

Driving downhill, Mack said, "I can't believe he actually showed up."

"Who, that agent guy?"

"No. Dash Riprock."

Now, in reality, she had named an A-list movie star that had been an A-list movie star for more than thirty years. Oscar-winner, larger than life, big time movie star. I will call him Dash Riprock for expediency.

"Dash Riprock? Dash Riprock was at that party?"

"Totally. Kelly told me he would be, but I didn't believe her."

"What the fuck, Mack? I love Dash Riprock. I have always loved Dash Riprock. Dash Riprock is part of why I even wanted to be an actress. I can't believe I didn't see him. Why didn't you tell me?"

"I'm sorry. I thought for sure you saw him. It is a tiny house."

"Turn the car around."

"What?"

"Turn this fucking car around. We are going back there!" I shouted.

"What? Really?"

"Heck to the yeah, really! I want to meet Dash Riprock!"

"Okay, but this is so unlike you," Mack laughed as she banged a U-turn.

"I know, but there are three people in the world that I would go back for. Tom Waits, Elvis Costello and Dash Riprock. Well, and Justin…"

"Townes Earle," she interrupted. "I know."

"For forty years I've been waiting to meet one of my heroes. We are going back, sistah!" I said and laughed excitedly.

"Forty years? I thought you were thirty-eight."

"What's with the third degree, Sherlock?"

"What?"

"What?"

"Oh, right," Mack nodded, as if anything had been said or cleared up. God bless alcohol. "But what are we going to say? We made such a big deal about leaving. Everyone will ask us why we are back."

"Shit. You're right. Fuck. What do we say?"

I was too drunk to think anything except, *I'm gonna meet Dash Riprock*!

"Oh! I'll say I lost an earring!" Mack suggested as we pulled up in front of the house again.

"Perfect! That is perfect. Okay, so, take out one of your earrings and let's get'r done!"

She removed an earring, dropped it into the console and we re-entered the party. Immediately upon walking in, Betty asked us why we had returned.

Dottie approached, too. "Hey, I thought you'd left. Where are your drinks?"

"I'll take a glass of red..." I said to Dottie and I looked to Mack for her order. She nodded agreement. "We did leave but before we got to the bottom of the hill, Mack realized she's lost an earring," I continued.

"Oh, dear. What kind of earring is it?" Betty asked.

Mack showed them her other earring, revealing to all of us, myself included, what sort of earring had been lost. It was a three-karat diamond stud.

"My dad gave me these earrings on my sixteenth birthday," Mack explained, laying it on thick. She looked at me for approval. I immediately regretted our plan.

"Oh, no!" Dottie exclaimed and started clapping her hands to get the attention of every party guest. "Everybody! Everybody! Mack here has lost a beautiful diamond earring! We have to help her find it!"

Dottie forgot all about our drinks. The party came to a halt so abruptly, I actually heard an imaginary needle drag along the vinyl of an imaginary record. The lights were turned up completely and virtually every guest dropped to their knees in the hunt for Mack's errant jewel.

"What's happening? Are the police here?" Kelly asked as she came downstairs to find the party at a standstill. "Why is everybody crawling around on the floor?"

"Mack lost an earring," I told her. "A huge Elizabeth Taylor diamond," I added, disgusted by what we had started. I looked across the room at Mack and saw her crying, actually crying, as she explained to three older men in suits the emotional significance of her loss. One of them was rubbing her back soothingly and another said he was off to fetch her a glass of water.

"Oh, thanks, Herb! But a merlot will be fine," she sniffled after him.

I got on my hands and knees, picked through a shag carpet and wondered how Mack could not have known that her diamond stud would cause this drama. I was wearing plastic beaded earrings from Fashion 21. Had I known what she was going to pretend to have misplaced, I would have been the one to feign the loss. After what felt like thirty years of futile searching, I got up and went over to Mack.

"They mean so much to me," she was saying as she sipped her wine. She'd stopped crying. Six old men standing around her were rapt. "My daddy bought me the earrings and my mom got me this boob job. They look almost as real as my diamonds are, huh?" she asked and corrected her posture to enhance her breasts.

"Mack," I interrupted. "Excuse me, gentlemen, but can I steal her away from you for just a moment?"

"Only if you promise to bring her right back," one quipped. There was some other muttering but I wasn't listening.

I grabbed Mack's arm and pulled her away from her admirers.

"Mack? What the fuck? Why didn't you tell me your earrings were valuable?"

"I thought that was the whole point."

"Any stupid earring would have been a god enough excuse to come back. Now look," I said and gestured around the house. It looked like *Meerkat Manor* in there with people scuttling around foraging and, occasionally, one person rising upright on their knees to check on the general progress only to drop back down to search through shag fibers. "It's like a monkey grooming ritual in there!"

"I know! Aren't they sweet?" she said, admiring the workers and sipping her wine.

I grabbed the wine out of her hand and drank some as our hostess approached us.

"Mack! I just feel awful," Kelly said and I saw her eyes well up. "I lost an earring similar to that once, too. And it was a gift from your father? Honestly, I am just sick."

"We'll find it, don't worry," I said.

"No. I insist. Take this," she said and pressed something into Mack's hand. *Probably a Valium*, I thought. This thing was spiraling way out of control.

Mack looked in her hand and said, "No, no, Kelly! I can't accept this."

I thanked God that Mack had the sense not to add prescription drug abuse to our list of mistakes tonight.

"Take it. I insist. I never found my other earring so that thing does me no good. I insist that you keep it."

I looked at the thing in Mack's hand. OMG. Kelly was giving Mack a huge diamond earring. We were now stealing the hostess's jewelry!

"NO! No! Kelly! Mack, give that back!" I said and took the stud from Mack and pressed it back into Kelly's palm. "Mack probably never had the earring on tonight at all. She was running late when I went by her house and I hurried her. Her earring is probably on her dressing table right now."

"Well, why not take this one just in case?" Kelly said to Mack.

"No," I insisted. "Why don't we check Mack's house first?" *Or the console of her fucking car*, I thought. "And if we can't find it, then Mack can… take your earring."

"Only if you are *sure*, Mack." Kelly was genuinely upset.

Mack agreed to my plan; we called off the search. The music went back up and the lights came back down.

"Seriously, Mack. Let's get out of here before we break something," I said as Mack opened the front door for us to make our final departure. I stepped over the threshold and, in my haste to escape the premises, literally walked directly into Dash Riprock. My boobs smashed against his chest and I bounced back.

"Whoa! Where are you ladies going so fast?" he asked, smiling.

I have no recollection of the next two minutes or so. There was the roaring sound of static in my ears as I engaged, Mack later told me, in a wise alec banter with Dash Riprock. Apparently, Dash and I were zinging each other fast and furious until Kelly appeared behind me at the door.

"Okay, you two. Break it up. This is a friendly party." She then took me by my shoulders, turned me away from Dash Riprock and led me back into the house.

"Mack. I can die now. My life has fulfilled its purpose."

"That was amazing! I think he likes you! You were so funny!"

"Great. I was? Great. Okay, let's go."

"What? You don't want to stay and hang around with Dash Riprock more?"

"Nope. That was all I wanted. I can't remember any of it but I have never felt more complete in my life. We can go," I said, lost in a hazy dream state.

"Okay, but I gotta pee. Wait here so I can find you. I am going upstairs real quick," she said and left.

I stood leaning against the railing tingling with gratification, I heard someone say, "Where'd your friend go?"

It was Dash Riprock, grinning wickedly.

"Uh… what?"

"Where'd your friend go?"

He kept smiling at me as if his teeth were in the act of hypnotizing me.

"She um… went upstairs to… um… the bathroom," I said, slowly coming to.

"Let's go out to my car."

What?

"What?" I said, ever the wit.

"Let's go out to my car for twenty minutes," he said and smiled at me more broadly.

"Your car? Why?" I asked and tried to keep my eyes away from his mouth, lest I be caught in a trance.

"Let's just go. Twenty minutes," he said, in that casual, seductive tone one uses trying to talk a jumper off of a bridge. His manner suggested I was in more danger not going to his car for twenty minutes than I was in following my own impulses.

"Twenty minutes? Your car? Why would I go to your car for twenty minutes?"

"Come on," he said and gestured toward the door.

The door was the river Styx. This was certainly Hades himself, beckoning me to my destruction.

I looked up the staircase where Mack had disappeared and then back to Dash Riprock.

"Um… but… what… why… twenty minutes? Your car?"

"Your friend is fine. Let's go." He reached his hand out to me.

"But to your car? I don't understand," I said, staring at his hand, his palm upward, fingers curled in invitation.

"Well, where do you want to go?" he asked.

"Um…"

"We can go anywhere you want. You name it," he said, and smiled a closed lip smile, lowering his chin and peering at me from beneath his brow.

I looked back up the stairs.

"Your friend is a big girl. She can find a ride home," he said.

"No, but, well, she drove. We came in her car…" I protested, weakening.

"Then you don't have to worry. Where do you want to go?" he said with his James Earl Jones baritone and total confidence. He'd sensed the crack in my resolve. No more need to hard sell. That might only scare me away.

"Anywhere you want. You tell me," he offered casually.

How bad could Hell be? Lots of fun people had to be there. Sure, they had herpes sores and hangovers, but they'd had fun getting them, right?

"Um, I don't know but I can tell you something..."

He smiled. He had me. He knew it. He made a rolling gesture with his hand, urging me to continue.

"I can tell you that... wherever we go... I am going to need a drink..."

Nodding accompanied his hand rolling now.

"...I am going to need to *like* you..."

No change from him.

"...and I am definitely going to need more than twenty minutes."

He laughed. He'd closed the deal and on terms far less favorable to me than he had been prepared to accept.

I looked up the stairs for Mack. I am a firm believer in the "dance with the one that brung you" philosophy and I had never left anyplace with a guy I'd just met in my entire life. Was that twenty minute thing somehow about a blowjob? A scenario flashed in my mind where Dash Riprock demanded a blowjob in his car and, enraged by my refusal, spat at me, "Why do you think I brought you out here? Because I *liked* you? What are you? Twelve?"

I looked back at Dash Riprock and, before I could speak, Kelly was upon us again.

"What did I tell you two? Break it up. This is a friendly party!" and this time she took Dash Riprock by the arm and led him away.

"Okay, you ready to go?" Mack asked.

"Oh, thank God you are back! Have I got a story to tell you! Let's go."

"YOU HAD A CHANCE to blow Dash Riprock and you didn't do it?!" Kate practically squealed into the phone the next day.

"I know. Part of me wanted to just for the story, you know? But the whole twenty minutes thing just made it seem so cheap."

"Darlin', blowing an old man in his car just because he is famous is pretty much as cheap as you get. The twenty minute thing is just icing on the cake. He was, at least, being upfront about it. I might have even taken him up on it. That man is a legend."

"You are probably right. About the twenty minutes. But it just gave me no room for plausible deniability, no way to kid myself it was anything but an act of prostitution. An act of prostitution leaving me hacking grey pubic hair like a fur ball and without the satisfying jingle of payday coins in my pocket as I did the walk of shame back to Mack. I choked. I understand if you are disappointed in me."

"Any movement on work?" she asked, changing the subject.

"No. At this point, I'm waiting for the sheriff to come padlock my front door."

"Anything we can do?"

"No, thanks, and I can't talk about it, okay?"

"Okay. Just remember that Wayne and I are out here and I meant my offer to stay with us. And we love you."

"I know. Thanks. I love you guys, too," I said and we hung up.

As soon as I hung up with Kate, I got a call from my agent, Kim, to tell me that that movie I'd done a small part in last year, *Getting High School*, was finally being released. One of the young actors in it had gotten famous in the interim and the producers decided to capitalize on his new success. There would be a big premiere in a month and Kim thought it would be good for me to be seen on the red carpet.

"So, you have a few weeks to get into extra good shape," she said. I heard the silent "fatso" loud and clear. I also heard the mailman slamming my mailbox shut. I hung up with Kim and went outside to find what new devastation the postal system may have just delivered to my door.

One piece of mail. It was from the unemployment office. I opened it hoping, expecting really, to see that I had been approved for the first tier of benefit extensions. I had been collecting nearly the maximum allowed for the previous twenty-six weeks based on a rare and lucky residual check I had received in the applicable base period. As expected, my claim was being continued but my award had dropped from a life-saving four hundred twenty-five dollars a week down to fifty-nine. Instant panic attack. I sat down and tried to calm my racing heart as I stared at the dollar amount, as if staring at the fifty-nine long enough would transform it into a four twenty-five. It didn't. Then I noticed a strange detail. The stub said that the claim had expired more than two years ago. My most recent claim had only been open nine months. So it was an error. This eased my mounting panic considerably. It was just a matter of calling the EDD and clearing up the mistake. I took a Xanax, got a beer from the fridge and sat down to begin the process of trying to actually get through to a human. After four hours of dialing and dutifully punching numbers and making selections, I only ever got as far as the recording which said something to this effect: "Due to an unusually high call volume and the number of callers already on hold, we are unable to take your call. Please try again later. Goodbye."—at which point the call got terminated, whether I liked it or not. Finally, at five o'clock, the message announced that the unemployment office was closed.

After an interminably long night of fitful sleep and nightmares about debtors' prison, I sat with my coffee poised to call EDD at 7:58 AM. I had to get through and clear up this error as soon as was humanly possible. The difference between seventeen hundred dollars a month and two hundred thirty-six dollars was the difference between me being able to eat or not. The seventeen hundred didn't even cover the minimum payments on my credit cards and my other monthly expenses, but it sure helped a lot. Two hundred dollars was almost useless.

My first attempt at calling resulted in a message telling me the EDD wasn't open. My very next call, a call that connected at exactly eight o'clock, got me the same message I had gotten for four hours the day before: "Due to an unusually high call volume and the number of callers already on hold, we are unable to take your call. Please try again later. Goodbye."

How could there already be so many people on hold that I could not join their ranks at the stroke of 8 AM? Infuriated, I redialed a dozen more times, sometimes being told immediately that call volume was too high and subsequently hung up upon, sometimes being asked to jump through a series of hoops before I got the same result. I wanted to beat myself to death with the phone.

I Googled the question, "How do I get a live person at EDD?" There were several dozen responses. I tried the one that most people seemed to have the best luck with. It involved pressing the number to check the amount of your last check and then, after a few more steps, they actually gave you the option to speak to an agent. Ten minutes later, a voice asked how they could help me.

Twenty minutes later, I held onto the phone, devastated. Apparently, some three-year-old claim with an award amount of fifty-nine dollars a week had already launched some process of the tiered extensions. I don't know. There was a lot of tersely stated information given to me that the roaring terror in my ears kept me from hearing adequately. What I did hear and was trying to confirm was that my unemployment insurance checks were going to be reduced to fifty-nine dollars a week.

"So, you are telling me that I have to live on fifty-nine dollars a week for the next year?"

"I'm not telling you that."

"Didn't you just say that you were going to reduce my checks to fifty-nine dollars?"

"I'm not reducing anything. Your award claim is based on..."

"Okay," I said, cutting her off. "My checks will now be fifty-nine dollars a week. For, approximately, the next year?"

"Not necessarily."

"What do you mean?"

A deep sigh of disgust from the other end of the line. I could feel her contempt and her utter lack of sympathy for me and I started to cry.

"How am I supposed to live on fifty-nine dollars a week?"

"Nobody is suggesting you do that," she answered.

"I don't follow..." I said, and sucked back my tears, expecting another more reasonable option. "What can I do?"

"Well, you could get a *job*."

If I could have crawled through the phone and killed this fucker, I would have.

"That's helpful advice. Thanks. Can you tell me why, if I had an open claim with an active extension, I haven't been getting the fifty-nine dollars a week for the last year or two or whatever?"

"You stopped returning the forms."

I looked into my file for that year and found a copy of the last check they'd sent me. It was dated the exact same day that my new stub indicated that claim had expired.

"I wouldn't have not returned them if you had sent them. As ridiculous as fifty-nine dollars is as something to try to live on, I certainly wouldn't have refused it."

"Why didn't you call us and ask where your continued claim forms were?"

"Probably because the last check I got was dated the same day as the claim expired. I probably thought I'd exhausted all my benefits."

Silence.

"It isn't fair that I am being punished now for not taking this money all along. Had I taken it, I would have had all that money and would have already exhausted all the tiers. I would now be eligible to file extensions on the four twenty-five award. I am being punished for a stupid mistake."

"It isn't a mistake. You should have returned the forms."

"YOU NEVER SENT THE FORMS!"

"Look, what resolution are you hoping for at the end of this call?"

"That I get my extensions at four twenty-five a week, not fifty-nine."

"Well, that's just not going to happen," she said, in the most patronizing tone imaginable. "So can I help you with anything else?"

"You haven't helped me at all. You are ruining my life. I am definitely going to lose my house now, because of this."

"Sorry to hear that. You should have called and..."

"Oh, go fuck yourself!" I screamed, cutting her off, and pressed the "end call" button with as much righteous fury as the world has ever seen. It was wildly unsatisfying.

I sat staring at the Google Chrome homepage for what felt like hours. Pandemonium and buzzing and a mishmash of half thoughts and suicidal fantasies occupied my mind until, finally, I burst into tears. A few minutes later, completely exhausted, I got up, washed my face and took my final Xanax. I then did the Thalidomide shuffle into my garage, got into the car and headed to Rite-Aid.

At Rite-Aid, too numb to worry about sounding like the pharming degenerate I knew I'd become, I asked the pharmacist for a refill of my benzo script. Apparently, a refill required approval from my doctor. I didn't have time to wait for an appointment and I couldn't afford to go to the doctor, anyway. I then asked if there was anything available over the counter to help me deal with the near-constant anxiety attacks I was having. She suggested some herbal and homeopathic stuff and pointed me in the direction of that aisle. I walked the walk of the undead over there and stood staring, uncomprehendingly, at the vast array of overpriced bullshit. Eventually, an employee stopped and asked if I needed help. I was flooded with gratitude and repeated—eyes welling up, chin quivering—the names of the things the pharmacist had suggested. The clerk must have sensed I was on the verge of a nervous breakdown. She collected the items I'd listed unnaturally slowly, as if not wanting to spook me with any sudden movements. She spoke to me in that soothing voice used for people on their deathbed or on the ledge of a high rise and then eased me toward the checkout stands. At the front of the store, I stood looking at all the self-serve registers with what must have been a completely helpless expression. The clerk offered to ring my items through for me and I let her, handing her my customer card to scan or my credit card, whatever it was she asked for in the sequence she requested it.

While she did that, my eyes wandered to a sign reading "Now Hiring" on the front doors.

"Excuse me, are you guys hiring?" I asked dully.

"I'm sorry?" she said as she bagged my items.

"The sign on the door says you are hiring. Can I apply for a job?"

She looked at me and, deciding I was joking, laughed. When I didn't join her, she looked embarrassed.

"I'm sorry. You want to apply for the stockroom job?"

"Yes, if I can."

"Okay. Yeah. Um. Let me get you an application," she said and headed toward the back somewhere.

A few minutes later, a sixty-ish, balding man approached me with papers in his hands.

"Did you want to apply for the stockroom job?" he asked from a few aisles away. As he got closer and could make out my face, his expression changed.

I must look seriously shell-shocked, I thought. *Everyone thinks I'm crazy.* I tried to adopt a saner expression and adjusted my posture to something I imagined looked more respectable.

Uh-oh! Maybe I have something on my face or hanging out of my nose, I suddenly thought. As a precaution, I wiped at the corners of my mouth and ran my sleeve across my nose.

"Yeah. If that is okay," I said, but I looked at the ground when I spoke to keep him from seeing anything on my face I might have missed. "I definitely need a job. Definitely need a job," I repeated, channeling Rain Man.

"Yeah, sure," he replied, hesitantly.

I risked peeking up at him for a second. He looked openly confused. His nametag read, "Jimbo—Manager."

"Why don't you follow me over to the photo center?" Jimbo suggested. "You can use the counter over there to fill out the application."

I nodded agreement and, as he turned away for me to follow, I wiped at my nose and mouth again. He sensed my motion and turned to look at me. His expression was one of wariness. Was he afraid I was going to attack him from behind? I decided to minimize any further unnecessary gestures or words, in an effort to come off as more enigmatic than psychotic.

At the photo center, I put my bag of homeopathic sedatives on the counter and took the application and pen Jimbo offered me. Jimbo stepped back a bit as I began filling out the paperwork. I could feel his eyes boring into me. I felt like Anthony Perkins at the end of *Psycho*, trying to act innocent for the suspicious viewers he feared were monitoring his movements.

"So, do you have any retail experience?" Jimbo asked, after several minutes of silent observation.

"A little. A long time ago," I mumbled, without looking up. I was fixated on the "previous experience" and "references" sections of the application. What could I put there? I hadn't had a real job in twenty years. No place I'd ever worked was still in business. Feeling Jimbo watching me, I pretended to fill those sections in by simply squiggling the pen just above the paper. That couldn't possibly do anything to deepen Jimbo's impression that I was a lunatic, escaped from an asylum.

"Have you any experience pricing things and stocking shelves?"

I shook my head no and kept my eyes on the application and continued my pretend writing.

"I'm sorry. This might sound crazy but... are you an actress?"

I looked up at him then and, misunderstanding what he meant, said, "No. I'm really filling this in. See?" I said and waved the application back and forth in front of him so he couldn't see that most of it was still blank. "See? I'm not crazy," I said and resumed filling out the application, or more accurately, began looking for a question on it for which I had a relevant answer.

I snuck another peek at Jimbo. He looked distinctly uncomfortable. He shifted his weight. My panic attack announced its return.

"No. I mean, aren't you an actress? Like, on TV?"

I stopped writing then and looked up at him, heart slowing.

"Oh. Yeah. Yes, I am."

"So? What? Are you doing this for a role or something? Are you doing a character?"

"No."

"You can tell me. I can keep a secret," he said and smiled conspiratorially.

"No. I really need a job."

"Oooh. Okay. I gotcha," he said and winked at me.

"No. Really. I need a job."

"Okay," Jimbo said, not even trying to hide that he didn't believe me. "Let's see whatcha got so far on that application."

Smiling, he reached out and tried to slide the application away from me. My heart began racing again. I didn't want him to see that I hadn't filled out anything beyond my name and address. I pressed my hand down to hold the paper in place. Jimbo pulled a little harder. I resisted by putting even more weight on the application. Now, I really was acting crazy and I knew it. The third time Jimbo pulled, I let him have it.

Jimbo slid the application away and looked at me with a confused, "What the Hell is wrong with you?" shake of his head, but he was still smiling. His smile faded as he reviewed what I'd written.

"Is this a joke?"

"No. I just haven't had a real job in so long, there isn't anything I can put on there that will help you determine if I am a good candidate to be a stock clerk. Can I ask you what it pays, by the way?"

"It is a part-time position. Twenty-hour week at minimum wage."

"Oh," I said. That didn't sound very promising. "What's minimum wage nowadays?"

"Eight bucks."

Eight bucks? That would be a hundred and sixty dollars a week. Before taxes.

"Really? That's it? Eight bucks? How do people live?"

"Not the kind of money you actors are used to making, eh?" Jimbo said, smiling again. He was certain, now, that I was just there researching a role.

"You'd be surprised."

"I bet!" Jimbo laughed, misunderstanding. "Well, okay..." Jimbo said, looking down at my application for my name, "...Ruby. Whattaya say I just keep this application on file here and if a job comes up that pays the big bucks, I'll give you a call."

Jimbo winked at me again. There was nothing I could do but agree with him, grab my bag and do the zombie-walk of total defeat back out to my car.

"So, I gotta lose twenty pounds and come up with about ten grand in the next four weeks," I said to Eliza and Mack at the Frolic Room, and then shoved a fried potato taco into my mouth whole.

"Shut up. You look great!" Eliza said and sipped her Guinness. She tried to suppress a grimace as she fought her gag reflex and I took the opportunity to ogle what she was wearing: jodhpurs, an ornate, boned vest that cinched her waist to wasp-like proportions, a turquoise, silk ascot, a tuxedo jacket with tails and what appeared to be a leather pilot helmet from the Wright brothers' era. Some antique-looking metal instrument was hanging from her heavy belt. "What do you need ten thousand dollars for?"

I realized I was in no mood to try again to explain my total, financial devastation to Eliza and Mack. Neither of them had ever had a single moment of real money woes. They each had steady income and, more importantly, rich parents that could and would bail them out if they had even the slightest situation on their hands. I knew that even if I told them every gory detail of my months-overdue mortgage and my towering credit card debt and my radically reduced unemployment and my total unhirability in both the theatrical and retail worlds, they still wouldn't experience the heart-racing panic I felt every day. They wouldn't even begin to understand the total life crisis terror I felt even thinking about how to word my predicament to them. Moreover, even if I could get them to grasp it, there was nothing either of them could do to relieve it. And I realized that, right then, in that moment, I resented them for that.

"Eliza, I feel I must comment on this stunning ensemble in which you are garbed tonight. You look like Adam Ant and Amelia Earhart had a kid," I said with the faintest hint of edge in my tone. I couldn't afford to buy bananas and this chick was a one-woman *Project Runway* gone whimsically amuck.

"Fuck you," she said, not hearing my tone, and unconsciously pushing her offensive pint of beer a few inches away.

"If you don't like Guinness, why are you drinking it?" I asked more pointedly than the question could possibly warrant.

Eliza just stared at me.

"What? Is that a 'thing,' now? Drinking guy beer or something?"

She definitely heard the attitude in my voice that time but, likely, hadn't guessed at its correct source. Eliza checked the time on a chained pocket watch she pulled from a breast pocket. This was a subtle way of warning me that my time allotment for being an asshole was rapidly ticking away. I was undeterred.

"I had no idea the vagitarians had broadened out so much from the flannels and Birkenstocks of yesteryear," I said, making grand hand gestures meant to direct everyone's attention to her attire. Everyone, including Eliza and Mack, ignored my display.

"Lesbians are into Birkenstocks?" Mack asked me through a mouth full of chicken taco.

"I don't know. I think so. Weren't they? Or am I thinking of hippies?"

"What is this look called, Eliza?" Mack asked and wiped her mouth with a tiny bar napkin.

"Steampunk. It's called steampunk," Eliza said, and then looked at me, her eyes stern and full of challenge.

"Hot Topic must have seen you coming. How much money have you spent on costumes in the last few months?" I asked.

"Costumes?"

"Okay, outfits?"

"Look, can we not talk about my clothing?"

"Okay! Let's talk about mine," Mack suggested. "Do these pants give me camel toe?"

Mack stepped away for us to examine her.

"Not exactly," I said, having given her pie at the Y a cursory glance.

"Not exactly?"

"Well, not camel toe…" Eliza said.

"But we can see your vulva cleavage and you are dressing left," I said, finishing Eliza's thought.

"Really?" Mack said and bent to investigate. "Wait, the vulva is on the inside."

"No. Your vulva is all the junk on the outside. We have had this conversation a thousand times."

"You have had *this* conversation a thousand times?" Eliza asked and cracked up.

"Yes, and I would like to put it to bed once and for all. Mack, the vulva is on the outside. Right, Eliza?"

"I don't think so. I looked it up and I am right," Mack insisted.

"Okay, so what do you call that thing you made us look at just now?"

"My honey pot," Mack replied in a baby voice.

"Oh, I stand corrected. 'Honey pot' *is* the technical term. My mistake."

"I didn't say that," Mack protested, but she was cut off by a text coming in for me. It was from an unknown number but it was a picture of me and the plastic surgery trio in the kitchen at the party of lost earring fame.

"This must be from Daniel!" I announced excitedly.

"Who's Daniel?" the girls asked in stereo.

"Daniel was the guy we met at that Dash Riprock party, Mack. He was really cute," I said, happy for a change of topic.

"Oh, right! The guy in the sweater vest. Text him back," Mack said.

"What do I say?"

"Invite him to join us here."

"Now? Really?"

"Yes!" they said, again in stereo.

8 Teen jesus

THIRTY MINUTES LATER, Daniel walked into the Frolic Room. He was even cuter than I remembered. He looked like one would if a young Billy Baldwin and an even younger Colin Farrell had had a son. Dark hair, pale skin and incredible, judgmental blue eyes.

Daniel introduced himself to Eliza and Mack, kissed my cheek hello and ordered a Manhattan. Drink in hand, he fixed me with those peepers and I felt it again. I felt the bizarre urge to defile him. I'd never understood Howard Stern's freaky fantasy about fucking Kathy Lee Gifford but sitting there looking at king of the preppies and basking in his superior air, it all began to make sense.

Daniel seemed at ease being in a bar with three women he hardly knew. The girls were grilling him and he answered every question with casual confidence.

"A Manhattan? That's an old man's drink. How old are you, Daniel?"

"Twenty-eight."

Twenty-eight. Ugh. I was a lot older than him. I felt a twinge of shame for having dirty thoughts about him.

"Where are you from, Daniel?"

"Arizona."

"What do you do?"

"I am a director of photography and camera operator."

"Do you know that Dash Riprock wanted Ruby to blow him in his car at that party?" Mack asked.

"No. I did not know that. How did that work out for you?" he asked and looked at me over his glass as he drained his cocktail.

"I didn't do it!" Suddenly, it was important that he have a high opinion of me. "He kept asking me to go to his car for twenty minutes and he wouldn't say why."

"He wanted a blowjob, right, Daniel?" Mack asked.

"I'd say so," Daniel replied and then ordered another Manhattan. "That wasn't very gentlemanly of him. You deserve more respect than that."

I felt myself beaming at him in response to his compliment. *He thinks I deserve respect*, I thought, oddly giddy.

Daniel asked me and Mack and Eliza various biographical details and the evening went by smoothly. He was a small guy, probably only five foot six. I've always had a weakness for the short guys, no idea why, despite the fact that they just make me look bigger by comparison. He was probably under a hundred and fifty pounds and he had a low and soothing, deep voice. By the time Daniel ordered his fifth Manhattan, his thigh was pressed against mine under the bar. I couldn't tell if it was intentional or if he was even aware it was there, but the contact electrified me. I could feel the muscle in his thigh and the body heat seeping through his chinos made me break out into a sweat.

"Well," I said, wiping my forehead with a cocktail napkin, "it's getting late. We should probably call it a night."

Daniel confessed to an early call time and we all agreed it was time to go. We paid for our drinks and headed out the door. By chance, Daniel's car was parked in the same direction as mine so we said our goodbyes to Eliza and Mack and they headed off in the opposite direction.

As we approached my car, I began to get butterflies. Why did this kid have such a strange effect on me? He was so buttoned down and so not my type but he made me feel nervous and girlish in a way I hadn't felt in a very long time. He watched me get into my truck and stood at the driver's window.

"I had fun. Thanks for inviting me out," he said and stared deeply into my eyes.

"Of course. I'm glad you could join us," I said, unable to tear my eyes from his. A tingling sensation started at the top of my head and trickled down my body like the dried beans in a rain stick.

"I'd really like to see you again," he said and stared at me even more intently.

As if hypnotized by his gaze, I mumbled, "Okay," and stared back at him powerlessly. I was so lost in his eyes that I didn't notice him leaning in. I jumped when his hands cupped my face and froze as he planted a soft, warm kiss on my closed mouth. He held it for three seconds and stepped back. I was finished.

"Good. I'd like that. A lot. I'll call you tomorrow. Okay?"

I nodded yes and watched him walk around the corner to his car.

"What the fuck just happened?" I asked myself aloud, and drove home on cloud nine.

True to his word, Daniel called the next morning and we made plans to meet at a local bar for happy hour. I was too nervous to meet him alone, so I invited Mack. Daniel showed up dressed like a Congressional page and, for some reason, that struck me as super sexy. Several drinks in, I compared notes with Mack in the ladies' room.

"I can't take it Mack. I just want to throw him down and rape him on the floor out there."

"Yeah, I don't get it. He is kinda nerdy."

"I know! I don't know why he affects me like he does. It makes no sense."

"You went five years without having sex and then had sex with Devonevans and his giant yam bag once and a caveman experience with Eddie Flagon. At least Daniel is pretty to look at."

"Pretty is exactly the right word. He is pretty, isn't he?"

Validated, I followed Mack back out to Daniel.

We chatted and drank and ordered appetizers and drank and then we drank some more. By eight o'clock, we were all hammered and I couldn't even let myself think about the amount of money I'd just spent. Mack suggested we go to a nearby nightclub and dance off some of our buzz.

"All the doormen are ex-models. I know them from my modeling days in Milan. They will totally let us in."

This was a critical element to the plan. The last time I had tried to take an out-of-town girlfriend to a local hotspot, the bouncers refused us entry at the first two joints and we had to do the walk of shame away from the door. The third time, we were turned away by the valet before we had even gotten out of the car. If you are over thirty, it is harder to get into a Hollywood nightclub that it is for a high school dropout to get into Princeton.

I was drunk enough that this dancing thing sounded like a good idea. Daniel didn't object so we caravanned the few blocks to Venus Envy.

As it happened, Mack did know the doorman and he did let us in, and for free. Because it was so early, we were among only a small handful of other patrons. Daniel ordered a Manhattan and stationed himself at the bar while Mack and I danced to what seemed to be five hundred versions of "Rhythm Is a Dancer" in an endless loop. I hoped that the moves I was busting out there looked young and sexy and not like I was sweating to the oldies or suffering some rare form of rhythm dyslexia. Occasionally, I would go to the bar to check in on Daniel or to get myself some water. I noticed

Daniel talking to another guy at one point and then they disappeared into the men's room. We he came back to his seat at the bar, I approached him while Mack went to the ladies' room.

"Was that someone you know?" I asked.

"No, I don't know him, but I just scored two hits of E and some coke. Do you want a bump?"

I have never done cocaine in my life. Sniffing drugs always seemed a degrading and desperate way to get high and the whole "you can know I have these drugs but don't tell so and so" always struck me as criminally antisocial.

"No, thanks. I'm trying to cut back," I said, hoping to sound cool and open-minded and not parental.

"I took a hit of E about an hour ago. Want one?"

It was then I noticed his saucered pupils. Were drugs the key to the intensity of his gaze? But E? At my age? Twelve hours of uncontrollable and ardent affection for everyone and a fascination with every texture sounded like Hell to me. I couldn't think of a young or cool way to reject his offer so I just said, "No, thanks," and began moving to the music a bit to distract him. He looked at me with those pretty baby blues of his and, even though he was the one buying drugs in toilet stalls, I still felt his look said, "I am better than you." His stare was intense.

Suddenly, I wondered if his prying eyes saw the lines on my face or the glint of silver from a stubborn grey. To escape his scrutiny, I leaned over the bar to get the bartender's attention. As I ordered a water, I felt a tap on my ass. I turned to find a girl in her twenties staring back at me.

"Excuse me," she said smiling. "I am sorry to bother you but..."

"No, that's okay. What?"

"I couldn't help but notice you and your friend dancing..."

Where the fuck was this going?

"Yes?"

"And I have a bet with my friend. I was hoping you could settle it for me."

I looked at Daniel and he shrugged his shoulders.

"Okay, shoot," I said.

"My friend over there," she said and pointed to a girl in a booth who waved back at us, "she thinks you are that girl from *Cooterville, PTA*."

"She does?" I said, feigning surprise.

"Yes. She thinks you played Stinky Browntown but I say she is wrong."

"Pinky," I corrected her.

"Stinky Pinky?"

"Pinky Browntown. How much is the bet for?"

"The next round of drinks. She loved *Cooterville, PTA* and Pinky was her favorite character.

This was terrific. Now, Daniel could see that his peers dug me, that I was far cooler than superficial evidence suggested.

"Well, bad news! You owe your friend a round," I said and, like a total dork, gave the girl in the booth a double thumbs up. Nothing says hip like mimicking the Fonz.

"No way! Really? You were that girl that played Pinky Browntown when I was a little kid?"

"Yes," I said, feeling younger and more relevant by the second.

"That is crazy! I mean, that is so weird. But, like, aren't you kind of *old* to be hanging out in *here*?"

I looked at her, trying to determine if she'd intended the cruelty of that question or if she was just a dumb cunt. Still too drunk to think properly, I simply excused myself and hightailed it to the john.

"Mack! Mack! You won't believe what this fucking douche out there just said to me."

Mack listened with her mouth open as I related the details.

"What a bitch! Let's go out there. Point her out to me."

"No, let's just go. I want to go home. I want to cry. I am afraid I am going to cry. I can't let her see me crying! I don't want to cry in front of Daniel, either. We have to go. Right now!"

I was relieved to see that Daniel was alone at the bar and the girl was nowhere in sight. We paid our tab and went out to the valet to get our cars.

"Are you okay?" Daniel asked, sensing the change in my mood.

I was too humiliated to cover effectively with anything clever. I said I was drunk, tired and wanted to get to bed. He accepted this explanation, hugged me goodbye for way too long while he rubbed the fabric of my shirt.

A week later, just as I was giving up any hope of hearing from Daniel again, he texted and invited me to a wrap party he was attending. I accepted and he offered to pick me up, which I also accepted.

The wrap party was for a little indie film and the crew there skewed very young. Nobody looked over thirty. After my recent Venus Envy experience, this made me somewhat anxious. In an effort to fit in with the hipsters all around me, I scanned the craft cocktail menu for a drink that would make me seem twenty-something—you know, a Prohibition Era libation or a complicated blend of small batch spirits, infusions and ingredients I'd never heard of or dreamed of combining. Then I looked at the prices. I ordered a tinny Pabst Blue Ribbon and sipped it with distaste as I scanned the room from the bar while Daniel spoke to a producer. I noted that every guy in the room had either a beard or a Frito Bandito mustache and they all wore glasses. Nearly all of them were wearing skinny jeans at least a size too small for their doughy physiques and their shirts, whether of the T or button-down variety, were all also unflatteringly snug. One guy wore a waist-length women's sweater with a geometric pattern spilling down the shoulders and a belted waist. While I let my eyes survey the male muffin-top milieu, two cute girls sidled up to me and introduced themselves as Megan and Tammy.

"So, you are Daniel's girlfriend? It is nice to finally meet you," Megan said.

"Girlfriend? No. We have just hung out a few times."

"Really? Because Daniel hasn't shut up about his new girlfriend for weeks," Tammy said.

Call me desperate, but I found this to be a gratifying ego boost rather than a creepy, stalkery distortion of reality. And I cannot overstate how refreshing it was for me to think about something else, anything else, than money and my future on skid row.

"Really?" I asked, hoping they'd reveal more.

"Totally! You are the first girl he has ever called his girlfriend. He likes you a lot," said Megan.

"Well, that is good to hear." I said, trying to hide how excited it made me feel.

"I have been dying to meet you. Daniel is like a little brother to us. We get very protective," Megan added.

"He's got a beautiful cock, I hear," Tammy said as casually as if she had said, "He just got a new haircut."

I made a sound that I hoped said both "Ah! Good to know" and "Don't I know it, sister" at the same time while nodding my head. I gulped my PBR.

Daniel reappeared. Nobody talked about his penis any more. I guess sister types only do that behind a guy's back. There was more chitchat and more drinks and, before I knew it, Daniel was dropping me off at my house. The evening had been surprisingly easy, nobody challenged my age or right to be there, and every time Daniel even accidentally brushed me with his arm, I had inappropriate thoughts about him. I was about to ask if he wanted to come in when he jumped out of the car on his own.

"Are you coming in?" I asked.

"If that is okay," he replied.

Inside, he met my dogs and I opened a bottle of wine.

"I'd make you a Manhattan but I don't have the stuff."

He said wine was fine and I handed him a very large glass. He put it down on the counter, pulled me to him and gave me a long and passionate kiss. He was a very good kisser. My knees felt all quivery. I broke the kiss and led him up to the living room so we could get more comfortable on the sofa, perhaps step it up a notch. As we sat down, he admired the art on my walls. The central piece over my sofa was an expressionist painting from the thirties depicting a group of people engaging in a séance.

"This is interesting. Why are their eyes rolling back in their heads?"

"Because I want to rip all your fucking clothes off and rub myself all over your twenty-eight-year-old skin and lick your abs and sit on your face and then dive into your eyeballs because you make me feel fucking deranged when you look at me. I want to destroy you and leave you fucking broken and weeping!"

I didn't say that. I said, "Because séances were trendy in the twenties. The artist is mocking the participants, depicting them in phony trances."

"I see. And are you not concerned that this painting might put out the wrong message?"

"What message?" I asked, genuinely lost.

"Séances are like Ouija boards. They are ways to communicate with Satan. You don't want people to think you are a devil-worshipper, do you?"

"Yeah, not too concerned," I laughed.

Daniel fixed me with those Goddamn eyes of his and I felt naked.

"Um," I stammered, suddenly serious. "The only kind of person that could be offended by something as silly as this painting would be, like, a Born Again Christian or some End of Days Rapture freak."

Daniel stared at me and said nothing.

"Right? I mean, does it offend you?"

"I am Born Again, yes."

I blinked back at him while I did a mental Rolodex accounting of things I knew about Daniel, among them that he used illegal drugs recreationally, drank heavily, drove under the influence, was into older chicks and self-defined sister-types knew he had a beautiful penis. I decided he was busting my balls and laughed.

"Fuck you! You are not some hardcore Christian."

"I actually am," he said, humorlessly.

"Come on. You mean your parents are Born Again."

"My father is a Baptist minister in Scottsdale. I went to church three times a week, growing up. I go to church every Sunday. I believe in the Rapture."

Jesus, I thought. *I am going to get cockblocked by Jesus.*

"Oh," I said. Admittedly a lame response but, I mean, what else can one say?

"Is that a problem?"

"Wait, so you believe everything in the Bible is literally true? Historical fact?"

"Yes. I do."

"Okay, that is just nuts! The Bible says things like *do not wear clothing made of two types of material.* You are sinning right now on my couch, what with your chinos and your cable knit sweater."

"I should go. This isn't a good idea."

"What? Really?"

"Yes. Religion is very important to me. I like you but I cannot tolerate you mocking my faith."

"Mocking? I just brought up something that is in your Bible. That isn't mocking. That is debating."

"This is no joke for me..." he said and began the process of leaving.

"Wait, I am sorry! I didn't mean to call you nuts. If you need... or... believe in that stuff, I can respect that," I said without adding, "if that's what it is going to take to get you naked."

"Are you sure?" he asked and penetrated me with his hypnotic blue orbs.

"Yes. I'm sorry. I was rude," I apologized, my tone thick with saccharin and faux regret.

Daniel bought it and settled back down on the sofa. I decided he needed a little more greasing.

"Sincerely. I didn't mean to make you feel uncomfortable. I just feel awful now."

I looked at him with my best hangdog expression and he responded by kissing me again. It was glorious.

"Say, Daniel," I said after fifteen minutes of making out with my teenage, Jesus-loving boyfriend. "I have an idea. What do you say we take a bubble bath?" It seemed crazy to attempt stepping it up so aggressively now that I knew he was a Bible-thumper but what did I have to lose? I wasn't going to be forever able to avoid the inevitable fights with him over Darwin and dinosaurs so time here was really of the essence.

"You want to take a bath? Now?"

"Yeah. I'll get the bottle of wine and draw a hot, bubbly bath and we can get in. My tub is huge."

He looked at me with a savior's eyes, eyes that radiated love and understanding, and he said simply, "Okay."

Afraid too much talk might change his mind, I sent him to the kitchen to fetch the bottle of wine and I went and filled the tub. I lit candles and added foaming bath salts and gulped the balance of my Cabernet.

"Oh, that looks nice," Daniel said as he entered the bathroom. He filled the empty glass I was holding and refilled his own. Now I had to take my clothes off in front of him. I hadn't had enough wine to do it with the confidence I hoped to project.

"Okay," I said like a gym coach. "Let's do this."

I ripped at my clothes and dunked under the bubbles in record time. Daniel was wearing lace-up boots and I now had the luxury of observing him undress from the relative privacy of the deep bath. He took off his boots and socks. I sipped my wine and tried to quell my nervousness. He took off his sweater, revealing a T-shirt beneath. With his right hand, he reached behind his neck and tugged the shirt off in one careless motion. He had a nicely subtle six pack, definitely there but not one that got all up in your face and said, "I never eat carbs." His skin was creamy gold. He dropped his pants, then the boxer briefs, and stood there in front of me as easy as you please.

Rumors about my teenage, Jesus-loving boyfriend were true, I was delighted to note. No half a roll of nickels and a pair of gumballs. No grapefruit-sized testicles and giant, overripe banana. Everything on Daniel was just right.

Daniel eased himself into the tub. We alternated between sipping wine and fooling around. I sent him to fetch a second bottle of wine while I added more hot water to the bath but no amount of thrashing my hand around under the stream would generate more bubbles so, when Daniel returned, I was sitting, feeling very exposed, in a nearly bubble-free bath. Daniel filled our glasses from the fresh bottle and dropped back into the tub.

"Cheers!" he said and we toasted. I leaned back against the back of the tub, hoping that the more reclined I was, the thinner I would look. I let my eyes run all over his body. This was much better than bathing with the Valance.

So the bubble-enhanced frolic continued, we drank more wine and I looked at his pretty face a lot. And then he said them, words I have never heard before nor dared hope to hear. Words that were in contradiction to everything I had ever thought about myself. He said, "You have the most beautiful stomach."

It was like the whole rest of the room was enveloped in a dense fog, visibility breaking through only in a tight circle around his lips. I focused on those lips and I mumbled, "What did you say?" I looked at the only thing my eyes could still see and watched as his lips again form the words, "You have the most beautiful stomach."

Now, maybe you have a beautiful stomach, or maybe you did in college or before the second kid, but I have always had a little bit more meat on my bones than I found to be ideal. I was a fat kid. I am the girl that wonders, "Do I look fat like this?" while I am having sex. So—when a twenty-eight year old, and lest you forget, a very pretty twenty-eight year old states, "You have the most beautiful stomach," unprovoked and in a tone that suggests that there really isn't any question about it—well—let's just say it worked.

I don't think I heard anything else he said for the next twenty minutes, but when I came out of my stupor, I could see those pretty lips moving still. And I heard him saying something else. Something shocking. Revealing, unasked, another fact about himself that I should have inquired about before the bath. Before the second bottle of wine. I heard him say these words and they make me shudder to this day. I heard him saying, "...the only person really qualified to restore America to greatness is Sarah Palin."

I was in the tub with a male Ann Coulter. Or is that redundant?

Anyway, before you go nuts on me, let me just say, I know. I know I should have asked if he was a Republican before I even let him into my house. And I know I should have thrown him out right then and there. I should have said, "Thank you for being willing to see me naked but you have gone too far. You ask too much. I have to withhold my affection and attractive abdominal area for another. Someone more responsible with their vote." Someone, you know, I won't want to stab to death as we fight over whether to watch Glenn Beck or Rachel Maddow.

But I didn't. I just poured us another glass of wine. Because, *fuck*, he was pretty. And he thought I had a beautiful stomach, so fuck you.

Seduced by his common flattery, I would have agreed to marry him right there in the bathtub. We drank and carried on some more until I felt that perfect penis of his pressed up against my lady garden. This broke me from my daze.

"Wait! Whoa, hang on a second there."

He backed off immediately.

"Oh, I'm sorry. Is that too far?" he asked politely.

"I think... yeah... I think we are moving really fast here. Don't you?"

"Yes, I guess so. I guess you are right," he agreed and sat back away from me.

"I'm sorry. I think I just need more time."

"No, I get it. You are right. I should go."

It was late and letting him stay over was not a good idea if I wanted to maintain this "no sex tonight" position I had taken, so I agreed to call it a night. I kissed him goodnight at the door wearing only a towel.

"MY TEENAGE, JESUS-LOVING REPUBLICAN boyfriend rules," I told Eliza on the phone the next morning. "Pretty to look at, drinks, is willing to nude the fuck up and get in the bathtub, nothing disturbing about his package and he thinks I am sexy."

"Teen Jesus there is Born Again and wishes Michele Bachmann had won the Republican nomination? Are you still drunk or something?"

"Shut up. Think about the guys I have been dealing with all year. They are rejects from the Island of Misfit Toys. So Teen Jesus likes to do coke and talk about his moral superiority. So what? The odds of this going anywhere significant are less than zero, sure. But, for once, I caught a guy in my snare that I don't find physically repellant. Why can't I just enjoy that for a while?"

Another call came in.

"Oh! It's Teen Jesus! I am gonna take it! Bye!" and without waiting to hear her goodbye, I clicked over to the incoming call. "Hello?"

"Good morning," he said in his yummy rumble. "How are you feeling today?"

"Great," I lied. I was pretty hung over. "You?"

"Great. So, Ruby. I wanted to talk to you about something."

"Yeah?" I asked, suddenly apprehensive.

"I want you to know that I really like you. A lot."

"Um-hm...?"

"And that I had a great time with you last night."

"Okay..."

"But I don't think it is a good idea if we keep seeing each other."

"Why?"

"Because we came very close to making a big mistake last night and I am afraid that if we spend more time together that we will cross the line."

"What line?"

"Intercourse."

Intercourse?

"Intercourse is what, I don't know... Mormons have... through a sheet... or in secret underwear. What we almost had would not fall into that category, trust me," I said, trying to sell myself.

Silence on his end.

"Are you there?"

"This is why it is not a good idea. You are not taking me seriously."

"I'm sorry. I... well... what are you saying? Are you a virgin?" I asked him.

"No."

"Okay. Have you ever had a girlfriend?"

"No."

"Who did you have sex with?" I asked, hoping he wasn't going to reveal some church scandal or the same obsession with hookers that Nick had.

"Girls."

He was not making this easy.

"Girls? But not your girlfriend?"

"No. I have had a few moments of weakness and done things I should not have done. But to hang out with you when I know that I will want to have intercourse..."

"Can you not call it intercourse, please?"

"Knowing that I would want to make love to you..."

Like a mammoth arsehole, I blushed with embarrassment. He wanted to make love to me! Egad! Something about this guy made me feel so goofy but hearing him say "making love" was still cringe-worthy.

"Yeah, you should maybe stick with intercourse."

"To do that, to have, you know, intercourse with you and then want to do it again and again..."

And again and again? My God. This was like phone sex. I was starting to breathe heavily.

"That would be willful disregard for the commandments."

"But wait. How many girls have you had sex with in your life?"

"I don't know."

"You don't know? So there were a lot?"

"Not a lot."

"How many?"

"I don't know. Maybe twenty. Or thirty."

That was more partners for him in twenty-eight years than I had had in my life.

"And these were all youthful indiscretions?"

"Yes."

"Meaning, you never had sex with any of them again?"

"No. That would have been willful..."

"Disregard for the commandments. I heard you. Wow. So in twenty-eight years, you have never had sex with a girlfriend, but you have had twenty or thirty one-night stands?"

"Yes, but they were all in moments of weakness."

"Look, I have had a few moments of weakness this year myself. I'm not proud and I ain't judging. But don't you think God would prefer you had sex with someone you really like over and over rather than over and over one-offs with random women you don't love, or even like, while you are drunk or high?"

"No."

Teen Jesus was an enigma.

"Well, I am very disappointed," I said, not adding, "but now I think I understand my mysterious desire to defile you and I mean to achieve this goal."

"I am sorry. I didn't mean to hurt you. I don't want to ruin your life."

"Ruin my life? Don't talk crazy," I said, waving my hand in dismissal and feeling cheerful and empowered though unsure why.

"I think you are a great girl."

"Look. Why don't you come over tonight? I can make us dinner and we can watch a movie. As friends."

"Really? You are not mad at me?"

"No. I get it. It's all good."

"Wow. Other girls have not been so understanding."

"No, I totally get it. You have a code you are trying to live by. I respect that. I admire that, actually," I said, laying it on thick.

"Well, if you are sure you are not mad, I suppose..."

"Great. Bring a bottle of red wine," I said and we made a date.

That evening, Teen Jesus showed up right on time. I fed him homemade gnocchi with mint and peas and we guzzled wine. We talked about movies and I played some of my favorite vinyl records for him, mostly vintage blues, on an old portable turntable I had dragged out of my garage. We talked about music and took turns playing DJ until the needle mutinied, betraying me as so many other things in my house had, by breaking off at the base. I resorted again to my iPad for music and Teen Jesus impressed me by requesting to hear something by Joshua Black Wilkins or Pokey LaFarge.

After dinner and on the second bottle of wine, we adjourned to the sofa to watch a movie. I sat next to him and deliberately leaned my thigh against his. As if I had flicked a switch, he was on top of me. Thirty minutes later, we were in the tub, chest-deep in bubbles. See? I got some game.

I parted the bubbles to better see a two-inch pendant hanging between his youthful pecs.

"That is some crucifix you have there. Do you think I am a vampire?"

He looked at me deciding whether or not to get out of the tub. I adopted an innocent expression and sipped my wine.

"It is a cross. Only you Catholics wear crucifixes," he said, evidently deciding that educating me was more fun than leaving in a huff.

"I'm not Catholic."

"Okay, well, the crucifix has Jesus on the cross. You guys like to focus on His suffering. We prefer to focus on The Resurrection."

"Ah. The Rapture."

"No."

"The Ascension?"

"No."

"No wonder you had to go to church three times a week. You guys got a lot going on there."

"You should come to church with me tomorrow."

I'd had quite enough of this and kissed him rather than answer.

An hour later, we had milked the bath for all its value. We got out of the tub and went into my bedroom. He stretched out on the bed nude and gestured for me to join him. For an uptight Christian, he was super comfortable with his own nudity, certainly more than I was with my own. It came off as innocent and endearing. I lay on the bed beside him. He leaned over me and I felt like he could see into my soul. His eyes were so beautiful, his lashes so lush, his expression so sincere and full of love. Maybe I had underestimated my own loneliness but there was something incredibly powerful about this pretty young boy accepting me as completely as he seemed to be, even though, on paper, I stood for everything he feared. Maybe the depth of his faith, his certainty that he was saved, maybe these things let me feel, for a little bit, that I could be saved, too, just not in the way he likely prayed I'd be. He was so quietly intense and that intensity radiated out of him dazzlingly. It was seductive to feel all that intensity directed unabashedly at me.

He kissed me and I felt loved for the first time in over a decade. Loved by this delicious little nutjob of right-wing, religious fundamentalism.

God has a fucked up sense of humor.

Teen Jesus got on top of me and I luxuriated in the decadence of his perfect and perfectly warm skin touching my skin everywhere. He was water on a wilting houseplant. Again, I was flooded with wildly disproportionate feelings of gratitude and the torrent of tangled emotions convinced me again that I wanted to marry this crazy little fuck. Maybe if he moved in and helped with the bills, I might not lose my house after all. Two could live as cheaply as one, they say, while bringing in the income of two. Or in this case, while bringing in one income, his, because I had none. These thoughts represented a new low for me and I knew it, but I didn't imagine foreclosure came with a big gift basket of high self-esteem so I allowed myself the luxury of dwelling on the fantasy. I'd been reduced to fantasizing about a man—a man who fulfilled my fantasy—my fantasy of having someone with whom I might split the utility bills. A new new low, seconds after the first.

As I was debasing myself in the alleys of my mind, Teen Jesus had positioned himself to commence the intercourse. I encouraged it as gently as I could. I wanted it to happen but I was afraid if I was too aggressive, and by too aggressive I mean "acknowledged it was happening," that he'd realize what he was about to do and abort, pardon the expression. Whatever I did or didn't do—it worked.

As he engaged in some routine thrusting, I turned my head to keep from having a tooth cracked by his flying Mr. T cross. I wondered if he was making things better or worse for himself by having that thing on while actively sinning. It amazed me that he could focus on what he was doing with it in between us and smashing me in the chin, but focus he did. For a little while, that is. After about a minute, he stopped and rolled off me. He had given no indication of a climax. I didn't think I had scared him because I had been as still as humanly possible, trying to support his moment of weakness without rubbing it in his face. My best guess was that God had gotten wind of what we were up to and had put the kibosh on it. It was okay with me. I was far less interested in what Teen Jesus had in his pants for me than I was in what he had in his eyes for me.

Incredibly, Teen Jesus made no further squabbles about us as a couple or the willful commandment-breaking we regularly engaged in. And he continued his self-denying, perhaps Tantric exercise forbidding orgasm. Or maybe religious compunction overwhelmed him each time before he could finish but, eventually, his trying to get it over with before Jesus showed up got frustrating for me.

One night after an exceptionally long and drunken bath debating whether Jesus would support tax subsidies for multinational corporations at the expense of Medicare, we tumbled into my bedroom for more intercourse. Teen Jesus had long since cleared up any confusion I might have had about why they called Evangelicals missionaries. This night, I must have been feeling unusually bold, confidence built by my weeks with Teen Jesus or maybe by wine, but I decided it was time to mix it up. I cannot report how I got it done because I don't know, but this night I managed to get on my hands and knees and Teen Jesus was behind me. This continued in the standard manner most of us are familiar with for a few moments, and I began to think I had underestimated Teen Jesus or maybe I had underestimated my own ability to corrupt. I was considering adopting a less passive participation when I heard Teen Jesus cry out behind me.

"Oh! My eye! My eye!" he wailed and froze mid-thrust.

I looked at my headboard in front of me and asked, "What? What's wrong?"

"My eye..." he said again, and made sounds suggesting something sharp had suddenly lodged there.

"Your eye?" I asked, more than a little awkward, doggy-style with Teen Jesus still inserted and talking about something decidedly not sexual. Frozen like a coffee table, I looked back over my shoulder at him to see what the matter was. His hands were to his eyes.

"Yes, ow!" he said, then he pulled his hips back and knelt behind me.

I was beginning to feel rather vulnerable, posed as I was with my ass in his face, but as I moved to turn onto my back, he hurried out of the room plaintively wailing, "My eye!"

What the fuck? I heard him lock the bathroom door behind him as I lay in bed wondering what could have gone wrong. Had he been stricken by a vengeful God for his flagrant debauchery? Had the view of my ass or his first look at a taint viciously burned his retinas? Was there something monstrous about me from that angle? I certainly had never had the opportunity to examine myself from that perspective. Maybe I should try. Maybe I needed to consider anal bleaching or a merciless ass waxing. It was twenty minutes before he returned.

"Are you okay?" I asked, afraid of his answer.

"Yeah. I'm okay now, thanks."

"Well," I pressed on despite sensing I'd regret it. "What happened?"

"I don't know. This sharp pain pierced my head through my eye. It was an instant eye migraine. I took some Advil I saw in there. It is better now."

Yeah, better now that your blues eyes aren't staring straight into my brown one, I thought.

"What do you think happened?"

"I don't know. I have never had anything like that happen before," he said, tucking himself under the covers.

I decided it definitely had to do with the eyeful of rear entry he'd just gotten, perhaps for the first time in his Christian life. Talking about it any longer would not lead anywhere good and, frankly, the idea that a peek at my bunghole had thrown him into paroxysms of ocular anguish was kind of embarrassing. I decided to throw him a bone.

"So, what time is church in the morning?"

"You want to go?" he asked with such excitement in his voice, I was glad I had offered.

"Yeah, why not? And afterward, I am hosting a Sunday supper here. You will come to that, right?"

"Of course. Thanks," he said, and then fixed me with the deep love eyes. I spooned his silky warmth and we fell asleep.

The next morning, we parked beside a little, white stucco and cinderblock Baptist church tucked away on a Hollywood side street. There were only a handful of worshippers in the sanctuary but each deserves description. There was an octogenarian, African American woman in her royal purple Sunday best. She was wearing an enormous purple hat with torn fishnet partially obscuring her face. Her dress was not long enough to hide the tops of her knee-high support hose and the support hose was not supportive enough to contain the swollen cankles that threatened to envelope her tiny feet. She shuffled up the center aisle in filthy slippers to a seat in a front pew.

There was a Hispanic man in his thirties in chinos and a wife-beater. His face and neck were nearly as heavily tattooed as his arms and back. He seemed to be doing some sort of maintenance at the church.

There was a woman with evident mental impairment in a faded "DRILL HERE—DRILL NOW" T-shirt greeting people as they entered the building. A homeless man with a single, thick grey dreadlock hanging past his ass sat in the back row. Another man of indeterminate age sat picking crusted meth scabs from his cheek. A pregnant and very young girl sat behind him.

"This is like a Fellini movie, Daniel," I gasped as we slid into a pew in the center of the room. "Is this your regular church?"

"No. Well, sometimes. I also go to a church up on Mulholland but this one is closer to your house."

As we settled in, a young couple sat immediately in front of us despite their entire row being empty. I looked at Daniel, irritated.

"What?" he whispered.

I didn't answer and turned a critical eye on the pair. The man looked like a stockbroker in a white dress shirt and suit pants. The woman was wearing what could only have been her clubbing dress from the night before, unless backless dresses with rhinestone halters are considered acceptable morning-prayer attire. Her hair was flat and matted in the back. When she leaned forward to pick up the hymnal from the rack in front of her, I spotted a telltale scab on her spine in the center of her back.

"Haha!" I said silently and pointed the scab out to Teen Jesus.

He looked and looked back at me confused.

I leaned in to his ear and whispered, "She has a rug burn on her back! That is a sex scab."

He looked at me, disgusted. "You don't know that," he whispered.

"Yes, I do. Look at her hair. Haha! She had sex on a rug last night and she did the walk of shame to church with bed-head. That doesn't seem very respectful," I said and donned my most prudish expression.

Teen Jesus looked at me like I had just peed on the floor. I stared back, defiantly. He shook his head, obviously disappointed in me, and turned his attention to the pulpit.

The sermon went on for about forty-five minutes. Teen Jesus stood and sat and testified or whatever and even sang hymns, though I could feel him squirm doing these things with me watching. I had to admire his commitment in the face of my potential scorn. Purple church lady spent most of the time on her feet, palms up like she was feeling for rain. The sermon mainly covered the evil that is homosexuality. The bullet points were:

- Homosexuality is a chosen behavior, not a naturally occurring sexual orientation.
- Poor parenting is likely to make a child more likely to choose to become homosexual.
- A homosexual orientation is an inherently disturbed mental state.
- Homosexual activity is immoral.
- Homosexuals can change or can and should choose celibacy over depravity.
- Homosexuals can convert to heterosexuality through prayer, becoming saved and perhaps by undergoing reparative therapy.

You will be relieved to hear that the church offered in-house counseling to those nasty gays that might have been there and who were ready to change their wicked ways. If there were any, I guess they were too ashamed to stand up and accept salvation with witnesses.

"We have gay friends, Daniel," I pointed out in the car on the ride home.

"They are not gay. Not really," he informed me.

"Yeah, I think they are. Your friends Bob and Tom have lived together for two years. Eliza is gay."

"No, she isn't."

I had my doubts about that one, too, so I let it go.

"Homosexuality doesn't exist. They are just acting out. It's a phase," he informed me.

"Your best friend is a lesbian."

"I don't believe that," he insisted.

"She told me some pretty graphic details about her sex life, Daniel. I think there are more than a few vaginas in town that could pick her tongue out of a line-up."

"I know what she says. She is just trying to be shocking, but she will come around soon."

"And when she 'comes around,' as you say, she can confess and be forgiven?"

He laughed dismissively at my delightful naiveté and said, "You are such a Catholic."

I am not Catholic and I said so.

"You don't know it, but you are."

"What does that even mean?"

"Your ideas about religion are all Catholic. Evangelicals do not have confession. There is no need. We are already saved."

"So it doesn't matter what you do? You are going to Heaven?"

"Yes."

"And I cannot confess or repent?"

"No. You must accept Jesus Christ as your Lord and Savior and be born again."

"But wait. What if I devote my life to others and live a sin-free life?"

"You will burn in Hell."

"I will burn in Hell but you can sin and go to Heaven?"

"Yes. We have been chosen by God, predestined to be saved."

"When? When did this popularity contest take place?"

"Before we were born. Only God can choose who is saved and who is not."

"But that priest..."

"Minister," he corrected.

"Minister said that homosexuals could cure themselves by becoming saved. Now you say the saving is predetermined."

"If they are chosen, they will be saved."

"What about people that never heard of Jesus? Primitive tribes unaware of Christianity but leading pure lives?"

"They will burn forever."

"Does this seem right to you?"

He just looked at me with something close to pity.

"Monogamous homosexual equals Hell? Slutty Christian equals Heaven?"

He nodded.

"So, Gandhi? In Hell? But you go to Heaven?"

"I am among the chosen," he nodded, and I could sense he was growing weary of my willful ignorance.

The chosen? This seemed pretty arrogant to me.

"How do you know this?" I challenged.

"I know it."

"And you like this petty, closed-minded God that commands most of his children to eternal Hellfire?"

He didn't respond. Sure he liked Him. Teen Jesus had already been picked for the A Team.

"But what if you are wrong? It is called faith, after all. Not knowledge. What if God wants you out there doing good deeds and feeding the poor? Voting for Democrats?"

"Ha! Catholic," he said and dismissed me in a tone that meant there was no point in discussing it further.

That evening I hosted a dinner party. Sunday supper was a casual open house sort of affair. Back in the day when I was more solvent, I'd host them frequently. Leaner times called for leaner measures and I was sure my guests expected more than the quinoa and brown rice my budget allowed. But this Sunday was special. I had been seeing Teen Jesus for over a month and only Eliza and Mack had met him. Others were curious about this man that had managed to hang in there for so long. So, I splurged and made the poor man's special occasion meal—lasagna.

Teen Jesus had been very helpful in the kitchen that day. We sipped wine while we prepared for our first guests to arrive. He was especially affectionate with me, flush from the success of having gotten me under God's roof even if I hadn't yet been born again.

At five, guests began arriving. Cocktails were flowing and I introduced Teen Jesus around. I left him on the patio with two male friends while I went to check on the lasagna. Just as I popped a cork out of a new bottle of red, I heard my friend Kevin scream, "You Bush cunt!" from the patio. In twenty years of knowing Kevin, I had never even heard him raise his voice. I put the bottle down and went to see what had happened but before I got out of the kitchen, Teen Jesus rushed in. He was wild-eyed, puffed up and terrified as a spooked cat.

"What happened?"

"I don't know," he said, nearly breathless. "We were talking about that Occupy Wall Street farce and gun control and the NRA and…"

"Uh-oh. What did you say?"

"I just said that if the government bans assault rifles, this country will become a Stalinist-style tyranny."

Oh, God. You are mentally ill, I thought, but said, "Kevin is a gun control activist, Daniel. Couldn't you just keep it light and talk about abortion or something?" I joked, trying to calm him down.

"He is a big guy. Is he going to kick my ass?"

"Who knows? I'll bet you're glad he doesn't own a gun now?"

Teen Jesus looked ill.

"I am kidding. He will probably avoid you for the rest of the party and I can promise you he will not try to beat you up."

I poured him a fresh glass of wine and pushed him back out amongst the guests. Minutes after Teen Jesus was gone, Kevin came into the kitchen.

"Are you high?"

"What?"

"You are dating a young Rick Santorum."

I knew Kevin was right but I wasn't ready to give up the deep love eyes. An hour later, as I was setting a lasagna out on the buffet, Kevin and Eliza came back into the kitchen.

"Teen Jesus is crying," Eliza whispered. She looked rather fetching, I noticed, in a pair of black tuxedo pants, a black vest with no shirt beneath it, black and white wingtips and a plaid fedora.

"What? Did he get into it with Kevin again?"

"No, Kevin has been keeping his distance. Your little Eric Cantor out there is crying about you."

"Me? What did I do?"

"After a long speech to me about praying away the gay, he got onto you and something about your soul and the next thing I knew, he was crying. He is crying for your soul. It's awesome." Eliza smirked.

I went on the patio and told everyone to go inside and start eating. Teen Jesus had his back to me and was looking out at the skyline view.

"Hey," I said softly and touched his shoulder. "Are you okay?"

He faced me and I could see from the redness in his eyes he had been crying.

"Yes, I'm sorry. I'm okay."

"What is it? Why are you upset?"

"It's nothing."

I pressed him until he spit it out.

"It's just like I was saying to Eliza and Mack. I care about you so much, you know that, right?"

"Yes…"

"And it kills me. It just kills me…"

"Have you been taking the pot?" I asked, suddenly suspicious.

"Yes. But that isn't it. It's that I love you. I love you and I know you are going to burn in Hell for eternity…" he said and a big, sloppy tear dropped down his cheek.

"Aw, come here," I said and embraced him, comforting him as I would a child devastated to discover there is no Santa Claus. "I will be okay."

"No, unless you accept Jesus Christ as your Lord and Savior, you will burn. It is eating me up inside."

"Sit down," I said, sitting down at the patio table. "Let me ask you this: do you agree that you live a less moral life, moral by your own standards, than I do?"

"What do you mean?" he sniffled and blinked, lashes thick with tears.

"I mean you swear, you smoke, you drink heavily, and you use all manner of illegal drugs. You have had, like, thirty one-night stands, yet I am the only girl you have ever had sex with that you care about at all. Your parents, meanwhile, think you are as pure as the day you were born."

"I was born into sin…" he corrected.

"Zip it, Pat Robertson, and listen to me. You have engaged in all this behavior that you, you yourself, deem to be immoral despite all the guidelines and pressures provided to you by your faith. You agree so far?"

He nodded and sipped his wine.

"Meanwhile, I do not smoke, use drugs and I have never, technically, had a one-night stand. I go years and years and years without sexual activity. Why am I able to live a better life—again, better by your standards—than you are and without the structure of religion?"

"What is your point?"

"I think God will look at the two of us and if we get graded on a curve, I'm gonna get better seats in Heaven than you do."

"You want me to answer your question?"

I nodded, confident I'd won the argument.

"You are not going to like the answer."

Now I had to hear it.

"The reason I go astray when I do, is because I am one of the chosen ones and Satan tempts me aggressively. Satan is jealous of my soul."

"Okay, and…"

"Satan already has your soul. You are a done deal," he said, eyes welling up. "No reason to waste time trying to win a prize he already has on his mantel."

I let this sink in for a few minutes.

"I told you that you wouldn't like it," he said, wiping his eyes, resolute.

"So, by that math, your purity is proven in exact proportion to how impurely you behave?"

"Sort of, yeah."

"Yeah. That's cute. That's cute how you did that," I said, patted his head, and I got up to get some lasagna.

After dinner, a few of us lingered in the living room sipping wine. Someone suggested we play board games, so I went to the garage to fetch Trivial Pursuit. When I came back, I saw my friend Tom standing in front of Teen Jesus, holding a business card.

"Director of Photography… patriot? Patriot?" Tom asked Teen Jesus in disbelief, waving Teen Jesus's card as Exhibit A.

"Yeah. I am a patriot," Teen Jesus answered.

"Define for me the ways in which you are patriotic."

"I pay taxes. I support the troops."

"Did you vote for George Bush?" And without waiting for confirmation. "For McCain/Palin after that? Who'd you vote for this last time?"

"I am a Republican, if that is what you are asking. I vote Republican."

"How old are you?"

"Twenty-eight."

I stood holding the game, frozen, helpless to stop the calamity I knew was coming.

"And you call yourself a patriot?"

"Yes."

"George Bush got us into two wars. Why didn't you enlist?"

"What?"

"You are the right age. How dare you vote for wars, send other peoples' kids to fight them, and then sit around in the Hollywood Hills sipping wine, passing out business cards that say *patriot*?"

I looked at Eliza. She looked nervous. Kevin was smiling.

"Why didn't you enlist in the service?"

"We have a volunteer army."

"Guys are serving multiple tours so you can sit here and say that, you little shit."

"Tom," I interjected, finally finding my voice.

"No," Tom said to me and turned back to Teen Jesus. "Tell me why you didn't enlist."

"Because I have duties here," Teen Jesus said far more confrontationally than seemed wise.

"What fucking duties? There are guys in hundred and thirty degree heat, getting shot at, missing their kids grow up. Dying. What duties do you have that are so important?"

"I am needed here. As a cameraman, I can do good here, get the word out to support the war."

"What? You said earlier you work on a reality TV show. How is that patriotic?"

"The camera I carry weighs about the same as the gun the guys over there use and..."

For the first time in maybe forever, I was seeing Teen Jesus for who he really was. I didn't see a pretty boy with beautiful blue eyes that looked at me with adoration. I saw a monstrous hypocrite, a man that quoted Christ while supporting wars he dared not fight himself. A man that had random one-night stands because he was too fucked up on illegal drugs to resist, but who would vote against any of the women involved having any choice were they to become accidentally pregnant by him. I saw a man who thought social safety nets like minimum wage and unemployment insurance were "entitlements," undeserved charities or Communist plots to fleece the wealthy. I saw a man that claimed to love the Constitution but also wished the Confederacy had won the Civil War. I saw a man I did not like. At all.

"You Liberals. Typical. You call us intolerant..." Teen Jesus was still talking.

"Daniel! Shut up," I shouted.

Daniel began to protest but I cut him off.

"Stop. Please. Can't you just sit there and look pretty?"

"Why? I have been listening to his predictable lefty rhetoric all day, encouraging a government takeover and a permanent welfare state. What's next on the agenda, Trotsky? Reparations? Legalized bestiality?"

"Stop. Please stop talking. If you can't just sit there and look pretty, you should probably go," I said in my flattest tone.

He looked at me for a few seconds. I said nothing more. He knew then that we were done.

Teen Jesus might have been a sick twist, but I never said he was stupid.

"I CAN'T BELIEVE you didn't kill him weeks ago," Eliza said, as we sipped champagne in my kitchen the following weekend. It was the night of my big movie premiere. Eliza was dressed like a Greek goddess. I was in a strapless, sequin number.

"I know. He is one of those Republicans that says the *Democrat Party*. What is that about? How are they hurting anyone by using improper grammar? Yet, it is definitely done intentionally. That alone should have been enough."

"I know. That's what I'm saying. He was in rare form at Sunday supper."

"He is always like that. You wouldn't believe the Rush Limbaugh propaganda he spouts. I guess I was just enjoying how much he seemed to like me. It felt good to see such admiration in someone's eyes. I am obviously an even lonelier pathetic loser than I realized. And these guys I've been hanging out with are just making it worse. Anyway, fuck it. Onward and upward."

We toasted with our champagne flutes.

"Speaking of onward and upward, I went crazy this week and had my frown line filled with, I don't know, Playdough or something and got Botox in my forehead."

"No way!" Eliza challenged with evident delight. "Lemme see!"

"Well, hang on. I'm kinda freaked out. I think he used too much Botox on my right side because my right eye feels sorta droopy."

"Stop. Lemme see."

I stood before her and looked directly at her with my face as relaxed as possible.

"You look great! I don't see anything."

"Okay, thanks, but wait. Right? Watch this. If I try to raise my eyebrows or if I smile too much or do anything that results in a significant change of expression, my right eye is frozen. I can actually feel my eyelid, heavy on my eye. The right side of my face feels like I just spent the last four hours crying," I said and sniffed. In truth, my puffy right eye was sending smoke signals to the right side of my nose that it was sob-city and time to get stuffed up.

"Stop. Lemme see."

I put my face through the various paces. After a minute or so with a lot of pointing and making expressions like The Joker, Eliza had to admit my right eye had a detectible droop.

"It's hardly noticeable at all," she lied. "Really."

"I just can't fucking believe it. Of all the nights in all my life. Tonight is my last chance at jump-starting my career. It has to go perfectly. And I have to look perfect, not like Marlon Brando in *On the Waterfront*. I'm like a poster girl for domestic abuse here."

"You are being crazy. You look beautiful and nobody is going to notice that teeny, tiny puffiness in one eye."

Whether she was right or not, talking about it all night wasn't going to change anything.

"How about you, Eliza? Any action there on Nappy Snatch?" I asked, changing the subject, and sniffed my Botox-induced runny nose.

"Nappy Dugout. Goddamn you. And yes, but still just in the chatting stages."

"You are going to have to nut up or shut up with one of those matches eventually, you know."

"Yeah, yeah, yeah. I know. Anyway," she said, changing the subject back to me, "you really look gorgeous."

"Thanks, but frankly, I ought to. I spent a fortune at the dermatologist for this Joe Louis makeover. I spent three hundred dollars I don't have on this stupid dress. I spent a hundred on this costume jewelry, fifty on a strapless pushup bra and another fifty on a pair of Spanx, which I love, FYI."

"Spanx are the best!"

"I bought new shoes, had my hair done and got a pedicure. Without even counting the dermatologist's bill, I am into this thing for nine hundred bucks. Nine hundred bucks for a twenty-minute walk down a red carpet. And I'd happily pay nine hundred more for a small handful of Xanax."

Eliza laughed as if I'd made a joke. I hadn't confessed my brief but glorious love affair with psychoactive, anxiolytic drugs to a soul. If I'd spent a depraved month or so belly-up to the Z-bar, that was my business.

"Well, you look great."

"As do you. This lipstick-lesbian Venus look is really working for you," I said and sniffed.

She had decided, apparently, not to bicker about my commentary this evening and let it slide without remark.

"Anyway," I continued, actually relieved that she hadn't taken my bait, "I've got to make the best of this. Do you realize that in over twenty years of being an actress, I have never been to the premiere of my own movie?"

"How is that possible?"

"I've been to a zillion premieres but this is the first time a movie I am in is getting the big push. At the Chinese Theater, no less. So old school. I won't feel like a fraud out there tonight. I am one of the leads in the damn movie. When the entertainment shows want to talk to me on the carpet, I'll have a legit reason for being there."

"That is going to be fun."

"All I know is, I haven't really worked in years. Little bullshit here and there but nothing worth mentioning, you know. More importantly, I haven't earned even a barista's income in nearly a decade. I know this for a fact because I applied for a job at Starbucks last month."

"You did not!"

"I did. A manager who looked all of about nineteen interviewed me. She was very gentle when she told me that my absolute and total lack of experience or references of any kind were going to be a serious hurdle between me and meaningful employment. Especially at my age. She actually said 'especially at your age' to my face."

"Did you kick her ass?"

"No. Her point was, as she stated it, that potential employers were unlikely to believe someone my age could afford to live on the sort of salary they were offering and that they couldn't afford to train me only to have me decide the job was a farce and move on. She also pointed out that most applicants that get hired there have a degree."

"A degree? You need a degree to get a job at Starbucks?"

"I guess so. It's brutal out there."

"You know, I read an article that said McDonald's is the largest employer of people over sixty-five."

"Really? Does McDonald's pay really well or something?" I asked and tried imagining myself as a high-paid fryalator operator in a red-and-yellow visor.

"No. Because all these people retired and then lost their retirement accounts in the crash. They've all been forced to go back to work."

"Oh, God. That's depressing."

"I know. But you are not going to end up working at Starbucks or McDonald's, anyway. You're an actress. An established actress. What the fuck? Wait it out."

She didn't get it. She didn't know that I had already waited myself into a desperate situation. She didn't know that I looked at every stranger I passed every single day and wondered what they did for a living and how they'd found their way to that occupation. I wondered what their jobs paid and how long it took them to learn to do it. I wondered how they afforded that new car or that purse or those Gucci boots. All of them. So many. They couldn't all be world-famous surgeons or attorneys to the stars. What the fuck did they all do for a living? Thousands of beautiful homes with perfectly and expensively manicured lawns. What paid for that? Millions, it seemed, eating lunches in restaurants with white linens. I'd drive by those people and wonder what they did that allowed them a two-martini lunch in Beverly Hills at midday on a Tuesday. Or I'd wonder what their husbands did and then I'd look at the waiter and try to calculate what a week of his tips might look like. A dog-walker would push past me on a sidewalk and I'd wonder how much she made and how many months it took her to build up that client list that had her walking eight fluffy, little purse-dogs in a single go. What does that valet's take-home pay look like? Nobody was safe from my scrutiny, nobody on any step of the ladder of success, because I knew I was on a rung beneath them all—and I needed back up, on whatever terms it took. Rather than try to make Eliza understand all this, I brought the conversation back to the event at hand.

"Ugh, Eliza. I hate the red carpet, but I need to make the best of this opportunity. That's why I maxed out three different credit cards getting ready for this night. I really think this is my last chance. I need to show everyone what I look like now, you know? I'm not Pinky Browntown anymore. This is the kind of thing that might actually help me. Not a stupid dinner at Pho Bich Nga."

"What is this movie, again?"

"A little indie film I did last year about a rural high school called *Getting High School.* You know, I don't know where I am supposed to put the emphasis on that title. Is it *Getting High* School or Getting *High School*? Anyway, it paid a hundred bucks a day but I had a great part. The kid that plays my son in it is now on some Nickelodeon show. He's gonna be Johnny-Depp-huge so a major studio picked it up. They are pushing the bejesus outta this film now, even though they were initially gonna shelve it. Huge stroke of luck for me. Anyway, you're sure I look okay?"

"You look awesome."

"And my eye really isn't just a giant brioche?" I asked and sniffed again.

"Absolutely not. You look beautiful."

"Thanks," I replied, unconvinced. "So do you," I said, draining my champagne. "All right! Let's do this."

PREDICTABLY, THINGS WENT WRONG almost immediately. I discovered I had not been issued the VIP parking pass required to park near the theater, though I saw several people I knew from the film being waved in. Eliza and I had to park our cars several blocks away and then walk in the cold, in ridiculous heels, through rubbernecking tourists and movie fans to the front of Mann's Chinese. I heard someone yell, "Pinky!" and picked up my pace. At the theater, security stopped us and demanded my credentials. Again, there had apparently been some oversight and I had not been issued anything security would accept. I stood there, impotently holding out my RSVP confirmation and tickets, feeling the boning of my dress dig into my ribcage.

"I swear, I am in the movie," I pleaded, but the guard was unmoved. I looked to Eliza then back at the guard. I couldn't believe I was getting turned away from my own premiere.

"Ruby?"

I looked beyond the security guy to see a woman wearing a dozen lanyards approaching us.

"Yes, I'm Ruby."

"She's okay. You can let her in," the woman said and the guard opened the velvet rope to let us through.

"I'm Rachel," the woman said, reaching to shake my hand.

"I'm Ruby and this is my friend, Eliza," I said, shaking her hand. "Thanks for rescuing us."

"I'm sorry he stopped you. I'm with the studio. I'll take care of you now," Rachel said and smiled reassuringly at me and Eliza. Then, leaning in a little closer to my face, she asked, "Are you okay, Ruby?"

Oh my God. What now? I sniffed and, ever elegant, swiped my wrist across my running nose and then tried to casually hover my hand over my droopy eye.

"Yes. Of course. Why?"

"You just look like you have been crying. Are you sure you are okay?"

"Yes. Absolutely. I'm... just... dealing with, you know? Allergies," I lied. "Just awful this time of year."

"Oh, don't I know it," Rachel said and put her hand on my arm in solidarity. "Mine are just awful. I'm so high on Sudafed right now, I had to take a Klonopin to calm myself down," she said and laughed, as if this was the most natural conversation in the world. "So, do you want to do the red carpet or shall I escort you two directly to your seats?"

"Oh, no, I'll do the red carpet!" I said, almost defensively. What? Was I some allergy-stricken eyesore that needed to be secreted past the press and into the theater through a side door? I was wearing a sequin sheath and rhinestone shoes, for fuck's sake. Wasn't it obvious that I had dressed to be seen? I was mad at myself for being so sensitive but this was just getting ridiculous.

"Okay, come this way. Eliza, you can come with me behind the carpet."

I handed Eliza her ticket and Rachel led me to the point where a huge phalanx of photographers were crusted ten-deep for twenty feet along the carpet. They were popping away and the flashbulbs were dizzying. They were screaming,

"Ashley! Ashley! Look at me! Here, Ashley! Straight ahead, Ashley! Let's see the back of your dress!" A blonde actress that I had never seen before was posing like a pro in front of them. She pivoted to reveal her backless dress and the prominent tramp stamp on the small of her back. Along the carpet in front of her were nearly a dozen other young actors and actresses, all of whom were being aggressively shouted at by the press by name. My heart was in my throat and my left eye began to twitch. I would have chewed Xanax like M&M's, had any been available. Why hadn't that bitch, Rachel, offered me a Klonopin? I focused on breathing through my mounting panic attack and, eventually, Ashley moved about five feet down the carpet. Finally, terrifyingly, it was my turn to step out.

I tried to calm the twitch in my left eye, be sure to keep my slumping right eye wide open and think about holding in my gut all while attempting to look relaxed and happy and glamorous as I carefully stepped in front of the gang of flashing cameras. I struck what I hoped was a flattering but unaffected pose and sniffed my running nose.

"Who are you?" a photographer called out.

"What's your name?" another called out.

I said my name and the photographers still in range to shoot that Ashley girl blatantly turned to snap a few more of her. The others politely took a few shots of me and then openly craned their necks and looked left for the next actor coming onto the carpet behind me. Mortified, I swept past the remaining still photographers. In all my days of being caught by paparazzi, I had never had to tell them who I was. How could I possibly have anticipated not being recognized at my own premiere? I had always heard that women become increasingly invisible in direct proportion to how small thirty looks in their rearview mirror of life—but this was too much. I felt as tiny as a citizen of Lilliput.

"Are you done with them?" Rachel asked, suddenly appearing at my side.

"Yes, I think so. Who are all those actors out there?"

"Oh, they are cast members from different Nickelodeon shows and a few are from that new Disney movie," she said after looking past me at them. "Do you want to do press?"

"Yes, sure. I'll talk to whomever's interested," I said and, ever the lady, tugged up on my strapless dress. "Got an extra Klonopin?" I was shocked to hear myself ask.

Rachel laughed. "I know, right? These things are crazy."

Fuck. She thought I was kidding. I decided it was best to pretend I was kidding and fake-laughed along with her.

As it turned out, the only people interested in talking to me were a Korean online shoe network, an American Internet fashion blog and a fourteen-year-old girl for her school's in-house radio station. None of these interviewers knew who I was or that I was in the movie.

I looked back to where the E! Network and other celebrity show cameras were set up. There were lines of gorgeous teens and their agents and managers and publicists standing twenty-deep before them.

"Do you want to talk to anyone else?" Rachel asked as she saw me scan the crowd.

"No, they look pretty busy," I said. The twitch in my eye had shifted down to my chin. I wanted to go home and cry. I wanted to go home and cry and eat bad things and drink good things. This night was a complete disaster. A really expensive disaster. I looked down at my three-hundred dollar dress and wondered if there would be any minimum-wage job interviews in my future at which a silver, sequin sheath might give me the edge required to land the job. I doubted it. Just then, I spotted the actor who had played my son in the film. I caught his eye and waved. His face lit up in recognition but before he could come to say hello, a handler grabbed his arm and led him to a woman holding an *ET* mic.

"Okay, follow me," Rachel said.

I looked back over the block behind me, a block full of opportunity and exposure and potential. I block that I'd hoped could help procure professional interest, re-introduce me to directors and inspire producers to hire me. A block that could breathe life into my flat-lining career. A block that had absolutely no interest in me whatsoever. I wished then that I had accepted Rachel's earlier offer to scoot me into the movie incognito. I wondered if she'd known that I would be largely ignored out there. I wondered if I was the last person on Earth to realize I really was a has-been—and not just a pouting wannabe. I blushed with embarrassment, slumped in resignation and let her lead me in to my seat.

"I'll hold onto your credentials and meet you outside after the movie. I'll walk you over to the after party," Rachel said and then took off typing on her gold iPhone.

I found Eliza and sat down beside her.

"How did it go out there?"

"Horrific. I'm done. And I don't want to talk about it."

Eliza took one look at my expression and, mercifully, asked nothing more.

Dejected, I sat there, the boning in my dress and the wiring in my bra competing with each other to be the first to actually puncture my flesh. The sequins on the dress were like sitting on gravel and they chaffed the soft skin inside my arms. I was miserable in every way.

Two hours later, the audience was applauding and the house lights came up. I sat staring, literally agape, at the heavy red drapes which had obscured the screen. My role had been almost entirely cut out. They had apparently done extensive reshoots to capitalize on the new fame of the film's young lead. The one scene that remained in which I had any dialogue was a scene between my character and her son. I was seated on his bed looking down at him. Every shot of me had been taken from his perspective. If you imagined what it would be like to look up into the face of an English bulldog while it leaned over you, you might have some idea of what gravity and bad lighting had done to my face. I was all jowls, eye bags and aging bloat. Seated on the bed, my boobs and my belly had become one big lumpy mound. It was devastating.

"That was cute!" Eliza said. "What did you think?"

"I looked a hundred and a hundred pounds overweight."

"No! You are being hard on yourself."

"Please. Don't patronize me," I said, feeling ten years older than I had when the evening had begun.

"Okay, well, I'll admit that Denny's shirt and mom jeans get-up wasn't very flattering but you didn't look bad."

I stared at her, the grim set of my mouth speaking for me.

"Well, you don't look like that in real life."

"Nobody sees me in my real life. Millions will see this film. I want to die."

Eliza offered a few more well-intentioned platitudes while I did my best not to take out my misery on her.

"Let's just get to the fucking after party. I need a drink. Badly," I said and we joined the flow of people out of the theater.

Two blocks away, security checked the credentials of everyone entering the soiree. Rachel had taken mine and she was nowhere to be seen.

"I am in the movie," I said and ignored the "Yeah, right" look on the guard's face. "Rachel, from the studio, she has my passes," I continued, and sniffed in the snot running out of my over-botulismed sinus.

"I don't know any Rachel."

"Well, is there a list or something?"

I tried to frown at the guard despite knowing my forehead was frozen in a recently purchased mask of expressionless youth. The guard was not impressed. He let out a deep sigh and picked up a clipboard with a half-inch-thick sheaf of paper. There had to be four thousand names in there. I gave him my name. Five minutes later, he still had not found me on the list. The bra/boning pain was getting so bad I began to feel claustrophobic panic. Hundreds of people were filing past us and into the party.

"Eliza, fuck this. Let's just go to a bar near here," I said, tugging at the dress for relief. "I don't want to go in there and have to pretend I am happy about the movie, anyway."

"Are you sure?"

I was. As we walked down the alley, I removed the strapless bra and stuck it in my purse. Sure, my boobs were an inch or two lower but I had improved my condition to merely very uncomfortable from absolute agony.

We found a dark, local joint and hunkered down at the bar. I filled Eliza in on what had happened on the red carpet and how different the movie we had just seen was from the movie I had expected.

"That sucks. They should have warned you."

"Yes."

"They should have prepped the press, too."

"I don't think the paparazzi ignored me so much because they weren't prepped. It was because I am old and my career has been over for years."

"Shut up. And you are not old!"

"I'm old in my industry and, now, I am beginning to accept it. There has to be more to life than this, Eliza. I'm not old. And I am not any less talented or hirable than I ever was. Even if I were ten years older or looked fifteen years older or weighed a hundred pounds more or twenty-five pounds less, there are roles for those people, too. But, for some reason, and while I wasn't looking, the universe or this town or I don't know what—something inside of me—decided that my acting career had run its course."

"You really think you might want to quit? What would you do instead?"

"I don't know. I mean, I don't want to quit but if I never have any auditions, what's the difference? Semantics. Who broke up with who, that kind of thing. If I am honest with myself, and I have not been for a long time, I don't think I will ever again pay for my life solely by what I earn as an actress. If I am stocking shelves at Home Depot or making smoothies at Jamba Juice for the bulk of my income, I am not a 'career' actress. I will then have a 'career' in the service industry."

"You are never going to be stocking shelves at Home Depot."

"Would it be so bad if I did? I remember hearing an interview with Marilyn Monroe that, I think, she gave in the last few months of her life. She mentioned driving to the studio and looking out the window and seeing people, like cleaning women or something, on the way to their jobs and being envious of them. Thinking, *I could be a cleaning woman*. You know?"

"No. Why would Marilyn Monroe want to be a maid?"

"Well, maybe because their lives were simple and predictable? Because nothing more than their basic job description was demanded of them. There was no expectation of them to stay thin or beautiful or young or sexy forever. That kinda thing. As an actress, every job feels like your last, too, and that takes a toll. It's very stressful. As a cleaning woman, the whole world doesn't get to view and criticize your work. They don't write magazine articles about how good or bad you looked in your uniform while you did your job. Nobody hassles the cleaning woman every time she is in public, always expecting her to look gorgeous and that she be in a gracious mood and ready to accommodate their every request. Anyway, I am off on a tangent here. My point was, I've begun to envy people with good old-fashioned regular jobs, too. I used to cringe at the idea of a nine-to-five and the idea of knowing where I would be in five or ten or fifteen years. And I didn't feel like

I was sacrificing anything when people like you would express awe that I could face a future with complete financial unpredictability. It felt like the only choice I had, as natural as breathing. I don't feel that way anymore. Or rather, I think the choice has been taken out of my hands," I said and sucked a nose-load of snot back up into my head.

Understandably, Eliza had nothing to say in response to that speech, a speech she probably thought was just a reaction to a really bad night. We sat in silence and, when we'd finished our fourth drink, I decided it was time to let Eliza off the hook.

"Okay. Let's call it. I need to go home so I can cry."

"Okay, I can't just not say anything here. I understand that you are disappointed but you are forgetting that you are *in that movie* and it will probably be a big hit with whatshisname, your son there, in it. You are a working actress. Try to spend a little time thinking about how many other actresses would kill to be in that film, even if they had to look fat and old to do it. Maybe you should claim you pulled a Charlize Theron from *Monster*. You might win an Oscar."

That had to be the wine talking but I responded as if she actually believed I could win an Academy Award, for anything, let alone my performance in *Getting High School*.

"Charlize Theron was already an A-list actress on the first day of shooting *Monster* and she returned to being her regular, goddess self within hours of wrapping that film. I didn't have to go out of my way to look like a bloated fishwife. In fact, I looked like one despite my best efforts to the contrary. And *Getting High School* is no *Monster*."

Eliza knew better than to continue trying to cheer me up. I wanted to go home and cry. I wanted to cry not only for my wounded vanity and my bruised ego but also because I was scared. That was the overwhelming feeling, fear. Fear of losing my home and everything I had worked so hard to achieve, fear of living, alone, in a shitty studio apartment in Reseda with a part-time, minimum-wage job bagging Maxi

Pads and discount brand cigarettes at the checkout stand in a dollar store. Fear of getting even older and even fatter and never one iota more interesting than I already was. Fear of my future sitting on a balcony in an apartment complex, judging my neighbors, drinking generic vodka out of Styrofoam cups, wearing "house dresses" and having three inches of grey roots because the $9.99 home hair color cost could be better put to use on another bottle of generic vodka. Fear of dying alone and having them take three weeks to find my corpse because I didn't matter to anyone and nobody had reported me missing because nobody, not even my teen boss—drunk on mouthwash and battling an eating disorder—had missed me. These thoughts were so depressing, the weight on my soul so heavy, that even my familiar panic attacks were cowed in their presence.

We walked past the red carpet on our way back to our cars. It was abandoned now, the excitement having migrated to the party we hadn't been admitted to. At the corner, I heard someone call my name. I turned and saw Rachel running up to us.

"Oh my God! I am so sorry! I looked all over for you and couldn't find you. I have your credentials," she said, handing them to me. "Come on. I'll walk you past security."

I explained that it was all good and that we were going to call it a night.

"No way! I can't let you go home without stopping by the party. I feel awful."

I looked at Eliza for support. The idea of the party now sounded worse than my fantasy future had.

"You should go," she said. "I have to work in the morning but you don't. Go back there and let everyone see how gorgeous you look tonight."

Motherfucker. Eliza would pay for this betrayal.

"Exactly!" Rachel agreed. "I am not taking no for an answer. Let's go," she said and took me by the arm.

"Are you sure you don't want to come, Eliza? Really?"

"Definitely. My shoes are killing me, too. I just want to get in my jammies and curl up with my puppy."

Eliza headed to her car and I cursed her black heart as I let Rachel lead me back to the party. There were dozens of autograph collectors swarming just outside the door.

"Pinky! Pinky Brownstone!" I heard someone yell. With that, the crowd turned like a pack of killer bees and engulfed me, arms outstretched, waving old photographs of me as Pinky. What kind of cruel joke was this? In a surreal state, I signed a few dozen pictures and then Rachel rescued me. We walked past security without incident and joined the festivities.

Having delivered me safely, Rachel looked at her iPhone, excused herself and headed off, texting on the go.

I headed straight for the bar and was lucky enough to find a seat in a dark corner. I ordered a drink and sipped it, scanning the room for a familiar face. I didn't recognize a soul. I ordered another drink and promised myself I would leave as soon as I finished it. Sitting at the bar in a three-hundred-dollar dress I could not afford, unrecognized and alone, at the premiere of my own movie felt like being the one in the wedding dress standing, awkward and alone, at the altar. The boning in the dress had ratcheted up its assault on my ribcage and I just wanted to go home, take the Goddamn dress off and begin the process of reconciling myself to my new life on square one.

"Hey, baby. S'cool if I chill here?" someone asked and I turned to face The Albino!

"Hey! Of course! Please, sit," I said, patting the stool beside me. I hoped he didn't hear the relief in my voice. Somebody I knew! I don't think I have ever been happier to see anyone in my life.

"Whoa! You look kickin' in that bling dress, yo!" he said and sat down and touched the rim of my glass.

I thought about the push-up bra in my purse and regretted having made that sacrifice to comfort. I tugged the dress up and wiped my wrist across my nose.

"So, wha's the dilly-o? What's goin' down, shorty?" he asked me and then made a gesture to the bartender. The bartender acknowledged him and began making a drink.

"You didn't see the movie tonight?" I asked, hoping against hope that he hadn't seen me and my impression of Winston Churchill in it.

"I saw it. My homeboy's the lead."

He was talking about the actor that played my son.

"I play his mother in the movie," I said, regarding The Albino with suspicion. His drink arrived.

"That was you? You were the mom in that scene at the crib?" he said and looked at me like I'd just confessed to believing in leprechauns. He gave my shoulder a quick and compulsive tap.

"I fucking love you!" I blurted.

"My bad, girl. I didn't recognize you at all," he said and touched my drink again. "You ain't busted like that mom was. Look atcha. You hella jiggy."

I beamed at him and raised my glass to toast. *That's right*, I thought. Not busted. I was hella jiggy.

"Cheers to you," I said. "I look fucking hideous in that movie and was ready to shoot myself in the face. You just made my night! Thank you."

"Seriously, babe. Look at you. You are phat."

I was so delighted with him, I didn't even waste a second wondering if he'd just said "fat."

I ordered another drink as I made a mental note that it was my sixth of the evening. I was pretty drunk.

The Albino—such a welcome diversion. We sat there and chatted happily for a long time. He had three drinks to my one. An hour later, emboldened by wine and The Albino's flattery, I asked, "So, what happened with us?"

"What do you mean?"

"Why didn't it go anywhere?"

The Albino got very serious and began telling me about various family issues he had; a troubled sister, an ill parent. As he was talking, he began crying. Not twisty-faced bawling, but the occasional tears fell on the bar in front of him. A huge surge of drunken empathy overtook me and I put my hand on his thigh as a gesture of comfort.

What am I doing with my hand on his thigh? I thought. *Is this appropriate? What am I doing? Do I really want to revisit the mystery and frustration and allergies that The Albino represented?*

I looked at his sad little face and watch a tear streak down his cheek. He was still talking but I had long since stopped listening. I was fixated on my hand and his thigh and why I'd put my hand there and what he thought of it there and how could I get it back or did I maybe want to leave it there—maybe feel around for evidence of masculinity.

"And that last part, you know, is why I was so jacked up," he was saying when I refocused. He swiped a tear. "I want to keep it real, my nizzle. I would hate for you to think I was flippin' the script, yo. You dig?"

It didn't dig, mostly because I hadn't heard a single word of his explanation but also because he was nearly impossible to understand even if you were listening. I pulled my hand from his leg and, nodding, said "Absolutely. You had nothing to explain."

That, of course, made no sense because I had brought it up and had asked for an explanation. Plus, I had no idea what he had confessed but if his emotional state was any indication, it had been a pretty heavy reveal. For months, I had wondered what the fuck was with this guy. I get the opportunity to confront him and he launches into a ten-minute sob-fest of an explanation and I don't bother to listen to it? When did I get so retarded? Or maybe I was more drunk than

I realized. Maybe I was having a mid-life crisis or a full-blown nervous breakdown.

"Honestly, don't worry about it," I added, being as non-specific as possible.

"You're great, shorty. Naw'mean?" he said and touched my earring.

"Yeah. Well, it was really great running into you," I said and finished my wine.

"You gonna flow off, boo?"

"Yeah. I've been in this dress far too long. And I don't need any more to drink. I should take off."

"Word," he said, amiably. I was moving in to hug him when his phone rang. He, predictably, dug in his front pocket for it and became immediately engrossed in a conversation with someone named "Cudie," to whom he said a cryptic, "Dude, tweet the deets," as I waved goodbye. I could swear I heard him human beat-boxing as I walked away.

Back in my car, I unzipped my dress several inches so I could breathe and get a break from the spines inside that had, I was sure, actually bruised my torso. I pulled out of the lot and was funneled by construction cones onto Hollywood Boulevard. I became acutely aware of my intoxication and felt dangerously exposed on the street that had so much traffic and so many tourists suicide-walking out from between parked cars and scores of runaways panhandling. Hollywood Boulevard should not be on anyone's drunk route home.

All the left turn lanes were blocked with construction signs and I was forced to drive ten or eleven blocks before I saw it—a sobriety checkpoint in the middle of the next block. The police had deliberately forced more cars to drive through it than might have happened without all those left lane closures. It looked like the Tijuana border with dozens of cop cars, lights rolling, and even more uniformed men milling around. I panicked.

I opened my moon roof and the passenger side windows. I had heard once that having the driver window open was a red flag to cops. I eyeballed my eBay breathalyzer sitting in the console and cursed myself. I fumbled with my right hand, looking for gum or mints, but found nothing. There was an old, half empty bottle of water on the backseat. Stopped in the line that had formed as cops inspected each passing car, I grabbed the water and rinsed my mouth a bit and drank it. There was nothing more I could do, so I adopted my best unconcerned demeanor and tried to look confident. I focused on something dangling from the back of the SUV in front of me for five minutes trying to will my heart to stop racing. Suddenly, it registered that the thing I'd been staring at was a chrome scrotum. The truck literally had balls. *Truck nuts*, I thought as I watched the cop ahead wave the testicularly-enhanced truck on through.

In the next moment, a cop was at my door. He gestured that I should roll down my window. I reached for the button and my dress nearly fell off. I had completely forgotten that I had partly unzipped it. I held it up with my right hand and rolled the window down with my left. He was a Hispanic guy with a wraparound mouth and a mustache so dense it looked like he had a strip of electrical tape on his upper lip.

"How are you doing tonight, ma'am?"

"Fine."

"Where are you coming from?" the Mustache asked and looked over me into my car.

"I was at a premiere. For a movie I'm in," I said, hoping he was impressed by D-list celebrity. If he was, he did a good job of hiding it.

The cop shined his flashlight into my back seat and, without looking at me, asked, "Have you had anything to drink tonight?"

My mind raced. Should I say yes but lie about how much—and risk having him think I was a liar? Or should I say no and risk having to blow and reveal myself, undeniably, to be a liar. I opted for plausible deniability.

"Yes."

He looked at me then. "How much?"

"I had a glass of wine or two at the after party."

"Two glasses of wine?"

I nodded and tried not to exhale in his direction. He asked for my license and registration. It was difficult to dig through my glove box and hold my dress up at the same time.

"Do you have a problem with your top?" he asked and gestured toward my dress. He took my license and registration and directed the beam of his flashlight into my eyes.

"Oh, um, no. I just unzipped it a little because it was poking me."

"Really?" he said with obvious disbelief. "You wouldn't be a working girl, now, would you?"

"What? No. I wish. I haven't really worked in years," I explained. Suddenly, it was important that he understand my situation. "This stupid premiere was supposed to get me back in business. It didn't. I'm fucking done."

"Would you mind watching your language, ma'am?"

This guy was totally missing my point.

"Sorry, but, not that you care, but, you know? A girl over thirty is invisible in this town. It's kinda sick."

"M-hmm," he nodded, penetrating me with his stare, and then turned his focus on my documentation. After he'd examined my license, registration and insurance card, he flashed his light back in my face. I held my breath.

"Pull the car over there, ma'am," he said finally and indicated the parking lot of a strip mall. In the lot, several other cars were already parked, their drivers being interviewed by police.

Fuckfuckfuckfuckfuck, I thought.

I pulled into the lot. Another cop stopped me and asked me to get out and hand him the keys. I struggled to get out of the car without falling out of my dress. Once on the pavement, he took my keys and drove my car to the other side of the property. The first cop approached me with his partner. I made a conscious decision to be upbeat and good-natured about the situation.

"Can I ask you a huge favor?"

"What?" the other cop asked.

"Can one of you guys zip up my dress?" I asked in a sexier voice than any of us expected.

They both looked at me as if I'd just pinched a loaf out onto the sidewalk. Unfazed, I turned my back to them and peeked over my shoulder a la Betty Grable. I tried to throw an alluring look their way but I realized too late that I was looking over my right shoulder. I could feel my droopy, Jake LaMotta eye lift slightly in the outside corner but I knew instinctively that I hadn't achieved a look anyone would call provocative. Grotesque—maybe. Attractive? Certainly not. I gave up on the seduction act and repeated my request.

"My zipper. I can't close it myself."

The Mustache looked at his partner and head-jerked him in my direction. The partner let out a sigh of irritation, approached me warily and stopped at arm's length. He zipped my dress from as far away from me as was physically possible and even clasped the hook and eye thingy. He was obviously a well-trained married man.

"Anything else we can do for you?" the Mustache asked with thick sarcasm.

I told him there wasn't and they led me to a corner in the lot.

"Okay. I want you to walk this line in the pavement with your hands at your sides, moving heel to toe for ten steps."

Two steps in, I knew a third step would prove calamitous so I stopped and assumed a wide stance for balance.

"That ain't gonna happen," I said, as if my failure was as meaningless as the poor toss of a dart. "These heels are very wobbly."

"Take them off," the Mustache said, humorlessly.

Fuck. I took them off and looked back at the cops.

"Let's go. Ten steps, heel to toe."

It went no better barefoot than it had in the stilettos.

"Nah, I can't do that," I volunteered cheerfully.

"Okay. Stand with your feet tight together," he said and waited for me to comply. "Keep your hands tight to your sides. Put your head all the way back and close your eyes." I did this, too. "Now count to thirty, silently. We want to gage your sense of time."

I was at twenty when they stopped me. For the record, I've since tried this trick sober and weaved visibly. It is harder than it sounds. The Mustache got right up in my grill and told me to follow a laser light with my eyes without moving my head. His reaction indicated I'd underperformed this stunt, too. Then the cop took a closer look at my right eye.

"Is something wrong with your eye?" he asked.

Standing there with a cop twelve inches from my face, his penlight burning into my retina like an interrogation lamp, I instinctively brought my hands to my Botox-botched face.

"Don't look at me! I'm hideous!"

That was when they busted out the breathalyzer.

"Take a deep breath and blow into this tube as hard as you can for ten seconds."

I dropped my hands and did what I was told while the two cops took turns yelling "Blow harder!" and looking at me with disgust.

"You have to blow hard. Take a deep breath!" the Mustache bellowed.

Honestly, I was doing my best to follow their instructions. I don't know what they thought I was trying to pull but nothing I did seemed to satisfy them. They made me blow five times.

"How'd I do?" I asked when it was clear that they had what they needed.

"Not good," the partner said.

Shit.

As I put my shoes back on, the paperwork came out. The Mustache put on a pair of over-the-counter reading glasses and grilled me for thirty minutes. He asked predictable things like my name, address and birthday. They asked me to confirm my story of the premiere and two glasses of wine, which I did.

"Are you a homosexual?" the Mustache asked without looking up from his clipboard.

"Excuse me?"

"Are you a *h-o-m-o-s-e-x-u-a-l?*" he repeated as if I were stupid and then looked at me over his glasses.

"How is that relevant?" I asked and then tried to remember if I'd pronounced the word correctly or if I'd said "revellant."

"Ma'am, I have to ask you these questions."

"Why? What possible difference could it make if I'm gay or not?"

"I don't write the questions. Are you a homosexual?"

"I don't see how this could possibly matter."

"Ma'am, this is protocol. We ask everyone. You're not special. Are you a homosexual?"

"No, I am not a homosexual, but I want to go on the record by saying that the question offends me."

"Note taken," the Mustache said and fixed his mouth in that "God, you're an asshole" expression.

The interrogation part of the process completed, the partner pulled out a pair of handcuffs and my world crashed around me. They were arresting me! They were taking me to jail! Somehow, that inevitability had escaped my consciousness until I heard the clatter of the cuffs and saw him look at me.

"Turn around please and put your hands behind your back," the Mustache said.

Handcuffing seemed like radical overkill for a person whose worst crime to date was jaywalking but I obeyed in silence and flinched as the partner slapped the cuffs on my wrists. He clamped them on far more tightly than was required. *These cuffs are too tight*, I thought, immediately aware of how cliché it would sound to say it out loud. The partner was, it appeared, less concerned with being cliché as he opened the squad car door and told me to watch my head as he shoved me into the backseat. He slammed the door and walked away.

The sequins of my dress made a loud scratching sound as I squirmed on the hard, molded bucket seat. My wrists screamed with pain as the unforgiving plastic pressed the iron cuffs deeper into them. My right nostril began to run. I sniffed up the deepest inhale that was humanly possible and then let that breath out again in an open-mouthed howl of deep anguish. The floodgates had been opened, the hounds released. I sobbed like a grieving sea cow for a solid five minutes. I was going to jail. Me. An unemployed, reclusive, pill-popping, wine-soaked, old lady has-been. I hadn't seen this appalling prison addition to my biography coming and I felt cruelly blindsided. I'd sobbed myself nearly breathless when the other back door opened. I quickly composed myself. My nose was stuffed to the breaking point but at least it had finally stopped running. Reflexively, I tried to wipes tears and mascara from my face, but the handcuffs weren't super cooperative. I had to face whatever happened next with a red, streaked face and an inability to properly enunciate any words that contained the letters N or M.

I heard the Mustache say, "Watch your head," and a man dropped into the back seat beside me. When the door closed, I said hello to him.

"Hi," he replied.

"What did they get you for?"

He looked at me and, shaking his said, made a sound that I took to mean, "I don't want to talk about it."

"What's your name?" I asked, actually saying a word that sounded more like "neb." *Just because we are going to jail is no reason to be uncivilized*, I thought. We were fellow outlaws, after all.

"Jamil."

"I'm Ruby."

No response from Jamil.

"They got me on a DUI."

Nothing. I looked out my window and watched other drunk fucks get hassled by the man. Again, I was thwarted by the cuffs in an impulse to wipe my face. I turned back to my companion.

"So, Jamil. Where are you frub?"

"West Virginia."

"Oh! West Virginia!" I said, as if that had some special significance for me. It didn't. "Lotsa… coal minink there."

Jamil looked at me like I was an idiot.

"West Virginia? Wait a minute! Don't tell me you're a fucking Republican!"

"My name is *Jamil*," he deadpanned. "What do *you* think, booze bag?"

Okay, so maybe I deserved the tone of his first remark, but the second crack seemed completely unnecessary to me. I couldn't help it if I appeared disheveled and had mascara all down my face. I'd just been arrested, for Chrissake, and my hands were bound. I tried to wipe my face on my shoulder but it was bare so the effort proved ineffective.

The Mustache opened my door and asked if I wanted to take my purse with me to the station or if they could leave it in my car.

"Are you towing my car?" I asked.

He said they were.

"I want my purse."

For five minutes, the Mustache tried to talk me out of taking it. He threatened that it would take four hours longer to book me if I brought it. I said I didn't care, that I didn't want it out there in the custody of random cops and tow truck drivers and impound lot attendants. Exasperated with me, he tossed my bag on the front seat.

The driver door opened and a new cop got behind the wheel. I didn't try to make any more small talk with my fellow captive and the new cop's ill humor proved equal to Jamil's. The three of us drove to the hoosegow in virtual silence.

9 A girl named carlos

AT THE STATION, I was handcuffed with my hands behind me to a ribbed, aluminum bench in a short hallway. The bench was so close to the wall that my knees almost touched the filthy paint there. The bright lights made me again self-conscious about my make-up and tear-streaked face. At least my crying jag had caused both of my eyes to swell to the point that they were once again a matching pair, and my nose had cleared. That was something. The sequins on my dress crunched against the treads of the bench. My shoes hurt my feet. The sequins and metal conspired to grind my ass and thighs like a cheese grater. The dress tore at my soft underarms. Boning stabbed at my ribcage and the manacles savaged my wrists.

"Can you loosen the cuffs a little?" I pleaded, discomfort overcoming my desire to appear the maverick, a renegade above clichés, beyond categorization.

Driver cop ignored me and took my purse into a room just around the corner. I resigned myself to my new realities and looked around.

"Face the wall!" a cop I hadn't seen screamed from behind me.

Obediently, I turned around, leaned forward a few inches and pressed my forehead to the wall. The main doors opened and a gust of cold air swept through the hallway. Four scary guys were led in and handcuffed to the bench behind me, facing the opposite wall.

"Hey, movie star!" one said, seeing my dress as he passed. His throat boasted a massive "213" tattoo in black ink in an old English font.

"Ha! If you only knew," I said, fraternally. These were my peeps. We were all badasses together.

"Shut up and face the wall!" the cop yelled again.

I threw 213 a look that I hoped expressed my solidarity with him and my shared disdain for Johnny Law.

"I said, face the wall!"

I gave in and faced the wall.

Three-and-a-half hours later and now virtually sober and remarkably calm, I noted proudly, I was relieved to see my first female companion. They handcuffed her to the bench right next to me. She was wearing black Capri leggings, a tank top and flip-flops. She had mascara streaks down her cheeks. She looked like a teenager.

"Loosen my cuffs!" she demanded. "My cuffs are too tight!"

I winced and waited for the slap-down to befall her, but the cop behind me promptly loosened her cuffs. I looked at her in surprise.

"Hi," she said.

"Hi. I'm Ruby."

"I'm Collette. What are you in for?"

"DUI. You?

"Same. My dad is gonna kill me."

"How old are you?"

"Nineteen."

"Where'd they get you?"

"There was a trap on Hollywood Boulevard."

I nodded knowingly, then asked, "Do you know somebody or something?"

She didn't understand my question.

"You asked that cop to loosen your cuffs and he did. I have been here almost four hours and nobody will loosen mine."

"No. I don't know anyone. My God! My dad is gonna be so pissed! How long do you think this is going to take?" she asked me.

"I have no idea."

"Hey!" she yelled toward the room my purse had disappeared into. "Hey! How long is this going to take?"

"You'd better pipe down," I whispered. "They are fucking cranky as shit around here."

"It won't be too long," the cop behind us said.

"So were you at the prom tonight or something?" she asked, indicating my dress.

"Something like that," I said. "Do I have mascara all over my face?"

"Yeah, kinda. Do I?"

"Kinda." I nodded.

She nodded back and we both faced the wall in reflection.

A few minutes later, Collette and I were released from the bench and led through a pair of doors and down a series of hallways. We made a pact to stick together as best we could.

The booking room was bustling.

"You should Facebook me when we get outta here," I suggested to Collette, at a loss for other small talk.

"Step up to this line," a female cop demanded, and before I could comply she screamed, "I said step up to this line!!"

"Okay, I'm coming. Give me a chance," I said, ill-accustomed to being treated like chattel by mean strangers.

"You a wise ass?" she asked, getting all up in my kitchen, channeling the drill sergeant from *Full Metal Jacket*. She had a neck like a mini-keg. It was really unsettling.

"No. But jeez..." I said weakly, leaning back from her glare.

"Put your feet on the spots indicated and lean forward forty-five degrees until your forehead is against the wall," another female cop demanded. I did as I was told. This second female cop began to pat me down while FullMetalJacket observed. I guess they feared I might have a shiv strapped to my inner thigh or something. Second cop's pat-down started normally but got increasingly invasive. She felt my bare armpits like she was feeling for tumors and felt my crotch so carefully she could have been called in as a witness to confirm or deny whether I'd had vaginal rejuvenation surgery.

"Are you going to buy me dinner after this?" I quipped.

"Is that a bribe!?" she screeched, standing up from her twat-inspection position.

"No. That was a joke. A bribe would be me offering to..." I hesitated as the two women glared at me. "...me offering to buy you dinner. See? It's a..."

I didn't bother to finish my thought. I stood there staring back at them while they, I guessed, decided whether or not to call the Feds.

Collette, meanwhile, was talking to two young male cops.

"What did a nice young lady like you do to find her way here?" one cop asked flirtatiously.

"They said I was drunk driving." she said and rolled her eyes, smiling.

Both cops smiled and nodded like she'd just reported having gotten straight A's on her report card and her parents had accused her of slacking. Their demeanor conveyed clearly that they were on her team.

"I just need to call my dad so he knows where I am. He is going to be worried sick. I mean, I *am* nineteen but... you know how fathers can be," she said and made a cutesy, pouty face.

I watched, stupefied as one of the cops reached for his own cell phone, dialed the number she told him and held his phone to her ear.

A booking window opened. I was next in line.

"Go to window two!" FullMetalJacket said, far more loudly than was required, and a second later repeated, "I said, step up to window TWO!"

I started to move and she stopped me with a staccato, "No! Wait! Okay! GO!"

Fuck. *Settle down, chickee*, I thought as I stepped up to window two, grateful to get away from FullMetalJacket and her no-penis overcompensation.

"Hi," I said to the clerk, hoping to find someone who just sucked rather than sucked unbelievably. The cop there smiled perfunctorily and I was grateful to the brink of weeping. He had my purse back there and dumped its contents on the counter between us. An inventory commenced. My cash was counted to the penny. Every item in my purse was noted on official paperwork, even the partially unwrapped OB tampon that had been rolling around the bottom of my bag for who knows how long. He powered my cell phone down and added it to the itemized list.

"You need to remove your jewelry, ma'am," the cop said.

Before I could react, I felt FullMetalJacket behind me removing the handcuffs. I rubbed my wrists and saw a bruise already forming on my right arm. I took off all my newly purchased premiere jewelry and placed it on the counter.

"Your earrings, too."

"They are just studs. What trouble could I possibly cause with two little diamond studs?"

"It isn't what we fear you will do, ma'am. We don't want any of the other prisoners hurting you to get them."

Other prisoners? It was one thing to sit chained to a bench and feel a sense of camaraderie with drug dealers and domestic abusers, shackled and silent with their backs to me.

It was another thing to be defined, out loud, as a prisoner, and to be told I needed to fear my cellmates. *Cellmates*. Oh my God.

I unscrewed the posts and removed the one-karat studs. They were the only valuable earrings I owned. The cop took them and said, "One pair of rhinestone, pierced stud earrings."

"Those are not rhinestones," I said, taking great umbrage as I rubbed my cuff sore wrists.

"They are rhinestones," the cop insisted.

"No. They are real. Can we get someone over here that might know?"

The cop leaned forward and said softly, "You don't want to do that. You don't want anyone here to be curious about these. If you want to get these back, they are *rhinestones*."

Oh! He was afraid that other cops might steal them.

"Oh…" I said, examining his face for its trustworthiness. "Okay. Rhinestones," I agreed and looked over my shoulder to see if anyone had witnessed our exchange.

"Okay, review the inventory and sign here if you agree it is complete and accurate," the cop said, drawing my attention back around.

I signed the form. As I handed it back to him, I wondered how much cops earned, if it was too late for me to become one and whether or not I'd just blown a career "on the job" by getting popped for a DUI. The cop eventually handed me a booking sheet and impressed upon me that if I misplaced it I might not get released from jail in this lifetime. I accepted that as fact and clutched the form to my chest like a safety vest.

FullMetalJacket led me past Collette standing at window six. Collette turned and smiled at me and I noticed her face was clean. I remembered my stained face and began licking my fingers and washing my face like a domestic cat.

"Stop right there!" FullMetalJacket shouted.

I stopped on a dime.

"I said stop!"

"I'm stopped! What the..." I tapered off and threw my arms up in helpless frustration.

FullMetalJacket opened the door to a glassed-in closet with a bench in it.

"Get in there!"

"Now?" I said, suddenly rebellious. What could she do? Put me in jail?

"Yes! Now! Move!"

I moved into the five-by-five room, sat down and resumed my feline hygiene routine. It felt so decadent to be able to move my arms. I might have purred if I had actually been a cat.

I looked through the glass and saw Collette joking it up with the cop that was booking her. The original two cops flanked her and nodded, laughing agreement with some observational comedy I imagined Collette had treated them to. "It's funny because it's true," their amused expressions seemed to say.

While I tried not to hate Collette for being nineteen and more appealing to men in her flip-flops than I was in my heels and my bloodthirsty prom dress, the door opened and another woman stepped into my fishbowl.

"Hi," I said. "I'm Ruby."

"Hi, I'm Laura," she replied and sat on the bench as the door was locked behind her.

"What did they get you for?" I asked.

"DUI," she said, and I said, "Yeah, me, too."

"Do I have mascara all over my face?" I asked.

"No, you look good."

"Thanks. So do you," I responded, anticipating her concern.

We compared arrest stories and bonded as we watched dozens of men and women filing through the room in front of us for booking. Eventually, a third woman was deposited in our cubicle. She was young, very thin and beautiful in a wild and unkempt way.

"Hi," Laura and I said in unison. "What's your name?"

The new girl tossed us a dirty look, did not respond and slumped onto the floor rather than share the bench with us. Laura scooted up tight to my thigh and made two thirds of the bench available for Scary Girl.

"There is plenty of room," Laura said. "You don't need to sit on the floor."

Scary Girl pulled her knees to her chest and started rocking back and forth. She reminded me of Fiona Apple in, by coincidence, the "Criminal" video. I noticed her skin was peppered with tiny scabs. *Probably from smoking cocaine or meth*, I thought, drawing on the knowledge I'd amassed watching marathon episodes of *Intervention*.

Cracky Crackerson didn't bother to acknowledge Laura, and Laura didn't move away from me and back to her original spot on the bench. I didn't blame her. Despite looking young and fragile, Cracky was intimidating.

Freaked out by Cracky, Laura and I sat in silence, too, and stared into the room beyond the glass. I gripped my booking sheet extra tightly. I was grateful now that I wasn't wearing my earrings or anything else that could be torn out of my head, swallowed, shat out the next day and traded for a rock on some seedy corner.

Four Hispanic kids that looked like gangsters were lined up along our window. Three of them turned around and began mocking us in our cell. The fourth one noticed what they were doing, shoved the one closest to him and said something we couldn't hear. One of his pals put his fingers in a V to his mouth and flicked his tongue out between them. I have always found that gesture to be exceptionally degrading but it was exponentially worse having it directed at me by a kid young enough to be my son as I sat drying off from a tongue bath I'd just given myself in a glass holding cell in a Hollywood jail. The fourth guy, the good gang guy, punched him in his arm and he stopped the obscene tongue thing. Good Gang Guy winked at us and turned away. I loved Good Gang Guy.

Eventually, the gang guys were processed and Collette went off somewhere with her admirers, probably to get a spa-style mani-pedi. Finally FullMetalJacket unlocked our door and commanded us to exit.

"Walk over there and stop at that red line! Stop there!" she shouted. After I had come to a complete halt, FullMetal-Jacket shouted a completely unnecessary, "I said stop right there!"

I don't usually say stuff like this, but FullMetalJacket needed to get laid and bad.

We were led and screamed at and led and halted and led some more like we were engaged in a nightmarish game of Nazi Simon Says. Cracky was having particular trouble dealing with FullMetalJacket's gunfire instructions and seemed to be trying to crawl inside her own skin. At a window in the middle of one hallway, we were each handed a thin, foam pillow and a scratchy square thing that the issuer informed me was a blanket.

Our destination was an empty prison cell with about ten or fifteen "beds" in it. The beds were comprised of upside down, U-shaped, tubed-metal headboards and footboards with a metal plank spanned between them. Atop these were blue vinyl pool floats. I chose the bed in the far right corner. Cracky chose the one next to me and Laura was next to her. It had to have been five o'clock in the morning by then and I was exhausted and hung over. I wanted to sleep, maybe sleep my way through the rest of my time in the big house, but I was afraid that if I let my guard down, Cracky would steal my booking sheet. Funny how being reduced to almost nothing increases the value of the most meaningless things that remain in your position. I once saw a homeless woman with a shopping cart and the one thing I could identify in it was a large bag of packing peanuts. *Why would a homeless woman want to cart around a bag of packing peanuts?* I'd thought.

But here I was, afraid that people were plotting to take my booking sheet which, in reality, had far less value than a bag of packing peanuts. *She could use those for a pillow, at least*, I thought. So I did the same thing. I tucked my booking sheet between my cheek and the airline pillow I had been allotted and eyed Cracky surreptitiously.

"There is a pay phone up here. Calls are free but you can only dial locally, in the three-two-three," FullMetalJacket said, and slammed our cell door closed for emphasis before she goose-stepped away.

A free phone sounds great, but how many telephone numbers can you remember off the top of your head? The only number I could recall was my mother's cell phone with a six-one-seven Bostonian area code. It was then that I realized nobody knew where I was. Nobody knew I had been arrested. None of my friends even knew what time I'd left the after party. Nobody would think to call The Albino, even if they knew I'd seen him, which they didn't. Nobody knew to post bail or call a lawyer.

I'd been disappeared.

I noticed neither Laura nor Cracky made a move for the phone, either.

"How long do you think we'll be in here?" Laura asked from two beds away.

I sat up and tucked my booking sheet under my thigh. No sense in tempting folks.

"No idea."

"We got arrested on a Friday," Laura said. All I heard was "We got arrested." It was still unbelievable to me. "Does that mean they won't indict us until Monday morning?"

Indict? Holy fuck.

"Or do we get arraigned?" she asked, but it seemed like she was thinking out loud more than anything else.

"They might let you out on OR," Cracky said.

Laura and I looked to her like she was the Wizard of Oz.

"OR?" we asked in tandem.

"Your own recognizance."

I looked past Cracky to Laura. She shrugged her shoulders and we both directed our attention back to Cracky.

"Unless they got you on the stroll," Cracky said, looking at me.

"The stroll?"

"Tricking," Cracky replied in a tone that made clear how tiresome she found me.

"I'm not a hooker!"

Cracky silently eyed my dress and stilettos.

"I was at a..." I began and then decided that it would be better if nobody ID'd me as an actress. I didn't need to cap the end of my career with a public DUI. I could already see the TMZ "Pinky in the pokey" headlines.

"...at a, um, prom," I said because I couldn't think of anything else.

Cracky literally laughed out loud, revealing a dearth of molars.

"As a chaperone," I added, pissy.

Cracky wasn't buying it but I didn't have to explain myself to her.

"Well, if they released us on OR, when would that happen?" Laura asked, uninterested in my career as a prostitute chaperone.

Cracky shrugged and said, "Whenever they feel like it."

That wasn't encouraging at all.

"And if they don't, what will happen?"

"They might keep you until Monday to put you before a judge."

Monday? I had three dogs at home that would starve, not to death, but miserably, if I didn't come back home for three days.

"I hope they keep us until Monday," Cracky volunteered. She really was on crack.

"I don't!" I objected, as if our fates were tied.

"Me, either," Laura agreed. "Why would you want that?"

"It's supposed to rain this weekend," she said.

I looked at Laura to see if this cleared it all up for her. She was staring at Cracky with a Botox-free, knitted brow. I decided to brave it.

"And... what does the rain have to do with... you know... wanting to spend three days in jail?"

"I live on the street. I don't want to be out there all weekend in the rain."

"Ah," I said. What else could I say?

Cracky's situation sucked the life out of the room for all of us. Thinking about her on the street in the rain, I realized I was cold, and wrapped myself in the itchy bath towel I'd been issued and crunched down in my sequin, hooker dress on my government-issue rubber raft. I put my booking slip under my cheek, rested my head and closed my eyes.

I guess I fell asleep but I had no idea for how long. I was awakened by FullMetalJacket clanking something hard against the bars of our cell.

"Okay, ladies. Rise and shine. Grab your pillow and blanket and follow me."

What followed was a disorienting sequence of drill sergeant commands to go and stop and go and take lefts and rights and more stopping. We were placed in several different cells during the night but never for very long. It was a sleep-deprivation torture to break our wills. We were placed in cells with other women and then a random selection of the collected group would be called to "Get your pillows and your blankets," and we would march down more glum hallways and get tossed into new holding pens. Some cells housed rows of mostly sleeping women; others held dozens of hostile inhabitants that glared frighteningly at newcomers. Some women sat on their beds and looked broken, some were fetal on their rubber mats, some paced manically. *Tweekers*,

I thought. My dress invited a lot of curious looks and more than a few derisive comments.

A new female cop opened the doors of the sixth or seventh destination on our journey and called out six names, mine and Laura's among them. Dutifully, we gathered our pillows and blankets and followed her out. There were no windows of any kind in any of the halls or cells so it was impossible to gage the time.

This must be what the early stages of deportation felt like, I thought. I'd been stripped of rights and free choice and my name had been changed to, "Fitzgerald, Ruby—Pillow-and-Blanket." If we dared ask questions of anyone in authority, they ignored us or threw us looks of scorn. Even the time was top secret. During this transient period, I must have crossed paths and shared cells with women guilty of much more and much less than I was. We were all treated like we had lice by the cops that were forced to deal with us even fleetingly. There were no concessions made for cooperating, no thought of who we might be in real life. The woman with no pants and a visible tampon string was treated the same as me and Laura. Polite or not, couth or not, we were all treated with aversion. Except for Collette. I hadn't seen her since the booking room. I imagined Collette surrounded by admiring officers and sipping a chai latte, drying her newly painted toes with one of those tiny fans salons have for that purpose.

"Do you need me to change the settings on your massage chair?" one cop whispered as he pressed his cell to Collette's ear. I imagined her shushing him with a wave of her hand, "Lindsay! O! M! G! You won't believe where I am," she squealed on the phone to her BFF.

Laura and I huddled together and followed our fellow inmates with trepidation.

"I can't believe that woman got in here like that with that tampon just hanging out," Laura whispered with a sour expression.

"Right? Couldn't they give her some striped prison pants or something and spare her and every one of us this indignity?"

"No. Well, yeah, but I mean, I tried to get a tampon out of my purse while they booked me and that dikey cop not only made me put it back but insisted I go in the restroom and remove the tampon I already had in."

"What the fuck? Why? Were they afraid you were going to try to hang yourself with it?"

"No talking!" our police escort bellowed back in our general direction. We complied.

Eventually, we were funneled into a cell different from the others in that it had two rows of ten or fifteen bunk beds, though these beds were also outfitted with the blue vinyl float "mattresses." The beds were placed about a foot apart. The bars had a Plexiglas barrier added to protect passers-by from us or visa-versa. I selected a top bunk in a bed pressed against the glass. A cartoon played on a TV mounted just outside. *Ice Age* was my best guess. On the opposite side of the cell, abutting the bars and glass, were two side-by-side toilets with no seats and a tiny sink mounted to the wall. There was absolutely nothing in the way of privacy provided. We were supposed to sit on the filthy porcelain in full view of the maintenance crew and any other personnel who might happen by.

The ladies who had entered this cell with me each settled into bunks. Laura was on the bottom bunk in the bed next to me. I noticed someone curled up sleeping on Laura's top bunk. I had to pee really badly but those toilets were beyond the pale.

"Ladies! Listen up! There is a phone here for you to use," she said, pointing to a wall-mounted pay phone a few inches from the toilets. "It only places collect calls and it only places calls to landlines. No cell phone calls will be connected."

Again, the only number I knew by heart was my mother's and she only had a cell phone. A profound sense of helpless loneliness washed over me. I looked at my booking sheet. I couldn't read it because I needed reading glasses on top of my contact lenses for reading small print. This really drove home the sense of deportation I'd felt earlier. Melodramatically, I imagined the different displaced people of history in unfamiliar and hostile places being spoken to or handed documents in a language they did not understand, and thought I was now much closer to understanding how they must have felt. My booking sheet might say right on it that I was to be jailed for days or weeks and I could not know. It might say I was being sent to an internment camp or that I owed an enormous fine but I had no way to know it. All I knew was that I had been told not to lose it or face dire consequences. I folded it back up and sat on it.

The boning in my dress had definitely caused bruising on my ribcage beneath my breasts. I squirmed and tugged at the dress but nothing helped. Both of my wrists were visibly puffed and there was maroon bruising evident there, too. How had my night come to this? How had my life come to this? Well, the fact was, I had been undeniably drunk when I got into my car to drive home. It was also a fact that it had not been the first time I had done it. Then I thought about how lucky I had been to have been caught in a garden-variety DUI at a sobriety checkpoint. I was lucky my arrest hadn't been the result of harm, injury or death I'd caused to something or someone, or myself. My drinking-and-driving career was officially over—this was also a fact—and I was relieved to note that nothing bad had ever happened, and now nothing ever would. I felt like I had been released from an onerous burden. One of the potential tragic ends to my dead-end future could be forever checked off the list. This cheered me up measurably.

A young African American woman rushed forward from the back bunks and puked delicately into one of the toilets. Everyone silently watched her. She quietly retched several times, spit, and then pushed the button over the sink that released the flow of water. She rinsed her mouth and then lurched back down the channel between the beds.

The cell door opened and an unfamiliar cop delivered two giggling girls. They stumbled in, appraised a few faces they found peering at them, and then ran arm-in-arm down to a mid-room bunk. They both crawled into the bottom bed and peered back out though the end. From my angle, they looked like a two-headed turtle. When they made eye contact with me, they pulled their heads back into their shell. I could still hear them giggling.

"Fitzgerald, Ruby?" the new and petite cop called out.

I raised my hand and said, "Here!"

"Leave your pillow and blanket. Take your booking sheet and come with me."

Am I getting released? I wondered. What if they did release me? How would I get to my car or home? This "going to jail" thing was so much more complicated than I had ever imagined.

Petite cop led me a few feet down the hall to the mugshot and fingerprinting station. Mugshot! I had completely forgotten about that. I licked my hands and tried to arrange my hair presentably. I repeated my earlier feline grooming on my face. I was determined to avoid the James Brown wild man shot and the weepy, sad sack Heather Locklear one. I was taking my cues from the mugshot queen, Paris Hilton. She always posed like she was poking her head through a painted carnival board, posing as the freak show fat lady or a saloon prostitute. Her expressions always radiated that she was in on a good joke.

"Stand on that red line and look up into the camera," petite cop instructed, politely.

I did what I was told, composed myself and then looked up at the camera smiling with my eyes. Tyra would have been proud. *Breathing in, I calm my body. Breathing out, I smile*, I thought.

Pop! The photo was taken. Petite cop wanted another for safety, so I looked down, thought happy thoughts and looked up, again. Pop!

I was pretty confident I wouldn't be ashamed of those if they wound up on the internet.

Next, fingerprinting. Petite cop pressed all of all ten fingers, not just the tips, into ink and then into a log. She pressed my entire palms, rolled from the backs of my pinkies to the outsides of my thumbs and pressed those into the log. Finally, she recorded the side of my hand from my wrist to the outside tip of my pinky. It was a very thorough documentation.

"Well, this is going to put a serious crimp in the burglary career I was about to launch," I said to petite cop.

"That's the idea," she replied, smiling.

Her civility was a jarring contrast to the abuse-of-power bitches I'd been dealing with all night.

The processing complete, I was led back to my cell. *Ice Age* was still playing in a loop on the TV outside the glass. I was relieved that we couldn't hear it.

As I climbed up into my bunk I heard my name. I turned to see the person in the bunk above Laura was awake and looking at me. It was Collette.

"Hi, Collette! Where have you been all night?"

"Here," she said, yawning. "Sleeping."

"Here? Right from the booking room?"

She nodded and asked, "Where have you been?"

Before I could answer, Laura got up and made a phone call. Everyone tried to eavesdrop but, it appeared, her call did not go through. When she was done, I decided, despite their no-cell-phone policy, to try my mother. After all, I had nothing better to do to fill my time.

I put the phone to my ear and noticed that the cord was only about twelve inches long, preventing me from sitting with the phone or even turning to face the room while I spoke. It dawned on me that a longer wire could be used to strangle someone. It was a surreal realization and amped my wariness of my cellmates. I threw a worried look over my shoulder and dialed the number. A series of clicks and silent pauses followed. Unbelievably, the call seemed to be going through and I was asked to record my name. "Ruby Fitzgerald," I said in monotone. A cop came by, made a note on a chart outside the cell and moved on without looking in at any of us. I waited through another period of silence and, losing faith, was just about to hang up when I heard the call connect. It was a prison miracle.

"Hello?" I heard my mother answer.

I said hello but she could not hear me. We both listened to a recorded voice say, "You have received a collect call from Los Angeles County Jail. Inmate [my voice saying *Ruby Fitzgerald*] has requested that you accept the charges for this call. Do you accept the charges?"

My mother accepted.

"Ruby?"

"Yes."

"Are you in jail?"

"Yes, I got busted for a DUI."

"At nine o'clock in the morning?"

"Is it already nine o'clock here?"

"Oh. No, it is nine here. It is six there. What happened?"

"Long story but I got caught in a checkpoint leaving that thing last night and..."

"Oh! That's right! How was the premiere? Did you look fabulous?" she interrupted.

"Ma, I'm in jail and I don't know how long I can talk. I just need you to Facebook Eliza and tell her where I am so someone can pick me up when I get released. She has a key to my place. Have her feed the dogs for me, too, okay?"

"Yes. Of course. Are you okay?"

I told her I was.

"So, the premiere. Did you practice your red-carpet poses like I told you to?"

Only my mother would be more concerned with my image on the red carpet than the fact that I was languishing in jail, masquerading as a prostitute to up my street cred.

"Ma, I can't talk about that now. People here think I am a hooker and I want to keep it that..."

I was cut off. At least the dogs would eat if I was there all weekend. I hung up the phone as FullMetalJacket delivered new cellies to our group. Good Gang Guy walked in first.

You could smell the confusion in the room as Good Gang Guy walked through the cell. Every eye was upon him as he selected a top bunk partway down my row.

Behind Good Gang Guy, a blonde in her early twenties wearing cut-off sweats and Uggs filed in. She had a black eye and a cut across her nose. She had obviously been crying, looked bewildered, and crumpled in a heap on the floor between my bunk and the one across the aisle.

When FullMetalJacket left, I asked the blonde if she was okay.

"Yeah," and she stifled a sob.

"They put a guy in our cell with us," Collette whispered to me, scandalized.

"That isn't a guy, Collette."

Collette whipped around to reassess Good Gang Guy. His hair was cropped almost to the scalp. He wore slip-on Vans, chinos slung below his ass and a Pendleton. He was pretty convincing, especially if you were a sheltered, nineteen-year-old suburban Daddy's girl.

Collette looked back at me with her eyes bugging out of her head. I just nodded in an all-knowing way.

"Are you sure you are okay?" Laura asked blonde girl.

"Why? Do I look bad?"

"You have a black eye, a broken blood vessel in your eye and a cut on your nose. What happened?" I asked, coming down to the floor with her.

"I totaled my car. My head hurts, too. Is my face messed up?"

"No, not bad. It'll be fine, but did you see a doctor?"

"No. They arrested me for drunk driving and brought me here."

"I think you should see a nurse. You might have a concussion," Laura said.

I agreed. Laura and I stood up and started banging on the bars. Eventually, FullMetalJacket appeared.

"What?"

"This girl," I said, indicating the blonde girl.

"What's your name?" Laura asked her.

"Sabrina."

"Sabrina needs to see a doctor," I told FullMetalJacket.

"Who asked you?" FullMetalJacket spat at me.

"Nobody."

"Did she put you up to this?" FullMetalJacket asked menacingly, meaning Sabrina.

"No. But look at her. She obviously needs to see a doctor. She might have a head injury."

FullMetalJacket regarded us all with evident suspicion.

"Do you want to see the doctor?" she finally asked Sabrina.

Sabrina nodded. FullMetalJacket got the keys and led Sabrina away.

Minutes later another cop came by with a street vendor cart.

"Lunch! Come on, ladies! Line up!"

Lunch? Had I missed breakfast, somehow? I looked back the length of the cell and watched people appear from nowhere like Munchkins coming out of their secret hiding places and revealing themselves for the first time to Dorothy. There were far more women in that cell than had been apparent.

We lined up obediently and were each handed two four-ounce cartons of cranberry juice, an apple and two cellophane-wrapped tubes. The cop placed the tubes in my hand with tongs through a slot in the bars. Initially, I thought the tongs were red hot and had branded my hand but the pain didn't stop when she pulled her tongs back. I dropped the wrapped things on my bunk.

"My God!" I wailed. "What are those things?"

"Chicken burritos. Careful, they are hot from the microwave," sadistic cop smirked.

Now I knew why they had fingerprinted us before feeding us. Those chicken burritos had just eliminated any identifying traits my right palm once had.

Everybody collected their food. Some went back to their bunks, some lingered at the front of the cell. Those that lingered introduced themselves to each other. In addition to me, Collette and Laura, there was a Hispanic girl named Maria, a teenage-looking girl also named Maria, the turtle twins who only giggled and did not reveal their names, and Good Gang Guy who introduced himself as Carlos.

"I don't eat chicken. Does anyone want my burritos?" I asked.

Carlos took one but there were no takers for the second. I tried to bite the apple but its flesh simply receded under the pressure of my teeth much as the meat on your forearm would if you lightly bit that. I was afraid if I pierced the skin, goo would ooze out on my chin. I threw the apple into the trash can outside the slit in the bars. I opened one of the tiny, baby cartons of cranberry juice and sipped it. It tasted like the glue that held the carton in shape. I threw that away, too.

"This apple looks delicious!" Carlos said, polishing it on his shirt. "I'm saving this honey for later."

I didn't have the heart to break the news to him.

As I sat on my bunk, the smell of the food, however disgusting, made me realize that I hadn't eaten in more than thirty-six hours. I watched an Asian girl in club kid attire squat over the urinal and pee. I'd had to pee for hours and, watching the Asian girl hover over the bowl, I realized I needed to shit, too. When the Asian girl was done, she disappeared again back from whence she'd come.

My abdomen cramped and I looked at those two toilets. As I considered whether I could risk squatting to pee without letting the poo out, a male cop walked up to the chart on the wall outside, made a notation and walked away. My turd got stage fright and retreated.

"What is he doing?" I asked nobody in particular.

"They mark an inspection every hour," Carlos said.

So, it was 7 AM.

"I meant, why is there a guy walking around out there?"

"They warn us when a guy is coming," Carlos said.

"They didn't just now," I pointed out.

Carlos smiled and shrugged his shoulders as FullMetalJacket returned Sabrina to us.

"What did they say?" I asked when FullMetalJacket had gone.

"Nothing. They checked my pupils and gave me four aspirin," she said, plopped onto the floor and sat Indian-style.

"You missed lunch. Do you want a burrito and a cranberry juice?"

I talked her into accepting my leftovers and I joined her on the floor as she ate. Collette, Laura and the two Marias joined us, too. Carlos moved a few bunks closer.

"So, why is everybody here?" I asked.

Everybody said they'd gotten a DUI, except Carlos. Carlos was here for the twenty-second time, this time for a parole violation. He had accepted a ride home from neighborhood felons and got busted in the car with them.

"I don't think they are gonna let me out this time, homie," Carlos told us. "I think I might do time now."

I noticed the two-headed turtle peeping out at us.

"How old are you guys?" I asked them.

"Sixteen," one answered.

"Why are you here?" Laura asked.

"B and E," the other said. "We broke into an abandoned house. They caught us drinking in there."

"I hope that teaches you a lesson," Carlos chastised, good-naturedly. "Crime don't pay."

FullMetalJacket reappeared and called out two names I did not know. It turned out they were the turtle twins. The girls held hands and gamboled their way out of the cell and down the corridor with FullMetalJacket.

At this point, we revealed our ages. Collette was nineteen, as was teenage Maria. Hispanic Maria was celebrating her twenty-fifth birthday as our cellmate. We all wished her a happy one. Sabrina was twenty-one, Laura was twenty-eight and Carlos was twenty. I, as you know, was older than all of them.

"What did you blow?" teenage Maria asked the group.

"How do you know what you blew?" I asked.

"Your booking slip."

"Ah," I said and unfolded my slip. I couldn't read it so I handed it to teenage Maria.

"Wow! You were really drunk!" she said and looked at me, impressed.

"What did I blow?"

"A .18 and a .17. Damn, girl!"

"What? What did you guys blow?"

Teenage Maria had blown a .07 but, because she was underage, zero tolerance required she be arrested. This was true for Collette, too, though she had at least been drunk with a .15. Hispanic Maria blew a .09 as did Laura. Sabrina had blown .13.

I was the eldest by years and was, by far, the drunkest when I'd gotten pulled over. Classy.

"You blew a .18?" Carlos said and made that "hot stuff" sort of chopping gesture with his hand and whistled. "I hope you learned your lesson, Holmes."

"Fuck you, Carlos. This is your twenty-second arrest."

Carlos pulled his shoulders to his ears, closed his eyes and laughed an audible "hee-hee-hee." Carlos was adorable.

For the next hour we traded our tales of arrest. Three of the woman claimed to have been arrested for having one drink. That seemed impossible but I couldn't imagine the point of fronting to your cellies so I believed them. I didn't mention my premiere. I said I'd come from a party and nobody questioned it.

"Maria Williams?" FullMetalJacket called out.

It was teenage Maria's turn to leave the cell. We all wished her luck as the jail door slammed locked behind her.

The need to pee was becoming agonizing. I'd held it for five hours or more. Now, the need to shit had subsided so I decided to give the pee thing a shot.

I lifted my sequin dress, wrangled my Spanx and hovered over the bowl. Nothing would come out. I could feel everyone watching though they all pretended they weren't. My legs began to tremble but no pee would come out.

"Won't your pee come out?" Collette asked.

"No."

"Come on, focus! You can do it!" Sabrina cheered. "Here, I'll run the water for you."

Sabrina pressed the button on the tiny sink and water sloshed out of the tap.

"Come on! You can do it," the African American girl said, coming forward from the shadows. "If I puked there, you can pee."

"If you don't pee, Holmes, the terrorists win," Carlos said, revealing a sense of humor I had guessed might be there.

"I peed!" I heard from the back of the room. "You can do it!"

Was that Asian club kid girl?

The room began chanting, "Come on, Ruby! You can do it!"

I didn't want to let everyone down but the pee was just not going to come and my legs were doing an exaggerated yoga wobble. I stood up and pulled my undies back on and my dress down.

"Did you go?" Sabrina asked.

When I said I hadn't, the whole room let out a disappointed moan. Dejected, I crawled back up into my bunk. The need to shit returned with a vengeance. I needed distraction.

"Maria," I said to Hispanic Maria. "Do you have any plans for your birthday tonight?

She explained that she had been unable to get a babysitter for tonight so had celebrated last night. She'd had only had one drink and was driving to meet her fiancé for dinner when she had been stopped for a broken tail light. Her fiancé, she explained, was shipping out to Iraq in three days.

"My guy is in Afghanistan now," Sabrina said.

Sabrina told the room that she had been unable to afford her rent after her boyfriend's tour got extended. She had been living out of her car for the last month.

"I don't have car insurance. If my car is totaled, I have nowhere to live. Plus, if they impound my car, I don't have money to get it out and everything I own is in it."

These stories were very depressing. They made me look at my own life from a different perspective. They reminded me that I still had a lot to be grateful for, despite a future that felt like stepping off a cliff into total darkness. At least I wasn't headed to Iraq. At least I had a home to lose. At least I wasn't looking at raising a baby alone while my husband dodged IEDs in Afghanistan.

At least I'm not looking at real time, like Carlos, I thought, as Carlos got up and made a series of phone calls. He only spoke in Spanish but he never got past the part where you record your name. It didn't sound to me like he was saying a name, though, not even a girl's name. Then I realized, he was leaving parts of a sentence that would be complete after a dozen attempted calls. The receiver would hear, "Do you accept a call from *I am in a Hollywood jail*." Then they would hear, "Do you accept a call from *I think they are revoking my parole*." This would go on until Carlos had imparted all he needed to. Very clever.

African American girl joined the group. She introduced herself as Violet.

"Where did everyone get arrested?" I asked.

Everyone had gotten caught either in the same trap I had or within half a mile of it.

"I was on the 101 near Sunset and they pulled me over," Violet told us. "They said I was swerving all over."

"You were," Hispanic Maria said. "I was in the backseat of the cop car, remember? You were swerving."

"I hope you know better now!" Carlos chimed in. "Drinking and driving is bad."

"Carlos, you hang out with felons," I said. "You are going to the big house from here."

Carlos treated us to his shrugging "hee-hee-hee."

"Carlos, how long are they going to hold us here?" I asked.

"They need to run your prints in the national database. If you have priors, it goes faster. If not, it can take a while, man. S'fucked up. Plus, they figure in how drunk you were and keep you until they think you are sober."

That was very bad news for me. I had no priors and I had the highest BAC. I was likely to be in jail longer than all the others, except for maybe Carlos.

A cop came and made a note on the chart, as she had several times already. It was now noon. Another cart of molten burritos appeared. I was amazed by how many people bothered to get them.

My need to shit made itself known again. I pinched my ass as hard as I could. Maybe I could sphincter-press that stool crazy hard and shit a diamond. At least the effort distracted me from the prolonged attack the boning in my dress had waged against my ribs.

"I am going to be so pissed if I don't get out of here in time to go to Burning Man," Collette said.

"Don't you live at home with your parents?" I asked, remembering her call from the booking room.

"Yes. Why? Do you think my father will keep me from going?"

"Um... you are in jail for a DUI. Jail. You are nineteen. I don't think Daddy is going to be happy with his little baby."

"You are right. Shit! I just *have* to go to *Burning Man*!" she whined. "What if I tell him I will accept any punishment he wants as long as I get to go to Burning Man?"

"You are not going to Burning Man," Laura agreed.

"Sister, you are going to accept any punishment he wants, no matter what," I agreed.

"I bet you are sorry you were drinking and driving now, huh?" Carlos teased.

"Fatima Fernandez?" FullMetalJacket called from outside the cell.

Everyone looked to see who responded to that name. Carlos grabbed his booking sheet and walked to the glass.

Fatima Fernandez? And I thought Carlos was going to be the last man standing in here.

"Bye, Carlos!" I called out, wondering if it would be smart to friend him on Facebook when I was released.

Carlos waved goodbye to the room and followed FullMetalJacket to an unknown destination. *I'll miss Carlos*, I thought. Then paranoia kicked in. Why had Carlos been released before the majority of us? It seemed, so far, they were letting the youngest ones out first. Was Carlos a plant, a mole, a stoolie? Had he sat amongst us, our trusted cellie, encouraging us all to confess our crimes only to betray us and testify against us in court later? This was a vexing thought, indeed, and left me feeling deeply betrayed.

The next several hours were killed by playing various games—most successfully, the movie game. This game required that each of us call out a movie title beginning with the letter A. When everyone got one, we moved to the next letter and so on. There were intermittent panic attacks to be quelled as one girl or another realized some new way this arrest was going to negatively impact their lives. Surprisingly, I was experiencing my longest stretch without a panic attack in as long as I could remember. Except for the unpleasant public toilet situation, inedible food and the absence of my dogs, I was finding the jail experience quite palatable. I enjoyed the company and I liked living in this entirely new definition of myself. Temporarily, anyway. Me, the fucking badass doing time in the joint. I really enjoyed my cellmates. I found myself wishing we could trade contact information and create a group that could reconvene every year and reminisce about our time here. Maybe we could get custom jackets made that read "Inimitable Inmates" or "Miss Demeanors" or something actually clever. You get the idea. *Maybe I should become a social worker*, I suddenly thought. *Then I could help rehabilitate girls like my new friends here. I wonder if there are degrees required, though. Degrees I don't have. I wonder what they earn in a year.*

The need to shit became oppressive again and insistently interrupted my visions of becoming a parole officer. I was considering using my blanket as a privacy barrier up on my bunk and sticking a finger up my ass to physically push the dirty bugger as far back up the chamber as possible when petite cop approached.

"Fitzgerald, Ruby?" she called out.

Shock and excitement did for my impending BM what I'd been about to attempt with my thumb. I jumped off my bunk.

"Yes?"

"Grab your booking sheet. Let's go!"

All the sentimental thoughts I'd been having for my new friends vanished. I was going to gain access to an actual toilet with an actual seat with actual walls for privacy!

I said goodbye and waved without even facing them. I needed to get out of there and to a restroom before these cops discovered they'd made some mistake.

"Minh Chen?" petite cop called out.

We waited until Asian club kid girl emerged from the back of the cell and then petite cop led us to the property room.

I signed for my purse and its contents. I checked for my earrings and, finding them safe and sound, said a silent thank you to the booking cop.

"What time is it?" I asked the cop who was processing us.

"Four."

I'd been in jail for fourteen hours. I hadn't slept really at all in nearly thirty-four hours and hadn't eaten in longer than that.

Once I drop this kid at the pool, I thought, *I bet I will have lost five pounds since my last meal.* So, you know, this was not completely without a silver lining.

As soon I was outside the actual jail part and released to the lobby of the station, I asked the cops there if there was a bathroom I could use.

"No, ma'am. If you want to use the bathroom, you have to go back to your cell."

Seriously. They actually made that suggestion.

I pushed through the glass doors and bounded down the steps into the bright, sunny day waiting for me. I scanned in every direction for anything that looked like it might have a public restroom.

"Ruby!"

It was Eliza and Dutch. They approached me with expressions of profound sympathy, like my whole family had just died.

"Jail was great!" I insisted and filled them in on my adventure as they drove me to the impound lot. Eliza had fed my dogs and was genius enough to have brought me a change of clothes. Twenty minutes later, we tumbled into the office of the towing company.

"I'm the dumbass that got popped for driving like a drunk asshole last night!" I declared as I approached the lone window clerk.

"You have an ID?" he asked, laughing.

"An ID? Shit!"

The cops had taken my license and had not returned it. What the fuck? How was I supposed to do anything... like get my car back, drive it, or fly anywhere or buy a drink? Then I remembered I had gotten a plastic card version of my passport the last time I renewed it. It was no good for travel anywhere except the land borders of Mexico and Canada but I hadn't realized that when I paid the fifteen dollars. The fact that it was basically useless informed my next ill-advised declaration.

"Oh! I have that fake passport thing!"

Everyone looked at me in surprise and I heard what I'd just said.

"I mean, it isn't fake. I was just... you know... it is a passport... it is just a plastic card one... not the book thingy... I just call it fake because you can't use it to fly or any... thing..." I trailed off, fearing I was making it worse.

The clerk laughed and waved me forward.

"Do you have a restroom?" I asked, handing him my passport card.

He thumbed to my right.

"Go ahead. We'll take care of this," Dutch said.

I locked the bathroom door behind me and simultaneously ripped the dress off and sat on the toilet. I looked under my breasts and saw spotted bruising and several cuts where the boning had either poked or scraped its way through. I massaged my ribcage and waited for the release I had been forcibly putting off for hours.

I'm going to get graphic here because I think if you are still reading at this point, you can handle it. The poop no longer had stage fright. It was right there in the wings, anxious to jump on stage. However, all the time it had spent wandering around backstage, told the house wasn't ready, told to go back to the dressing rooms or hang out in the green room, all this killing time had resulted in the poop gaining some girth it might not have had when it first made its presence known. I had now amassed a cannonball in my colon that was far too wide to shoot out the barrel. I pushed and pushed and crowning was the best I could do. I looked around the bathroom for something, a spoon maybe, that I could rinse off and then shove up my ass to scoop around the poop softball and catapult it out. Nothing.

I touched the skin around my asshole with my fingers and it felt as strained and tight as the vagina of a woman giving birth. From what I could tell, this thing had a six-inch diameter and it didn't have the common decency to fold in on itself like the head of an infant.

Twenty minutes went by. *Eliza and Dutch must be wondering if I committed suicide in here*, I panicked. I took a deep breath and gave the mightiest push of my life. I felt the pop of a tear and the cannonball slipped out a bit. *Oh, thank God*, I thought, but then it stopped. I took another deep breath and pressed with everything I had. Another tear but I didn't care if I hemorrhaged to death getting this thing out of me. Hell or high water, it was coming out. It seemed I might die either way and I couldn't let them find me like I was, with

Punxsutawney Phil's head out my ass, looking for his shadow. I had to get this job done and soon.

I pushed again. This time, there was a satisfying shift and I imagined it wouldn't be long now.

Ten minutes later, I sat there looking between my legs at my progress. I could see the Duraflame log reaching out toward the blood-pinked water but, perhaps afraid the water was cold, it had again refused to progress. What was I supposed to do? Grab it like the grip of a baseball bat and yank it out? I had never had a predicament like this in my life. I got mad.

"One more push and then I am cutting you off," I said out loud to my turd. "You are no match for me! I've done time, motherfucker!"

I took a final deep breath, squeezed my face tight and pushed. *I must look like Eddie Flagon does when he paddle-fucks someone*, I thought. The memory of Eddie pissed me off even more and I upped my effort. The poop slid out another inch.

"That's it. You're cut off!" I said, gritting my teeth.

I pinched my ass as hard as I could, but I was no match for the petrified log that had been calcifying in my colon for half a day. Finally, I had to put my fingers on the stretched and bleeding sides of my a-hole and pinch in manually. It worked and I was unpleasantly splashed with the bloody water from the basin. The other half of the severed poop retreated back up inside in terror.

That's right. Run, you miserable fuck. I'll see you later, I thought.

I gingerly wiped my threadbare anus. I was glad I couldn't see it because it had to really be showing its age at that point.

I stood up—nude now, mind you—and admired my work in the bowl. I upped my weight loss estimate by a pound and flushed the toilet.

Washing my hands, I looked at the damage the dress and handcuffs had done and thought about how much sympathy mileage this experience could get me in the right circles. I was surprised to note that I really had no self-pity, though. I had kinda gotten what I deserved and the worst part of the whole experience had been this last half hour. For sure, my ass had taken the brunt of my jail experience. Maybe that is what they really mean when they ask ex-cons if their asses hurt. I knew mine did.

Eliza and Dutch had to know I'd been in here taking a dump. What else could I have possibly been doing for thirty minutes? I looked in the toilet and was horrified to see that the shit was still there, giving me the finger. I flushed again and stared it down. The second attempt achieved no more than the first. I wanted to flush again but if Eliza and Dutch heard me flushing over and over after I'd spent forty minutes in the john they might imagine I was having trouble flushing a shit almost as big as the one I was actually trying to flush. How embarrassing would that be?

I looked over my shoulder for witnesses and then wrapped my hands in tissue. Still naked, I reached into the bowl and carefully plucked the Yule log from the basin and dropped it into the trash can inches away. I covered it with more tissue and twenty feet of paper towels. Fuck the environment. I had a situation on my hands.

I washed my hands again, got dressed in the change of clothes Eliza had brought for me and washed my hands another time. I washed my face and then wet my hair. Maybe wet hair would throw them off the scent. I walked back out into the lobby.

"We were beginning to worry about you," Dutch said.

"Sorry! I had to give myself a whore's bath in there to get the stink of the clink off me."

Eliza and Dutch nodded as if that was what they'd thought all along. Or perhaps they were just being kind.

My dogs greeted me enthusiastically when I walked in. I explained why I had been detained and they readily accepted my apology. I fed them, nuked a freezer-burned Lean Cuisine pizza, had a glass of wine, a long bath, and went to bed.

I WOKE UP THE NEXT MORNING with an unfamiliar feeling. Was going to jail like losing your virginity—leaving you forever changed? Or was it just that I had woken up without a hangover for the first time in months? I made a pot of coffee and reflected again upon my life as the coffee brewed. I hadn't had meaningful work in ages, I was several months behind on my mortgage, chin-deep in credit card debt, on a Welfare diet, and I was coming dangerously close to being unable to afford my daily doses of grape-based self-medication. I'd attempted relationships with four or five of the craziest losers on my romantic résumé and had actually been struck in the face by one of them during sex. I'd just been completely invisible at the premiere of my own film, despite my best efforts to the contrary, and I'd been arrested and spent my first night in jail. My future had no professional or romantic prospects but was riddled with expenses I couldn't meet and the fallout from the first criminal offense of my life. I'd been willfully plodding ahead in my life with my hands clapped over my ears to drown out the increasingly loud information that my life was collapsing all around me. With the aid of wine, Xanax, the diversion of inappropriate men and epic denial, I had been able to pretend to myself that everything would right itself, that my life would get itself back in order if only I could wait it out. All that thumbing my nose at reality had gotten me where? *Jail*, I thought. Fucking jail. I think jail is a red flag in pretty much everyone's life. Maybe it was time to honestly reassess my life and my approach to it. Jail wasn't how my life was supposed to turn out. I was supposed to be happily ensconced in both a loving relationship with a wonderful man and a great role on a long-running and critically acclaimed television series, direct a few episodes, land a beauty product contract, found a dog rescue charity and maybe have my own line of clothing at Target. And early on, I'd come very close to making most of that happen. Well, at least I had a recurring role on a television show. How had all that promise and momentum been washed away? How had I been reduced to the total loser I'd become? When did I drop the ball?

"It will all be okay, you'll see. All it takes is one job and everything will turn around again," my mother always said, and I'd let myself be convinced because it all had to be okay. It had to be. What else was there for me? And she was right. One job really can turn a career around. Look at what *Pulp Fiction* did for Travolta. I'd actually wondered once if there was any chance Tarantino had been a Pinky Browntown fan. It wasn't impossible. Maybe he was preparing to bring me out of my campy obscurity to play an iconic role in his next feature film. Just because I couldn't actually see my resurrection coming, that didn't mean it wasn't. You can't see sound waves, either. That doesn't mean they don't exist. So I'd kept the blinders on and the wine in stock and waited. Waited my ass fifteen pounds heavier, my face ten years older and myself right into the slammer.

Coffee in hand, I sat in front of my computer and investigated just what damage my DUI was going to do to the hanging shreds of life I had left. The news was not good. For a first-time misdemeanor DUI conviction with no mitigating factors (like an injury or a minor in the car), the punishment included:

$400-$2000 in fines.

Informal or "summary" probation for 3-5 years.

Up to six months in county jail which can sometimes be converted to work service or additional fines.

A three- or nine-month court-approved alcohol and drug education class that costs $100-$500.

A three-month total driving suspension followed by a six- to ten-month restricted license. A restricted license enables you to drive during the course of your employment, and to and from work, school, and/or California DUI school and AA meetings.

At least six, but up to fifty-two, Alcoholics Anonymous meetings.

A negotiated amount of community service hours.

You must maintain SR22 insurance (an expensive auto insurance policy designed for DUI offenders and other high-risk drivers) for three years after your driving privileges are restored.

Canada will likely refuse you admittance into the country for ten years as Canada considers all DUI convictions felonies.

If you are caught driving with a BAC of .01 or higher for three years following conviction, it is considered a probation violation and jail time is required.

A DUI is priorable for a second DUI offense for ten years.

Holy shit! Who knew? And what's up with Canada? Half my résumé had been shot in Canada. If an actor cannot travel to Canada, work opportunity is reduced dramatically. Not that I could ever get a job that shot in Canada because 1) I never had auditions anymore and 2) now I wouldn't be able to drive to one if I got one, but still. A ten-year banishment seems kind of excessive.

How do normal people comply with these terms? People with real jobs. Jobs they need to drive to. Jobs that won't be understanding about a three-month leave of absence. Who has that kind of money for fines and extra time for community service? It seemed to me that one DUI could take an otherwise-together person's life and destroy it. Three months without driving must lose a lot of people their jobs and, subsequently, maybe even their homes.

My phone rang. It was my mother.

"So, how are you doing?" she asked, tentatively.

"You mean jail?"

"Um, yeah..."

"Jail was fine. Jail will go down as a singular and not entirely unpleasant event in my life. Jail is someplace I was never supposed to land but I'm kinda glad I did. I'm not the adventurous sort and, I guess, it has been a long time since something that unexpected and unique has happened to me."

"Well, that's a good attitude. I guess," she said. I could tell she wasn't convinced that I was as okay with my imprisonment as I was. Even I was aware of how monotone I sounded, so I couldn't blame her for her suspicion.

"Jail was nothing. Whatever with that. I have been drinking too much and rolling the dice with the driving for too long. Now I won't anymore. And at least nobody got hurt. Nothing was damaged."

"That is good. So then, why do you sound so defeated?"

The word "defeated" tipped the first in a row of emotional dominoes and I was flooded with a dozen feelings in rapid sequence: humiliation, fear, sadness, anxiety, exhaustion, anger, disappointment, resentment, dread, rejection, abandonment, shame—and then defeat. I was defeated. She'd hit the nail on the head.

"Because I am defeated," I said and burst into tears. "And not by jail. By everything else in my life. Jail was practically fun compared to the wasteland that is my real life."

"What's going on? Did the premiere not go well?"

"NO! No, the premiere did not go well. But that's not it. You know, I always believed that we all have different lessons to learn in life and that the opportunities to learn those lessons are continually put in front of us. If we choose to ignore those opportunities or squander them, life hits us harder and harder, making the lessons more difficult to avoid each time. While I am genuinely baffled about what it is I am not learning here, it seems undeniable that life is trying to get me to see something. I feel like I was getting hit in the face with pies for the last few years and, because I laughed them off as life's little pranks, I am now getting hit in the face with a frying pan.

Do I keep ignoring it until I get hit with a Mack truck? What am I doing wrong? Do you see what it is I am supposed to be learning or understanding or changing here? Because if you do, please tell me!"

"I don't. I honestly do not."

I sat and sobbed into the phone for a solid minute as my mother listened in agonized silence.

"I wish there was something I could do," she said when my sobs finally exhausted themselves.

"I'm going to lose the house," I said and, for the first time, really let myself believe it. I felt three hundred pounds heavier with the acceptance of that reality. "I am months behind on the mortgage. I have nothing in the bank, no retirement accounts of any kind and I am deep into a five-figure credit card debt. This DUI is going to cost me thousands of dollars that I do not have and, effectively, put me under house arrest for the better part of a year. I have to accept that my career isn't likely to recover to the point that it will ever again support me, especially if I can't go to Canada for ten years."

"Why can't you go to Canada?"

"Canada considers a DUI a felony and we felons are not allowed over the border."

"That seems harsh."

"I know but whatever. Fuck Canada. Aren't they responsible for Justin Bieber?"

"I don't know? Are they?"

"I don't know. I think so. Anyway, that is the reality of it. No going to Canada for a decade. I tried to apply for a few real jobs around here but either people do not think I am serious or I am unqualified. Even for the most basic jobs, jobs I thought I was better than while I was still in high school. Joke's on me now. I have absolutely no marketable skills. I'm pretty much fucked," I said and giggled deliriously, like a schizophrenic. Sometimes pressure breeds odd reactions.

"Please don't bite my head off for suggesting this..."

"Eh, fuck it. Go for it. I'm already an unemployable, bankrupt felon on the verge of homelessness. How much worse could you make it?"

"Why don't you sell the house? Move home, back to Boston?"

"What? And give up show business?" I said and laughed wryly.

"I know you are joking but I am not. Yeah. Give up show business. I mean, when was the last time your job made you happy?"

"Probably right about the last time I had a job."

My mother didn't respond, so I continued.

"Then again, the last time I had a job worth mentioning is so far back, I can't even remember."

"That's a long time to not be happy."

She was right but, despite talking about it all the time, I had never seriously considered giving up acting. Not proactively, anyway. Not decisively. I had been just trying to roll with the punches, downsize my life and expectations, as acting gave up on me, hoping it wouldn't quit me completely and that I could forever eke out some kind of living, however meager. Suddenly, I felt like a pathetic, clingy woman tearfully clutching at the ankles of a disgusted boyfriend who had long ago fallen out of love but who still felt enough pity not to savagely kick loose of my grasp. I was embarrassed for myself. No wonder I'd tried to avoid clarity.

"You must have some equity in that house..."

"I have a lot, I think," I answered, microscopically more open to her suggestions.

"More than your credit card debt?"

"By a lot probably, yeah. But no bank will let me touch it because I have no income. Sick twist, really. I will lose my house even though I have lots of equity in it."

"You don't lose your house. You sell it. You take that equity. Move home. Live with us. You don't have anything to prove to anyone out there. Or anywhere."

Something to prove? It was like an epiphany. All of a sudden I realized that I had always felt like I had something to prove—to myself and to the people in Boston that had sworn I'd never "make it" and to every other person who had rejected me on one professional level or another. I'd been gritting my teeth and pushing back tears and I'd been trying to will the life I thought I wanted into being with such focus that I hadn't ever taken the time to reassess—to investigate if the goals I'd set when I was eighteen were still goals that were possible to reach, or even if I still wanted to reach them.

"Acting isn't making you happy anymore. Find something else you love."

Something else I loved. That sounded so simple. Could it be that easy?

"Reinvent," my mother said.

Reinvent. The thing I had resented Eliza for. Maybe I resented her for doing what I was not ready to face doing myself. I let the word sink in. It no longer sounded threatening. It sounded so full of hope now. Reinvent. Inexplicably, I saw myself smiling, wearing a fifties cotton frock in the spotless kitchen of a sunny bungalow somewhere, my freshly baked pie steaming on the windowsill. What the fuck is that about? Apparently, I secretly wanted to be June Cleaver. I thought about that, too. I saw myself setting out a dinner, a man coming in, me handing him something freshly stirred in a Tom Collins glass, dogs bouncing at his feet. This man didn't say things like "I have a huge cock and I'm gonna tear your shit up," nor did he weep over my future in Hell. He didn't have an audition the next day, a screenplay in the works, aspirations to direct and, more importantly, neither did I. We both had regular, stable jobs that didn't come home with us or end every three months. He was probably an electrician or maybe he owned a local hardware store. Everybody loved him. But what did I do? Where was my place in this new world? Then I saw it. I owned a small café or diner. Or maybe I just worked there but hoped to buy it one day from the aging proprietor. I made simple but fresh and hearty homemade foods. I joked with customers, sometimes arousing feigned horror in them as I let a curse word "slip" or made a particularly crisp political observation. I gave the local homeless guy a hot meal every day for sweeping the sidewalk. I endlessly topped off coffees. I served beer. I had daily specials. Everybody loved me. I was that girl from that show but now I lived thousands of miles and millions of years from that version of myself. I was a regular person among regular people doing regular things and it was easy. Easier, anyway.

This life was a relief. A huge fucking relief.

"What if I did that?"

"What? Moved home?"

"Yeah," I said as a wave of nervous nausea rolled through me and my heart raced as I let myself actually consider throwing in the towel. "Yeah. What if I stopped this whole farce out here? Why am I white-knuckling this bullshit? When I first became an actor, I wanted to be one of those actors like Gene Hackman or Jessica Lange or Sissy Spacek—you know? I wanted a well-respected résumé with exciting and varied projects on it. I wanted to leave an impression. That ship has sailed. I am too old and un-established now to ever get anything substantial accomplished. And I had reconciled myself to that, too, as long as I was allowed to make a reasonable income as a worker bee actor in the Hollywood hive. Even that now feels so out of reach..." I said, without finishing the sentence, and drifted off into thought.

"So sell the house. Isn't Kate a realtor?"

"Yeah, she is. Do I really want to spend the rest of my life scraping by, living in a shitty apartment, praying for an audition for three lines on the latest utterly forgettable, victim-of-the-week show? Won't I just end up bitter and lonely, fingers permanently dyed orange from a steady diet of Cheetos and cheap, canned beer?"

"Well..." my mother said and, realizing she had nothing more to say, fell silent. Or maybe she sensed I was seriously considering moving home and she didn't want to spook me off with the wrong words at the wrong moment.

"Can I call you back in a little bit?" I asked after a few moments.

"Of course. It's all going to be okay. You'll see."

"I know," I said, beginning to let myself believe her.

I OPENED A BEER and went out into the yard with the dogs. I looked around the property and back up at my house. I loved the house, both for its charms and for what it represented. It was the sole monument to my achievement as an artist. None of the work I had gotten to do had ever been special or particularly memorable. I wasn't ashamed of any of it. That wasn't the problem. It was just that I had never achieved any real status, at least not the sort of status that allows an actor to choose jobs and not just be forced to accept the ones they are lucky enough to get. My résumé did not reflect my taste in cinema, or even in TV. It was just a long list of paying jobs I was fortunate enough to have been hired to do. But there was no DeNiro "You talking to me?" scene or a Nicholson "I am the motherfucking shore patrol, motherfucker!" No Bette Davis "Fasten your seatbelts. It's going to be a bumpy night." Not one great moment. My only claim to fame was TV's bad girl, Pinky Browntown, a recurring guest on a cheesy but classic television show. I was a modern Pinky Tuscadero—right down to sharing her name. And where was Pinky Tuscadero now? I went inside and looked it up. Oh God. Arrests involving firing a shotgun through a neighbor's window and into several other neighbors' cars, plus jail time for assaulting someone else—with her cane, no less. I'd already done jail time. I really was the next Pinky Tuscadero. I had to end the similarities now. Today. I had to stop clinging to the past. I had to step out of the darkness of denial and into the sunshine of reinvention. I called Kate.

"I'm selling the house, Kate. I'm done."

"Are you sure?"

"Yeah. I'm drowning financially. In fact, I can't even imagine ever having a career again that would make all the rejection, uncertainty and instability worth it. I'm getting too old to live hand to mouth, dreaming of the days when I will have, if I am very lucky, a supporting role on a poorly written TV show."

"You'd be lucky to get a poorly written TV show?"

"Yes! Because 99.99% of them are poorly written. So getting a great show is virtually impossible. Most of us are out here scrambling and praying and begging for roles on shows we know are shit and getting one is like hitting the lottery. It is hilarious, actually," I said and laughed.

"For a gal who was in jail twenty-four hours ago—you seem in remarkably good spirits. Are you drunk?"

"Not drunk. Not even hung over! It's a new me! I love acting. I love this house. But neither of those things are me. I let them define me for so long and fought so hard to hold onto them—letting go is like having a huge weight lifted off my shoulders."

"Really?"

"Yes. And I am as surprised as you are."

"If you sell the house, what will you do?"

"I will put all my shit in storage here and pack the dogs up and drive to Boston before my DUI sentence kicks in and I can't drive for nine months."

"Wayne wants you to know he will handle your DUI case here for free, by the way," Kate interjected.

"Thank you. That is very generous of him. Tell him I will take him up on that."

"I spoke to him about it last night and he said he will look for some extenuating circumstances that might get the case dismissed. If there are none and you agree to simply plead guilty or no contest—you don't even have to be present. I think he can handle it all for you from here."

"That's great. Thanks. So anyway, once I am in Boston, I might try to get a job in my parents' neighborhood. At a restaurant. I can work for almost nothing, as I'll probably have to, because I will be living with my parents and not driving, so I shouldn't have a lot of expenses. Plus, I will have the money from the house to pay off my credit card bills, et cetera. Then, my plan so far, and this is just off the cuff, is to learn as much as I can about running a kitchen and a restaurant, with an eye to eventually opening one myself. Maybe I will find a great old dining car somewhere and buy it, have it shipped to Massachusetts and open a gourmet diner. Who knows? I can't remember ever looking at my future and thinking I had options. Options. So decadent. It's really exciting to think about!"

"I'm happy. You sound really good. For the first time in a long time. I want to run an idea by you, though. I haven't brought this up before because I didn't want you to think I was pushing something on you before you were ready. Have you considered not selling the house?"

"That's all I've considered since I bought it. I don't have a choice anymore."

"You do, though. You could probably rent it for more than what your mortgage costs. My company could manage the property for you, get you good tenants, collect the rent and all. That way, you can keep the house, not only as an investment but as a back-up plan if going to Boston sucks, and even get a little income from it. In a year, or anytime, if you want to come back, the house is still yours. Or you can choose to sell it down the road when you are not under such pressure."

This seemed too good to be true.

"Really?"

"Yeah. Really."

"What do I have to do to make that happen?"

"Just let me know how soon you plan to go east."

"Okay," I said. "Lemme put this in my pipe and smoke it a bit."

"You got it. Everything is going to work out great. You'll see."

More and more, I was beginning to believe that, too.

I GOT ANOTHER BEER and, with unexplained butterflies in my stomach, looked up the American Diner Museum. To my shock and delight, there were dining cars for sale there from every era and in every condition from trashed to fully restored. More surprising was the cost. They ranged in price from ten thousand to a hundred thousand dollars. Butterflies picked up their pace. There was one Valentine diner in Estelline, Texas, south of Amarillo, that was for sale and looked so much like my fantasy café I'd envisioned earlier, I felt almost faint. But it looked like a stationary building and not a traditional dining car. It didn't look very movable. Route 66 seemed to have an endless supply of diners, some up and running, others in various states of abandonment. I determined then that I would take Route 66 as far as I could on my drive across country and educate myself as much as possible on the various models and menus and locations. I also decided right then and there that I would take Kate up on her offer to rent out my house. I would hire a handyman to come in and repair all the little nagging broken things that I had put off dealing with because of money woes. I would pack everything up, have a painting/goodbye party week with my friends so I could get the house cleaned up, and spend some quality time with everyone. I would call Kim, my agent, and tell her that I was moving back to Boston and that I could work there, if anything came up. No sense closing that door completely. I would then put the dogs in the car with some clothes, my computer and a few other important items and I would hit the road. The Mother Road. I was going to road trip it to my new, reinvented life.

I hadn't felt better about myself or my future in a decade. It made no sense. I was moving home in defeat, to my parents, at middle-age, with dreams to be a restaurateur. Restaurants were notorious in that they required you work twenty hours a day and still lost money. Restaurants failed nearly as often as acting careers. But the idea of taking charge of my own day, my own fate, in a way that was so much more hands-on than sitting around cursing my agent and waiting for an audition for a job I wasn't going to get, anyway, was incredibly empowering. Who even knew if my agent was submitting me on things? But if I ran a café, I'd know everything: ingredients, delivery times, staff pay, customer tastes. Success or failure seemed to rest so much more on application and elbow grease and not the whims and opinions of others. It seemed you could make it anything you wanted if you were willing to work, and I was desperate to work. I was already fantasizing about the potential menu when I looked up the numbers of various long-term storage companies in town.

A MONTH LATER, the contents of my house had been packed up, picked up and taken off to storage. My friends had helped me repaint every surface and all the minor and major repairs that were needed had been completed. It had been a whirlwind of excitement and promise. It is incredible what you can get done when you have a clear plan and some drive. Maybe because of the physical exercise of packing and painting, maybe because of my lightened mood, I don't know, but ten pounds had fallen away without effort. I felt great. I was genuinely happy.

"You look happy," Eliza said as she, Mack, Kate and I sat around my kitchen counter eating bagels and drinking champagne from paper cups. It was my final morning in Los Angeles. The girls were over for one last goodbye. I would leave with them, hand my house keys to Kate and begin my drive to Boston.

"I am. And excited," I said and noted that Eliza was dressed in an outfit that looked very Banana Republic. I wondered what niche she was currently representing.

"I am. I really am. Two months ago, if you'd told me I'd be retiring from acting, putting everything I owned in storage and moving home to live with my parents in Boston to work for minimum wage in a restaurant kitchen, I would have wanted to kill you. Or myself. I'm as surprised as anyone to watch my reaction through all this."

"Are you really retiring from acting?" Mack asked, not looking at me but, rather, brushing at her nipple through her shirt, as if it were a piece of lint she was trying to flick away.

"No. Not in any official way. I suppose I can get an agent in Boston, too, and pursue local stuff while I try to develop some restaurant skills."

"You know? If you love something, set it free," Mack said and began addressing invisible lint on her other nipple.

The rest of us looked at one another, bewildered as to where that came from.

"What the fuck are you talking about?" I asked, finally.

"It's just that it's funny. You know? It is like you were not allowed to find a way to keep your house until you gave up trying to keep your house," she said and, at last, looked up at the rest of us.

All three of us sat in silence, digesting the fact that Mack had said the first genuinely insightful thing of her life. I realized I was staring at her boobs and looked at Kate and Eliza to distract myself. I noted then that they, too, had been hypnotized by Mack's lintless tits.

"I'm excited for you, Ruby," Kate said when my stare finally broke her trance. "I'm going to miss you. A lot. But I think this is going to be great for you. I have great tenants moving in here next week. Two guys. Costumers over at Paramount. They're lovely. And Wayne and I will handle all the rest of the house and court details from here. But it's going to suck to have you gone so far away," Kate said.

"I still don't know why it all had to happen so fast," Eliza said. "It just seems so sudden and impulsive and... I don't know..."

"It had to happen fast so that I could get it done before the bank started foreclosure proceedings on my house and before my impending conviction takes my driving privileges away."

"Conviction? It's like you are a criminal or something," Mack said.

"I am. I think it will add flair to my new persona as a 'bossy, busty café owner with a past.' I should frame my mugshot and hang it behind the register. When I have a register, that is. In other news, Eliza, what's up with this outfit?"

"What? It's... what?"

"It's regular," I replied.

"And?"

"You haven't opted to look like your regular self in ages. What will the baby dykes think of you looking all J. Crew on them?"

"Who cares?"

"Indeed?" I said, and Mack, Kate and I all turned our full focus onto Eliza. Eliza stared back innocently.

"What?" Eliza asked again.

"You tell us."

"Okay, fine. I had a date last week. With a woman."

A chorus of reactions erupted from the three of us.

"Calm down. Let me just tell you and get this out of the way."

We all complied. I sipped champagne.

"So, anyway, we went to The Abbey and had dinner and a million drinks. She was this gorgeous, mixed race Rae Dawn Chong thing with this amazing curly hair. Anyway, we were at my place afterward and there was wine and I had set candles everywhere but she was on me like white on rice so I never got any of the candles lit."

A three-throated squeal filled my kitchen.

"And?" we all asked in unison.

"Will you guys stop! If you don't behave, I won't tell you what happened."

"Okay, okay…"

"So anyway, it was my first time kissing a woman. I was nervous but I liked it. And without the candles, the room was a bit darker. It built my courage up. We kissed a long time and then the next thing I knew, our tops were off and we were rolling all over my couch. She had nice boobs. We did… boob things."

"Boob things?!"

More squealing and laughter from the peanut gallery but, this time, Eliza ignored us and pressed on.

"Boobs are nice. I like boobs. I like my own boobs."

"Thank you!" Mack said and looked at the rest of us, nodding accusatorily, as if Eliza's statement had finally proven a point Mack had been trying to make to us her whole life.

"We all love your boobs, Mack. We see them more than our own," Kate said.

"What are you saying?" Mack demanded.

"People? Here. Focus," Eliza said, pointing at herself with both hands. Satisfied she had our attention again, she continued. "I was relieved to discover that I enjoyed doing… things… to her boobs. And she sure knew her way around a nipple."

"I might puke," I blurted.

"Why? You got a problem with boobs?" Eliza challenged, defensively.

"No. I don't know. This whole story has me feeling like I'm going to explode! It might be the best story I've ever heard in my life. Continue. Hurry!"

After a deep sigh and a "Can you believe her?" look at the other ladies, Eliza continued.

"So the boob thing went on for a while and, inevitably, she moved onto my… downtown. I was wearing a dress at the time so she got access pretty quickly. I closed my eyes and let her perform cunnilingus on me…"

"Isn't 'cunnilingus' the dirtiest sounding thing ever?" I couldn't help but interject.

"It is if you do it right," said Kate and nodded, smiling lasciviously with one eyebrow arched.

This got all of our attentions.

"I'm just saying. Sometimes those swingers' parties get pretty wild. I've been known to go off the reservation here and there. I'm not above going down…" she said and cut herself off. "But this is Eliza's story. Go on, Eliza."

All of us stared at Kate for a few seconds, reassessing her in our minds, then Eliza continued.

"So she manages to get the job done in record time."

"How many songs, do you think?" Mack asked.

"How many songs what?" Eliza replied.

"How many songs did it take you to cum?"

"Oh, right," she said, remembering Mack's insecurity. "Honestly, I don't think it would have even been one. It was really fast."

"I knew it. I take too long to cum," Mack said.

"What is she talking about?" Kate asked me.

"Some guy told her she takes too long and now she counts songs to guesstimate her performance time."

Kate stared at Mack, her head tipped and her face fixed with sympathy, but I needed to hear where Eliza's story was going.

"Eliza, focus. So you came faster than a fourteen-year-old boy. What next?" I said, urging her on.

"She waited for me to return the favor. She put my hand on the button of her jeans. I froze. She seemed unfazed, and just took her own pants and underwear off. She had the most amazing body but I was still frozen. She pushed my head to her stomach and I didn't know what to do, so I kissed it. And I kept kissing it, all around, then on her thighs and stuff. She seemed to like it so I just kept doing it. Finally, she spread her legs and I was suddenly staring it right in the face."

No squeals. The three of us were riveted.

"I approached it, slowly, like one would a woodland squirrel one wanted to photograph…"

"Aaah! A woodland squirrel?" I said and erupted into peals of laughter. "This is definitely the best story I have ever heard!"

"So, I get right up to it but I can't bring myself to kiss it. So, I didn't know what to do, so I just kind of opened it up with my fingers."

This time Kate screamed with laughter. Eliza was this far in and chose to ignore our reactions and get the story out.

"Have you ever looked at one of those things? There's a lot going on in there."

Mack nodded, somber, knowing.

"It was like a… mini roast beef sandwich. All kinds of nooks and crannies and then I saw it. It looked like a teeny, tiny penis poking out. I touched it with my finger and she groaned and pressed her hips forward. I diddled it a little more. She groaned more. Everything got really wet and she seemed pretty happy with what was going on but I couldn't bring myself to put my mouth on it."

"So? What did you do? Give her a pity handy?"

"I didn't know what to do. I don't know how many songs this went on for but it seemed like all of a double album. I had to do something. I had to get out of this. So while I was poking around her junk, I scanned the room with my eyes, looking for inspiration. And then I saw it. I knew what to do. And I did it."

"What the fuck did you do?"

"I'm not proud. I want you to know, I am not proud."

"Fuck you! I feel like your date! Finish this off!"

"Okay. Okay. So, while I was diddling and poking with one hand, I reached over to the coffee table and… oh my God!"

"What?"

"I took a candle off the table. I took a candle off the table and stuck it in her!"

Pandemonium in the kitchen.

"Oh my God! You stuck a lit candle up her twat?"

"No! No! It wasn't lit. Remember?"

"Oh, right. But you still stuck a candle in her cooch!"

"No. I didn't. I stuck it up her ass."

Full-blown riot. Mack and Kate and I took five minutes to stop laughing. Wiping at tears and exhausted, we returned out attention to Eliza, who was ashen.

"So, okay. Oh my God. Why her ass?"

"I don't know! It was dark! There's a lotta stuff down there! I panicked!"

"Ha! And? Did she like it?"

"No, she didn't like it! You woulda thought I put a hot poker up her butt. She freaked out. She jumped up and began ripping her clothes back on. She saw me there, kneeling over the sofa, buck naked, still holding the damned candle, face drenched in guilt. 'Did you just stick that candle in my ass? What the fuck is wrong with you?' she screamed. I was too stupefied to put the candle down or to stand up or to get dressed. I just kneeled there, holding the candle like a torch and said, stupidly, 'No.'"

More laughter from her audience.

"Anyway, needless to say, I am lucky to be sitting here. I seriously thought she might kill me. She was really tough! But eventually she calmed down enough to storm out and slam the door behind her. I think my career as a lesbian is over."

"I should say so!" Kate said.

"That is seriously the greatest story in the history of mankind! I am so going to miss you guys!" I said and my laughter turned, instantly, to tears.

"Oh, no! Don't start that! You are going to get me going," Kate said and burst into tears. This caused both Mack and Eliza to start crying, too. We collected into a group hug and cried some more.

"I love you guys," I said. "Thank you, for everything!"

My cell phone rang. I broke the hug and looked at it. It was Kim.

"Shit! It is my agent. I forgot to tell her I was moving back east..." I said and answered the call.

"Hi, Kim! What's up?"

"Well, I have some good news and some bad news."

"Okay..."

"I got a job possibility here for you. Some producer saw you in *Getting High School* and fell in love. I guess they just fired one of their actresses and he wants to offer you the gig."

"Okay. What's the job?"

"It is a co-star spot in the pilot of new television show. Want me to email you the material?"

"Yeah, but what's the job?"

"Not much. A couple of lines. Feel free to pass on it. You would be the ex-wife of the lead guy. They are describing the show as sort of *Tender Mercies* thing."

"I love *Tender Mercies*! This sounds like really good news. I don't care how small the part is. What's the bad news?"

"They don't have the budget to bring you in. They need you to work as a local."

"Work where?" I asked, heart sinking, knowing that her answer was going to be Canada.

"Texas. Some town south of Amarillo."

"Well," I said, afraid to believe what I was hearing. "Um, that doesn't sound like bad news."

"They need you there in three days. Your character works this week."

"What is the offer?"

"You fly yourself to Texas, you put yourself up, and the offer is three thousand dollars for two days' work."

I stood there, stunned and silent, trying to absorb this unexpected development. Eliza, Kate and Mack were all staring at me, trying to figure out what was going on.

"Hello? Are you there?"

"Yeah. I'm here. I'm sorry. So, um, is there nudity or something?"

"No. It is a network show."

"Yeah. Okay. I'll take it."

"Don't you want to read it first?"

"No."

"Do you think you can get a flight and a hotel cheap enough that you break even? Given that you will only make three grand?"

"Yes. I'm not worried about the money."

"Okay. And there is like a twenty-percent possibility the character could recur in the future, assuming you and their lead have the chemistry they are looking for. But there are no guarantees. And remember, there are only a few lines. This is smaller than anything you have ever done. Are you sure you want to do this?"

"Yes. Whatever. I don't care. Tell them I'll take it and that I am driving there. I can leave in five minutes."

"You are driving to Texas and you are leaving in five minutes?" Kim said and laughed, as if I were kidding. "Are you drunk?"

"No, and I'm not joking. I was leaving here today to drive Route 66 through Texas—through Amarillo, actually—anyway. Can you believe that? I happen to know that Amarillo is about sixteen hours away. I can do that in two days, easy!" I said and laughed the giddy laugh of a lottery winner. "Just email me the material and all the contact info and give them my cell number and, you know, tell them I'm on my way."

"Okay. That was easy. Congratulations, I guess."

I thanked her and hung up. The girls all stared at me, expectantly.

"You won't believe it."

"What?" they asked in unison.

"I just got a job. An acting job. In Texas."

"That's great! Congratulations!" Kate said.

"Yeah! Congratulations. What is it?" Mack asked.

"Some new show based on *Tender Mercies* or something. I don't know. It's only a few lines but I don't care. All I know is, they need me in three days. It is an easy two-day drive. I'll stop in Flagstaff tonight and hit Texas tomorrow night. I couldn't possibly have pulled this off, what with the dogs and everything else, if I hadn't already packed my car up for a cross-country trip that involved taking the dogs. This is amazing."

"See? If you love something, set it free," Mack said. Again.

"This again? What are you talking about?"

"Just like the house. I think you were not allowed to have what you wanted until you let go of wanting it so bad. It's all about surrender. Holding on to the past is like holding on to your breath. You will die. If you love something, set it free. If it comes back, it will be yours forever."

We all stared at her, absorbing this.

"Well, thank you, Sting, but let's not get crazy," I said. "It is a few lines for three grand, not the lead in a big-budget feature."

"Why do you need to quantify the blessing? Why must you always be negative and downplay stuff? Why can't you just accept this for everything it is and for everything it might become?"

I looked at Eliza and Kate for backup but they were both staring at Mack with expressions that suggested they were each doing complicated math problems in their heads.

"Every time you are tempted to react in the same old way, ask if you want to be a prisoner of the past or a pioneer of the future," Mack continued.

"What is going on here? Did you get some Dalai Lama quote toilet paper or something?" I asked.

"That was a Deepak Chopra quote," Mack replied with evident pity.

There was definitely something in the air. Something strange and different. Getting philosophized by Mack felt foreign, even embarrassing. But she was right.

"You know what? I'm gonna go with your take on this one. Thank you."

"Good! See? There is more to me than my perfect tits and Brazilian laser job, you know."

There was no comeback to that, so we all let it hang in the air for a moment.

"Okay, guys," I said at last. "This is it. I'm going."

"When you make a choice, you change the future," Mack said in her most superior "and may peace be with you" voice.

"Okay. Knock it off. You're getting weird."

"Okay," Mack said, simply. She then polished off her champagne and picked again at some non-existent lint on her breast.

I looked at Kate and Eliza and noticed that, though they were both partly watching Mack's fixation with her own nipples, they both had tears in their eyes.

I was going to miss these crazy bitches.

After another thirty minutes of hugging and crying, I took one last look around my empty living room, noting that I felt no deep sense of loss or sadness about the house, even though I didn't know if I'd ever live in it again. I closed and locked the front door. I handed Kate the keys, hugged everyone one last time and got into my car with the dogs. I started the car and pulled away, watching the girls wave goodbye in my rear view window. I plugged my iPhone in and Justin Townes Earle's "Far Away In Another Town" filled my car. The lyrics were about a man preferring loneliness on his own terms, but it seemed like he was singing about me escaping my past. The song made me cry bittersweet tears. Leaving Los Angeles and my home and my friends was the scariest thing I'd ever done. But I had my dogs and a silly little job waiting for me in Texas, a job that had a tiny chance of being something more than it seemed. I was only two days away from starting an entirely new chapter of my life. New places, new people, new experiences. And when that new phase was over, whenever that panned out to be, I'd head to Boston and start over. Again. And despite my tears, I knew inside, actually believed—for the first time in years—that everything was going to be all right. Or better, at least. Maybe. I hope.

Fuck. Who was I kidding? Pulling this off was going to take a lot of luck. And balls. Huge balls. Huge, lucky balls the size of Devonevans'. And alcohol. Copious alcohol. I eyeballed a case of red wine I had packed in the back of the car. It calmed me considerably. I put on a top forty station, got on the Hollywood freeway and headed south.

THE END

About the author

Christine Elise McCarthy has been acting professionally for 25 years and is recognized primarily for her roles as U4EA-popping bad girl, Emily Valentine, on *Beverly Hills, 90210*, as Harper Tracy on *ER*, and as Kyle, the gal who killed Chucky in *Child's Play 2*. She has also appeared in recurring roles on *China Beach*, *In the Heat of the Night*, and *Tell Me You Love Me*. Among her other film roles are Abel Ferrara's *Body Snatchers* and two films starring Viggo Mortensen: *Vanishing Point* and *Boiling Point*.

As a writer, she has written three episodes of *Beverly Hills, 90210* as well as characters and storylines for the series, a pilot that was optioned by Aaron Spelling, and comical true-life essays that she performed at the Upright Citizens Brigade and Naked Angels theaters in LA. She maintains an irreverent food porn blog called www.DelightfulDeliciousDelovely.com for which she provides recipes, photographs and sometimes shares details of the triumphs and, more frequently, the humiliations of her own life. She has a great passion for photography (www.MyPinUpArt.com) and has shown her pin-up and decaying Americana imagery in the United States & Paris. She has been on the selection committee of Michigan's Waterfront Film Festival since its inception in 1999, she is co-director of the Victoria Texas Independent Film Festival, programs for the Self-Medicated Film Festival and The Lady Filmmakers Film Festival, and consults & judges for many others. Her directorial debut, *Bathing & the Single Girl*, was accepted into over 100 film festivals and won 20 awards.

Bathing & the Single Girl, inspired by her short film, is her debut novel.

Made in the USA
Columbia, SC
05 November 2020

23982583R00224